Growing up near London, Carley-Ann Osborn has always had a love of books and especially loved the ones that take you on a character's journey through their eyes. Writing was more for her own entertainment in her youth but was left on the back burner as a young adult. It wasn't until her mid-30s that the love for reading and writing came back into her life, and she hasn't been able to stop since.

This is dedicated to all those who have continued to support and encourage me. I love and cherish you all.

Carley-Ann Osborn

PRETEND WITH ME

AUSTIN MACAULEY PUBLISHERS™
LONDON * CAMBRIDGE * NEW YORK * SHARJAH

A CIP catalogue record for this title is available from the British Library.

ISBN 9781035843862 (Paperback)
ISBN 9781035843879 (ePub e-book)

www.austinmacauley.com

First Published 2024
Austin Macauley Publishers Ltd®
1 Canada Square
Canary Wharf
London
E14 5AA

Chapter 1

<u>Catherine</u>

Have you ever felt lost?

Stuck in a life that is no longer yours?

Trapped by somebody else's life choices?

Daydreaming, I sit and stare out into the swarm of souls that surround me: those who I once considered to be my 'close' family and friends, and I come to realise now, they are not—at least, they are not anymore.

They are *his*.

They don't know me—not really. The people who were once my confidants are now just faces in the crowd, acquaintances I see because it's 'good social practice' rather than needing or wanting to see them.

Ultimately, not one of them would understand this, even if I were to recount it—this loneliness and utter emptiness that float around my being like a swarm of wasps stinging incessantly, hacking away at my soul. My isolation forces me to retreat into myself, to pull on my smile and pretend like everything is ok, to keep sinking into this self-made trap with no one around to pull me out.

I'm here, by myself, nursing a glass of some expensive wine that I don't really like, just because that's what everyone else here enjoys gulping down, so it *must* also be what I am expected to like as well.

I am taking this moment, looking out over the garden festivities from a quiet corner near the house, just to recompose myself before I have to plaster that smile back on my face. Soon I would need to venture out and socialise with the grace taught to me by my father—an actress's trick to misdirect others away from your own dilemmas. Speaking of the devil…

"There you are, sweetheart! Your mother and I were wondering where you had disappeared off to, you ok?" Standing up from my perch to face him full-on, the well-practiced smile fixed firmly in place, and I brush the imaginary dirt from around my garish, bright yellow summer dress. He looks the pinnacle of ease in green cargo shorts and a grey top, with a sophisticated short beard speckled with various shades of grey. He may be in his 60s, but he certainly doesn't look or act like it; age has done well with him.

"I am here; I just needed a minute," pointing to the wine glass, "I must have drunk a bit too quickly and went a little to my head. I'm ok now," I lie.

"Ok sweetheart, come on, Uncle Jerome wants to talk to you about Vanessa's school prom. I think he was hoping you would take her dress shopping."

I desperately try and hold in the eye roll that is threatening to make its unwelcome appearance, because apparently dress shopping is all I am capable of now a days. Gone are my dreams, aspirations I spent endless hours fantasising over, working towards, dreams I gave up when priorities changed, leaving behind this; this is all I am now.

"Sure, I'll be over in a minute," I may have uttered a little too high a pitch to cover my disappointment.

"Ok honey," Rubbing my shoulder as he strolls back out to the sea of faces, his confidence and charm just oozing out of him, encompassing all those within its vicinity.

He has always been like that, able to hold a room with ease and be comfortable in whatever company he finds himself in. Who am I kidding? So could I, once upon a time, I learned from the best after all. Sniggering at myself, I remember a better time: the 'Belle of the Ball', that was me. I would relish the notion that all eyes were on me when I entered a room, a time when making friends and attending social events was practically a hobby, one I used to enjoy and seek out.

Now I just feel like I am suffocating. Like, I am drowning in a sea of expectations and etiquette. Trapped. A newfound claustrophobia tugging at my fear, like my soul is struggling and dying under its weight. Giving myself over to this new me, where my body is present but my mind remains vacant, lost in a whirlwind of misery and misplaced thought, going through the motions because that's what everyone else wants from me and expects from me.

I'm not sure how much longer I can continue like this. In this spiral of self-pity, remorse, anger, and loneliness, I drag myself down into the pits of an inevitable depression, unable to stop myself from tumbling.

For two years, I have surrounded myself in it, trapped in a cocoon of someone else's making, unable to escape; and unable to reach out to anybody for help. I have to find a way to break free—by myself—to pull myself out of these binds before I am lost forever with no conceivable way back. If I can find the strength to take the first step, maybe the natural path to freedom will be laid out for me to follow.

Fighting back tears of remorse for my fallen former self, I school my features into those of practiced contented happiness and head back out into the crowd.

Chapter 2

<u>Jackson</u>

"Oh my god! It's him; I know it is. Oh my god! Oh my god! Oh my god!" I hear the hushed squeals emanating from across the café. Turning my head slightly, I can see in my peripheral vision where the delightful noise is coming from. A group of three young girls in the corner appear to be the culprits; they are sitting ogling in my direction with an all-telling look of awe evident on their faces, fidgeting in their seats, playing with strands of their hair, and grinning and giggling stupendously, like they just cannot contain themselves. Yes, that would be them.

"Oh my god, he's better looking in person; he is so pretty," I can't help the self-assured grin that unfurls across my face, followed by a slight chuckle.

I'll never tire of these reactions; in fact, I relish them. They are what keep me motivated when I am getting my ass up at 5 in the morning and heading to the gym. They are why it takes me that extra 10 minutes to choose my outfit each day. I *must* make sure it somewhat matches whatever I happen to be doing, that it hugs every muscle, and that it exposes my most attractive assets and best features. Today's example is simple: a dark blue pair of jeans with a grey crew neck jumper, one that is slightly too tight and extenuates my chest and upper arms; perfect for a morning sitting, drinking coffee, reading the paper, pre-empting paparazzi cameras, and last but not least: exciting my young, enthusiastic fans.

"I'm going to go talk to him."

"We should all go."

"Oh my god! I'm so nervous," I look up to face them; it seems that at this point, it is fruitless trying to pretend I haven't heard them. It is so obvious that they are talking about me, so I might as well acknowledge it directly. With my best-practiced 'movie star' teeth-baring smile, I offer just the slightest of waves in their direction, followed by a well-timed cheeky wink for good measure.

"Ahh!" They all scream together, their high-pitch squeals causing me to wince, squinting my eyes a little before chuckling to myself again while I look back down towards my newspaper. It never gets old.

It isn't long, however, before they have plucked up the courage to come over, fidgeting uncontrollably from foot to foot as they position themselves next to my table.

"Jackson Hunter?" I turn towards the array of giddy faces and address them. "That's me."

"Oh my god, I *love* your movies. I have your poster on my wall."

"So do I," chimes in another, slightly bouncing on her heels in excitement. That earns them another low chuckle and a toothy smile.

To be honest, I still haven't decided if I find that particular part of fame creepy or not. Knowing my image is pinned up on a young girl's bedroom walls feels peculiar to me.

"Thank you; you flatter me," cue another round of pleasing giggles.

"Will you sign my breasts?" Interjects the overzealous girl in the middle; the request itself is not uncommon, so it doesn't shock me as such; however, it enters dangerous territory. Looking at these girls, they cannot be more than 15–16 years old, making it highly inappropriate to even consider it. Nonetheless, these girls are clearly excited, influential, and…well…I really don't want to offend them, so some tack is in order here to control the situation without damaging their fragile, youthful egos. Not to mention I have my reputation to think about; talking about fragile, wrong move here can break my very credible standing in this world. It is a very fine line we must walk across.

"Unfortunately, girls, I *am* so sorry, but I do draw the line at body autographs; they just don't last long enough. How about you ask for a couple of napkins from the counter, and I'll sign those instead? I'll even pose for some photos if you have a camera with you?" A flash of disappointment crosses her face, but it is quickly replaced by some more giggles as they panda off to find something for me to sign.

Do I miss going out uninterrupted and having a normal life? Privacy? Sometimes…rarely. For the most part, I love it—being the centre of attention, invited to all the best places, the glamour. It's like I was made for this life. It took me a while to learn how to turn my natural charm into a tool of the trade—mind you—one that I can flip for any occasion, or to any problem, or in this case, to any fan I may come across. As part of my contract with my agency, I am allowed to have a life—of course, but I have to stay out of trouble. No negative press if I can help it, which means I am constantly having to keep myself in check, which also means—of course, no inappropriate touching of young fans, even if it is *just* to sign an autograph.

When they return, I sign some napkins, pose for some photos, and engage in some idol conversation with them, mainly focused on the films I have had the good fortune of being a part of and their favourite scenes. I even give them a little behind-the-scenes banter, which they seem to get a kick out of.

A few minutes into our meeting, I hear my phone's ring tone pulsing on the table behind me. A quick glance tells me it's Harry.

"Sorry ladies, I have to get this; it's been lovely to meet you all." A round of more childish laughter and excited goodbyes later, I turn to answer my phone, seeing now that's the second time he has tried to call.

"Harry! How are you?"

"Why didn't you answer your phone the first time? I already told you to be on standby and wait for my call today; that is literally all you had to do," Oh Harry! Harry Davis is the best agent I could have asked for, but he expects the same professionalism that he affords you 100% of the time.

"Sorry, Hars, I was talking to some fans; I didn't want to be rude; *you* taught me that!"

"Yes, well, I am calling to let you know you got the part from Adrien. They start production of 'Adrien's Hel' in 4 months."

"Of course, I did. I got the impression the audition was just a formality on their part," Considering they *asked* me to audition, it's the least I expected.

"Be that as it may, they have requested that you attend the other casting auditions next week, in particular that of your leading lady." Really? That's unusual.

"Oh, any particular reason? I have never had an input into the hiring of my cast members before."

"Apparently the director is very keen for the two leads to have…how did he put it…" I hear the rustling papers through the phone. "Undeniable onscreen chemistry."—*Excuse me?*

"What do they mean by that? Does he think I can't act? Or *they* can't act?"

"No, no, it's not that. They have the choices down to a select number of actresses already, but I think he is just looking for that 'spark' you know? Between the two main characters in particular, he is keen to see how his final line-up interacts directly with you and how that translates onto the camera. It's not really that uncommon; you have just never been asked to give your input before."

"Oh, ok. Well, whatever they need, I suppose, where do I need to be? What do I need to do?"

"So, the final auditions for Helen's role are in London; they are booked to go on over three days from Monday to Wednesday. I believe they are down to the final ten. They have sent over a dummy script for you to learn and act out with them, so I suppose you just go, act out the scenes with the actresses, and offer any input you think is relevant, which might help with their decision," It sounds simple enough.

"Ok. Send me the details, and I'll be there. Is there anyone on the short list I would know of, do you know?"

"Umm, no, I don't think so. From what I can tell, they are opting for an unknown; I am going to assume they want the main focus to be around their A-list character, which is obviously you."—*Haha, damn right!*

"Ok, I'm not going to argue with that. Not a problem. Talk soon, Hars."

"Oh! Don't forget the premiere this weekend! Speak soon, Hunter," and with that, he hung up.

Me…forget the premier this weekend? Ha! As if!

"Good evening, viewers. We are here, lining the red carpet today, at the premiere of the latest Starmen film, 'Angels by Day'. It is a star-studded event today, with so many A-listers here. I am honestly 'Starmen' struck myself! Haha. What do you think, Drew?"

"Oh, I agree, Samantha, and can I just say you are looking star-studded yourself tonight! Do you mind giving us a twirl?"

"Why thank you, Drew? I do try to fit in, haha. Oh, quick Andrea, Andrea Reyes, can we ask you a couple of questions, please?"

"Of course, darling. Who are you guys with today?"

"We are with 'Entertainment Tonight'. It's good to see you here this evening. Now obviously, you are playing the gorgeous Penelope in Angels by Day. What was it like working with Hugh Starmen? This is your first film together, right?"

"Yes, that's right. You know what? When you are working with someone as decorated as Hugh, you just have to go with his flow, you know? He had such a

vision for this film and how he wanted it to look, and I am really looking forward to seeing how it has all come together on the big screen."

"We heard there were a couple of setbacks—you broke a finger?"

"Hahaha, not quite so dramatic, but yes, I dislocated one, this little pinky here. I got a little too zealous in one scene in Chicago, but nothing too serious…"

"Ah!"

"Ahhhh! Oh my god! Jackson Hunter! You made me jump; you tease! Do you have to creep up on me like that? This one, I tell you, was always pranking us on set; I swear, I was a nervous wreck by the end of filming."

"Haha, you love it Andrea!"

"Jackson Hunter, Drew from 'Entertainment Tonight', thank you for coming over. You played the role of Theo in 'Angels by Day'. So, a bit of a prankster on set, were you? What's the worst thing he did during filming Andrea?"

"Oh, most of it included locking doors and misplacing props, but you know there was this one scene, without giving too much away, where we were having an argument, with vases and nonsense being thrown around the set. At one point, I was supposed to storm through a door, but as I went to open it, he had hung some sort of Halloween costume there."

"Haha, I found it in the prop department; you should have seen her on…the…floor!"

"So were you Jackson!"

"This is true. The difference was I was in hysterics; I have never seen anything so funny as you nearly pooping your pants!"

"Jackson!"

"Haha! Hilarious! Is it fair to say you two enjoyed yourselves making this movie Jackson Hunter?"

"Oh yes, I have really had great fun working with Andrea, and you know she is such a pro at what she does and the elegance she has just come through in her characters. It's been a great honour working with her, and I really hope we get the opportunity to work with each other again."

"Ahh, that's so nice to say, Jackson. Me too; I think his youth might just be rubbing off on me."

"Haha, well, thank you both for talking with us today. I hope you enjoy the movie."

"Oh, me too! Come now, Jackson, the least you can do is walk me in after that mini heart attack."

"It will be my pleasure, dear Andrea."

"Andrea Reyes and Jackson Hunter were there. So, it seems like it was all fun and games working on set for the stars of 'Angels by Day'. I wonder if the director, Hugh Starmen, would agree."

"To be honest, Samantha I don't think he would; Jackson is notorious for his antics. I can't imagine a lot of work getting done when he is on set."

"Haha, but then again, Drew, I bet it's not only his great physique that put him on the 'UKs top 20 most sexiest men alive', this year, I think, a little bit of that cheeky schoolboy charm that we all seem to find so endearing also contributes to his fast-growing popularity, don't you think?"

"Haha, very likely, Samantha, very likely…oh but now who is this coming out of the black limo…"

Chapter 3

Catherine

'Ok, Catherine, you got yourself this far; all you have to do is walk through the door.' Nerves dance through my abdomen as I stare at the oak double doors leading into the temporary casting set—the very one that holds my future like a dangling carrot on a stick, tempting me inside—but my stubborn legs won't go. On instinct, I wrap my stomach in my arms, cradling it as if that will calm the tumbling waves that are threatening to burst out at the seams.

"Just walk through," a mantra I have repeated several times in the last 10 minutes or so. Why is it so difficult? I wanted to get back to doing what I love and claw back some of my old life. It's been so long, however—too long! My last audition must have been 9 years ago, I think. Yes, I remember now, it was that TV show where I played 'victim number 2', which I thought at the time was my breakthrough into television. This, though, is the big league, far bigger than I thought I'd achieve this early. A film!

When Josh pushed me to go for the original auditions, claiming the experience alone would help me immensely, I never dreamed I'd get this far, down to the final 10! Apparently, I have something the director is looking for—for the lead, no less! *'Yeah, you and 10 others.'*

"Oooo weee," I blow out the breath I've been holding, expelling my very own sound effects; surprisingly, not one person in the street looks around. Well, this is London after all; they are probably used to all sorts of crazy nonsense.

This is definitely more than I expected. I feel like I am being thrown into the deep end when it's been 9 years since your last swim. What doesn't help matters is the little titbit of information the casting directors bestowed on me during my call back: Jackson Hunter is in there. They graciously informed us that he has been cast as the male lead and will be present at today's auditions. I have seen a few of his movies, and let me tell you, he is *swoon*-worthy! The dark hair that he wears swept back and longish, not enough for a ponytail but enough where you can imagine your fingers intertwining between their strands, and it is thick enough that I can envision said fingers getting lost in the pull of their neat curls. The permanent stubble he carries, complements his carefree lifestyle; I'm not even sure he has ever been pictured (outside of filming, that is) clean-shaven either—not that I have stalked enough of his pictures to make that judgement.

However, it is his eyes that have always captivated me—brown, the colour of dark chocolate. When he looks at you, you are seeing into his very depths; he uses and manipulates them skilfully to draw you into his character without ever having to say a word; he can tell you a whole story with just one look. Of course, I cannot talk about Jackson Hunter without mentioning his most famous attribute, his incredible physique! With broad shoulders, pecks, abs, and biceps that you can visibly see through every piece of clothing he wears just because he couldn't possibly get any more gorgeous, The Devine had to throw in that great body too. I am pretty certain he must have a clause written into every contract that states he has to take his shirt off at least once in every film because, I swear to God, it's *every* film!

Nope, him being in here does nothing to shatter these nerves rising up within me, almost making me nauseous in anticipation of meeting him alone, not to mention the monumental connotations attached to everything else today represents.

When we were briefed last week that these auditions included him *and* the directors, they also informed us that they would be looking closely at our interactions today as well as our interpretation and re-enactment of the script they sent us. *'Ha! No pressure then!'*

Arms around my abdomen: *'breathe, Catherine, you got this. This is your path, your way out.'* I can't screw this up!

'Definitely no pressure then!'

Jackson

Well, yesterday was interesting. The actresses were essentially given a brief 'here's the script, act it out', i.e., no direction and definitely no context. The consequences were pretty…disorganised. Each actress had a slightly different interpretation of the script, which was tricky to say the least, as I had to adapt to their whims along the way; it has proved for some interesting interactions, I can tell you. One, who clearly was a follow-the-director's-instructions kinda girl, just went over the top with the lines in a very clear display of what we like to call 'over acting' which was a very clear indication of her over-compensating to cover her lack of originality. Another took on the role of a dominatrix, clearly a role she was—How do I put this delicately? 'Experienced' in? She even came in her own costume!

One thing was evidently clear, however, that Harry was right, the director was aiming for the unknown, which while can be a good thing in some respects, means inexperience, which ultimately equates to more work for me. Not one of those ladies yesterday displayed what I assume the director was looking for—that 'Spark', or at least have the skills to pretend!

Today is Tuesday, and the second half of the applicants are auditioning today. Which means another fun-filled day of playing catch-up to whatever interpretation these wannabes could come up with. As entertaining as they are…it's exhausting. Hopefully they will find what they are looking for today—maybe?

Already two applicants in, and I have a headache. The first one, Melissa, seemed so awestruck that she kept fumbling and forgetting her lines, not the way to make a good impression. I mean, how is she supposed to work with me if she can't even get her words out?

"Ok. Can you send in the next applicant, please, Catherine Carell?" Announces Gary, the head casting director, while staring down at his sheet, blowing out a stream of air while puffing out his cheeks. He must be as fed up as I am. The director is coming tomorrow to view the final 3, and I am pretty sure only 1 out of the 7 we have seen already has any real potential, in regard to this movie anyway.

The PA comes back in, holding open the door to allow one of *the* most stunning women I have ever met to enter the room beside her. I take a brief moment just to stare and admire her beauty as she walks to her position in front of the panel of our three casting directors. Long blonde hair, set in waves cascading down her back, with some falling to her front. She isn't overly tall, but her beautifully toned legs are on display beneath a grey pleated dress that sits halfway up her thigh. The vision of her making her entrance gives me cause to check myself before I am caught ogling too long. I can't see her eyes though, or much of her face for that matter, as she looks slightly downwards towards the floor with her hair partially covering her features; glimpses are caught as it sways gracefully from side to side with her movements, her lips are tucked into her mouth as a slight blush creeps up her face.

'*Damn*' I curse to myself; she is another shy one; she can't even look at me, but damn if I don't mind a few months working with her, especially in *this* film where I *know* contact is inevitable. '*God, I am such a creep!*'

"Good morning, Catherine; it's good to see you again," Gary proclaims; his familiarity with her suggests he must have met her before, possibly from her original audition. From what I can gather, these three conducted the initial auditions separately, likely so they could cover more ground in a shorter period of time. Well, I suppose when you're finding an unknown, you've got to dig a little deeper! "This is Francesca to my right, and Sophie to my left; they will be assisting me today, and of course you must have heard of Jackson Hunter," Gesturing his open-palmed hand towards me.

"Hi, please meet you," I mutter with a little wave, '*What the fuck was that, acting like a bloody fan girl?*' As she looks up to reply, I can finally see her, petite features sitting happily upon her face, flawless, and her eyes the truest blue, like sapphires glimmering back, catching my breath slightly. '*Stunning.*' Unfortunately, her reply does nothing to re-ignite my hope that she may, in fact, be the one. It is a very small, barely there, "Hi," Before she looks back towards Gary and his band of merry casting directors, she once again hides her face behind her hair.

"Ok Catherine, are you happy with the script we gave you?"

"Yes."

"Excellent, so just remember that this isn't the script for the film we are making, but the characters it portrays, and in particular the chemistry we want to see between you and Jackson, are there. That's what we want to see from you today. Do you think you can pull it off?" She nods slightly. I notice he is being particularly nice to this girl, more than he has with the others. What does he see that I don't? Isn't it clear to everyone here that this girl has no natural charisma? The skill that this role most definitely demands!

"Great, so props are around you; take a few minutes to take a look and see if any will help you with your portrayal, which includes Jackson. He will follow your lead, but if you need him to do anything in particular, let him know beforehand."

"Will do, thank you."

She does as she is told. Looking around, she doesn't give me any further instructions, but she does move a chair to the top of a raised platform, making a clear stepped pathway between that and where I am standing.

"Ok ready." She claims.

"Great, now, like before, we will be recording this for playback later; are you ok with this?" Another small nod. "Fantastic. So, Ralph is here," Pointing to my pre-empted 'co-star' beside me, "is playing the role of troll; your line begins after his queue. Positions!" The room falls silent. She takes a seat in the chair on top of the platform, head tilted down towards the floor so her hair covers the whole of her face, hands on either side of the chair resting on its arms. She waits for her queue.

"And action…" In comes 'Troll', aka Ralph, beside me.

"My queen, Abigor is here to see you," his well-practiced line comes out flawlessly. Well, he has said it 8 times now!

What happens next, however, is so far removed from my realm of expectation that it almost stuns me into silence. She raises her head slowly and purposely, revealing not only a smirk on her face, reminiscent of evil stepmother vibes, but in her eyes a look of determination so transformed from the shy girl here not 2 minutes before. This glare portrays a unique combination of anger, power, and strength with a very subtle hint of desire—maybe passion? I can't quite work it out; either way, it has me bewitched, settling so well into the role of the character that it's almost scary.

"Ahh Abigor," she starts in a voice so silkily low and sultry, carrying throughout the room effortlessly; like an echo, it hits me way down low in my abdomen. Rising from her chair in one fluid motion, she extenuates her neck, still staring me down with those piercing blues, power emanating from her ora at her portrayal.

Very slowly, she moves one foot in front of the other, careful to extend her legs as far out as she can to elongate the preened lines running from her throat to the tips of her toes, as she steps down from the platform towards me. Every one of her movements is so well executed; they're not jagged or clumsy; they're just fluid, almost as though she were walking underwater, her limbs a flowing extension of her form. "What news do you bring me from the surface?" She journeys down the steps, taking her place next to me as she delivers her line. Her hands just reach out so her fingers flutter lightly across my collarbone. *'Oh, right fuck, my line.'*

"The heroes have scattered my queen," She begins to move, encircling me, her hand never leaving my body, instead tracing the skin atop my V-neck opened shirt, following the path from my collarbone, around my shoulders, and across my back. "The people are once again divided. It is only a matter of time before one of them breaks," she moves in a full circle and is once again positioned at my front, her hand now resting on my chest as my breathing regulates to follow hers. Pains of nerves pinprick low in my abdomen. With our faces now in line, our eyes are locked, unable to tear mine away. I am captivated.

"Good, then all is coming together; we will soon have our war," the word 'war' is emphasised by a deep sound coming forth from the depths of her throat and by the forming of her lips into a delicious 'o' shape, uncontrollably drawing my eyes to glance at them briefly before hurriedly returning my gaze back to hers.

"As you predicted, my queen," Those pools of sapphire burning their desire deep into mine—we are now so close, her breasts mere centimetres from my body, and both our chests rise and fall in sync, increasing in speed and depth through no other force than the attraction that has ignited between us.

"You may leave us now, Troll," her eyes never leave mine.

"But your majesty, this is Abigor; you must not…" Like tearing apart a pulse from its current, she looks towards Ralph with a glaring intensity no longer filled with desire but that of rage.

"I said leave us!" She commands—not a shout, but that of authority mixed deliciously with the right amount of hostility. I am unable to look away; her presence in this moment demands attention and respect. I am in sheer awe over how she has been able to effortlessly turn into this goddess before me, especially considering it came in the form of that little timid girl mere moments ago. Images of her in my bedroom, dressed only in lingerie…and that look, that confidence, dances at the forefront of my mind. She turns back to face me, once again schooling her features into another realm, this one back to passion and desire. I can sense the longing radiating off her.

"Trolls," she continues, eyes half-lidded, her intensity never losing its momentum. "I am surrounded by trolls," her voice, directed at me, has turned seductive and enticing. It is taking a lot of willpower right now *not* to get a hard-on in her presence.

"My love," I ad lib, reaching up to cup the side of her neck in the palm of my hand; she responds to my touch by stretching it out further, giving me full access while my other hand finds its way to her hip. It would be so easy to pretend these interactions are real—a snippet of our actual lives. "If you did not need me on the surface, I would never leave your side," with one hand still resting on my chest, her other now reaches out to cradle my cheek, stroking at the stubble growth. Neither of us is able to look away.

"Ok and cut," With that, I can visibly see the shutters come down within her eyes. Suddenly the timid girl is back as she takes one huge step back away from me, untangling herself from my hold. The moment is well and truly gone. *'Wow, that was intense!'*

"Well done, you two. That was good, very good. Were you happy with that, Catherine?" Her full body forcibly turns away from me towards Gary, giving him another one of her curt nods as she did. "Great! Now if you don't mind either coming back around 3 or maybe just hanging around, we'll be able to let you know then whether to come back tomorrow. Is that, ok?"

"Yes, of course. Thank you so much for the opportunity," Half turning around back to face me, "And thank you, Mr Hunter," I am left speechless from the whole interaction; all I can offer her is my own slight nod as she turns to make her way out of the room. I'm pretty sure I currently have a frown occupying my face, while I still struggle to comprehend the whole ordeal.

Once the doors are closed, I immediately turn to address Gary, Sophie, and Francesca.

"That one!" I point towards the doors as though they are the physical representation of her. "You wanted chemistry, that was it! I have never *seen* an intensity like that."

"I admit she *was* good; I saw it in her audition too, definitely got massive potential," turning to address his co-workers next to him, "she has an ability to school her features into any character I have so far thrown at her."

"I can see that," I interrupt, determined to put in my 10 pence.

"She has some factors that work against her though," he comments while he sucks in his lips between his teeth.

"Like what?"

"Ones I can't disclose to you right now. But you are right; she will definitely make the cut for the final three. We will have to see how she does in front of Cameron tomorrow and how she handles everything else," Back to his professionalism, he re addresses his PA, "Can you call in the next one, please, an Elisabeth Wisemen?"

The last two candidates pass by like a blur; they do not hold a candle to Catherine. These idiots are fools if they pass by a talent like her; unfortunately, like so many other times in the world of filmography, this is quite often the case.

The next day comes quickly enough. As promised, we are graced with the presence of our all-seeing director, Cameron Elliott. He *is* a true visionary of his field, but alas, he is as pompous an ass as many of the others I have worked with. I am pretty sure if he could direct, write, cast, star, and edit these films all by himself, he would. He is very particular about what he wants the outcome of this film to look like, and it starts with the actors, hence this whole fiasco.

Anticipation builds as we plough through the first two finalists. Catherine is the third and last to come in, and once again, her shy exterior exhumes as she enters. I smile a little, knowing exactly what passion is actually lurking beneath—a fire just waiting for the word 'action'.

"Good morning, Catherine," Gary welcomes.

"Good morning,"

"You know everybody else from yesterday; however, this is Cameron Elliot," he states, pointing to Cameron sitting next to him without even glancing up from his paper. "He is the film's director and ultimately has the final say over who is hired today. Like we have mentioned before, what we are looking for is a chemistry between the lead female character and that of the lead male, which is being portrayed by Jackson Hunter," she nods in agreement.

I wait on bated breath; today will really be a testament to how she will respond to me and to the demands of the role. I already know what he is going to ask her; the question is, will her timid self-take over, or can she reign it in to release her inner portrayal of the confident, sexy persona she showed us yesterday?

"So, we are still sticking with the same script you worked with yesterday, so you don't need to worry about that. You should know, Cameron has already looked over the footage and was very impressed. However, today we would like to push you a little further," he pauses; even he must know by looking at her current demeanour, that this might be pushing it a little with her.

"As you may or may not be aware, the film becomes quite physical, so we would like to see what that looks like with you and Jackson, which inevitably means we would like to see you kiss and, consequently, whatever that kiss may progress onto," I can visibly see her take a gulp as she processes this information.

"Are you ok to proceed?" she gives a brief nod of her head, no hesitation; I like that.

"Ok, talk to Jackson; see what you can work out between you; remember, we want to see chemistry and passion."

"Show us what you are capable of, Miss Carell," Cameron finally speaks up after allowing Gary to take the lead so far.

She comes to me, a new resolution now masked in her features.

"What are you thinking, Catherine?"

"Umm," she looks around at the props scattered about us, resolution evident in the tone of her voice as she speaks, "I am thinking just a kiss isn't going to cut it. It seems from the extract that these two have been together prior to this encounter, so we need to make it look like the world comes together at the same time they do."

"What are you suggesting?"

"When things truly, I mean really truly, come together, it isn't frantic, it isn't uncontrolled, it's natural, and these are two people who belong together, however evil they may be," she pauses a moment to think. I am going by her lead here; it's her audition. "How much can you carry?"

"Well, if you are talking about in a gym…"

"I mean, can you carry me?" I take a step towards her, positioning my hands under her arms to lift her slightly off the ground.

"Yes, easy."

"Then that's what we do, we come together, make it look as natural as we can, pick me up and take me over there, and lay me down where we will simulate us becoming one. Can you do that?"

"Of course,"

"Ok then. Same as yesterday, then." A slight nod tells them we are ready. *'Come on, Catherine, you can do this.'*

Back in position, we repeat our performance.

Re-enters Ralph, the troll.

"My queen, Abigor is here to see you."

"Ahh Abigor. What news do you bring to me from the surface?" So professional, exactly as she did yesterday.

"The heroes have scattered, my queen. The people are once again divided. It is only a matter of time before one of them breaks."

"Good, then all is coming together; we will soon have our war."

"As you predicted, my queen."

"You may leave us now, Troll."

"But your majesty, this is Abigor; you must not…"

"I said leave us!" A pause as she turns back to face me, "Trolls. I am surrounded by trolls."

"My love," I reach up once again to cup the side of her neck while my other hand finds its way to her hip, moving slightly more towards her ass this time. "If you did not need me on the surface, I would never leave your side," This time, when her hand reaches out to touch my cheek, there are no words of cut, no reprieve. This is it, if she wants the job; if I want to work with her, then we have to make this count.

Her eyes, once locked on mine, are filled with that same impulse of desire; they momentarily glance down towards my lips before fluttering close, issuing me my queue. Our lips come together, and I swear I feel the electricity spark off of them penetrating mine. She opens almost immediately, allowing my tongue to enter and play with hers. When her hand moves from my cheek into my hair, sliding through it as if it has done it a thousand times before, spasms of arousal head directly south.

I am starting to lose myself in the momentum of the kiss. Her hand, which began on my chest, now has my shirt balled up in her fist as she holds on, giving herself over to the entirety of it. My hand begins to massage the back of her neck as I attempt to deepen our connection further, grinding my hips against hers. *'My god, but does this feel real?'* But it's not; I have to remind myself. *'Oh shit!'* I forgot she wanted me to lift her for our next move.

Bracing both hands against her ass, I give her a little squeeze to tell her I am ready. Her hands now find their way around my neck, and with a slight jump, we land it effortlessly. Her legs wrapped around my hips, my hands under her thighs, not once breaking the hold around our lips. I carry her over to the pre-determined area I am to lay her down, doing so carefully as I position myself, so I am draped over her.

It's only then that we break the kiss, opting to rest my head on top of hers, chest heaving, and bringing my hips down to meet her own. I have no idea if I am going too far or if she's as part of this as I am. She lifts her head, exposing her neck; fingers once again intertwine between the stands of hair at the back of my head and I take the hint, sinking down to rest my head, in the shallows of her nap, ready to kiss her exposed skin.

It's then that we are here, the words 'cut' echoing off in the distance. I open my eyes and lift my face to meet hers the same time she opens hers. A flicker of something flashes across them before the shutters come back down, bringing her back into the world of reality, out of her 'acting zone'. I, however, remain there a little longer, relishing the notions growing in the pits of my stomach. *'Holly shit, was she as into that as I was?'* No time to ask, nor is it appropriate now. She has already pushed me up and out of the way so she can roll out of position and head back over towards the director.

"Was that what you were looking for, sir?"

"Yes, thank you, Catherine. Now tell me you're 30. Is that correct?" Cameron asks, as though it isn't a completely obnoxious move to come out and state her age with no regard for her right to privacy. I come to stand slightly behind her, attempting to ignore the tightness in my trousers as I listen intently to their comments.

"Yes, it is," A brief glance of annoyance enters her otherwise composed demeanour. Cameron leans slightly closer to Gary before stating as though we are not even there to witness it.

"Older than the other girls," he gives a displeased sucking noise between his teeth as he evaluates his notes. Gary gave a nod in agreement.

"And what does that matter?" I interject.

"Only that I was hoping for someone a little younger, that's all," he addresses me. Then back to her, "No offence, Miss Carell; it's just the nature of the business."

"I don't think that should even matter; in fact, it *really* shouldn't," I add, giving over to my own annoyance. "This way, at least she is closer to my age than the other two; a bit more believable, don't you think? You asked me here because you wanted to find someone who shared the same energy as me on screen. Well, you're looking at her, and I think she just proved to you that she has no hesitation performing some of the more intimate scenes you have planned with very little prompting. Her age shouldn't be a factor if everything else fits, surely."

"Thank you, Jackson. Thank you, Catherine; we'll be in touch to let you know our decision," And like that, Gary has dismissed us. *'Fuck!'*

She gathers up her things, thanking the nobheads for their time, and heads out the door. I follow, escorting her out into the main lobby.

"Hay, um, sorry, directors can be ruthless asses," I offer an apology. She returns with a wide smile; it spreads across her face, allowing me a quick glance at her perfect teeth, but somehow, despite its beauty, it still feels false.

"Thank you for sticking up for me, but don't worry, I know all about directors," I attempt to give her a genuine smile in the hope she reciprocates. She doesn't, with the false one remaining instead.

"Look, um, do you want to go get a drink or something? You know, possible future co-workers and all that?" I shoot my shot.

"Umm, I am going to say no; I have to get back. I am sorry. Thank you, though," my heart sinks, *'Denied.'* "Fingers crossed; I'll see you though," she adds.

"Yeah?" Hope dancing in my chest.

"Yeah, when filming starts, maybe?" *'Face palm!'*

"Of course, yeah, fingers crossed."

"Fingers crossed. See you, Mr Hunter," Holding out her hand as a gesture. I take it. She is being a complete professional, whereas here I am crushing hard like some immature school kid!

"Yeah, see you around, Miss Carell."

With that, she heads off towards the underground station. Taking with her any hopes of getting to know her any better—for today at least. Let's just hope these asses get their heads out of their butt holes and realise what a talent she really is, because this film will be ever more worthless without her in it, and the real kick in the teeth…I'll probably never see her again.

Catherine

"Hi, Catherine, it's Josh!" His voice rings through as soon as my phone reaches my ear, excitement evident in his voice.

"Josh, hi, how are you? What news do you have for me?"

"I am good thanking you, my lovely. Exciting news, Cathy! You got it! They loved your audition, and your intensity and want to offer you the role of Helen!"

Oh, my goodness. I pause in shock in the middle of the pavement, causing the person behind me to almost collide straight into me.

"Oh my god, you sure?"

"Sure, as sure, baby! I have already sent you the script; it should be with you in the next few days, but I have also emailed it to you so you can start looking over it in preparation. Production starts in a little over 3 months; once I have an actual start date and place, I'll email it over to you. Filming is predicted to take around 5 months over various locations, predominantly in London."

"Ok, what about accommodation?"

"They are sorting all that out, baby; don't you worry, you just need to learn your lines, show up, and show them exactly what you're made of, sweetheart."

"Oh Josh, thank you so much!" Excitement bubbles inside me; those flutters of butterflies are now back with a vengeance.

"Hay, no thanks necessarily, babe; you are the one with the talent; I just pushed you through the door. This is your new start, sweetheart; grab it with both hands. If this film is a success, it will propel you to bigger things, I promise." Josh, my amazing new agent, my enthusiastic advocate, 'pushed' me here; more like threw me across the threshold and got me the audition.

"Thank you, Josh. Talk to you soon."

"Talk soon, sweetheart," Oh my, this could be my chance. For the first time in a while, a smile beams across my face, and that smile lasts all the way home.

Chapter 4

Catherine

It has been a long time since I was on set, even longer since being on one of this magnitude. The last time (on one of this size at least) must have been when I was a little girl; although everything seemed so much bigger to me back then, it doesn't detract from the magnificence of it now. Before heading out the back, I stop to take a moment to breathe in the scent of the atmosphere around me, and that overwhelming, familiar feeling of belonging takes hold. Finally, I feel like I am home.

It's easy to forget just how many people it takes to create a motion picture. With so many bodies bustling about, setting up cameras, connecting cables, and creating sets, it's only really those in this industry who can truly appreciate the complexity of it all—us actors; we're just a small part of the overall production.

I decide to take just a little longer to absorb the dynamics of it all before heading out back to the conference room. This being our first day of table script reading, all the essential cast members and production team are there, including Jackson Hunter. I haven't seen nor heard from him since our encounters at those momentous casting auditions, the ones I haven't been able to stop thinking about since they penetrated my imagination's defences.

My mind wonders as I consider my own thoughts: Why would I have heard from him? I know in my mind we were acting; I know people were watching; I *know* it probably meant no more to him than just another role, another kiss, but those notions that stirred in me that day have all but consumed my thoughts…my fantasies. Just staring into those impossibly deep brown eyes that have always captivated mine was enough to want to give myself over to those impulses shooting across my groin. Being as close as we were, I could see they were not the truest brown as perceived behind a lens but contained the tiniest flecks of gold, which had me mesmerised. It took all that I had to turn and look away when I needed to and to play out the role I had built up in my head.

When he caught and carried me off as though I weighed nothing more than a feather, I was already gone, waves of arousal already dictating my actions. I had no conscious thought running through my mind in those brief few minutes he held me in his embrace, only an instinctual need to have him. That man has awakened something in me I thought I had long forgotten: need, lust, want…notions I thought were dead and buried along with whatever other hopes I had of a future where I wasn't so damn miserable.

Yet I know, in my niggling consciousness, that he is just another reminder of something I cannot have—something I will never be able to have again. My invisible prison is ever more prominent when faced with yet more things I want but will forever be out of my reach.

At least I can take this, take back my career, my passion for acting, and tell a story for the world to see. I will just have to reign in everything else and keep them secluded from the real world and retrained to my fantasies. I can do that. I have been pretending for years to be something I am not; to want something so much that I just cannot have. What's one more longing to add to the pile? I'll use this pent-up yearning and direct it towards my dramatics; let it leak out of my pores for only the camera to see.

I take in a final inhale to brace my confidence before I head in the direction of the conference room. I can do this; I can face him and not desire more; I can be just as professional as he can.

Right?

Jackson

There she is, ceremoniously the last one to enter the conference room, gliding in in her form fitted black pencil skirt and pale pink blouse, her hair exactly as I remember it: flicking it back as she enters, almost as though she is dramatizing for added effect, allowing it to cascade in waves descending down her back. Her face wears a beautiful, natural-looking smile that radiates through to the rest of her features. I like that she appears more confident today; it allows her true self to shine through rather than hiding away behind a veil of hair.

I have thought about her a few times these last few months. Well, it appears she is impossible to forget, and as she sits opposite me, reading through her lines with us, I can see exactly why, *'still stunning.'* A permanent smirk rests on my face as I watch her from across the table, practically suffocating me with her beauty and her passion. Even in this crowded room, her talent for completely transforming her expression, her voice, and her whole demeanour into that of her characters have me awestruck. She has thoroughly been enveloped in this role of a confident, immoral seductress, succumbing to my own character's flaws. Fleeting thoughts pass through my consciousness, *'how good would she look under me, screaming my name as she came?'*

God, these thoughts *are* dangerous and only make me sound more and more like some creepy perv who can't keep his mind out of the gutter, especially as she has given me no real indication that she feels even remotely the same. She has been nothing but professional this whole time, addressing me only when the script deems it necessary, breaking character only when there is a need to address a question or a submission from someone else in the room, to change a prospective or a different approach.

I am almost relieved that when Cameron suggests we break for the day, we are told to prepare a run-through of the scene tomorrow in front of the set to see how our ideas and interpretations translate onto camera. I need to reign myself in before these thoughts run away from me.

That was *before* someone else suggested a nightcap in the hotel bar.

We have all been put up in the same hotel while we're shooting the scenes at the studio in London, a hotel that comes equipped with its own downstairs bar. The idea (I presume) is to limit our risk of being seen by the paparazzi; it also means we are not all dotted here, there, and everywhere around the capital. Efficient, but it also means none of us really have an excuse not to go for a quick drink with our new colleagues, or else face the accusations of rudeness.

'Well, actually, why not?' I think to myself that it really isn't unusual for me to have a few nights out with my fellow cast members during filming; in fact, it's usually me who suggests it. Why should I let an unhealthy attraction towards a person of that cast affect that? It might be good, actually, to get to know her better; maybe I can get her to want to know me better; maybe I can get her to want me back? Or maybe I'll find a flaw that will get me over this infatuation sooner rather than later. What is the worst that can happen?

A few hours later, and oh my god—the worst has happened. The more time I have spent in her company this evening, the *more* enticing she has become, her personality well and truly shining through, and yet she still shows no signs that this is even remotely reciprocated!

"So, there I am, 4 years old," she re-tells, "being told to eat the most disgusting soup I have ever had in…my…life!" It turns out she was a child actress, starting off in commercials, apparently. There are 9 of us left sitting here at the hotel bar, and she has had each one of us in stitches for most of the evening while she recalls the antics of past directors and what they used to do to get her to cooperate during shooting. Gone is the shy girl who auditioned a mere 3 months ago; this one exudes confidence, exaggerates in gestures, and has me even more entranced than ever. It seems I am not the only one who has been drawn into her charm; however, in only a few short hours, she has mesmerised the whole table, all engaged in her antics; all eyes on her.

"And every time I ate a spoon and said that god awful line…" holding her finger up to accentuate her point, "…without wincing, mind you! My mother's hand would shoot up from under the table to pop a piece of chocolate in my mouth!"

"She sat under the table the whole time," Louise, another cast member who is due to play Caroline, interjects with eyes wide in disbelief.

"The whole time! Goodness knows how she sat under there for so long with her neck crocked like that. Her other arm was then pinned across my lap under the table to stop me from fidgeting, and I swear you look back on some of the outtakes and there she is," Her arm then shot straight into the air, exaggerating the action! I cannot help but chuckle along with them to her storytelling, she really does tell them well.

"Maybe they should do that with us tomorrow? An ingenious way of keeping us engaged, no?" I add mockingly. She turns to me laughing, directing her eyes to mine, schooling her features into that familiar look of feigned seduction in line with that of her character, and adjusting her hand so that it gently cradles my cheek.

"Adrien, you know my need for you runs deeper than that of mere lust," she mimics a line from our upcoming script. Recognising her prompt, I quickly snatched a couple of chips from a bowl that was conveniently placed in the centre of the table, stuffing them straight into her mouth, causing her to giggle slightly in time with others around the table.

"Helen, if only you knew what I would do to you without the company you keep," she, in return, grabs a slightly larger cluster of chips, playfully shoving them into *my* mouth, which provokes me to cough and choke a little while I try and suppress my laugh, resulting in a cascade of laughter from around the table.

It's then that her façade breaks, a full smile spread widely across her face for the first time, I think, *not* her fake one, and it is aimed directly at me.

"Show me," she muffles. Still sniggering, I take the opportunity to grab another handful of chips, stuffing her so her face is full. Her whole body convulses as it becomes involved in her fits of giggles. I can't help it; making her laugh has me feeling higher than the sky. Her laugh is intoxicating, and I need her to keep laughing and to keep feeding me with her beautiful smile. With my mouth still full, I continue.

"Glad...ph...ly, now phucker up, spheetheart," Grabbing hold of her shoulders, I try to fake kiss her. This earns me her wide eyes and a small, muffled shriek as she tries to get away.

"No!" She tries to scream out amongst the mouth full of chips and giggles that she is very unsuccessfully trying to retain. I aim for the side of her face, smearing greased chip residue all up her neck and chin.

"Oh my god, Jackson!" She cries out. I let her go. I was worried I may have gone too far. Those worries were soon put aside, however, as her continued smile and childish giggles let me know I didn't. She takes a napkin to wipe off the chip residue, and her eyes, once again, find mine—those blues holding my own browns for one beat too long, enough for me to catch what maybe no one else has—that is before she catches herself and turns back to face the others. *'Attraction?'* I can't tell, but it was there, something else, I saw it briefly before when we broke that kiss at the audition, *'is she...reacting to me?'* Could she be that good of an actress that she can even mask her own body responses?

Two flashes of something I can't quite make out are not enough for me to act on, though. Too much is at stake if I get this wrong. Shit we are only on day 1, and we still have 5 months of shooting to do! If I make this awkward now, we may not recover. No, it's one thing to be attracted to someone and another to act on it when the feelings are not entirely reciprocated.

We all continue to converse a little while longer before collectively deciding to call it a night, opting for a good night's rest rather than enter day 2 tired and possibly slightly hungover.

Lying on my hotel bed, thoughts of Catherine dance around my head. How does someone as beautiful, funny, and talented as she, end up so self-conscious and afraid of herself, she hides it from most of the world, choosing instead to mask herself behind a ruse of fake smiles and feigned interest?

I want more: more of her smiles that force anyone who is lucky enough to have seen them to want to return their shine; more of her infectious laugh that makes me want to draw it from her time and time again. I want more of *her*.

As I start to drift off to sleep, all I can think about is how beautiful she would be in my arms, how amazing she would feel on my lips, and how perfect she would look coming with my cock buried deep inside her and my name expelling from her mouth, her face flushed with a look of pure pleasure. God, I don't think I've wanted anything more in my life.

Maybe 5 months is enough time to convince her that she could want more of me too?

Chapter 5

Catherine

"Fuck!" A growl echoes loudly through the halls, originating from the room down towards the end of the corridor.

"Urgh, fuck!" Another I realise is coming from the very direction I am headed. A deep flutter of nerves hit my abdomen as I started to recognise the owner of the grunt. *'Oh, this is a bad idea; turn back and abort! Abort!'* However, my stubborn feet do not seem to get the message, venturing on.

While heading to my room last night, I decided it was best to stick to my regular routines as best I could, and considering this movie involves a fair bit of exposed skin on my part, one particular routine was best not skipped: my daily trip to the gym. I have my own gym at home, which makes using it on a daily basis a lot more convenient. I only really aim for around half an hour to an hour at a time; it isn't enough to bulk up, but enough to keep me in shape. However, I am usually alone, so all these self-conscious notions are never really an issue. This is the hotel's gym, though, and while my sheepish brain wants to turn tails and run, my stubborn pride keeps me on course. Getting up at 5 this morning to head down here, I honestly didn't expect to find anyone else about, *'but of course he would be here!'* Why hadn't the thought occurred to me that *he* would never miss a gym session? No way does he maintain that body by doing anything less.

"Urgh!" Another low grunt reverberates down the empty corridor. I pause just to the left, outside the open door, hesitant to go in. *'Don't be silly; you can't avoid him; you need these routines!'* Taking a final look at my attire, I brace myself. I am clad in black workout leggings sporting a pink strip running up the outside leg and a matching sports crop top; my hair is tied up in a simple high ponytail. Brushing away all self-conscious thoughts directed at my exposed abdomen and makeup-free face, I breathe in a deep breath, bracing myself as I enter.

Only to be halted abruptly in the doorway by the sheer force of lust. There he is in all his glory, wearing just a pair of tight workout shorts and a baggy vest top soaked completely through with sweat. Jackson, his hair slicked back, wet with perspiration and even more dripping down from his temples. He is occupying the weights machine, working on a pulley system, and every time he pulls down on the bar, the muscles on his arms flex in the most delicious motion, causing them to glisten against the wetness of his skin. "Fuck!" He goes again, clearly working against the strain of the weight. Fuck indeed, every inch of him screams testosterone. What I wouldn't give to run my hand over those muscles, to feel their firmness against the lightness of my fingertips, I can't help but bite my bottom lip unconsciously at the sight of him.

It was at that moment, however, that he unexpectedly let go of the weights with a grunt and stood to turn suddenly, locking eyes with mine. *'Shit he caught me staring.'* I expect him to call me out for my blatant perversion. Instead of being rude, though, a sly smile creeps across his face.

"Good morning," A low, deep purr expels his greeting. Can those words even be said seductively? Such a normal acknowledgement, yet coming from his mouth, is the sexiest thing I have ever heard.

"Good morning. Sorry I…ur…was shocked to find someone else in here; it seems I am not the only morning person in the group," he offers a throaty chuckle as he grabs his towel, which was draped over another piece of equipment, using it to wipe the sweat from his face and arms.

"Nope, not the only one; try not to miss a day; going at it in the morning gets me motivated to take on the rest of the day."

"Same here; usually this time is the only time I get to myself, so it has sort of become routine."

"Great! I'll be grateful for the company; I gotta warn you though, I get kinda loud, as you most probably heard," I give a little chuckle to cover the truth that unbeknownst to him, his loudness is my arousal.

"Oh yes, to be honest, I wasn't sure I was *even* heading to the gym this morning; thought I might be walking in to find you filming a porno!" *'Did I just say that?'* His deep chuckle that follows vibrates through me and hitches my breath. He bites the corner of his bottom lip as his gaze surveys the length of my body.

"Trust me, darling, my sex noises are not nearly as aggressive."

"Duly noted," A touch of excitement courses through my body, *'is he checking me out?'* Stop it, Catherine; he is clearly a player with a capital P. He probably checks out every girl, with or without the very skimpy clothing I decided to dress myself in this morning.

Remembering what I was actually there for, I head on over to the cross trainer and begin my workout. I hear him behind me arranging the dumbbells. I no longer need to look at him to envision how he looks lifting them; the image of his contracting muscles is now forever scorched into my brain.

Not surprisingly, I find myself exercising more vigorously than before…*'Umm I wonder why?'* Ha! There is no question as to why when motivation comes in the form of a very sexy man-god, behind me. My arousal is making my blood pump harder, faster, and warmer than ever before. *'Damn you, pheromones.'*

"Hay, would you mind helping me out a minute?" he calls out, *'Oh, only too happy to!'* Shush, shut up, stupid brain; get yourself out of the gutter. Snapping myself out of my sickening lustful thoughts, I turn back to what Jackson is actually asking me for.

"I just need someone to spot me."

"Uh huh, sure," Oh dear.

I head over and position myself behind him while he lays down on the bench, lining himself up with his weight and, consequently, my pelvis.

"So, is this all you do for fun? What else do you get up to?" He asks nonchalantly. Shit! I can't tell him the truth. What? Actually, I don't have much free time. That this job is more like a holiday than work.

"Not much, really, you?"

"Oh, the usual, basking in the joys fame brings mostly, I find that opportunities for adventure tend to come knocking more often than me having to seek them out," he takes the weight off the bar in his hands, bringing them down towards his chest, uttering another one of his subtle grunts as he does. His peck peaks out on the side of his baggy vest, perfectly toned and flexing with the movement of his arms. *'You…are…a…perv…Catherine! Stop staring!'*

"What made you apply for the role of Helen?" He asks as he strains against the weight, bringing it back up again.

"I didn't really; I auditioned for the movie and thought I'd get a small part. Gary seemed to see something in me and put me forward for Helen."

"You definitely have something…" he manages, straining against the weight, lowering it slowly, only to raise it once more. "What made you stop acting originally?"

"Not sure, really. Life just got away from me; I suppose," he places the bar back on its hooks to sit up, turning 180° to face me, each leg straddling either side of the bench.

"Well, for what's it worth, I am very glad you chose now to start again; I really am enjoying getting to know you and working with you, of course."

"Thanks," I was tucking a few strands of escaped hair behind my ear. "You too, even if *all* I have really learned so far is that you are as loud in the gym as two mating foxes in heat," I tease.

"Hay!" he jumps up, ready to chase me in jest, a broad grin filling out his face. "What did you say?" I edge myself around the bench as he pursues me, all while I squeal in laughter.

"No, Jackson!"

"Come here so I can show you just how loud I can be."

"Ahh, no, you keep those things," pointing to his bulging arm muscles, "away from me; those should be certified weapons!" He throws his head back while letting out one of his deep-throated laughs.

"Ok, I am going to head out for a shower. See you at rehearsals, Catherine, where you'll get to see these *guns* up close and personal."

"Alright, Mr Chauvinistic, get out of here before your head is too big to fit through the door!"

"Haha impossible! Have you seen the size of these doors?" He leaves, granting me a sly side glance as he does. Leaving me to reel in the whirlwind of our interaction, a small smile still resting on my face, which doesn't seem to lose its effect as I head over to the treadmill. It's genuine; Jackson seems to bring that out of me, and his charm and schoolboy humour spark a light that was once shut off.

'Don't get carried away, Catherine.' Its lust, that's all it is; he is so ludicrously attractive it would be damn near impossible not to fantasise over him, and he would most likely fuck anyone who gave him any inclination that they wanted to in return.

'But maybe,' I wonder, *'just maybe that might be exactly what I need.'*

I shouldn't have done it, but I did, and now I can't undo it.

I have never been a fan girl; I haven't had the urge to cyber-stalk someone since the days of teenage crushes. Somehow, however, the impulse to look up at Jackson Hunter became too much as I ran out of my sexual tension on the treadmill. Thoughts of one-night stands and living out fantasies running through my mind—the dangerous idea that for one brief moment I could have what I want.

Out came the laptop as soon as I made it into my room, and now any stupid notion I had of having him in my bed is dashed.

Jackson Hunter, one of the UK's most eligible bachelors, 'doesn't do one-night stands,' as quoted by 'Real Gos' magazine. 'I have a unique desire to connect with my partner; you just don't get that short-term.' He states this in the interview conducted just last year. 'If you're with me, then you are only with me; there is no one else.'

Well, that's shit. I mean, looking at his track record, he doesn't *seem* to be able to hold a girlfriend for more than a few months at a time, so clearly has a short attention span, and there doesn't seem to be any shortage of them, so it's not an inability to find them, but, alas, no recent record of anyone coming into his life being able to just take away what they need.

So, there is that, I will not let him compromise his morals, nor will I allow him to get me into a position where I can admit to mine. It looks like I'll back off. Keep this professional; it was my intention from the beginning after all, *'that was before you caught him checking you out, and that was before his sweat-soaked form did things to your lady parts you thought were dead!'* Never mind, back on the pile of things I'm not allowed. I am sure it won't be long before he has another gorgeous girl on his arm, and his attention will veer away from me to them. It looks like he is overdue for one, 4 months since he was last pictured with a girlfriend on his arm. I'll just have to control myself till then.

Chapter 6

<u>Jackson</u>

"Hels, I...I don't understand; how is this possible?" She moves ever closer to me in a practiced move that almost appears like she's gliding across thin ice. Coming so close, her breasts rested against my chest, her arms entangled around my waist, twisting up my back as she reaches up to grasp my shoulders and lips so incredibly close I can feel her breath against mine.

"You underestimate me, my love."

"Never, only in awe," Covering her mouth with my own, our faces meld into one in a frantic dance of passion. Backing her up towards the wall behind us. Before colliding with it, however, we briefly separate so I can throw her against it, forcefully pinning her against the plasterboard. Taking her mouth back against mine in a furious embrace, my whole body dominating and covering hers: she sends so many confusing signals coursing through my mind, across my chest, and to every nerve ending.

"I need you," The words escape her mouth in a hushed command, while I find her neck and lips promptly connecting with them. She smells so sweetly like vanilla and tastes just as intoxicating. "Take me, Adrien."

"Ok, cut, thank you," Cameron's voice rings out in my ears; it is a physical force to pull myself away from the one thing in this room I want. I hear rather than see Cameron approach us from behind, "Are you ok there, Catherine?" Addressing her.

"Yes, I'm fine. Why?"

"Just being thrown against the wall there. That was new! And quite forceful!" A false laugh escapes her lips as she replies.

"Ha, I'm not going to break; you know, Cameron, I'm fine," she places her hand on his arm in reassurance. Is there no one she can't charm?

"Good, cause I liked it. It really added to the moment," Looking around to address me, "You happy with that?"

"Of course."

"Good, then that's how I want it; good job. We *are* going to have to re-enforce this wall, however, because that will not withstand many more of those; it shook quite significantly as you did it; can't have that on camera," he winks, then walks off in the direction of the construction manager.

"You alright? Honestly?" I ask, realising I hadn't warned her I was going to do that. To be honest, I wasn't exactly planning on it; just kind of got caught up in the passion of it all, like so many other times we have gone at it on set these past few weeks.

"Ha, yes, I *am* fine! It was good; even I was beginning to believe it," Believe it, please! The desires that I thought were actually growing between us have all but dissipated, and trust me, not from my lack of trying! That morning in the gym, I thought it was a turning point: she was flirty and smiley, and I really did get the impression she liked me; I caught her gawking, for goodness's sake! I thought that maybe it was the start of something, but even as soon as later the same bloody day she shut down again.

I thought it may have been the presence of other people; maybe she wasn't used to showing affection in public. A bit contradictory with what we had been doing for the camera all day, but giving her the benefit of the doubt, I waited until the next morning. Back in the gym with it being the two of us again, I tried, only to be shut down, locked out, and our interactions minimal; the warmth that I saw in her eyes that first morning was gone and back to curt pleasantries.

She isn't cold; far from it, she is more indifferent. We have gone to the hotel bar a few times as a group the past few weeks, even ventured out to some nearby clubs, and while she continues to be the life of the party, being able to entice and engage us all, she pays me no more particular attention than she does to everybody else. Yet every moment I spend in her company, the more I want her. Other girls have tried to flirt to get my attention, and while remaining a gentleman to all, I only have eyes for her.

Having to be this close to her on set is definitely not helping. I just want to give myself over to these impulses, but I am constantly having to rein them in at the sound of the word 'cut', turning on and off my cock like a goddamn flashlight. I am so conflicted with the range of impulses surging through me that I am even starting to second-guess myself!

This, not knowing where I stand, is my problem. There is clearly something between us, but without knowing exactly what it is, I can't get my head around it, or her. I have waited around long enough for her actions to reveal their true intentions; clearly, I need to take a more direct approach to this. Ask her outright, get my answer, and then move on, with or without her on my arm. If she likes me as much as I seem to like her, then we can start making a go of it and see where it goes. If she doesn't, then maybe my body will finally get the message, the disappointing conclusion that it isn't going to happen, that I was mistaken, and we can just concentrate on the rest of the movie.

Tonight. It's Thursday, and we have gotten into the habit these last few weeks that while we are on a Monday to Friday rota our nights out should try to be on a Thursday. Not everyone comes to them, but there is at least enough to make it fun. Most of the other cast and crew head home on a Friday night to be with their families, so it seemed logical, as long as none of us had too much to drink.

We have arranged to leave the hotel tonight. There is a club a short walk from it, where we have ended up a few times before. It has good music, good vibes, and a great VIP section to keep us separate from the rest of the club. Going out, however, involves dressing up a little more than usual, so I know she will already be in her room getting ready. This is where I will make my stand.

As I wait outside her hotel room door, preparing to knock, I take a moment to inhale deep breaths to calm my nerves. It is an odd sensation to be on the precipice of something life changing. Never before has asking a girl out caused such a surge of agitation. Of course, I know the reason for this; never before have I ever been unsure of a woman's feelings for me; normally, they are so obvious with their affections that I know outright whether I will be rejected or not. This, however, is nerve-racking! After tonight, it will either be the beginning of something or the end of something, and I really can't tell you which way it will go or what either scenario will look like, because, being honest with myself, I don't actually know a whole lot about her. I know I enjoy her company; I know I find her insanely attractive; I know some part of me is craving more of her; but beyond that is the unknown. Maybe that is the reason why this feels so different from any of the others before her—the enigma of it?

I knock.

All or nothing, I have to try. I have to resolve this one way or another.

The door opens, and she's dressed in nothing but a white towel tied haphazardly around her body, her hair dripping wet and draped across one shoulder. Her face, which started as a scowl, has turned into the brightest of smiles upon seeing me on the other side of the door. What I wouldn't give to be the creator of that smile every damn day.

"Hay you," she greets, resting one hand on her hip and shooting it out in an angled stance in the doorway. I realise I have been holding my breath in an attempt to calm the warm arousal creeping downwards, taking all my effort not to act like a creep by objectifying her body as she stands there, trusting me explicitly, while she has barely anything on, and not really showing any signs of being at all uncomfortable with me being there either.

"Hay yourself," I answer, finally.

"You, ok? Oh, I am not running late, am I?" She twirls around, back into the room in a slight panic, grabbing her phone off the bed to see the time. I use this opportunity to step inside, closing the door behind me so no one else has a view of this stunning, half-naked enchantress in front of me. Bending slightly over the bed, staring down at her phone, the towel riding up her thigh, barely grazing the base of her ass, she still seems so at ease.

"No, no, you're ok," Trying to look everywhere else other than at the site of her scarcely covered backside. "Still have plenty of time before we're due to meet the others; don't worry," I can see her take a visible sigh of relief before taking a seat in front of the vanity unit.

"Oh good, I thought I had lost track of time. You know, this is the third shower I have had since I got back; this damn stage makeup just won't come off! It's all in my hairline look," she pushes back the front of her hair to reveal that, yes, indeed, it still retained traces of makeup at its roots.

"I am sure no one will notice, and even if they do, no one will care," she seriously doesn't appear to have any issues with me being in her room, dressed the way she is, and addressing me in the same way she would any other day. It is such a stark contradiction to my very over-baring awkwardness; it's like I am an old friend, and this interaction is just a platonic scenario we have done a dozen times. *'Oh shit, is that how she sees me? Have I read this all wrong? Has she just been seeing me as a friend this whole time? What should I do? Should I back down?'*

No, I need answers, even if it is just so my brain can put my dick back on reprimand.

"I…um…" Shit I am acting like a prepubescent school kid again. *'Get your head in the game, man; you're Jackson Hunter!'* "Catherine…Shit…Catherine, tell me I'm an idiot," I resign dejectedly, dropping my fidgeting hands down to my side. I just have to rip the band aid off and hope it doesn't sting. She stares at me deadpan, her face unreadable.

"Ok, you're an idiot," she returns, completely nonchalant, before turning back towards the mirror and carrying the widest of grins on her face. "Now remind me, why are you an idiot again?"

"Because I can't stop thinking about you."

She pauses, mid-application of whatever potion she is rubbing into her skin. She isn't looking at me, nor is she even making any attempt to move, instead choosing to stare blankly at her reflection in the mirror.

I cannot stand the silence, replacing it instead with ramblings that seem to be tumbling from my mouth like verbal diarrhoea, feeling like I am digging myself a bigger hole but unable to stop.

"Every time I kiss you on set, it feels real to me, Catherine. I want it to be real. There is something I can't quite make out between us, and I want to explore it, but I don't know if it's reciprocated or not. Sometimes, I think so, and then sometimes I question whether I saw or felt it because you act completely different from how I would expect you to…and so I am here, I suppose, to find out if it is or if I am acting like a complete idiot. If I am, just tell me, and we can forget we ever had this conversation, and it'll be over. I'll move on…but if I'm not, and this is real, god, Catherine…I dunno…shit, I just…I don't know."

Her eyes have drifted down to focus on some inanimate object on the table; she still hasn't said a word. I move a little closer, placing my hand on the unit in an attempt to redirect her attention back to me.

"Shit, say something, Catherine, please, your silence is killing me here," she still doesn't look at me. Still lost in a trance to whatever is so damn interesting on the table.

After a long moment, she finally breaks, placing her hand over mine and allowing her eyes to follow the movement there but not to look directly at my face. Muttering in a hushed whisper, she responds.

"I think you should go," With these 5 words my insides shatter. I laid it out, asked for what I wanted, and got denied. Swiftly removing her hand, she gets up from the table and moves past the bed, choosing to stare out the window at the passing world outside.

I have been dismissed. The stone currently lodged in my throat makes it difficult to swallow. Slowly, I closed my eyes and turned to leave, resigned to the notion that I was wrong.

So why does *this* feel so wrong? This isn't how it's supposed to be.

It wasn't until I nearly reached the door, though, that I realised I had missed something. *'Am I wrong?'*

"You didn't deny my claims," she ignores me, continuing to stare out of the window, out over the roaring city below, as I make my way back across the room to where she is stood.

"You weren't disgusted by them either; you didn't outright tell me I was wrong. So, am I? Am I so far off base here?" Again, her silence is all the reply I receive: anger and the worst kind of irritation start to build up inside me. "I'm not, am I? I'm not alone in this; you feel something."

"Jackson, please!" She quietly begs.

"No! You feel something, but you're denying yourself. Why?" Nothing. "Shit! Catherine, talk to me!" I slowly approach her from behind. I know she can see me in the window's reflection, so it's no surprise to her that I am there. That anger still continues to simmer away at me, but it doesn't seem to be getting me the reaction I need to move this forward; maybe something else will, something I feel like she has no control over.

Against all impulses, I keep my hands to myself, but I do bring my mouth down, so it is next to her ear. Her breath hitches as I place one gentle kiss sweetly on her neck. When she doesn't say anything and doesn't make any motion to move away or, at the very least, move me, I am encouraged to go further.

"Tell me to stop," I whisper before placing another kiss slightly lower on her neck this time. She moves her head to the side, extenuating it to give me access. She *is* enjoying this; *'I knew it!'* With another kiss at the base of her neck on her shoulder, I continued to trace her lines until I met the top of her arm. It is when I reach out to touch her, however, that I hear a very tiny—and might I add, unenthusiastic—whisper, "Stop."

I do, pausing to hoover just above her shoulder blade, bare from the towel. I take a moment to deliberate on my next move.

Eventually, with a slight nod, I back off and move away.

"Ok, Catherine, I'll respect that, even though I know you didn't really want me to."

I start backing away towards the door, contemplating my next move while biting my bottom lip.

"I know you want this, Catherine; I can see it and feel it emanating from you, but for some reason you're scared. It's ok; I'm not giving up on you, though, now that I know. I think this could be something special, you know? And that's worth giving a damn," she pulls her arms around her waist; her classic defensive move I have seen her use a few times now. That shy girl from the audition is back, the one I know isn't her true self but rears its ugly head none the less. "I'll see you in a bit, Catherine. We're meeting down in the lobby."

With that, I leave the room. One hundred and one plans start formulating in my mind. I know now that she wants me too; her involuntary reaction to my intimate kiss was more than enough to convince me. I need to find out what has created that barrier—the one that causes her to deny the things she wants—that stops her from showing herself fully to the world. If I can crack that, maybe I'll have a chance.

Catherine

Why couldn't I just say no? Why couldn't I have just lied and told him I felt nothing? Then maybe he would have left, hurt, maybe dejected, but he would have recovered, and I would have been left to wallow in this misery alone. Now I have given him hope and a drive towards something that can never happen. I *need* to stop this, push him away, and make it abundantly clear that I am not good for him before this goes too far. Why did it have to be him, the epitome of sex on legs? I am not only fighting against his unrelenting ability to see hope where there is none, but against that of my own body, which just wants to throw myself at him, to beg him to take me away to a place so far from here that I no longer have to restrain myself.

But I can't.

I have to stop this, and I have to be as assertive and resilient as I am. Any sign of that unsure little girl I displayed earlier, and he will call bullshit.

Heading down the lift, I brace myself, drawing on my strengths and the well-practiced skills I have to take on the roles of aloof, indifferent, and promiscuous. I can't take back my lapse earlier; he knows I like him. What I need to show him is that I am no good for him and that I can't be what he wants in a woman. It's not entirely untrue, but I need him to believe I am all the things he despises rather than the truth. Oh, the truth is that if I could, I would give him everything.

He isn't alone as I reach the lobby. Being in a group will give me plenty of people to bounce between, so both my own and his focus won't be so completely on each other. I opted for a little red number today, red clearly being the universal colour of seductress, because that's all this is, right, nothing more than sexual attraction; that's all I need to elude to. I feel Jackson's gaze running the length of my body as he takes me in; it takes all my willpower not to meet it. I hear Rodney, a scoundrel straight from the lighting department, give off a very loud wolf whistle. I can't help offering a smile and a twirl of the 'goods' for added effect.

"You look amazing!" Rodney takes my hand, holding me out to survey me.

"Why thank you," That's right, available to everyone; that's the impression I want. I can't see Jackson; he must have moved behind me, but I know he must be watching this. "Shall we head out?" All together, we head in the direction of the club, arms linked firmly in Rodney's grasp.

The club is alive! Vibrations from the music move through me, causing my whole body to move to its rhythm. It has been a while since I have felt like this— to truly lose myself in the moment, surrounded by people who enjoy my company and who know nothing of my former life. I don't need to justify myself to these people, nor do I have to live up to any unrealistic expectations; I can just be me for a few short hours. My laughter beams out of me as I move, shake, and twirl along with everybody else, trying not to overthink it for fear my demons will ruin the euphoria coursing through me.

A few guys have come over and danced just a little too close. I let them, continuing my ruse that Jackson means no more to me than just another guy in the crowd, that I am no longer affected by him than by anyone else. It isn't true, of course; my skin crawls with every new touch, but I need to dismiss any traction of hope that he took away from our interaction earlier. I have paid him little to no attention all night, which is probably why he caught me by surprise when I heard his deep, penetrative voice purr behind me.

"Having fun?" *'Shit, keep dancing, keep acting like this is a very normal interaction.'*

"I am actually the DJ has played some great tunes tonight," he closes the gap between us; I can feel his pelvis grazing lightly over my arse.

"Don't think I don't know what you're doing."

"And what is it you think I am doing?"

"You think if you make it look like you are promiscuous, coming onto everything with a pulse and a cock, it'll make me want you less. Make me leave you alone," *'Shit, was I really that transparent?'* He is so close to my ear I can smell his earthy cologne, his voice reverberating through my mind, louder than the music thumping through the speakers.

"But I see you. I see you wince whenever someone touches you; it's subtle; it is like you want to move away but you are forcing yourself to stay. But with me…" he gently glides his fingers down my arm, coming to rest in my hand.

"You like this; your body responds to me involuntarily," Damn it, why does he have to be so intuitive? *'You can't have him; you can't have him.'* I have to keep reminding myself.

I turn on the spot to face him; the move removes my ass from the bulge growing in his pants; my heels, however, make it easier to see him eye-to-eye. In response, he takes my hands in his and places them around his neck. I do nothing to stop him, though; *'damn you, ovaries!'*

"So why don't you tell me what this is really about so we can get through this and share in something truly amazing, hay?"

I take a deep breath. I want to; I really want to tell him everything. I want to finally let someone else in, but I know I can't; he won't understand, and even if he did, it wouldn't change anything. This is still the life I am trapped in; even if I am in a temporary reprieve, dragging him down with me wouldn't solve a goddamn thing.

"I can't give you what you want," It's vague, but the truth.

"And what is it you think I want, sweet girl?" he brings his hand up to brush his knuckles softly across my cheek, opening his palm up to rest it on the side of my head, fingers entangled in the hair at the base of my neck. He answers himself, without waiting for my response to his question.

"I want you. Your body writhing under mine, relishing in the delicious contact of our bodies coming together, I want to see you come over and over again, loving the feel of my body in yours."

His lips are so close to mine without touching: I once again find myself holding my breath as my head begins to swim at the connotation of his words, *'Oh, how I want that too.'*

"But I don't just want your body, Catherine," he continues, "I want to take you out, show you what it is to be cherished, and I want to know everything about you…everything. I want to wake up next to you and be the reason for that radiant smile that charms everyone within its viewing range every damn day! I want that laugh that hits my insides every time I am able to draw it from you. But most of all, I want you, all of you. That's what I want from you, Catherine."

I feel my heart crack and break under the enormity of his words, another life they are all I would have wanted to hear, but now.

"I can't give you that," I whisper, almost inaudible, but I know he heard it.

"Then what *can* you give me?" I have to, I have to say the words I know will turn him away, make him see the worst in me, but it's the only way, just let him take with him any conclusions from them as he will.

"I can give it to you tonight," Clearly dejected, he rests his forehead against mine, releasing a deep sigh, hinting at his disappointment.

"Is that all?"

"That's all I have."

"Nope. That's not going to fly with me, Catherine," he shakes his head, rubbing it against mine while sucking in his lips.

"I don't do one-night stands; they are empty and meaningless." I hear his anger spit out his words, bubbling up inside him.

"I want something real. I want something real with you."

"I can't give you that," I push back against the strength of his hold and say, "I'm sorry," promptly walking away from him towards the rest of the group at a table towards the back of the club.

"I'm going to go; get an early start with makeup; stay out any later, and they'll have to deal with these eye bags as well as everything else," Gesturing towards the whole of my face, attempted to joke as a way of distracting from the clenching currently residing within my chest.

"Will see you all in the morning," I turn to Jackson, whose face now holds a scowl that could riffle the bitterest of bitter old men!

"See you in the morning."

Brushing past him as I leave. *'It's for the best.'* I tell myself.

So why does it feel like every nerve ending in my body is screaming at me? Telling me I have made the biggest mistake of my life. Telling me I am wrong.

Chapter 7

<u>Jackson</u>

She hasn't come to the gym this morning. I have no doubt it's because she is trying to avoid me. That's fine; it gives me the chance to burn off some of this excess aggression I have been building up since the revelations last night.

Expectedly, I am pushing myself harder than I usually do, trying to push out her last words to me from my conscious, *'I can't give you what you want.'* Why? She has still left me with no explanation, no satisfactory answer, and nothing I can use to tell my cock to calm the fuck down. I am still left with more questions than answers, and I am even more confused than I was to begin with.

"Urgh!" Harder! Anger begins to rage through me: anger at her; at myself for not being able to walk away; her behaviour; these games; and these unanswered questions. Offering me just one night, she thinks that low of me that I would actually accept? She is no good for me; I know this, and even *she* is telling me this.

So why can't I stop thinking about her? Why can't I push out this notion that it's all wrong, that there is a truth somewhere in her defence, that I am missing something from a far bigger picture? What am I missing, Catherine Carell?

These questions follow me around for the rest of the morning, hovering over my head like a damn comic book strip.

"Hels, I-I don't understand; how is this possible?" she moves that much closer to me. I try, but I can't. I just can't look at her straight, instead I attempt to focus on a piece of scenery just to the right of her face. As I feel her arms snake around my waist and her lips close in, my heart starts beating erratically, and the mixed notions of anger and self-pity sink lower into my chest.

"You underestimate me, my love," she is such a pro, exactly like yesterday, as if the events of the evening didn't even take place. She is so completely unaffected by me that there is not a shred of regret or remorse evident in her demeanour. How can she affect me so much, and yet she can stand there like the ice queen herself? *'Snap out of it, Jackson!'*

"Never, only in awe," I kiss her, but it isn't the same; the intensity is gone, the urgency dissipates and as I back her up against the wall, I don't throw her; I only push and then pin her against it. The mood for that sort of passion is missing, extinguished by my state of mind.

The fact is, when I first did it, I was so caught up in the moment that the physicality of it felt right. Now…now we might as well be two strangers. I am drawing on my professionalism and my skill as an actor to get through this scene, but that electricity that usually runs through us…is gone.

"Cut!" I hear Cameron yell from somewhere in the distance. We break, and I see Catherine head towards the drinks table, and I watch as Cameron takes very determined strides in my direction, the disgruntled look of annoyance evident across his face. "What was that?" Oh no, clearly, drawing on my 'skills as an actor' is not paying off.

"Do you have criticism?"

"You know I do. Where the hell is my chemistry?" I sucked in my bottom lip to bite down on it hard, hiding my frustration. "Come and look!" He drags me over to view one of the small screens next to the camera, playing back the last few minutes of take.

Yes, I can see it: the sheer lack of interest clearly written across my face, the negativity radiating off me like an aura. You look at Catherine, and you can still see that desire and strength warping her beautiful features into that of her character, but I look like a bloody dog who lost his bone. "What's happened, Hunter?" He finally asks once the playback has finished.

"I know, I'm sorry; I don't think I am quite with it today."

"Well, get with it!"

"I will; can you just give me a half hour?"

"Fine, but you had better come back with some balls, I swear to god!" He walks off to start yelling at a lighting hand, while I turn on my heel to make my way back to my on-set trailer. I need to get out of my head, and I have half an hour to do it.

Firmly closing the door behind me, I enter my trailer, leaning my head against the door. *'Fucking man up you, fuckwit! She isn't yours; she clearly never will be.'* Well, that's the problem now, isn't it? That's why I feel so down, because I want something I can't have. For a brief moment yesterday afternoon,

I thought I could, but now I am forced to accept her decision, even though I have no idea why. This *was* ultimately what it boils down to, no matter how angry, disappointed, or frustrated I am, it's completely out of my control, and if I am honest with myself, it's my own fault for believing in false hopes, because for a time I thought attraction was all we needed.

I hear a faint knock at the door behind me. Surely it hasn't been half an hour yet? Composing myself, I turn to open it, coming face-to-face…with her; the one person I am trying my very best to rearrange my thoughts over so we can get back on track.

"Hay, you ok?" I ask, still unable to look at her properly.

"Can I come in?" Curt, short, is not the vibrant Catherine I am normally received with, nor is she the shy, timid one. This appears to be a whole new side to her, one that has probably come to reprimand me and remind me to get my head on straight.

"Um, sure," I stand to one side to let her pass, partially closing the door behind her.

"Listen, I know I am not with it; I got a lot on my mind, just…" Without warning, she pushes herself against me so hard that I stumble back against the door, effectively closing it completely with a thump. One hand quickly finds itself entangling at the back of my head with the small wisps of hair there, while the other lands on my chest. She moves her face so it lines up with mine, those blue sapphires locked, our lips a mere centimetre apart; only giving me that moment notice, before her mouth then makes contact. She waits there without moving, her lips crushing into mine. Apprehension maybe? Waiting to see how I would react to her intrusion.

Wait no more, I'm taking this moment, finally an intimacy away from the cameras, away from the scrutiny of directors. This isn't acting; this is us. Returning the kiss with as much force and passion as I have been reeling in these past few weeks, I let go of the frustration of the last few days and give in, angling my head and opening my mouth to accept her awaiting tongue. My hand rests happily on the side of her face; fingers lost, buried in her hair, my other hand finds her hip, dragging her pelvis closer to mine, pinning ourselves against the force of the other.

The kiss is heavy, filled with all the masked sexual frustration and desire that's been threatening for weeks to erupt between us. I can hear and feel on my cheek that both our breaths have become erratic, more intense, and desperate, as we continue to deepen our connection. With my hand squeezing her hip, hers balled up, gripping my shirt so tightly, almost as if we believed that by letting go, the other would float away.

I don't want this to end. I don't want the reality of the situation to come barraging in like a runaway freight train. Eventually, however, our lips unlock, but our mouths remain close, allowing only our noses to slightly nudge at each other's, each breathing heavily. Taken aback by the force of our connection, her eyes once again find mine. This time, the lust and desire I had seen in them in the past, doesn't pass by in a flash; she isn't hiding them behind the shutters of her mind; she is allowing me to see them; she wants me to see her want for me. I don't know how long we have been here lost in each other's mouths, but however long it was, it wasn't long enough. I want more. I'll always want more.

After a time to allow ourselves to be lost in the moment, she slowly starts to back away, regaining her composure, straightening out her clothes, and brushing off imagined dust in order to readdress me.

"So, you are still capable then," she responds, finally allowing those shutters to close in order to conceal her true thoughts. The puzzled look on my face must be saying it all as she continues.

"You are still capable of feeling that passion and acting out arousal? Good, I think you forget the whole reason I got this job was because of that. If we can't deliver now, well…I'm not sure. Now sort yourself out and bring it to the set; we have a scene to shoot," Pushing past me to find the door, she exits out back towards the set.

I watch as she walks away from me. She is right; this is a job. If I can't act myself out of this slump, then what the hell am I doing here? One thing is for sure, that little display really *has* fired up a desire from within, propelling all other feelings of sexual frustration and rage to the forefront of my mind and dictating the direction my body wants.

I head back out to the set, finding Cameron quickly while these sensations are still running rampant through my veins.

"Ok, I'm good," I say briefly before moving past him onto the scene behind where Catherine is waiting.

"Ok great. Positions!" With a point of his finger, he signals action.

"Hels, I…I don't understand; how is this possible?" This time my eyes stare intensely into hers; no longer shy about touching her, I place my hand behind her neck to keep her face pinned, staring back into mine.

"You underestimate me, my love," she looks at me like she wants to tear my clothes off there, and then, extenuating her neck to give me a perfect view of its delicateness, I lower my face to lightly brush my lips across the skin there.

"Never," I whisper into her ear, "only in awe," We don't hold back as our mouths close over one another; we mirror that same intensity from my trailer. Backing her towards the wall, I unintentionally threw her against it again, this time with such additional velocity that I felt a breath escape from her as I braced myself against her not two seconds later.

Our mouths meet in a frantic need coursing through from my body into hers, my arms leaning against the wall either side of her head while hers grip my shirt, drawing me closer.

"I need you," my mouth leaves hers to find her delicious neck again while I continue to grind my pelvis into hers, pinning her between them and the wall. She places both her hands open palmed on each side of my face, dragging it back to meet hers, her mouth slightly agape, breathing heavily. "Take me, Adrien."

"Cut!" Cameron's voice rings out while he claps his hands for added effect. "Fantastic! That was it!" I back away from her, my eyes still entranced by hers, only breaking the hold as I felt a hand slap me on the back. "I don't know what you did, Jackson, but that was perfect, both of you! On Monday, we will film it! I want it exactly like that, so whatever shit you're dealing with, leave it at the door. Understood!"

"Loud and clear," I reply, the sting of the kiss still lingering on my lips, provoking me to suck them in to savour the sensation. Her reply is just one of her curt nods as she tries not to look at me. It seems the sheer impact of our moment has clearly left a bit more of an impression on her today.

"Great, let's move on and practice scene 5 while we still have our day. Umm, Catherine," he turns back to address her. "You are not in this one, but do you mind hanging around a bit? I know Jonathan in makeup wanted to get a mould of you so he can get a head start on the effects for scenes 16 through 18 before we head out on location. Is that, ok?"

"Of course."

"Great, well done today!" She heads off in the direction of the makeup department while I wait for props to set up the next scene. I can't say I am not relieved to have a reprieve from her. I need time to realign the signals misfiring between my brain and my body, because right now, all my body wants to do is follow her, give into these impulses, and give her exactly what we both need, not caring for who is watching…and those impulses are dangerous.

Catherine

This afternoon required very little effort, but god, was it tedious. Jonathon spent it making a complete mould of my face, chest, and arms so he could recreate 'markings and injuries' later on in the filming, tailored to my body shape. Essentially, I had to sit and wait for plaster and silicon to dry all afternoon with straws sticking out my nose…fun!

By the time I am back in my hotel room and see my half-filled suitcase sat on the bed, I let off a very audible groan, *'Urgh!'* the last thing I want to do is pack. As it is Friday, I always head home to Dorset.

In a feeble attempt to gain some momentum to finish the task and go, I opt to shower first. That, however, did not have the desired effect; instead, it allowed my mind to wander back to today. As the warm waves of the shower's comfort wash over me, I am once again transported back to Jackson's trailer, with the feel of his hands on me, a tight grip on my hip like he couldn't bear to let go, the softness of his lips in contrast to the firmness of his kiss, taking his want for me. I knew it was wrong; I knew it was pushing the boundaries I had attempted to put in place the night before, but I also knew he was struggling. I knew, because when I looked at his face, I saw it was a reflection of the same struggle within me. The only difference between us is that I have had years to perfect the outward appearance of 'ok', of pretending the feelings I have for people I am intimate with are completely different from the ones I show to the world.

Now, however, the guilt of dragging him back in is eating away at me, the heaviness of the burden pitting in the depths of my stomach.

I head out after only a very short-lived shower; it is doing nothing more for me than giving my brain free will to overthink this whole situation with Jackson, which is not what I need right now. Pulling on a plain tee-shirt and joggers from the pile on my bed, I stop to stare at the case next to it, *'the suitcase,'* right? That should give me something to do to distract me and focus on the job of going home, back to my life, even if just for the weekend.

I heard a loud knock on my hotel room door. I am not expecting anyone; I am not expected to be anywhere. Tentatively, I head towards it, peeking out at the peephole to see who is visiting me at this hour.

Jackson!

"Shit!" I curse to myself under my breath so he doesn't hear me through the door. In the time it is taking me to get my breathing under control and my thoughts in order, he is knocking again, louder this time. *'Shit, if he doesn't let up, he will alert the whole damn corridor that he is here.'* After schooling my features and bracing myself for an argument about today's episode, I open the door to him.

Before I can get the door fully open, however, and pre-empting the inevitable conversation, he pushes his way into the room, closing the door behind him. His hands quickly find my cheeks on either side of my face, and he is kissing me, pushing me back so I am against the wall, pinned between him and it. My body responds of its own accord; no longer in control of my mouth, it instantly opens up to his, pelvis pushing back against the incessant grind of his hips and hands resting on his chest; they can go nowhere else, my body completely engulfed by the sheer size of his. Fumbling our way into the room, my hip collides with a side table, knocking over whatever inanimate objects were sitting on top of it. We are only made aware of our clumsiness by the clatter the items make as they tumbled down onto the hotel room floor.

He stops but doesn't back away, his body still painfully pressed against mine, backed against the far wall. Face still incredibly close, with his lips just grazing over the top of mine as he speaks.

"Give it to me," he breathes through the sound of his evident need. "Give me my night," he takes my mouth again, completely entrapping mine against his, his tongue dancing alongside my own in a battle of blatant want.

Unable to use my voice to answer him, as we are still locked in our tongue tango, I start to unbutton his shirt in reply, stripping it from his shoulders and chucking it across the floor. Inadvertently, I break the kiss at the unveiling of his strikingly well-sculpted form, in order to take in the vision of it, one I have only ever seen in its entirety before on the big screen.

This sight before me, however, one that I can see, touch, and gently trace with the tips of my fingers, is enough to fill my sexual fantasies for the rest of my *life*! In a brief moment of distraction, Jackson has taken the opportunity to find my neck, kissing at my sensitive spot just below my ear. I can't help but let out a small whimper as he does. This seems to egg him on, turning his affections less gentle and more assertive, using his hand on the other side of my head to bring my neck closer to his mouth, almost biting.

"I need you," he whispers into my ear, sending even more pulses of arousal straight down to my core. Any sensible thought has left my conscious brain as I give into him, into this, into our bodies as they are drawn to each other, frantically trying to get closer.

He backs up a little as I move my hands to the base of my shirt, lifting it up over my head and revealing to him my bare chest. His mouth agapes as he takes in the picture in front of him; tentatively reaching up to cup my breast in his hand, he gently massages it, using his forefinger and thumb to subtly pinch the nipple standing to attention, sending through me the urge to arch my back, pushing my chest out to meet him.

Quickly, our impulses turn our bodies frantic and excessively needy once more. I want him…now; I want his body inside mine. Desperately, I start pulling at his jeans. He pulls a condom out of the back pocket as I work on unbuttoning them, pushing them down at the same time as his boxers, releasing from their constraints his erection, ready for me. With no other thought than the sheer desire bubbling away in the depths of my body, I take hold of it in my hand, reclaiming his lips as I do, swallowing down his hiss of approval.

With a few soft strokes, he turns animalistic; within seconds, he has me back pinned against the wall, and I feel his erection rubbing along the crease between my sex and my groin. With a low growl emanating from deep in his throat, I can tell he has reached his breaking point. I gesture to the condom in his hand. As he tears it open to clothe his sheath, I grab hold of my joggers, pushing them off my hips so they can drop to the floor alongside his.

With our now-naked bodies pressed up against each other, he takes my arse into his hands, giving my cheeks a quick squeeze. I know from our filming that this is his gesture for me to jump, knowing he will catch me and bring my legs around his waist and my hands around his neck. Using the wall as leverage, he angles his hips so his cock lines up with my entrance, hovering there teasingly for a moment before lowering me down onto him. I fling my head back, resting it against the wall, embracing the feeling as I take him in.

I had forgotten how this felt—to feel the nerve endings within, fire away as he penetrates me, sending sensations of pleasure shooting to all corners of my body. This feeling of fullness as he buries himself completely—why have I denied myself this for so long?

I'm not sure what image is depicting on my face, but it has given Jackson cause for concern when I feel one hand leave the back of my leg to find my cheek.

"Catherine, are you ok? Have I hurt you?" The short laugh I release is laced with all the sexual need I now have coursing through me at a million miles an hour on loop! Placing a hand on *his* cheek in mirrored form, I bring my head back down so my eyes meet with his, hoping they can convey more than my words can.

"No, Jackson, you feel perfect," The Cheshire grin on my face is reflected back to me as once again our passion takes over and our mouths lock as he starts to move beneath me. Each thrust penetrates so deeply it hits that magic spot deep within, bringing forth cries of pleasure and, with it, a building warmth down low in my abdomen.

"J…Jackson…God I'm so close…ahhh!" My orgasm rips through me, so intense it causes all muscles to contract as it cascades through my body, consequently fuelling Jackson's own when I feel his movements become jerky and erratic, before a deep-throated roar erupts uncontrollably from him, finishing with a few more thrusts while he rides his out.

As our muscles begin to relax, his hands drop from my arse; with them, my legs from around his waist. Standing on my slightly shaky legs, I lean my back against the wall for support while he rests his hands and arms on the wall on either side of me, his head resting in the crook of my neck. I run my fingers through his hair reassuringly as we try to slow down our breathing and heart rates to some form of normalcy.

Still with his face in my neck, he leans it closer to my ear as he finally speaks.

"Why can't I have you?"

My heart breaks under the weight of the enormity of what we just did, it all comes crashing down upon me in waves of guilt. *'What have I done?'*

I can't answer him; I can't even comprehend the most basic of thoughts right now. Instead, I rely on my tried-and-tested method of being indifferent. I bring his face up to meet mine with one hand while I send the other to reach down low.

"I'll see you Monday," I pull the condom off him and head off in the direction of the bathroom, closing the door behind me.

Putting the reminiscence of what we did in the bin, I sink down onto the floor, cradling my legs up close to my chest. After a few minutes, I hear the door to the room slam shut. It's only then that I let the tears fall, repeating over and over in my head, '*I can't have him. I can't have him!*' So, my body may finally start listening to my brain! He is better off without getting sucked into my world of bullshit: that although in those few minutes I have felt more complete than I ever have done in my life, that life isn't mine, and Jackson deserves more than I can ever give him.

'*What have I done?*'

Chapter 8

Jackson

I am home, in my personal gym, pushing myself through this morning's workout. Music blares through my surrounding speakers as I attempt to drown out errant thoughts of Catherine—what we did last night—thoughts that are accompanied by stray notions of disappointment, distaste, and that overwhelming feeling of regret. This is why I don't do one-night stands anymore; I always walk away feeling empty. Not once have they ever left me fulfilled. The more famous I got, the more women would just throw themselves at me, all wanting a little bit of Jackson Hunter, something to boast to their friends about and sell to the gossip rags. Like I say, meaningless.

That's how it feels now—like she used me. She took what she wanted from my body and effectively dismissed me from her sight. I realised I am being a little hypocritical. I went there with the sole purpose of having sex with her and taking from her the night she offered me; I couldn't help it! After our little moment in my trailer, it was the only coherent thought occupying my mind.

After spending the afternoon focusing on running through scenes that didn't involve her, I thought it would help dampen the notions created by our little romp. I was wrong; they still plagued me. I didn't even bother heading to my room first; I went from the studio straight to hers, hoping I would catch her before she took off for the weekend.

Although the event was rushed and frantic, in the moment, it felt incredible. Just touching her body, feeling it pressed up against mine, hearing her moan around the sensations from my cock as I thrust deep inside her against the wall, crying out my name as she came.

I wanted to go again! I thought maybe, more like hoped, throughout the night we would have a chance to talk. Try and figure out the enigma that is Catherine Carell between breaks of unbelievable sex. When she went and hid herself away in the bathroom, however, almost immediately after our act of lust, that hope was dashed. She got what she wanted, and I felt disgusted with myself for lowering my own morals to give in to her, then angry with her for letting me.

I am jolted out of my thoughts by a hand coming to rest on my shoulder, sending my body into panic mode and ready to fight whatever intruder has come into my space, stumbling off the treadmill in a panic. Turning around, ready to pounce, I am halted by the very bemused look of Harry, my agent.

Recomposing myself, a little breathless, I called out into the room.

"Alexa, music off," before redirecting my attention back to Harry. "Jesus Harry, you can't just creep up on people like that!" He lets out a hearty chuckle as I reach out to grab a towel to wipe the perspiration from my face.

"Ha there really wasn't any other way; you had the music blaring so loudly you clearly didn't hear your phone or the doorbell! Luckily, I know the gate key code; I had to let myself in."

"Yeah lucky," I gesture to the gym's doorway for him to follow me out towards the kitchen. "Coffee?"

"I wouldn't say no," I start preparing a pot for him while gathering up ingredients for a shake and positioning them neatly beside my blender.

"So, what can I do for you today?" I ask suspiciously as I start unceremoniously cutting up the fruit and veg and dumping them in the jug.

"What? I can't be in the neighbourhood and pop in to see my favourite client?" I raise an inquisitive eyebrow at him.

"You can...you very rarely do, though."

"Well, I am today. Part of my job is to make sure you're happy. Do you need anything from me, Jack?"

"Not really, I'm happy," I lie as I punctuate it with a curt smirk, keeping my focus on my task.

"You don't seem it. You seem off."

"What do you mean?" Chopping and placing more veg into the blender. I hear the coffee machine click off, and without hesitation, I turn, taking the coffee from the machine to hand it to Harry as I faff about with more bits of fruit that are laid out in front of me.

"Well, whenever I have seen you after a workout, you usually seem pumped and raring to go. Today you just seem...dejected," I blow out my cheeks as I finally place the lid on the blender, pressing the button to hear it roar to life next to me. '*Am I really that obvious?*'

I allow the blender to finish before I answer him.

"I'm ok, Hars; just a lot on my mind, that's all," Pouring out my now-green cocktail.

"A girl?" My eyes dart to his. *'How does he do that?'* "You kinda have that look." My face must have asked what my mouth didn't. "Not that one you're working with, I hope?"

"What no! Don't shit where you eat, man," I lie. Whatever the reason for Catherine's reluctance, what is very clear is her need for secrecy; she trusts me, and whatever I may hope for us in the future, breaking that now would jeopardise any chances I may have, even if those chances are non-existent at this point.

"Ok, that's good. The last thing you need is bad press on set! Ok, so what? Your usual bullshit of offering them the world didn't work."

"It's not bullshit, Hars," I begin to clear up the worktop from the mess I created.

"Ok, ok! So you're not bullshit…bullshit didn't work. So what, one girl on this entire planet said, 'no,' move on; if she doesn't want you, it's clearly not going to happen."

"But there's the thing," pointing the knife at him as though it were an extension of my finger, "She does want me."

"You slept with her?"

"Yeah,"

"And she doesn't want anything more?"

"That's what she says," I point to him again, like I am in some sort of debate justifying my answer, "but her body says something different."

"You broke your 'no one nightstand' rule for her?"

"I couldn't help it Hars. She's different, and now that I have, I think that might be all I get, so now I'm kicking myself for giving in before I have a chance to find out why. I don't know, I feel kinda used, man; I didn't get what I wanted from the interaction, you know? Well yeah, I *did* get what I wanted, but you know what I mean, right?"

"You really like this girl! I've never seen you so beaten out of shape for someone, even the ones you're actually dating!"

"You are not telling me anything I don't already know about Hars. It's driving me mad. I can't help it; it's like I am drawn to her or something. I can't stop thinking about her."

I begin pacing around the kitchen island, smoothie in hand, while I try to formulate my incoherent thoughts.

"She tells me she 'can't'; she 'can't be with me', she *'can't* give me what I want'. But I don't understand what that means 'cause she won't talk to me about it. What possible force in this world could possibly stop her from being with me if that's what she really wants?"

"She 'can't' or she doesn't want to?"

"Well, that's it! It's that she 'can't', like something outside her control is stopping her, but not actually herself, you know what I mean? But I *know* she wants to," Exasperated, I lean back against the counter, taking a swig of my drink, continuing to try and make sense of this predicament. Saying it out loud has made it no easier to make any sense of it at all. Harry just sits in silence for a while, sipping away at his coffee while he contemplates.

Finally, he pipes up.

"Did I ever tell you how I met my wife?"

"Rachel? No," I stare at him in anticipation, waiting for him to continue.

"We met at Uni. I had just gotten out of a long-term relationship with my childhood sweetheart, someone I'd known since we were kids, but the 'couple' thing just didn't work. I was heartbroken; you know, I thought she was the real deal."

I can see the pained look across his face as he stares down at his coffee, recalling the memories from that time.

"My friends took me out to a bar, told me I had to 'get back out there', have a couple of 'one-nighters' to get me out of my 'rut', as they called it," he places his coffee on the counter while he continues to recall his story. "My friends started to chat up a group of girls, one of them being Rachel. I thought she was attractive, but my heart just wasn't in it, you know?" I nod, oh, I know all too well the amount of times I had been dragged out to 'get laid', by well-meaning friends, because that's apparently the answer to all life's problems. "Well, she ended up jumping in bed with one of my mates."

"Shit!"

"No, it wasn't like that; as I said, I wasn't looking for her then; to me at the time, she was just another girl in the crowd. Well, she actually started dating my friend for quite a while too, and for a little over 2 years they were together. In that time, we became good friends, hung out in the same circles, and all that. At the end of Uni, they broke up; a long distance thing didn't work for them, and she had a tough time of it, but we remained friends; talked online a few times a month, sometimes weekly; we always found time for each other," he starts tapping his fingers on the tabletop.

"It wasn't until around 3 years after that, we met up as part of our yearly get-together. It was probably the only time we had in our whole time together that *one* of us, at least, wasn't in a relationship. Well, things just sort of happened," He has a broad smile across his face as he pauses to contemplate his next words.

"You know what she said to me on our wedding day? When we first met, I wasn't ready for her, then…she wasn't ready for me…it wasn't until that *one* day that we both found ourselves ready for each other."

I look down thoughtfully to the floor, trying to comprehend the 'life lesson' Harry was attempting to bestow upon me here. He must have been able to read my face again because he let out an amusing low chuckle before adding.

"My point is, Jack, you may be ready for her, but she may not be ready for you. It doesn't mean you're not meant for each other; it might just mean she is dealing with some shit right now, shit you can't even imagine, and she needs space to work through that before she *is* ready."

"So, you think I should back off?"

"I think you need to show her you are there for her in whatever capacity that is, and when *she* is ready, she'll come to you, if it is truly meant to be," I nod slightly at his words, letting them sink in to contemplate their morals.

"You may be right, Hars. Hay, if this agent gig gives you grief, maybe you could start up an agony aunt column!" He pushes his empty mug away from me, chuckling to himself as he does.

"Yeah, maybe when hell freezes over, plus with you on my roster I'll be laughing my way into retirement long before the need for that!"

I return his laugh as he starts heading towards the door, I begin following him out when all of a sudden, he turns on his heel to face me.

"Oh, all this mushy shit made me forget the actual reason I came over. I have a couple of auditions in the pipeline for you; one of them is due to start filming almost directly after this one. Are you ok with that, or are you hoping for a reprieve before jumping into your next role? Just say the word, and I'll tell them you're not interested."

"Send over the scripts. I'll take a look; if it's worthwhile, it might be worth scraping a holiday this year."

"Ha, that's what I like to hear. Open mind! I'll have them sent over by this afternoon. Cheerio Jack. Good luck with…you know…everything."

"Thanks, Hars; talk to you soon." Not 15 minutes after he entered, he was gone again. Efficient.

It's left me time alone to think about what he said. Maybe he's right. No, he *is* right. Whatever she has going on is clearly well beyond the scope of my imagination; I just need to trust that it is a good enough reason, and maybe if I could just find a way of staying in her life, just enough so she doesn't push me away, it may just happen on its own. At the very least, she'll grow to trust me enough to share with me her reasoning as to why the hell not.

Patience, however, has never been my strong suit.

Chapter 9

<u>Catherine</u>

I'm not sure what to expect from Jackson when I walk onto the set Monday morning. I've had knots in my stomach all weekend, anticipating what his reaction would be, but it certainly wasn't this.

I got here at seven am; we're shooting scenes for the final cut today, so full makeup and costume were required, which of course took time to apply. As a result, I didn't even have a glimpse of him until I walked onto set, fully dolled up in my costume and stage makeup and with him the same.

Jackson's get-up consisted of a tight pair of stonewashed blue jeans and a low-cut V-neck top that looks to be a size too small as it stretches out over his torso, and I can also see an edging of a tattoo poking out of it where his skin is exposed.

I thought maybe we might see a repeat of Friday's withdrawal, or maybe more likely anger from our little rendezvous, especially with the way I had treated him after. But today he seems…happy, excitable even, back to the regular Jackson Hunter you often see mucking about in interviews. He talks enigmatically to a small group, consisting of Rodney, Louise, and another cast member, Rebecca, also in full makeup; he bounces around animatedly, regaling some theatrical story to them.

Maybe this is it; maybe Friday night was just about getting all that sexual frustration out on each other, and now we can just move past it. Mixed feelings parade my thoughts at this notion. On one hand, its good; it's what I wanted; it's what was *needed*; it would be unfair to allow him to start feeling things for me when it will never amount to anything, so moving on for him is the best course of action. On the other hand, I'm a little disappointed that it has just proven what I already knew, that all men want is sex. It doesn't matter what I felt or what I thought he felt; he didn't really want anything long-term with me; sex was enough.

Plastering on my usual façade I smile at the four of them as I approach. We are still waiting for the final preparations to be put into place, so there is very little else for us to do but wait. Jackson spots me over Rebecca's shoulder as I get closer, his enthusiastic smile growing wide while his expression darkens into that all-knowing look.

"Catherine! Did you have a good weekend?" He asks, acknowledging my presence in the group, causing a chain reaction of hi's and hello's from everyone else. Rodney lets out another one of his wayward wolf whistles as he surveys my costume. It's nothing much…literally…a classic skimpy black and red-clad 'female bad guy' outfit…'Original'.

"You look incredible, Catherine; do you have full use of that outfit or is it for on-set purposes only?" Rodney, ever the creep, but he owns the title; he never seems to want to hide the fact that he objectifies women's bodies openly, but nonetheless, he somehow gets away with it with a boyish charm.

"Ha, on set only, I am afraid; only Jackson gets to cop a feel of these bad boys," I look down to come breast to face with them!

"Well, aren't I the lucky one?" A sarcastic tone falls from Jackson's voice as his small smile turns to that of a half-smirk.

"How does that costume have the unique ability to push up and out your tits without actually showing the nipple? It's like you're defying physics with those things!" Rebecca chimes in with a jest causing the group to chuckle along with her.

"Ahh, my dear Rebecca, it's called 'tit tape'!" I add, giving my breasts a quick tap for added effect. "Keeps me decent," Rodney and Jackson both snort as they double over in laughter, while the others giggle away.

"You are far from decent!" Rodney cries!

"Well Rodney I wouldn't be a very good 'raiser of hell' if I came out in your mother's Sunday best now, would I?" I retort with mock outrage.

Looking to change the subject away from my outfit…or in reality, the lack of one—I turn to Rebecca.

"Did you have a good weekend? You planned a night out, didn't you?"

"It was great," Rebecca starts, "went to go see 'Les Misérables' in the city with my husband," she isn't from here, Canada, I think she mentioned the other night; she was quite excited to be part of her first film here in the UK. "Figured while we are here, we might as well see the sites."

"I went a few years ago and loved it; what did you think?" I reply, happy that I had successfully managed to steer the conversation.

"Amazing, but then I loved the film, so not surprising."

"Have you seen what they have put on Jackson?" Louise interjects, gesturing to Jackson's new 'ink'.

"I did spot it; what the hell is it?" I ask. Jackson replies by pulling back the neck of the top, revealing a mixture of patterns and shapes that are intricately interwoven into a unique design.

"Not sure," he stares down at it, "It must be relevant to the movie somehow, probably trying to make Adrien look more 'devilish'," he airs quotes. "I think it looks quite cool; actually, been thinking about getting it done for real, or maybe something similar. What do you think?"

"It does look good on you, actually." Rodney chimes in.

"Yeah, it gives you a sort of bad boy look," adds Louise.

"Yeah," I agree, "maybe something more relevant to you though, that design doesn't look quite right."

"Umm, interesting," he repositions his top, making sure his 'new ink' is clearly on display.

The conversation dies as the five of us stare out onto the half-assembled set.

"You ready for today, Catherine?" Jackson interrupts the silence, still sporting his wide Cheshire cat grin as he takes a sip of water.

"Of course, are you?"

"Been looking forward to it; throwing you about the set has become one of my favourite pastimes," Bastard.

"I'm sure it has, I've been tempted this morning, to ask costume for added padding under this get-up."

"Haha, but where would they put it?" Louise interjects and is rewarded with another round of giggles.

"Don't worry, Catherine, I won't hurt you," he winks, like he had to point out the double entrant to me.

"Ha! Yeah, right, the way you two go at it, you would think this was your very own private porno! If it wasn't for the way this one," Rodney points his thumb, gesturing to me, "Composing herself 98% of the time off camera, I would swear you were *actually* going at it, but she clearly has no interest."

Involuntarily, I tensed up, and I felt a blush start to fill my cheeks. Jackson must have seen this, and despite him trying to provoke me earlier, he unexpectedly began to divert their comments.

"Haha, if Catherine and I were really going at it, her feet wouldn't even touch the ground!" Adding, "And do you really think you'd still be standing there with no black eye to your name with the way you perv over her Rods?"

"Me? I don't know what you're talking about."

"Ha, you couldn't be more obvious if you tried Rodders…thankfully for all of us, not just Catherine, she is way out of your league!"

"Hey, Asshole!" He playfully punches Jackson in the arm and then turns to me. "You'd go out with me, right, Catherine?" I push out my lips and make an exaggerated sucking noise as I play along, pretending to contemplate this prosperous conversation.

"Sorry Rodney!" I answer, tilting my head and pouting my lips. He bows his head in mock disappointment.

"So, what would you rather date 'built like a fucking wall' Jackson, I mean, look at him; there is nothing cute or snuggly about that! At least my body is more realistically human!" He pokes his finger into Jackson's upper arm for added emphasis.

Rocking my head from side to side, pouting my lips again in pretend contemplation.

"Come on, Rod," Jackson interjects. "It's a no-brainier man; it's a brawn thing, and I'm clearly the better choice." Flexing his upper arm muscle for added effect. "Right, Catherine?"

When he sees I am still 'thinking', his voice goes slightly higher, as though he was offended. "Right?" I make the same sucking noise again, before I answer.

"Sorry Jackson…leagues," A roar of laughter emanates from a small group as Jackson feigns being insulted.

"Ok, I think we're ready to do a quick run-through before the first take, all bodies on set!" We hear Cameron shout out over the hustle of the room.

"Right, come on then leaguer, time to shoot some sexy business!" Positioning myself behind Jackson to try and push him towards the set, clearly to no avail, I couldn't move him with a dump truck!

"You know you're going to pay for that comment, right?" He smirks while I giggle behind him, "Just saying lots of walls on this set; maybe I fancy a little more throwing practice today."

"Bring it on, big boy!"

"You may just regret that."

Wow, just wow. This has been an intensive morning. We have re-shot it more times than I can count, with Cameron barking orders for different camera angles, more lighting, and less lighting. 'Freeze just there so we can re-position!' Right, so I should stay right here with my legs wrapped around Jackson's waist and his cock uncomfortably poking into my thigh while you rearrange the equipment around us.

The raunchiness of the whole thing, coupled with my memories of Friday night and knowing how he actually feels inside me, has left me a little hot under the collar, and each time we have to reshoot I can feel myself getting more and more aroused.

"I need to take five Cameron; I'll be in my trailer," I call out as I head off, not really waiting for a response.

"No problem, wait there, I'll send in makeup for a touch-up. I want to reshoot this angle briefly before we move on this afternoon."

"Fantastic!" I hope that didn't come out sounding too sarcastic!

Reaching my trailer, I close the door firmly behind me, and I lean up against it for support. I need to calm this down before I do something stupid—well something else stupid…Speaking of which…

"Knock knock," I hear Jackson's voice behind the door. Nope, not what I need right now.

"Two secs!" '*Compose yourself Catherine.*' Breathing out a long sigh against the metallic doorway. I then opened it to allow him in, and I have no doubt why he is here—very likely a payback for my intrusion into his trailer last week. As the door closes behind him, I expect a repeat of our previous interaction: frantic, impulsive, and passionate.

Instead, however, this time he is different. While his eyes still contain that hint of desire, they are somehow softer and more passive. He reaches out to stroke my cheek gently with the back of his fingers as he moves in closer, his face stopping a few mere inches from mine…but he doesn't make contact; his warm breath brushes gently against my cheek. This pause of hesitation has given me time to think and to rebuff his advance.

"Jackson, we can't; someone will walk in any moment."

"It's ok," he replies in an almost whisper. "They won't be here yet, and even if they do walk in, we'll just say we are rehearsing; they won't know the difference."

"What do you want from me?"

"You know what I want, but you tell me that can't happen. So now I am asking for something different."

"And what might that be?" My voice is heated, my breasts rising and falling heavily along with my deepened breaths. I want him to kiss me and connect with my body in another furious embrace, but he is still hovering around my face, teasing me with the promise of his lips.

"I enjoyed the other night, but it ended too soon for my liking. I want more from you, Catherine," I swallowed a large stone in my throat as his lips brushed gently across my skin, slowly trailing to the base of my neck, lightly brushing the sensitive skin he found there. "I need you," A light kiss makes contact, which releases a gasp from within me. "And I can see you need me too."

I feel his smiles broaden against my skin; his nose softly grazes my neck.

"Let me come to you tonight? I want it to be slow this time; I want to relish in your body and soak in the feel of it against mine," bringing his lips back up so close to mine that they are just a splinter away, "I want to taste you."

I start to let out a whimper of arousal, but before I can, he swallows it, threading his hand through my hair to the back of my head and deepening the kiss. I don't protest, giving in immediately to those impulses once again. So turned on now, the word 'stop' and 'no' are like a distant memory, replaced with a consistent 'yes!' Ringing through my consciousness on repeat, over and over incessantly. His other hand finds the exposed skin around my abdomen, holding me in place, and as it makes contact, it sends shivers through me, lighting up every nerve it hits.

The kiss is slow but no less passionate. By the time he lets go of my mouth, I am breathless, with no rational thought to be found as I find myself agreeing with him.

"I want you," I breathe out in a low husk before I am able to construct any reasonable thought. His smile now exudes his male pride, no doubt his ego relishing the fact he has reduced me to a whimpering mess in his arms.

"I'll come to you after the end of the day; I'll be discreet, I promise."

"No, I'll come to you," I counter, and suddenly my logic drive starts to kick in. "I'll probably need time to get this stupid stage makeup off anyway; I'll come when I am ready."

"I look forward to it, sweet girl," he tucks his bottom lip under his teeth as he slowly starts backing away from me towards the door. "Until later."

"Later," he leaves with a cocky stride in his walk as he heads off in another direction.

'Shit, what have I just agreed to?'

Jackson

Ok, I may have played a little dirty to get what I wanted. Harry said to stay in her life in whatever capacity that may be. Well, this is as close as she will allow me to get right now, so if I have to manipulate her sexual need for me to get close to her, so be it. The fact is, without sex, she just tries to push me away anyway, and that isn't helpful to anyone. To be honest, I am far from complaining; sex with her again will sate this overwhelming sexual desire to be with her, and as a bonus, maybe if we do this regularly enough, over time I may be able to find a way to get her to open up and talk about the real reason she is holding back. It's a win-win in my books, regular sex, and a chance. *'We're all winners!'*

The impatient wait for her to come to my room is excruciating! All afternoon, I have thought of nothing else but having her in my arms again. This time it will be different: it was over too quickly last time, more like two rampant teenagers around the back of a bowling alley than two consenting adults. This time, I am determined to take my time. That's if she doesn't chicken out, of course; she clearly has a tendency to overthink things. I just hope the fuel of passion that has been passing through us all day didn't fizzle out when she got back to her room; it certainly hasn't dissipated from my own body. My need for her is as strong now as it usually is.

It's nearly 7; she should have gotten back from the studio around 2 hours ago. *'What is taking so long?'* I am sitting on my bed, phone in hand, thumb suspended over the call button.

I told you, I am not a very patient man!

It's then that I hear a very slight knocking at the door; if I wasn't otherwise waiting for it, I might not have heard it.

Opening the off-white, wooden hotel room door, I am blown away by the vision of her standing on the other side of it. She is not so strikingly dressed—in comparison to how I usually see her, that is. There is no designer dress hugging her form, no fashion accessory to off-set a particular colour or feature. This vision of her is stunning nonetheless, natural; it's clear she has makeup on, but it is subtle: the dress she has on is cream, plain looking, with matching sandals. The simplicity of her attire, however, only extenuates her more natural features: golden locks that frame her face and fall past her shoulders, those deep sapphire eyes that continue to have me entranced whenever I stare too long into them, and the way her clothes sit happily on her frame, revealing her petite and well-toned body.

As I stare at her face a tad too long, I notice for the first time she has tiny freckles dancing across her nose and cheeks; those freckles continue down her chest and arms, and they make me smile, absorbing in the idea that although they are uneven and so to the untrained eye 'must' be making her skin appear 'imperfect'—to me, she still appears flawless.

I step to one side to allow her to enter the room, getting a waft of her scented perfume as she does, floral and delicate, just like her.

"Drink?" I offer.

"Please. Wi…" she starts.

"And don't say wine," I interject before she finishes. "I know you hate it," she offers me a slight smirk as her stance takes on a more assertive posture.

"I always drink wine; I don't think I have had anything else, alcohol-wise that is, since I've known you."

"I know, and I see you grimace every time you take a sip. Why would you drink something you clearly don't like?"

"Habit, I suppose."

"Well, I got us some champagne for today. I hope that's ok? That is, until you tell me what you actually like?"

"Champagne is great; thank you," I pop the cork and pour out two glasses, offering her one. Her stern stance takes on a more placid one as she receives the glass, twirling herself around to take a turn about the room, her dress swaying with the movement of her legs. It is not lost on me that she is still not comfortable enough to just sit down, so I take on the initiative and sit on the bed first, gesturing for her to follow suit next to me. She doesn't, however, choosing to stay standing…establishing a clear, awkward boundary by keeping her distance from me.

I use the uncomfortable silence between us to start a topic with a question that I most definitely think desperately needs asking.

"So, Catherine…what is this?"

"What is what?" She answers coyly, clearly attempting to deflect.

"This, us? It's clearly something, but you have rebuffed any attempts I have made to define it."

"You need it to be defined?"

"I do," she ponders for a moment, taking another sip of champagne before she answers.

"This…this is lust."

"Lust?" She hums a little tune to the sound of 'ah ha'. "You think that's all this is?"

"That's all it ever is," Suddenly, her whole demeanour changes again. She almost seems angry, but not at me, but more at the conversation.

"I don't understand."

"I mean, people get together because they are sexually attracted to each other; they give into that lust and think they can build a foundation on it. Eventually boredom sets in, one or both end up drifting apart, eyes wonder to find different things to fulfil their needs, then the relationship ends, sex being the only real meaningful thing about the whole interaction," Is this seriously how she views all relationships?

"It's not always like that."

"No?"

"No, some survive."

"The stronger ones maybe, the ones based on more than just sex, or the ones willing to fight to work through the 'boredom' phase; the majority, however, won't make it past that; someone almost always wonders."

"And you think that will be us?"

"I *know* that will be us, sex; it's the only real definitive thing between us."

"No, I think we could be different."

She lets out what sounds like a very sarcastic chuckle as she turns away from me, looking out the window, once again taking the moment to contemplate her answer.

"Tell me, Jackson, how many girlfriends have you had in the past year?"

"That's different."

"How?"

"We didn't drift apart because of boredom; more often than not, it's because we realised we weren't working out; affection dies out, so the relationship had a very clear end."

"Same thing. After a while, someone wants something the other can't give; they no longer want each other; more than that, they want something or *someone* else, so they look elsewhere to seek it out."

"And this is why you won't give us a chance?" She turns back to face me, her appearance changed again to one of sympathy.

"This is why I *can't*. You are who you are, Jackson, and I have too much to lose if this were made public. I can't just give into this lust for you and date, only to end up being another notch on your bedpost later on down the line." And this is what she thinks of me? I just date girls until I get bored of them, ruining their reputations in the process. That's not me at all.

"So, we still haven't defined what this is. 'Cause I want you, Catherine, more than I have wanted anything, and I don't think this want, or 'lust' as you call it, is going to be put to rest after a couple of quick fucks," Taking another sip of her drink, she continues her musings. I polish mine off, sucking in my lips between my teeth in frustration, reaching over for the bottle to pour another. She finally takes a seat next to me, gesturing to her glass so I can refill it.

"Umm, how about this?" She turns her whole body so it is facing me, one leg curled under her on the bed. "We have sex, just sex whenever we are both in the mood. No expectations, no need for chivalry. We just give in to what our bodies want, scratching this nagging 'itch', as it were, until either one of us gets bored, in which case we'll just stop. Just until the end of filming, that is, then it'll have a very definitive expiration date where we don't have to worry about letting the other one down; we can then go our separate ways, back to our own normal lives, no harm, no fuse."

"And you're so sure we won't last? So sure that, this is what is going to happen with us?"

"That's what almost always happens when sex is the driving force. It's just life," This isn't what I want, not at all. Relationships mean more to me than just sex, but I can't find it in me to say no to her, I want her, and if this is the extent of what she is giving me, I have to take it. Maybe with time I can show her we can be so much more; we have four months left of filming and four months to prove to her that I can offer more than what she thinks I can.

In an attempt to justify it to myself more than anything, I find I am reasoning with her logic, because really, what *is* the worst that can happen? I get her exclusively for the next four months, and then she is proven right—that one of us gets bored and the connection we have comes to a very natural ending.

I start to nod my head before the two fractures of my psyche have really come into alignment over the decision. She takes another sip of her drink before her eyes find my face again, her free hand resting on top of mine.

"Ground rules, though," she has a look of seriousness about her as she continues. "No one can find out. No one. No public displays of affection, no talking about it to anybody else, and no photos. Everything we do stays within the confines of our rooms."

Once again, I find myself nodding without fully comprehending what it is she is asking, but that bright smile that has found her face is worth sacrificing a few of my own principles for now. If it means I get her to myself for a while, then it's worth it, *'isn't it?'*

I downed the rest of my champagne and gestured for her to do the same. I need her now; I need the feel of her body against mine to help me feel at ease about this whole setup. I need to know I have made the right choice by agreeing with her. Cupping her cheek in my hand, I make no hesitation about capturing her lips in mine, tasting the sweetness of the champagne on her lips. She didn't resist, instantly giving in and allowing me access to the fullness of her mouth.

Tearing herself away, she starts to trace a trail of soft kisses along my jawline. Flutters of arousal find their way south; her lips lightly brush against my stubble before finding my earlobe, which she bites ever so gently as she whispers.

"Take off your shirt."

I am not sure even Superman could have whipped off his shirt quicker than I could under those instructions, with or without his bloody telephone box!

I toss my unwanted clothing to the floor, then bring my focus back to her and those luscious lips, which were slightly agape as she stared shamelessly at my torso.

"I couldn't stop staring at you, you know? Those mornings we shared at the gym," she starts to delicately dance her fingers across my chest and abdomen, encircling the outline of the muscles protruding there. "All I wanted to do was touch you like this," A shot of egotistical pride elevates my mood, resulting in a broad smile that overtakes my face. I have always believed my motivation to maintain my body was for my work, even myself, but watching *her* and hearing how *she* wants me, for her to get so aroused by it, does more to me than any hoard of screaming fans.

"You didn't need to hold back, sweet girl," I thread my fingers through her hair, holding her head so it is closer to mine and my mouth closer to her ear. "I'm all yours," I hear her breath hitch at the words as her fingers continue to play along my torso, sending little tickles of pleasure along those nerve endings.

I promised myself I would take my time tonight, but feeling the heat of arousal emanate from her body, it's turning me on faster than I can comprehend.

I place my other hand on her thigh, beginning to lightly brush at the sensitive skin along the inside, mirroring her own painfully subtle movements on my chest. Her breathing becomes heavier under my touch and audibly less consistent. She looks back up to meet my eyes briefly before we are once again locked in an embrace, our tongues now taking on a will of their own, seeking each other out.

Impulses are signalling my need to take this further; the overwhelming need to be inside her tries to take over to hasten my actions, but there is something I want to do first. Something I have been thinking about the whole damn day.

I use the momentum of the moment to push her backwards onto the bed, pushing her down into it with the weight of my body, using one arm placed next to her head for leverage so I don't *completely* crush her!

The kiss continues while I use my other open-palmed hand to trace a line from her neck down the length of her body, carefully manoeuvring around every one of her curves as I go, until my hand finds what it has been looking for. Lifting her dress slightly, I tuck my hand inside the elastic of her underwear. *'Oh my god!'* I let out a carnal groan when I felt what was waiting for me.

"Catherine," I moan against her lips. "So wet, sweet girl, anyone would think you were waiting for me," she gives a soft smile as she captures my lips for a quick kiss.

"I *have* been waiting for you," Another low growl comes from the depths of my throat, shortly followed by a more softly uttered moan coming from Catherine when I allow my finger to glide through her, settling on her little sensitive bud, playing teasingly with it.

As her body begins to move beneath me in tune to the movements of my hands, I turn my lips away from her mouth to her neck, seeking out her trigger point between the ear and her nape.

"You're so beautiful, Catherine," I whisper, "I want to see you," Removing my hand from her crotch to run it back up her body underneath the dress, she gets the hint immediately, shifting so she can hoist it up over her head. She then arches her back to give her access to the clasps for her bra at the back, removing that as well to toss it across the room with the rest of our clothes.

"Beautiful," Is all I muster before desire takes over? Taking her nipple into my mouth while my hand massages her breast, her back arches off the bed in response to a desperate need to be closer to me. Leaving one breast to momentarily give attention to the other, I then gradually began laying light kisses across her abdomen, relishing in the softness of her skin, and positioning myself comfortably between her legs.

Finally reaching for her underwear, I hook my fingers into its elastic, pulling them down, first one leg, then the other. While playing lazily with her now exposed clit with my fingers, I take a moment to soak in the sight before me. Catherine lay out naked on my hotel bed, eyes closed, breathing erratically and heavily, hands curled up, gripping the sheets as she allows herself to get lost in my touch.

Once again, like all my interactions with her, my body starts to move before my brain can register what the hell it's doing. Lowering my head and body, I close in on her sex, replacing my fingers with my tongue. My mouth is instantly flooded with her taste, which sends electric signals of arousal, finding my cock instantly, motivated further by the ever-growing volume of moans and sighs she is exuding in front of me.

When I can't take the throbbing of my cock any longer, I move back up the bed, nestling my face back into the crock of her neck.

"Are you ready for me, sweet?" She answers me with a heated kiss, doing more for my state of mind than any words.

I leave her briefly to remove my own joggers and pants, find the condoms I left on the bedside table, and quickly make light work of dressing my member before returning to her, capturing her lips once again, and manoeuvring back between her legs.

Her body seems to respond instantly to me, wrapping her legs around my back and giving my hips full access to hers.

She breaks our kiss momentarily to pierce my eyes with hers, giving me permission to go. Lining myself up, I am unable to break our eye contact as I slowly enter, her warm and inviting body encompassing mine in its embrace. We both let out a low moan as I continue, finally burying myself completely inside before reclaiming her lips with mine.

'Slow' I have to remind myself. Easing out and back in again. She moves with me, and together we find our rhythm. Losing myself to the moment, I am unable to maintain the kiss any longer. I push out all negative thoughts so I can just enjoy being with her; inside her.

I can feel the pressure mounting. The overriding need to come shooting sparks of pleasure through my body.

"Jackson!" She sighs, while I feel the digging of her fingernails in my back; she is close too. Using the opportunity, I start to speed up, ploughing my dick harder and faster into her, pulling from her cries of pleasure over and over. With another arch on her back and a cry of my name on her lips, I feel her internal muscles clamp around my cock, drawing from me my own carnal growl, which bellows out more like a roar as delicious amounts of pleasure implode throughout me, emptying out into the condom.

Dumbfounded and breathless, I collapsed on top of her, having enough wit about me to place the majority of my weight on my arms that had fallen to either side of her body, and I let my face fall to her chest, buried between her breasts, with her arms lying flat on my back.

"You lied," she says in between breaths, and I lift my head to look at her questionably.

"Never!"

"Uh huh, you told me your sex noises were not as aggressive as your workout noises. I think we have just proven that you're a little liar," A wide grin spreads across her face as she jests. I return one of my own.

"'Little liar?' You can give me slightly more credit than that surely; there is nothing little about me!" We both chuckle while still attempting to calm our bodies down.

"Ok, yeah, I grant you that," I go back to resting my head on her chest.

After a few more minutes, I finally have the energy to move, planting another firm kiss on her lips before moving to lie next to her on the bed, still attempting to stabilise my heart's rhythm to its usual pace.

She, however, takes the moment to get up, quickly finding her clothes, which were scattered across the room's floor, to redress.

"You don't have to go, you know. You are welcome to stay here, a little while longer, at least," I say to her, following her movements around the room with my eyes while staying firmly on the bed. I want to go to her, hold her, and kiss her again, but then I know I'll find myself asking those questions that have only ever yielded me cryptic answers and a quick escape, and that completely defeats the object of this whole 'taking my time' plan.

"I do. Better to go now while the corridors are quiet than risk staying too late," I nod my head. I don't really have a choice but to agree at this point, but instincts dictate I cannot stay on the bed much longer while she ventures around the room, preparing to leave me.

Shooting up, disposing of the condom as I do, I wait for her to be fully dressed before wrapping my hands around her waist from behind, pulling her arse into my hips and my face into her neck.

"At least tell me what your favourite drink is; if we're going to be doing this regularly, I'd like to know, so I can prepare for next time," She releases a slight chuckle as she untangles herself from my grasp and pulls away, heading towards the door, pausing briefly before opening it.

"Amaretto over ice. Simple and sweet,"

"A perfect reflection of you, then," As if punctuating my compliment, she returns it with a sweet smile and a blush on her cheeks.

"Goodnight, Jackson."

"Goodnight, sweet girl." And with that, she is out the door. Leaving me naked, standing in the middle of the room, the smell of sex and her floral scent still lingering in the air.

I'm already starting to anticipate our next interaction, a smile creeping across my face. I may not have her the way I want…not yet, but tonight was more than I had yesterday, and tomorrow is yet to come.

Chapter 10

<u>Catherine</u>

"Morning, anyone seen Jackson?" Cameron struts onto the set, his usual look of professional determination prominent over his features. We came in this morning ready to run through the next scene on the roaster, with *both* Cameron and Jackson nowhere to be seen. Upon further inquiry, we discovered that Cameron had been held up in a production meeting this morning and left us with instructions to run lines and be ready to begin as soon as he arrived. This doesn't, however, explain the missing Jackson.

It's been a couple of weeks since Jackson and I came to our little 'arrangement'. We have been meeting up almost every night that we are on set, and I have to say I am already noticing a significant change in, well, me. I am beginning to naturally feel more like my old, confident, carefree self, in contrast to the pretend façade I had adopted over the years. It has allowed me to actually start to enjoy myself—on *and* off the set—giving in to random moments of silliness, which is very easy to do around Jackson's school boyish antics. It definitely made for some interesting outtakes for the blooper reel, I can tell you!

It isn't just the sex, though; it's him. He is so attentive and always has a way of making me feel like the most important person in the room; it's almost like he has made it his mission to make me smile at least once a day. I haven't had this kind of attention for years, and I am not ashamed to say that I am really enjoying and relishing it.

He was fine when I saw him this morning in the gym, so where is he now?

"Right, I am not delaying any longer; we have already lost an hour. Let's get moving. Matt, grab the script, and you'll read Adrien's part for the time being. Ok positions!" With a brief scattering of bodies, we all find our places; thankfully, today's scene doesn't really involve much intimacy, so reading through with Matt shouldn't be too problematic.

"Ok and…run scene!" Cameron calls out, staring intently at the little screen next to his chair.

"Adrien, this is not what you promised!"

"We have faced some setbacks, my love," Matt's tone is flat and generic; it is no surprise; he is a set hand after all, not an actor. Luckily, it isn't that hard for me to envision Jackson in front of me instead of him.

"What setbacks?" I yell, taking on Helen's god complex personality, mixed in with a little bit of prepubescent teenager, for the character's role. "You promised me that woman's blood in a pitcher, Adrien; where is my blood?" I pick up the pre-determined glass to the side of me, pretending to throw it in Matt's direction. "I am starting to wonder if you even care for me at all."

"You doubt my loyalty to you?"

"I doubt your competency to complete even the most rudimentary of tasks!"

"How dare you?"

"Then prove me wrong, my love…hang on, Cameron!" I break the scene to address our director, "Do you think when Adrien says his line, it would contribute to his character and his change of direction if that anger was directed physically as well?"

"Go on?"

"Well, if his sexual encounters with her were *that* violent, I would imagine his anger would be equally so, if not more, so maybe a grab of the throat, a pin against the wall, something like that? It would just show early on that he doesn't feel threatened by her, you know? And isn't averse to betraying her."

"Good ideas; when we track down Jackson, we'll explore it."

"Ok, right, um, ok…." Right, focus, I'm Helen again now! "Then prove me wrong me love."

"Gladly," I keep my eyes on Matt as I move about the set, doing my best to portray this persona of ambiguity. "Tell me, Adrien, where *have* you been these past few days?"

"Here!" The set's dummy doors fly open behind us, causing me to involuntarily jump and spin around on the spot where I am faced with an image of Jackson covered in gruesome wounds, bloody stains, and overall, looking completely dishevelled, more like a horrifying zombie than my handsome co-star; to top it off, he is sporting a huge menacing grin plastered creepily across his face. The sight before me creates an instant, terrifying scream that emanates from not only myself but also a number of other members of the crew as well, who are scattered about the room. The palpitations in my heart weaken my knees as I attempt to get away, unable to make it, I find myself collapsing onto a nearby chair.

The sound of laughter starts to fill the room, most notably that of Jackson's, who's cackle echoes about the vast space. Looking over, I see that he himself has sunk down onto the floor to his knees, holding his chest and abdomen as he cries out in hysterical laughter.

It takes a few moments to absorb what has happened exactly, and it isn't long until my look of shock is replaced with humour, *'fucking git!'*

"I'm sorry…I'm sorry," he gets out in between giggles, holding his hands up in surrender and standing up to make his way over to me. He proceeds to hoist me up out of the chair and wrap his arms around me, resting his head on top of mine in a feeble attempt to apologise. "I couldn't resist!" I allow myself a brief moment in his arms before pushing back against his chest to stare up at him. On closer inspection, I can now see the cuts and scars on his face are just makeup, and the blood on his clothes is clearly stage blood.

"What the hell, J, where did you get this from?"

"I got here early, and when I heard Cameron was held up in a meeting, I paid makeup a visit. It looks good, right?"

"You're lucky you didn't take out your leading lady! I nearly had a heart attack!"

"Ha! I am sure your heart is made of tougher stuff," he walks off towards Cameron, peeling off the makeup as he goes. "Sorry Cameron, give me 5 I'll wash this off." I see even Cameron has an amused look with his hands on his hips as he addresses him.

"It's ok, I think we can all appreciate the light relief this morning, but enough fooling around for today; we only have a month left of the set before we go on location; we need to crack on."

"Yes sir, boss sir," Jackson makes a mock salute as he heads off.

"I'm just going to take 5 and get a glass of water,"

"No problem, Catherine; I think we will all take 5 while we wait for Jackson," I nod and head off towards the snack and drinks table, with Rebecca shortly behind.

"Jackson's something else, huh?" She questions, as she reaches for the coffee pot.

"You're telling me! Still trying to get my heart to stop its arrhythmia!" We both chuckle, turning back towards the set as the guys start replacing the props we moved.

"You coming to the bar tonight? I think we are keeping it local to the hotel this week."

"Of course, when do I ever miss a night out with you guys?"

"Is Jackson coming?"

"Not sure; you'll have to ask him,"

"Oh, I thought cause you two are close, you probably know where each other is at?"

"Close?"

"Yeah, you always seem to be joking and giggling about something or other; I thought you were…well, you know?" All my insides start misfiring all at once, and with a blaring alarm ringing inside my head, I can practically see the red and blue siren dancing in front of my eyes. Thank goodness, it seems my ability to suppress my emotions is holding strong, as it doesn't appear to be showing.

"Ha, we're friends Becs, we don't live in each other's pockets. I don't know what his plans are; I think this morning's events are testimony to that!"

"I know, but you can be, like, touchy-feely sometimes."

"I suppose I never noticed it as anything different; well, I would think we couldn't do what *we* do with each other all day without creating different boundaries in our private lives, but he *is* a great friend to have."

"Yeah, he is, certainly makes things more interesting around here!" We giggle, then turn our heads off in different directions before she adds, "hay I am going to go catch Rodney to see if he is coming out."

"Sure, don't forget to ask Jackson and let me know what everyone is doing."

"No problem; see you in a bit."

"See you in a bit," Disaster is averted for now. Shit, we have to be more careful though. Rebecca seems to be a little more intuitive than most, so hopefully nobody else has noticed, or at least not enough to say something about it.

I see Jackson making his entrance from the back; the reminiscence of the stage makeup can still be seen, but it doesn't really matter for today as it is just a run-through.

Right game face on, Helen is in.

Jackson

Shit! That was the funniest thing I'd seen all shoot, and it definitely set the mood for the rest of the day: the look on her face! We couldn't stop giggling and cracking jokes for the rest of the day, and you know, it was nice to see everyone just relax a bit, especially Catherine. In fact, she has done nothing but relax since…well…you know, and the more she does, the more I just want to spend time with her. A bit cheesy, I know, but it's true. I just enjoy being around her. When we are together, she sparks an exhilarating energy within me, as well as a contrasting calmness that I have never felt before.

"You challenge me? Do you have any idea of the power…"

"That you *do not* yet possess! And if I am not mistaken, you need *me* to do th…" the line is interrupted by the raising of her hand to my chest, just as I am yanked back by the harness attached around my waist, catapulting me into the safety mat behind. The action catches me off guard and stuns me momentarily as the action steals my breath. I lose track of my lines or even what I am supposed to do next as I try and compose myself.

The look on my face must have been a picture, because I hear Catherine cracking up and laughing in front of me while a set hand offers to help me up. I falter a little while I find my feet, laughing alongside her.

"Fucking hell, that thing has some kick, huh?"

"It looked good though…as long as the camera doesn't focus too much on your face!" She mimics what my face must have looked like, wide eyes and an open mouth. Yep, shocked is an understatement!

"Come on, then, you have a go!" I start to feign untying the equipment around my waist. "See how composed yourself when you're being hurled backwards at stupid miles per hour!"

"Oh no, we don't need to see that!"

"Oh yeah!" I lunge towards her, restricted by the length of the elastic but managing to just about grab hold, wrapping my arms tightly around her chest and arms while I relax my legs, hurling us both backwards into the mat.

"Jackson!" She screams just before we make contact, crashing spectacularly into it. I am prepared this time, managing to keep hold of us both and land us safely. After we regain our wits, we end up in just balls of giggle fits, rolling around on the crash mat!

"Yep, I like that," We hear Cameron call out in all seriousness, seemingly oblivious to our antics, "That really worked, but yeah, Catherine's right, your face is off; we need to work on that."

"Ha, we will; it was my first time in it. Give me a couple of goes, I'll get used to it. It was kinda fun, actually!"

"Good, I think we'll call it a day for now. See you all in the morning, bright and early. I want this nailed before the weekend to film on Monday!"

Still curled up on the mat, we take a moment just to ourselves while everyone else is busy pottering about around us. We are no longer touching, but we are facing each other, lazily grinning at each other.

"You heading to the bar later?" I ask, resisting the urge to add 'with me' at the end.

"Of course, I wouldn't miss a night out, but I have to warn you, I think we need to rein in our antics. Rebecca cornered me earlier; she *actually* thought we were sleeping together. We don't want to start rumours for the gossip rags, now do we?" I know she is putting on a show for anyone who may be hearing it, but I know it is actually a warning, directed at me. What she really means is 'stop breaking the clause of our little arrangement before the world and her donkey finds out'.

I can't say it doesn't feel a bit like a kick to the gut. I thought…well, I must have thought wrong, because for me, this still feels real—in fact, more real than it was a few weeks ago. This want for her doesn't seem to be fading, but clearly for her, the boundaries are still in place—and she just reminded me of them.

"Done," Promptly, I get up from my place on the mat. The moment is ruined. I quickly removed the harness around me to drop it to the floor before walking off, leaving her alone on the mat.

For the first time in weeks, I am beginning to think this arrangement was a really bad idea.

We ended up having a great night at the bar. Catherine kept her distance for the most part, but I expected that. I'm pretty sure the only reason she was playful with Rodney most of the night was for the very same reason. She wants people to think her playfulness is for everyone's enjoyment and not only reserved for me. For her sake, I too keep up the charade, joking around like usual with some of the others in the group, pretending she means no more to me than they do.

By the time the night ends, everyone scatters into their own separate rooms. There has been no hint or communication between us like there usually is if we had a plan to rendezvous, so I'm not sure if she is expecting me or not. I go, nonetheless.

I probably shouldn't be; the events of the morning in contrast to those of the afternoon and into the evening have messed with my mood and are causing odd notions in my brain, but I can't help it; the pull of her is too much, and I am drawn in by the mere thought of her.

Softly knocking at her door, I wait for an answer, nervously looking around for anyone else in the corridor.

As soon as she answers, I am on her, kissing her frantically and uncontrollably like I did the first night. This should be my warning sign, the massive red flag screaming at me that I shouldn't be here with my mind and body acting like two separate entities, but she responds instantly, and I am lost. Pushing her back towards the bed, we collapse down onto it.

She quickly turns us over, straddling my pelvis, grinding down on it with her hips relentlessly, pulling from me a grunt that so often makes an appearance when we are like this; close.

Breaking the kiss, I lean back to stare into her eyes, slowing down this racing, lust-filled romp by cupping her cheek with my hand. My other hand finds her pelvis, attempting to still the movements of her hips, and I say that one dangerous thing I know deep down I shouldn't but am unable to reign in my stupid sub-conscious.

"Why won't you be with me?" Shit, instant regrets sit in my chest. Here goes my long-term game plan. Stupid brain: stupid alcohol, loosening my tongue.

The expression that glares back at me, however, is not one of anger like I expected; it is pain. I can see it in her eyes as they turn over all glassy.

Catching herself, she swiftly climbs off me to put a sizeable distance between us.

"You need to go," she says quietly, edging further back.

I close my eyes in an attempt to control myself to avoid saying anything else, but I can't. It's out now, and while she may not be angry about my words, I sure as hell am. I need answers, and I need them tonight!

"No!" I yell, standing up to follow her. "No, I won't go until I know. I need to know, Catherine, why you won't be with me; why you're ashamed of me!

Why the fuck does every damn fibre of my being tell me I belong to you, but you're telling me I don't? You need to tell me *why,* Catherine!"

She doesn't answer; instead, she turns away, moving towards her vanity unit. Opening the front draw, she pulls out a tiny object, leaving it on the desk.

A ring.

Turning back to me, she repeats it in a hushed whisper. "You need to go now," Before heading towards the bathroom, locking the door behind her as she goes.

A ring—a wedding ring, to be exact. I look on in disbelief at that damn atrocity staring back at me, taunting me with its meaning from its place on her desk. *'She isn't mine because she belongs to someone else.'* The picturesque ideal I had of Catherine comes crashing down around me, tainted with this new knowledge.

She locked herself in the bathroom to essentially dismiss me again. Well, not this time! She has some fucking explaining to do, and I'll be damned if I leave this room until she has given me a reasonable, goddamn excuse for her betrayal.

I head over to the hotel room door, opening it, only to slam it shut again, strutting back to sit on the bed, waiting for her to come back out.

A few minutes later, she emerges, patting a tissue against her eyes, clearly not expecting me to still be here. Once she notices, however, that I am staring daggers at her from my position on the bed, her whole demeanour once again changes.

"In case you didn't get the hint, that was your cue to go," she is trying to pull off harsh; unaffected, but she has quickly forgotten, I have already seen how upset she was the moment she vacated the bathroom.

"You're married?" I am trying to remain calm; I am not sure I have said that to my face, however; pretty sure anger—perhaps more rage—is the residing look I am currently offering. I keep trying to tell myself that *'there's an explanation; there is a bloody explanation.'*

"Yes," her only response, but she offers up nothing else to explain herself.

"So, you have been cheating with me this whole time?" She scoffs, turning away. She reaches for the bottle of Amaretto that must have been left here from the other night, pouring herself a glass; it's then that I see, despite her short answers and hard exterior, that her hands are shaking.

"I've not been cheating," Bringing the glass to her lips, her other hand appears to be attempting to steady herself against the vanity unit.

"So what? You and your husband have some fucked up open marriage thing where you get to fuck whoever you want as long as you end up in the same bed at the end of the fucking day?"

"Something like that," she emits, under her breath, defeated. "So go; now that you know what a piece of shit I am, why don't you just go?" She looks down to the floor; her free hand moves from the unit to then find its place around her abdomen, hugging herself.

I need to keep going, to push her while she is still willing to answer my questions. I cannot, however, contain the harshness in my tone; as calm as I am trying to be, the outrage still pumps red through my veins.

"So, you have been fucking us both?" She scoffs again, this time turning her head to look out the window.

"No, Jackson, you don't need to worry; I haven't been dipped in by someone else's pen; you're safe."

"Then help me understand, Catherine, what the fuck is all this? Why are you fucking other people when you are still with your fucking husband?" A stray tear rolls down her cheek, and it almost makes me feel guilty for shouting. "Catherine, you have to answer me!"

"Because I can't bear even the *thought* of him touching me, let alone actually letting him…" her arms squeeze around herself more tightly. Unable to contain it any longer, I involuntarily leapt from the bed, grasping at her glass and placing it on the table, while I wrapped my arms around her in a feeble attempt to comfort her.

The gesture must have broken her because suddenly she turns, her face collapsing into my chest, and her whole body relaxes into my arms, my own strength being the only thing keeping her from falling to the ground. I feel the wetness against my shirt from her tears while she balls up the fabric in her hands as they become fists against my chest. "He cheated on me," I hear her speak out against the strain of her grief. In an attempt to appear understanding, I bring my hand up to gently caress her hair, letting her know it's ok to continue. "Eight damn years we were married," *'Shit!'*

"How did you find out?"

"His mistress came and told me. She said she couldn't bear to lie to me once she found out he was married," I felt a light tap against my chest as her fist gently hit out against the hurt. "Even after the fact, I couldn't help but wonder, just how many times had he stepped out on me, and I just didn't know about it? Only for the simple fact that it came from her rather than him. It made me sick; he still makes me want to vomit just thinking about it."

"Then why the hell don't you leave his cheating ass?" Hesitating briefly, she takes the steps to break out of my hold, backing herself away again. *'No, no, no. We are so close.'*

"You wouldn't understand."

"Try me?"

"Jackson…" She pauses before letting out a cry in frustration. "God Jackson, I have children. My two boys. They love their father; they…" Upon hearing this knowledge, although obviously shocked and temporarily taken aback, it doesn't seem to impact me like I thought I would otherwise expect it to. The fact she has children doesn't seem to faze me at all atop of everything else she is throwing at me tonight!

"Children adapt to broken homes, Catherine; you shouldn't have to sacrifice…"

"My name isn't Carell," she interrupts and then pauses again, like that one statement alone explains this whole damn mess.

"Then…"

"Carell is a stage name; my father's name is LeMond," A sudden realisation hits me like a fucking bat to the head. LeMond, fucking Christian LeMond, he is only *royalty* in the world of Hollywood from back in the late 70s, 80s, *and* 90s! There isn't a soul out there that hasn't heard of him; shit he was one of my inspirations coming into the industry.

"My husband's name is Carter, William Carter, son of Patrick Carter," Oh, my fucking lord, the truth is hitting me like a boulder to the chest—another one of the acting greats! In fact, come to think about it, it is well known that LeMond and Carter are long-term friends in the inner circle. The enormity of this information is overwhelming, involuntarily forcing me backwards away from her into the empty vacuum of the room.

She continues.

"William and I grew up together; we were a power couple, you know. I really thought we were meant to be together, with the closeness of our families and everything, so we married young. I thought we were happy," she pauses. I can see she is trying to keep it together. How long has she been holding this in?

"And then he cheated. Why didn't you leave then?"

"At the time, I didn't know what to do. He begged me to forgive him: to think of the children, the impact on our families, their reputation; his reputation if it got out, and to give him a chance to make it up to me. He promised me that he would spend the rest of his life doing so," she can't even look at me as she explains. "He is a respectable businessman in his own right; you know, even without his father, he feared that if our marriage didn't work because of his infidelity, especially with the notability of our families, it would damage not only his reputation but also that of the ones we love. On top of that, both our families are so intricately intertwined and so well known, that there is no way to manage a separation without the fallout cascading and rippling out, affecting them as well, not to mention what would happen if the press found out, what effect a controversy like this would have on their careers, their social standing…"

"So, how did we get here if you gave him another chance?"

"Because the idea of those same hands that had touched her touching me made me sick, and I couldn't…" Another tear falls down her cheek as she spits out those words. "It took him two weeks to find someone else."

"Shit Catherine!"

"He doesn't even try to hide it from me anymore. He just goes and does what he likes. We pretend to the world, my friends, and my family that we are still a happy couple, but in reality, we haven't been for a long time."

"How long?"

"It's been two years."

"Shit!" I run my hand across my mouth as I continue to try and absorb this information. "Have you spoken to anyone else about anything that has happened?"

"No."

"Why not?"

"I told you, everyone I know is all intertwined with him; I can't talk about it without it getting out to somebody else like Chinese fucking whispers, and of course, in *my* circle *and* being the children of LeMond *and* Carter, you never know who will sell you out to the press to make a quick buck. I can't be *seen* with you, Jackson, because when this movie comes out, it is only a matter of time before some journalist figures out who I am. I can't risk the affect it will have on everyone I love."

I can physically feel the heaviness sitting on my chest, almost as if by her alleviating her load, it now rests on me. I am stunned and confused and have so many other questions swimming around in my mind, but I don't think tonight is the night to elaborate on myself.

"I'm sorry," I finally say. I truly am. If I knew the pressure she was under, I never would have pushed. "I get it now; I don't know what it is like to grow up in your world, but I can imagine, and I can understand the pressure of maintaining outward perceptions. You feel you are stuck between a hard place and a very large rock through no fault of your own, and you made the choice to sacrifice so others wouldn't be impacted by the alternative."

When I see her falter, I move forward to catch her again, the emotional toll on her right now must be immense. I hold her tightly in my arms, lightly stroking her hair. That subtle smell of vanilla is helping to calm my bewildered mind. When she looks up at me for the first time since she came out of the bathroom, she catches my eye with hers. Feeling closer to her now than ever, I can't help but capture her lips with mine, entangling my fingers into the hair at the back of her head. It isn't a passionate kiss; it's just the only way I know how to show I care for her.

"Let me stay with you tonight and wake up in my arms tomorrow," she looks at me like I have just spoken absolute jargon. "I don't want sex," I correct defensively, "just…you have been so open with me tonight; opened yourself up to being vulnerable; it doesn't feel right just leaving you like this. Don't make me leave you alone tonight. Please." The look of relief washes over her as she bravely nods her head.

I lead her over to the bed, stripping her outer clothes to lie her down, after which I strip off on my own, down to my boxers to get in next to her. Switching off the light and snuggling in close, bringing her flush against my chest and wrapping my arms around her protectively. Softly, I start to stroke the arm that is stretched out around my torso, hoping the touch helps, even slightly, to ease her stress.

"Catherine?" I question her to see if she is still awake.

"Humm," she hums out sleepily.

"Look at me," she tilts her head up, and I can just about make out her features against the lights of the city streaking in from the window. Cupping her cheek in my hand and lightly brushing my thumb across her cheek, I suggest, "Let's pretend," I hope these next words do not come across as too patronising. "For the final few months we have left, let's just create a bubble around us in the safety of our rooms, where no one can touch us, where we can be who we want to be, be open with each other, and be ourselves," I capture her lips in mine, attempting to take with me all the pain from the night. "Let's pretend that you are mine and I am yours," Lightly tracing the outline of her lips with mine, I whisper, "Pretend with me, Catherine."

She makes the final push forward to connect my lips with hers as her reply. After indulging in it for a few moments, I break away, once again bringing her form closely next to mine. It isn't long before I hear the faintness of her subtle snoring telling me she has fallen asleep, and it isn't long after that I too fall into a contented rest.

Waking up with her in my arms feels like the most natural thing in the world. She belongs here, with me. Floods from last night permeate my mind like flashes from a horror movie.

'She isn't yours because she belongs to somebody else.'

Yeah, a douchebag cheater who should have lost all rights to call her his wife the moment he laid eyes on another woman. I cannot even try and fathom the kind of life she has had to lead the last two years—the one she has had to mentally prepare herself to continue living, it's no wonder her behaviour has been so conflicting. Her social status in life tells her she needs to behave one way, but she is desperate to want to be someone else.

Well, now I know. The way I see it, I have two options laid before me. Either I accept the decision she has made, accept that it is out of my hands. Who am I to question the choices she has had to make? I don't have a hell of a lot to lose if it all goes wrong, but she could lose everything!

Or I can fight for her. I am guessing, from everything I know so far, that her presiding fear is that she cannot take the risk or subject her family to the fallout for a relationship that she worries won't last. Well, maybe I can show her that I mean what I say—that I really do care for her, that I am worth dealing with the fall so we can have a real shot at a future together—that I am worth the risk.

I look down at her sleeping against my chest, *'so beautiful.'* I start to brush stray strands of her hair away from her face, causing her to stir against my touch.

"I'm sorry, I didn't mean to wake you," a say as she hums against me; she starts to stretch out across the bed.

"It's ok, I am a light sleeper anyway," Instead of moving away like I expected her to, she snuggles in closer, hugging my waist tighter. *'Not snuggly, my arse Rodders!'*

"You, ok?"

"I am actually, thank you; it feels good to finally have someone who knows and kinda understand…even if you don't really," we both lightly chuckle as I take her hand in mine, intertwining our fingers and circling her knuckle with my thumb.

"Can I ask you something?" I ask.

"Sure,"

"You said this has been going on for two years?" I pause, trying to tactfully find the right words. "Umm, how many times have you, you know…"

"Slept with someone else?"

"Yeah,"

"Only you," the pause after gives me time to absorb the enormity of that answer before she continues. "It never felt right before; I never needed it, but I couldn't stop myself with you, Jackson. I'm sorry."

"Hay, no sorrys! I couldn't help myself either," Another light chuckle as I pulled her closer.

Well, that seals it. I have to try, don't I? I can't just let her pass me by without trying; my affections for her are clearly mutual; she is just better at hiding it then I am.

"Come on!" I start pulling us out of this mental and emotional cocoon we are building. "If we don't get up now, we won't make it to the gym this morning," Turning her head to smile up at me, I can see she appreciates the gesture. "Well, we're pretending, right? And in our pretend world, we definitely gym it together," Laughing, she disentangles herself from my hold while rolling over to get out of bed.

"Definitely."

"Great, I'll go to mine, get my gym gear, and meet you down there?" I smile at her.

"Definitely," she smiles back while I quickly gather up my bits, then start to throw on my clothes that are littering across the floor.

"And in our pretend world, we definitely kiss, like all the time." I add, cheekily stealing a quick kiss as she graces me with another one of her warm smiles.

"Definitely," she repeats still smiling. As I go to leave, I turn to take another glance at the beautiful woman before me, I make myself a mental promise, all while I throw my own toothy grin back at her. *'I'm going to show you, Catherine, what it is to be cherished. If for nothing else, then just to show you that you are the kind of woman who deserves it.'*

Three and a half months left.

Chapter 11

Catherine

"Mum!" Axel came bounding down the stairs as soon as I got home, coming at full speed as he leaps to embrace me, which causes me to stumble a couple of steps backwards. At 4 years old, he isn't quite big enough to knock me over just yet: my 7-year-old son on the other hand…

"Mum! You're home," Crash! I fall to the ground, catching them both, as Callen comes charging in to join his brother. We fall to the floor in fits of giggles. God, I miss these two.

"Guess what, Mum?" Callen begins, "We did an obstacle course today in PE, and Mrs Fallon said I was the fastest! I even beat Susie!"

"Wow, that's so good, baby."

"Oh Mum, Mum, I drew you a picture. Dad! Where is my picture?" Axel elbows my ribs as he struggles to his feet, bounding into the adjoining room.

"I put it on the fridge, buddy," William calls, the whole room appearing to darken as he enters the hallway, buttoning up his cuff links absentmindedly as he walks by. Light shining in from the adjoining rooms cast shadows from the wooden carvings that decorate the hallway furniture; from my position on the floor, they loom over me like monstrous creatures creeping out of their daytime hideaways. The image quickens my breath as I watch Axel dart from one side of the room to the other, running between the living room and the kitchen. Callen suddenly remembers something else running towards the living room. Their movements cause the shadows to flicker and move.

An overbearing silhouette remains, however, casting its darkness directly over me, engulfing my own into its empty void.

"You alright?" He questions nonchalantly, not really looking at me but at the direction of his belongings.

"Of course," I cough, "are you heading out?"

"Yes. Don't expect me back; kids have been fed."

"Don't forget, it's your parents party tomorrow."

"What? Shit!" Staring down at his watch, "Can't you go by yourself?"

"They're *your* parents! I'm pretty sure your mum will have something to say if you're not there! I already covered for you last time."

"Shit, ok fine, I'll make sure I'm back early; just make sure you're ready to go by the time I get here; I'm not hanging around waiting for you."

"Fine."

"And in the future, if you say you're going to be back by 7, make sure you stick to it; it's nearly 8."

"Shooting over ran slightly."

"Still stands. Bye boys!" He calls out, no longer prepared to acknowledge me. I am used to that by now.

"Bye Dad!" They call together, and with that, he snatches up his keys and is out the door.

I close my eyes in silent relief after expecting a tyrant of verbal abuse upon walking in through the door for my tardiness; he spared me tonight. At least I don't have to spend another minute in his company; tomorrow will be hard enough! This evening, I can spend my time with the most important people in my life.

"Ok, boys, who wants to watch a movie?"

"Yay!" I hear them scream from their different positions around the house.

"Great, go get yourselves comfy and choose what film you want; I'll grab the popcorn."

I hear them shuffling about the house, gathering up duvets, pillows, and soft toys, and dragging them into the living room while I head towards the kitchen to fix some snacks for us. I see Axel's picture on the fridge; it's a picture of 4 little stick people with giant heads and smiley faces. It makes me smile, his innocence a shining beacon through the mist of bullshit.

After the popcorn is finished popping away in the microwave, I head back out into the living room, armed with it and a handful of their favourite snacks. The boys are waiting, cosied up on the sofa. Snugging in the middle of them both, we settle down for the movie, one boy under each arm.

They are so engrossed in their animated adventure they don't notice I am not really paying attention; I am too busy daydreaming about the last 24 hours with Jackson. Fantasies dance through my mind of a different life, one where he is here with me, still making me feel like the most important person in the world, instead of yet another inconvenience, with us all sitting here, watching a film together after a long week of filming. Another life away from this suffocating prison *he* has built around me, where being in the arms of another woman is more important than spending time like this as a family.

Involuntarily, I kiss both boys on the head and pull them closer, hugging them tighter.

"You ok, Mum?" Callen asks, still not taking his eyes away from the television screen.

"Yeah, baby, I'm fine. Missed you guys, that's all," he then returns my hug, snuggling in closer still. He has no idea the extent of the meaning behind such a gesture, but it hits my emotional heartstrings, nonetheless.

"Miss you too, Mum."

I don't know what this is with Jackson or why it's only him that makes me feel this way. It's like, when I'm with him, I can have the world and that damn cake as well. But we both know it's only temporary, so I will indulge in these fantasies while I can pretend. As long as I always get to come home to these two, though, that will be all I need.

Monday morning comes around far too quickly, yet not quick enough in equal measure. I do not get to spend a lot of time with my boys at the moment, and so I cherish the time I do. In addition, this weekend has been the first one I feel I have been able to mentally cope with (with everything going on around me, that is) without it affecting my confidence or my time with my family.

At the same time, I cannot wait to see Jackson again. Excitement builds in my abdomen with anticipation over seeing him this morning, ready to embrace this new level of acceptance; he knows everything now, and I no longer have to hide anything from him.

By the time I actually get onto set, I have already been in makeup for nearly 2 hours! Once again, we have to wait while the stagehands finish putting together the props and set them ready for shooting. As I approached the group, that have been set up in our regular place next to the drinks table, I spot Rebecca regaling a story of what, I can assume, was what she and her husband got up to over the weekend.

It's then that I spot Jackson behind her, leaning against the table with his legs outstretched, his eyes already finding mine as a sweet smile plays on his lips. I return it with one of my own, which I try to conceal behind the curtain of my hair; however, it does appear he is as pleased to see me as I am to see him, which I find incredibly reassuring.

I prop up next to him, slightly away from the overly excited group next to us.

"Good weekend?" He asks, blasé-like and lower in tone, so as not to entice anybody else into our conversation.

"I did actually, saw family. Yourself?"

"Yeah, it was alright; I spent most of it wishing I were somewhere else," I don't miss the glint in his eye, signifying exactly where the 'somewhere else' might have been.

"Me too."

"Ok, all hands on set. We'll do a couple of quick runs-throughs before filming. I hope you're ready for this, Jackson," Cameron gestures towards the harness and mat, all set up just for him.

"Of course!" He exclaimed, grasping his hands together for added emphasis.

"Great, let's get to it!" As everyone turns to walk towards the set, Jackson gently takes my arm by the elbow to briefly hold me back.

"Tonight?" He questions, in all seriousness, but I must have looked just like the cat that got the cream as my smile widened at the prospect.

"Tonight," I whisper back. I yank on his arm to pull him to stand, dragging him towards the set. "Now come on, you. I hope you have been practicing your game face. Can't have you being propelled into a wall by the force of my power, looking like a constipated baboon," That earns me a deep chuckle, not only from him but from some of the other crew members that we passed along the way.

"Oh, don't worry, darling, I will be the epitome of a 'sexy hero'," he air quotes, "pout and all, you'll see," I reward him with a chuckle. Shooting the rest of this movie may just have become the most satisfying thing I have ever done.

Later that afternoon, after we have finished up, I am back in my hotel room, once again finding myself scrubbing at the hair follicles on top of my head in an attempt to remove this ridiculously thick stage makeup.

It is almost 6 when I hear a soft rapping at my door. Inquisitively, I look towards it. I am not expecting anyone else accept Jackson, and we usually do not rendezvous until closer to 7. Heading out of the bathroom towards it in just my towel, I check through the peephole to confirm that it is indeed Jackson before opening.

As soon as he enters, however, I am given no notice as he grasps my hips with his hands, pulling me towards him, dropping a bag next to me, and kicking the door closed with his foot.

"I have wanted you all day," he professes as his mouth finds mine, finding their now familiar rhythm as they become merged into one. Flexing slightly to brace my pelvis around his, it is almost effortless for him to pick me up and carry me over to the bed, laying me down gently across it as he stretches himself out next to me. His mouth finds the sensitive spot under my ear, kissing and nipping at it while his hand creeps up my leg, tracing patterns along the way, leaving a trail of goose bumps in its wake. It has not taken him long to become acutely in tune with my body's responses, being able to turn me on in very little time at all.

His hand skims past my groin, where I prematurely moan in its presence, only for him to tear open the towel, leaving me bare before him. As he firmly guides his hand over my now-unveiled body, I feel his lips leave my neck so he can look down to where his hand is. I hear his breathing becoming hitched, his movements become slightly erratic, and his mouth agape as he continues to stare at me lying bare before him. I should feel self-conscious, exposed, and vulnerable, but I don't; instead, I *feel sexy and* powerful. *I* am doing this to him, creating this level of arousal at the sight of my body alone.

"Beautiful," he says simply, but the connotations in his tone reek of desire.

As confidence shoots through me I quickly turn him over to straddle him, and his hands instantly find my hips as they grind purposely into his. I let out a small moan, looking up to the ceiling when I felt his member through his jeans, rubbing up against my clit.

"So needy," I hear him beneath me. "Tell me what you want, sweet girl."

"I want you to touch me," I breathe.

Eager to oblige, I feel his thumb come to rest on my clit, slowly beginning to circle its bud while the rest of me continues to grind down on the spot to try and relieve some of the mounting tension building there.

"Come here, sweet," his hands fall to my arse, gesturing them to move forward. Following their guidance, I edged my way up his body, and he doesn't stop me until my exposed sex hovers over his mouth. With no hesitation, he engulfs me in it, sending waves of pleasure shooting through all my nerves to all corners of my body and expelling from me a cry that must have sounded almost carnal. I want to get closer, but I force myself to remain still, desperately trying not to grind myself against his face. While his tongue and mouth give all their attention to my clit, I feel the penetration of his fingers, one shortly followed by two, easily finding the secret spot hidden deep within me.

A familiar building of warmth starts rising in my abdomen; the coursing sensations through me have peeked, causing my body to start shaking slightly under the onslaught of my sex.

"Jack...son!" I cry out; pleasure comes like waves crashing around me; no longer able to control my body's movements and feeling weak, I am unable to hold myself up or effectively regulate my breathing. Jackson must have sensed this, suddenly finding myself on my back after briefly blacking out, vaguely aware of the feeling of his gentle kisses spraying across my body, relaying sweet nothings as he does.

"You sound so pretty when you come, sweet girl," I have never felt as cherished as I do right now, with him, still coming down from the orgasm he has bestowed upon me, all while *he* still remains fully clothed.

I start to gently pull at his top, dragging it up over his head.

"It's ok sweet," he starts. "I can wait," I pull him up, so his face lines up with mine, his body laid out over me as I softly cup his cheeks in my hands.

"I can't; I need you, Jackson. I want to feel you inside me," Our lips lock, and I can taste myself on him. Edging my hands down his torso to the edge of his jeans; I am able to undo the button there, guiding them down past his sculpted arse so he can kick them off the edge of the bed. Next are his boxers, springing free his member, so hard I can see the pre-come glistening as it escapes out its tip. Eagerly, I take it in my hand, stroking it gently before giving him a few firm pumps; he rewards me with his deep-throated growl.

"Catherine," he whispers, heated by the intensity of his lust. Quickly, while we are caught in the moment, I reach out to the nightstand for the condoms, ripping one out of its packet and making light work of dressing him.

Moments later, he is there, pressing up against my entrance and pushing the tip inside. We both look down to watch as my body completely engulfs him, pausing briefly as both of us relish the sensations now surging through us. As he starts moving, the feelings of pleasure, which hadn't quite dissipated before, are on the rise once again. Holding on to Jackson's shoulders for dear life, he really begins to plough into me, causing the bed to rock with his movements. The mounting pleasure within me starts to cause my internal muscles to contract, making his movements jerkier and wild.

"Shit…Catherine!" He grunts out, which turns into a growl as I feel his cock tense and contract while he rides out his own orgasm.

Shortly after, he collapses onto the bed next to me. Instinctively, I wrap him up in my arms and legs, holding him so impossibly close, allowing myself to enjoy the comfort of having him here with me.

I am not sure how long we lay there; we had loosened our grip on each other's bodies some time ago, but his body remained cuddled up to mine. His hand sweetly stroking my arm, along my collarbone, dancing over my breasts, then back again, with neither of us really in any hurry to move.

It's my phone's ring tone that finally breaks the silence. After a fleeting moment of confusion, realisation hits as I quickly jump out of bed, remembering what I am supposed to be doing. Hurriedly, I snatch up my dressing gown out of the half-unpacked suitcase on the floor.

"Who is it?" Jackson asks, clearly bewildered.

"I forgot the time; I'm supposed to be ready for them."

"Ready for who?"

"My kids, now shush while I take this; just stay there," I sit up at the vanity unit, carefully placing my phone upright while angling it so it doesn't line up with the bed, and pat down my hair using the phone's reflection for guidance before pressing the green answer button.

Flashing up on the screen are the faces of my beautiful boys, smiling and giggling into the phone.

"Mum!" They cry in unison.

"Hay babies, how was school?"

Jackson

"Hay babies, how was school?" She returns, cheerily, down the phone as I attempt to stay motionless on the bed.

"Good."

"Good," I hear them both reply.

"What did you do today?" She continues cheerfully.

"Umm, nothing."

"I don't remember," laughing mockingly at them, she throws her hands up enthusiastically.

"I really do need to get your brains checked out," and with that, they are all giggling. They spend the next 10–15 minutes or so chatting and laughing away. I can't see them, but they sound cute, and she obviously has such a genuine connection with them. Another puzzle piece falls into place as I suddenly realise why she has never met up before 7pm, *'its cause she talks to her kids every evening. Dur!'*

The sound of high-pitch laughter and chatter is quickly replaced by a deep male voice coming over the speaker.

"Alright, go on, boys. Find your pyjamas. I need to talk to your mother."

"Ok Dad. Good night Mum."

"Night, Mum, I love you."

"Good night babies. Love you too. Talk to you tomorrow," The male voice then returns.

"You alright?" It's a stern, unwelcoming tone in contrast to the excited chatter from a few moments ago. In return, her own voice becomes bland and unforgiving.

"Yes, I am fine. Is everything ok there?"

"Yes, just that it's half term next week, in case *you* have forgotten."

"Of course I haven't; I have already spoken to the director to try and get a little more time off."

"Well, I thought I could bring the kids to you. It might be good for them to see what you are getting up to all week instead of spending time with *them*. They clearly miss you when you're not here," So, you don't have to deal with them by yourself, you mean?

"I miss them too. Of course, I'll talk to the director and the hotel to see if I can upgrade the room to a family one for the week." It's interesting; their responses to each other are emotionless. If I only based their relationship on this one interaction alone and knew nothing else about them, I would almost think they had never even met each other!

"Good," he pauses for a moment before continuing. "I think, Catherine, we need to reconsider you going back to work," Excuse me? This pricks my ears and gets my immediate attention, unconsciously causing me to sit up straight in bed, as though moving alone will help me hear better.

"Why, what's happened?"

"Nothing in particular; I just think that *you* need to *really* think about what is best for this family, and I don't think *you* are right now." Why that manipulative fuckwit?

"I am William; of course, I am, but I also need to think about what is good for me. The boys have you when I am not there, when filming is finished, I will have plenty of time with them before my next job."

"If *we* decide you take the next job. The boys need you here with them…" As if she suddenly remembers I am here, she cuts him short.

"We will talk when I get home, William. This isn't a quick discussion to have over a face call."

"I didn't think it needed a discussion."

"Talk the weekend; bye, William," she hangs up on him, blowing out her breath through puffed-out cheeks, before she turns to readdress me.

"Sorry about that; he doesn't usually want to talk."

"It's ok, sweet; is he usually such a jackass?" She chuckles as she makes her way back over to me.

"Yeah, actually."

"Your kids sound cute, though; I would have loved to meet them."

"Well, looks like you will, sort of."

"With him, though," she hums her yes. "You won't let him make you quit, will you? You have such a talent, babe; you need this."

"I won't; don't worry. Anyway, I don't want to think about him, not when I have a much better subject laid out before me." My back is against the headboard as she straddles my lap again, planting a firm kiss on my lips. My hands immediately find her hips.

"Umm, I agree," I moan, "I *am* a much better topic of conversation," we smile into each other's mouths, reclaiming the moment we previously lost. "Umm, while we wait for the Jolly Roger to regain the wind in his sails, shall we order something to eat? You hungry?"

"Famished! I'll order up some bits," without completely leaving my lap with one leg remaining across over mine as she reaches, stretching herself out over the bed for the hotel phone to order room service. While she laughs and jokes over the phone with the receptionist, I take the time to admire her sprawled out in front of me. How different this confident girl is from the one I first met—that she can now lie here with me in just a flimsy dressing gown ridden so far up her butt, it is practically out in all its glory, just for me. She didn't even flinch as I caress the back of her leg, stroking her calf up into the folds between them. How amazing would it be to see her like this every day, to touch her without the fear of those around us?

I hear her hang up, then manoeuvre back to me, capturing my lips once more. I am really starting to like this position, her on top of me; it almost puts her in control, and that's all I want—for her to know she is safe, with me. The thought of hurting her *now* sickens me to my core; I could never do that to her.

"By the way, what's with the bag?" She asks, pulling away slightly, dragging me from my thoughts.

"Hay!" Exclaiming excitedly and suddenly remembering, "I thought of the perfect cover to stay overnight. We both go to the gym stupidly early, right? When no one else is about! All the staff already know our routine. So, it'll make no difference if we both leave at the same time; they're not to know if we came from separate rooms or not. So, I brought my gym gear to change into in the morning," A genuine, impressed smile appears on her face as she gazes into my eyes. I see hers glistening back at me.

"You're really ok with all this?"

"No, I'm not," I say it honestly, taking her hand in mine and kissing the back of it tenderly. "I think you should leave that jackass, if not for me then for yourself, but like I said, I do understand why you feel you can't," Gently, I reach up to stroke her cheek, cupping it in my hand. "I just want to be with you, Catherine, and if this is all I can have, then I'm taking it," I pause briefly to steal a quick kiss on her waiting lips to halt their quiver. "And if that also means finding solutions to the little problems we face to do so, then I'll do that too," No more needs to be said; we leave our bodies to do the rest of the talking, continuing on into the night.

Chapter 12

Jackson

How do you juxtapose living out *the* most perfect week with one of the worst?

In the week that followed the 'revelations' (as I am choosing to call it), you could unequivocally say it was a massive turning point for us. Without the big secret lurking over her head, threatening to expose itself, Catherine just allowed herself to be with me. I'd like to think of it as her unfiltered self, even if it was in the confines of our rooms. Within those walls, I am not ashamed to say I have, without a doubt, fallen for her…hard. Drawing from her those tiny giggles has become my favourite hobby. Whether it be from some poorly timed joke, playing about acting like kids, or from little compliments I offer up when I get the chance, to rise from her that little blush. Those moments light me up in a way no woman has ever done before. I just want to keep drawing them out of her, taking them for myself over and over.

That last Thursday evening, before she was due to go home—bringing back with her that asshole—I laid awake, listening to her softly snore curled up into my side. I knew it would be over a week before I got to see her like this again. I tried to memorise every feature of her delicate face and every curve and contour of her body. I didn't want to let her go. I had to keep telling myself over and over that this thing between us was just temporary; it had a best-before date, but I didn't then, and I still don't want to listen to my own reasoning. She *feels* like she belongs to me, and that's the notion my mind has chosen to latch onto.

I didn't see her come in that Monday morning; she must have gone straight into costume. We are not ready for full makeup yet, but we have found that her costume doesn't always want to behave itself when I am throwing her about the set, so we have gotten in the habit of rehearsing with it on, for most of the time at least, so we can see what moves we can actually get away with.

It was around 8am when she finally emerged: the costume was on, but it was underneath a tied-up cardigan, no doubt to make it seem a little more conservative with *him* coming on set. Our group, like always, was congregated around the drinks table while we wait for the set crew to finish up.

"So, you guys should know something," Catherine throws in suspiciously after a brief moment of silence. The group all turned to her, but I already knew what she was about to say. "I have some special guests coming to see us today," They looked at each other, confused. "My husband and my children, Callen and Axel, will be here soon."

"Children!?" "Husband?!" A couple of them exclaimed, startled by her admission.

"How do you have children?" Rodney blurted out, "There is no way!" Catherine started chuckling to herself while nodding her head and sucking her lips between her teeth.

"Why didn't you tell us you were married?" asked Rebecca.

"I don't know, to be honest. I suppose I never saw an opportunity to just blurt it out." The group all began murmuring at once, firing questions this way and that at Catherine, which she attempted to answer, all in quick succession. I just stood back, watching off in the distance, appearing on the surface to be watching the set hands, but in reality, I was just lost in my own world. Soon I would be faced with him, the man who has everything I want but who doesn't damn well appreciate it.

"Ok, on set," Cameron cried out, breaking up the conversation as we all manoeuvre from our place to find our positions.

It wasn't long into rehearsal when I heard a small commotion happening to the far right of the set; they shortly followed. I could tell it's them, not only because it was a man walking along with two small boys in tow, but also because the guy had an aura of arrogance following him around like a bad stench. He stood tall, and as much as it pains me to say, handsome *and* well built, so clearly looks after himself, clad in a V-neck green jumper and tight blue jeans.

"Permission for five minutes, Cameron?" I heard Catherine calling from beside me.

"Of course," the brightest grin appeared on her face, the same one I saw when she spoke to her children over the face call.

It took her a moment to wriggle out of the harness she was in, but once she was free, she ran hastily over to them as they, in turn, ran to her, colliding into a heap on the floor. As the small party giggled away, it radiated into chuckles, proceeding to make its way throughout the crew, including myself. Not him, however, but in its place, he portrayed a touch of annoyance as he looked on at the spectacle.

"Hay babies, did you enjoy the tour?"

"Uh huh!" said the older boy, "Makeup was the coolest! Look, look!" He jutted out his arm from under his sleeve, revealing a very gruesome-looking cut.

"I got this one!" The smaller boy lifted up his shirt to reveal a pretty impressive scar.

"They do look really cool," she replied in a pretend 'impressive' tone. After a little more banter between them, she goes to stand in order to address her husband, kissing him on the cheek while his hand finds her waist. That simple gesture set off a pit inside me, jealously prevailed and overrode my senses. "Have you been enjoying yourself too? It must have been a while since you have been on a set."

"Nothing really changes," he replied in a dismissively flat tone, clearly unimpressed. His gaze dropped as he inspected her outfit. "Is this what they have you wearing?"

"Yes, it's my costume," she replied defensively, pulling her cardigan closer around herself and hugging her waist protectively.

"Couldn't they have chosen something better suited? One that covers you up a bit more? I mean for Christ sake you're not exactly 18 anymore."

"I didn't really have much say in the matter; it isn't my movie, but, you know, it's fine; I don't mind it; it suits the character," he looked away, slightly irritated, sucking in his cheek as a clear physical indication that he was trying to hold his tongue.

Rebecca went over first to break the tension.

"Hi, I am Rebecca; you must be Catherine's family. So nice to finally meet you. Shall I introduce you to everyone?" She proceeded to go around, introducing us all. Ever the actress, Catherine played the doting wife well, staying by her husband's side as they walked around the set. You would never know the truth behind her façade unless you knew it prior, which I of course, did, and each time he touched her, it pinged at my rage, *'He shouldn't get to do that.'*

When they got to my position, still on the set, the kids started to jump up and down excitedly.

"Jackson Hunter!" The older boy cried out. "Wow, I saw you in that movie with computers and the future and the motorbike, but it wasn't really a motorbike because it was *flying*, but it was so cool you were like, 'watch me'. And you sped off…"

"Hay Bud, glad you liked it; what's your name then?" Taking a leaf out of Catherine's book and masking my true feelings behind a veil of friendliness.

"I'm Callen, and this is my brother Axel; he likes your films too, but some of them are a little too old for him, so he doesn't watch as many as I do because I'm nearly 8!"

"Wow, so you'll be really big then, huh?"

"Yeah, and Dad says when I am 8, I can get a motorbike!"

"Wow," I looked up to him, "That'll be cool," I stood to offer him a smile and my hand; I had to play the part, even if it sickened me to even acknowledge him. "Hay, Jackson Hunter."

"Yes, I have seen your films," he gave me an annoyingly smug smile back, taking my outstretched hand. "Pleased to meet you," I can't say the feeling was entirely mutual.

"Ok, back on set!"

"I have to get back to work; do you want to see Mummy rehearse?" Directing her attention back to the children.

"Yeah!"

"But you have to be *real* quiet, ok?" They nodded their heads, eyes widened in unison while pulling in their lips, mimicking silence. Ha, they *are* cute kids!

Getting back into her harness, we took our positions. The children looked on in amazement.

"That is enough, Helen!" I started as I pushed my way through the set, getting so close to her that our mouths were a mere centimetre apart.

"Oh, my love, don't tell me you're suddenly growing a conscience now," she stood tall, projecting her breasts out into my chest. Continuing with our rehearsed scene, I push her up against the wall, resuming my onslaught; she smiled back sadistically.

"It's not too late, Helen; you can stop this," I captured her lips in mine briefly before pulling back, and gazed into her face. She rewarded me with a deep, callous laugh.

"Why would I do that, Adrien?"

"For me, do it for me…for us," I turned my tone into a plea. She throws her head back and continued with her malicious laugh: chairs and props flying across the set around us on cue.

"Oh Adrien, there is no us." The harness attached to her waist pulled her suddenly upwards, indicting for me to be propelled backwards, just like in the way we had rehearsed. She found her next stance easily, like the devil's angel taking to the skies.

"Ok, that's great. Thank you," exclaimed Cameron, "ok, take 5 while we reset."

Catherine landed safely back on the ground, unlocking her harness easily. "That was great, Catherine," Cameron added, "You still need to watch your feet's position, it needs to be a little more pointed."

"No problem, I'll work on it," he nodded as she turned to address her children, kneeling to their height. "Hay, so what'd guys think?"

"You were great, Mummy," Axel said excitedly, and he hugged her tightly around her waist.

"Yeah, Mum, that was so cool," I smiled softly from a distance at the interaction between them—that is, until I spot *him* looming over the three of them.

"Catherine, can I have a *word*?"

"Umm, sure, hay why don't you guys help yourself to something off the food table? Mummy and Daddy will just be over here." Pointing to a vacant section of the room off in the distance, away from the set. The boys darted off towards the food as I watch them walk off in a different direction.

It's then, that I saw the sourness of their body language before my eyes. His face depicted that of fury, pushing her forward by the elbow away from us, like a parent scolding a naughty child, whereas she, in response, retreated into herself, she continued to pull at that cardigan, wrapping it tightly around her torso.

I was not having that! Rage started to bubble away inside me; I couldn't just stand there while he belittled her like that. I began to head over, my fists balling beside me. It must have caught Cameron's attention as well, as I saw in my peripheral vision that he, too, followed suit. This ass-crack didn't seem to hear my approach, but as I got closer, I could hear him berating her.

"Are you trying to humiliate me?"

"No, Will, of course not; I am just trying to do my job."

"*This* is not what *I* agreed to when *I* let you go back to work."

"This is acting; I don't know what else you expected."

"I expect you to know how to present yourself; you're a 30-year-old mother for Christ's sake; mothers do *not* parade about with their arses hanging out! I cannot believe how selfish you are being; you're not even considering *me* or the boys when you prance around, acting like *that*!"

Glancing past Williams' arm, she spotted me, and her eyes opened wide in alarm. As I approached, I schooled my features so as not to appear too angry as I placed my hand on his shoulder reassuringly, forcing his attention to focus on me instead of her.

"Hey Will, Catherine, are you alright over here?"

"Yes, we are fine; I am just having a private conversation with *my wife*," he spat out.

"I can see that," I almost seethe back.

"William, I'm Cameron, the director," Cameron interjected. He nodded slightly, taking William's hand into his own to shake while I took a step back, using the moment of distraction to direct my gaze towards Catherine, but she was no longer able to look at me.

"So, you are the one who put my wife in next to nothing?" Facing Cameron head-on, broad shoulders squared off as if he were preparing for a standoff.

"Look, I know it isn't easy seeing your wife be intimate with another man on camera; trust me, I know, my wife is also an actress. Those first few scenes watching her perform were torture for me. But you should know this is just acting; we are all professionals here, Jackson more than most, I assure you."

He gestured towards me with a nod to his head. I remained stern beside them. "Your misses is a damn fine actress, mate; even *I* find it hard to tell she is acting, and I have worked with my own fair share, but as soon as I say cut, they all return to their usual selves, and I can *promise* you, although yes, I admit that outfit is small, no part of her intimate body is exposed at any point in the movie," I could tell Dickwad wanted to say something more, but he was holding his tongue as the two of us stare at him, clearly realising he was outnumbered.

After a moment, he caved under the social pressure of us all glaring at him, he half turned towards Catherine, simply saying, "We'll talk later," and stormed off in the direction of the boys. Catherine ran up behind him, asking where he was going, "I'm taking the children out; they shouldn't have to see this," I heard him sternly say in response.

Catherine nodded silently, trying, once again to wrap her cardigan ever more tightly around herself. Resigned to defeat, she hugged the boys tightly as they all say their goodbyes.

Once they had all left, unable to help myself, I took Catherine in my arms and offer her a hug of my own.

"You alright?" I asked, trying not to give away to Cameron that I knew more about that interaction than anybody.

"I'm fine," she offered us one of her all-telling fake smiles. "He wouldn't be a proper husband if he didn't get a little jealous," she covered. I hated that; I hate the fact she had to make an excuse for him.

"No, I suppose not. Take another five, then meet us back on set."

"Thank you, Cameron," she pulled away from me, and headed towards her trailer. I wish I could have gone after her, giving her all the comfort she needed, but I couldn't; I had to keep my distance, at least for this one week.

Catherine was different for the rest of the afternoon. While keeping her usual professionalism, her regular smile was gone; once the room was filled with her radiant laughter and an upbeat personality, she was withdrawn, she had chosen to spend her downtime locked away in her trailer instead of with us.

Her change in personality, as well as our forced separation, played dangerous games with my mind. Propping up ideas in there that had no place, nor very little foundation, but once there, I could do nothing but dwell on them, I fixated on the possibility of them, and twisted facts to fit my proof. *'What is she afraid of? Would he actually be capable of harming her? Over this?'*

I could not get that damn thought out of my head—the way he was, the way he spoke to her, how he seemed to dominate her. Would he? She wasn't afraid nor had she ever felt the need to run from me when my own anger reared its ugly head. Why? Was it because she was already used to aggression; used to violence?

It was not helped by the fact that she did not come to work on Tuesday; claiming she was spending the day with her children instead, which Cameron granted.

I wanted to find her, text, or ring just to make sure she was ok; it took all my willpower not to. My fear was that *he* would see the message instead, and then I would only have made things worse for her, but I could not help the worry.

Rage boiled within me right until I got back to the hotel Tuesday evening. Restless, I by-passed my room—the room that held my most intimate memories of her, and headed down to the bar, choosing to drown out those incessant thoughts with alcohol instead.

It is here that I see them, entering the hotel lobby while I watch on from a distance. She didn't seem to notice me, but she was grinning and laughing away with her children, his arm was wrapped possessively around her waist. *'Get off her, I swear to god!'* "Fuck!" I cursed under my breath.

As they headed up the stairs, more thoughts flailed aimlessly in my mind. *'Are they sleeping in the same bed? Are they kissing goodnight?'* Ahh! I was driving myself mad, my imagination running wild with these insane rogue images.

A little while later, around 8pm, I was still sitting alone in the bar, nursing my third whiskey, when my eyes were drawn to the ping of the elevator across the lobby.

It was him.

But he was by himself. Dressed to the nines. I watched as he adjusted the cuff links on his shirt and he made his way across the lobby, out the main door.

No one else would have battered an eyelid, but I *knew*. I knew exactly where he was going. *'You fucking prick!'* Annoyance and rage bubbled away, causing pains of frustration to overwhelm every damn one of my nerves. *'You really don't deserve her, you fucking dick!'*

I downed my drink. No longer thinking clearly, I rose out of my seat to follow the prick, intent on releasing some of this pent-up aggression building within me, preferably on him. I was almost near the entrance of the lobby, where I could see him outside waiting for a cab. Clenching my fists ready to take him out, it was then that I had a sudden realisation. He was here, which means he was not with her.

Hurriedly retrieving my phone from my back pocket, I quickly search for her number, shooting a message.

Me: Hay, I missed you today. Is everything okay? I'm worried.

It was not long before I saw the familiar 3 dots on the screen, indicating she was writing her reply.

Helen: I'm fine, thank you. Yes, been out with the boys today; they are knackered. I am just sitting here watching a film with them. I'll be back at work tomorrow x.

A touch of relief washed over me.

Me: That's good; it's not the same without you.
Helen: Lol missing your throwing partner? X
Me: Something like that. I am glad you're ok.
Helen: See you tomorrow, Jackson x.
Me: See you tomorrow.

At least I knew I would see her on Wednesday, which temporarily eased my mind. Heading back to my room, I hoped that knowledge alone would calm down the chaos swimming throughout my consciousness.

The rest of the week was agonising, knowing she was there…but wasn't. Ever the professional though, her true acting ability came forth in her everyday interactions with those around her; you would not have known any the wiser for her dispiritedness if you did not otherwise know her as personally as I did.

Her eyes held a glaze that hid her true self from me, and I missed it. Those thoughts that had been plaguing me earlier in the week did not dissipate; in fact, they grew worse as each day passed, festering, especially when on Thursday she insisted on wearing her own clothes in rehearsal, simply saying she felt a bit 'bleh' and just wanted to be comfortable, adding more fuel to the fiery fury. I kept asking if she was ok, secretly begging her to tell me she wasn't just so I had an excuse to beat the crap out of this guy! She was, however, insistent that everything was fine and that the kids had just been running her ragged all week.

The weekend was the worst though, and my imagination got the better of me. Knowing there was no reprieve for her being in the same house as him, no excuse for hotel walls being too thin, or having to be on set the next day; what would she be facing?

The following Monday, however, she was different; she seemed happier, no doubt because she didn't have the threat of him hovering over her, telling her what she *should* be doing instead of what she *chose* to do.

Rehearsals and shooting went well, and I was ecstatic to see the smile back on her face as she laughed and joked with the rest of us. Nevertheless, the questions of the previous week still haunted me, prompting me to act on impulse rather than rational thought, impulsively heading straight to her room as soon as the workday was finished. I had to see her, I had to know, and I had to have her in my arms once more.

So here I am, outside her door, lightly knocking and waiting patiently for her to answer.

Catherine

I had just walked in the door of my hotel room when I heard a slight knocking at my door. I laugh inwardly. I know Jackson is impatient. It must have been tough this last week to hold off: to pretend we mean nothing more to each other than co-workers, but even this is quick *'give me a chance to have a shower at least!'*

I open the door with a huge grin on my face, expecting to be met with the same mischievous one looking back at me that I am used to, ready to pounce. Instead, however, I am taken aback, Jackson looks almost…pained.

Without hesitation, he takes my head in his hands, thumbs resting on my jaw while the rest of his palms spread themselves across my neck and hairline. Without a care for who might see me in the corridor, he pushes me into the room, claiming my lips and holding my face to his. As my back collides against the wall to the right of the room, he briefly lets go of my face to close the door. With my hands finding their home on his back and under his shirt, he then uses his whole body to envelope me in his embrace. His hands, seemingly unsure of where they want to be, roam from my jaw into my hair, then glide their way down my back. So far from the frenzied, passionate attacks we have partaken in the past, this is wary and in an almost frantic display, trying to take me all in at once. I am unable to keep up with or understand what he needs.

All of a sudden, he stops, resting his head on top of mine, connected by our foreheads, one hand on the side of my neck, the other keeping him steady against the wall. I open my eyes to find his closed in concentration and that same painful expression on his face. Bringing my hands from his back to find his face, I try to get him to look at me, but to no avail.

"Jackson?" I question in a worried whisper, still trying to draw his attention. He reacts unexpectedly, expelling a sharp and loud, "fuck!" As he hits his hand against the wall beside my head. After a slight pause in thought, it is followed by him hitting the same spot again and again, repeatedly with the palm of his hand, in what appears to be a desperate act of frustration.

"Hay, hay! Jackson look at me," I attempt to calm him, guiding his face back to meet mine, waiting for his eyes to open. His deep browns are penetrating as he slowly opens them, looking deep into the depths of mine. "What's going on?" His breathing appears laboured, and his gaze remains intense.

"Did he…" he starts, struggling to form the words through gritted teeth, "Did he hurt you?"

"What? No! Of course not!" My heart races as I try to calm him down.

"You'd tell me…You'd tell me if he did. Right?"

"Jackson, look at me; I'm fine, see?" He seems to be calming down a little, resting his head on top of mine in an attempt to regulate himself. I have never seen him so worked up, so upset; my cheeky, carefree Jackson has been turned into this…because of me.

"No, he just fucking spins his control over you instead! Got you right where he wants you, hasn't he?" He sniffs quite audibly as his panic seems to morph into rage. "God Catherine, the way he spoke to you, talked down to you like you were a piece of shit on his fucking shoe. Please tell me you don't listen to his bull crap!"

"Hay," I begin, guiding my hand to gently stroke his cheek and lightly kiss his lips in an attempt to calm him down. "Where has all *this* come from?" He pushes away from me in frustration, racking his hands through his hair. Resentment and anger are still very evident on his face and in his demeanour.

"All week…" he's now pacing the room, "I have watched him touch you, play happy families, and get to pretend you're some perfect fucking family! Fuck Catherine, that should be me!" He shouts, using both his hands to gesticulate towards himself. "He doesn't fucking deserve you; it should be fucking me!" And once again, my heart breaks. The realisation that this isn't some scratch we are itching for anymore; this is real for him; I can't do this to him anymore; it just isn't fair.

"Jackson, I think we need to put an end to this now," My arms fall to my side in defeat as the reality of what I have just said hits. It's the right thing to do, I know, but it doesn't rein in my heart as it screams hysterically at me to retract everything I have just said. My heart is not the only one, it seems, as he jerks his head up, staring at me in a panic.

"What? No!" He exclaims. His whole posture warps into something else; desperation. He comes close to me, grabbing at my shoulders in an attempt to hold on. I hold his face again, trying to stop the tears now glazing my eyes, turning him and everything else around him blurry.

"Look at you! Look at what *I am* doing to you! This isn't you. This isn't who you are. I'm hurting you."

"No! Catherine, please, please don't end this," he brings his head down to mine again, eyes closed, shaking his head in silent resistance. "No, I'm not ready for this to be over." I feel a slight tremble in his hands as he glides them up and down my arms and up again to find my face. "I'm fine, I promise. I'll be fine. Just moronic thoughts, that's all. I'm fine now. Please, please don't let me go. Give me more time."

"I don't want to hurt you."

"You won't, I promise; it was just the first time. Seeing you and him, it hit me more than I thought it would, but I'm fine now…now I know you're ok, I'll be fine, I promise. Please don't let me go yet," I hate this. I hate it because I can't deny him; I can't say no because I, too, don't want to let him go. I do not yet want to say goodbye.

Foolishly, I agree, unable to speak, so I find myself just nodding stupidly along, taking his lips back to mine in a desperate attempt to let go of all the pain we have shared in the last 10 minutes. Giving into our bodies, we once again embrace, letting our mouths overtake our good sense and giving in to the moment we have allowed ourselves to indulge in, but it isn't frantic or rushed; it's just us.

Stepping back a little, ashamed to say with a couple of sniffles, I put on my prized smile for him to see, giving my best try to get things back to the way they were a week ago.

Grabbing his shirt with my fists, I pull him closer towards me, taking back some control over our emotions.

"Come on you, we have had a long day; how about we grab a shower first?"

"Together?" There's my Cheshire cat smile I missed, a telling sign of all the naughty things he has spinning around his mind.

"Together," I confirm, heading towards the bathroom, one fist still intertwined in his shirt, pulling him along behind me.

He pulls his shirt over his head, tossing it to the ground and catching my now empty hand in his. He pulls it up to place a soft kiss on the back of it. I mirror him, pulling off my top and pushing down my skirt, leaving them both in a pile next to the door. I turn to enter the bathroom, jutting out my hips exaggeratedly as I go.

I feel him come up behind me, gently playing with the back of my bra, teasing at its clasp. As he carefully undoes it, I feel his lips find the side of my neck, immediately finding the sensitive spot there while I fiddle with the knobs on the shower fitting. I feel his hand snake forward into my underwear, his finger gliding over my sex, and leisurely play around the skin surrounding my clit. Letting out a sigh of approval, I tilt my head back to rest on his shoulder as he continues to tease, using his other hand to play with my now exposed breasts.

"My sweet girl," he whispers in my ear, "I've missed you," Reclaiming my neck in his mouth, his movements become more forceful, squeezing my nipple between his fingers while his other one enters me, stroking its way from my opening to the sensitive nub at its hilt. Having him touch me like this again feels like home, with the intense waves of pleasure shooting through my body as I lean back into him, allowing him to take my weight as he continues his onslaught. I feel his cock slide in lengthways between my arse cheeks, nestling in between them, causing them to clench around his shaft; my hips begin to rock between the feel of his penis and that of his fingers.

Bringing one arm up over my head to rest around his neck, my other hand finds my other breast accompanying Jackson's, attempting to mirror his actions. Releasing a long moan, he increases his tempo, knocking out the stability of my legs in the process, but he is resilient, holding me up while sinking two of his fingers inside me, continuing his assault.

Pushing me into the side of the shower, I use both my hands to press up against the clear glass to hold me steady. As he moves his hand behind me, I jut my arse out to meet him to give him better access to my sex as he continues his attention inside me—faster, deeper, hitting that spot deep within again and again, causing my body to spasm against his touch.

"J…" I make out just as he moves his fingers back to my clit finishing me off, feeling my climax pulse spread like a warmth around my abdomen, causing my body to shake uncontrollably. Catching my breath against the coolness of the glass, I feel him move behind me, vaguely aware of him pulling me under the soothing warmth of the shower's water now beating down on my overly sensitive body.

While soaking in the water's embrace, I can feel Jackson's body flash up against mine, tenderly capturing my lips with his. He feels so good against me, feeling his hands lathering me up with soap upon my waist and my breasts, washing my body like I am his to wash, and cherish.

I opened my eyes for the first time since our interaction began, bringing them into focus to gaze upon his form, a chest so well maintained I can never help myself; I have to touch. Taking the soap in my hands, I return my admiration, lathering him up and massaging his muscles to the glorious sight of him flinging his head back at my firm touch. Encouraged, I move my hand lower, encasing his engorged erection in my slick hand to gently stroke it from base to tip, reviling in his gasps of low grunts and soft sighs. I want this. I want to make him feel just as good as he makes me feel, to make him forget about the shit from the past week and just enjoy us. Like this. Together.

Briefly guiding him under the shower's spray to rinse him of the suds, I then meet him under the water, kissing him affectionately across from his neck to his chest, taking the time to enjoy the feeling of him against me, surrendering to my touch, and trusting me explicitly.

My back to the wall, I start kissing my way down his body, skating my hands across his waist and down his legs. I kneel in front of him, coming face to face with *him*. I want him *now;* I want him to come undone before me. Watching his reaction as I leave a sweet kiss on the tip of his member, I smile, seeing his mouth slightly agape as he draws in his breath, waiting for me to continue. So as not to be cruel, I don't leave him waiting too long, taking him into my mouth as deep as I can before quickly retreating out once again. The jerky movement of his hand having to rest against the wall of the shower to keep him upright tells me he is enjoying it. Eager to continue, I take him in again, using my tongue to press against the underside of his erection, tracking it along and back up to its end, swirling around the tip.

"Catherine," I hear him gasp under his breath, his head bent downward and staring at me, allowing the water to trickle down through his hair around his face as I take him whole again. He watches me, as entranced as I am.

It isn't long before I feel his hips start to thrust to the movements of my mouth, but I sense his restraint; he is trying not to fuck too hard, trying not to hurt me. I take my moment, sucking harder, taking him so deep that his cock touches the back of my throat. Holding back the need to gag, I do it again.

"God Catherine...I'm gunna..." With a final jerk forward, he roars, expelling from him his seed, filling my mouth as I struggle to drink it down with the continued movements of his hips. I continue to allow him to ride out his orgasm in my mouth, waiting for him to stop before releasing my hold.

His breathing is staggered and straining while he still tries to hold himself up against the side of the shower. Standing, I position myself between him and the wall, the water now beating down on the both of us. One hand comes to rest on my neck and shoulder, his head on top of mine, while he regains himself.

I thread my hand through his wet hair, entangling my fingers at the roots and using my nails to gently massage his scalp; in return, he turns his head to meet my hand, enjoying the feel of it there, a low moan escaping his throat.

"Come on!" I whisper after a while, enjoying this simple intimacy between us. I turn off the tap, finding the towels on the rail outside the shower screen door. I use one to quickly dry myself off first, running it through my hair before wrapping it around my body. The others I use to dry him. I take my time with him, however, starting at his face, dabbing at his toned chest, down to his stomach, and then his legs, savouring the time to adore him in his entirety, all the while he watches me intently, not saying a word as I do. The intimacy of the act sparks like an electrical current running between us, depicting more than our words ever could.

Once he is dry, not completely, but to my satisfaction, I take his hand, guiding him out and over to the bed. Lying down next to each other, we are slightly turned inwards, but with my arms wrapped around him, his leg over mine, and his head on my breasts, we lie there for a while, neither of us saying a word, almost scared that if we speak, it'll break the connection we just shared and the comfort exchange between us.

"Can I ask you something?" He asks finally, interrupting the silence as he lazily traces tiny circles along my abdomen.

"Anything."

"Why did you give up acting in the first place?"

Well, there is a question: why did I? Why did I give up the one thing that was only mine, which gave me so much joy in my life?

"I can't remember the exact moment I decided not to go back," I continue to ponder as I try to answer his question. "I had just gotten pregnant with Callen. It was shortly after I married Will. I remember him telling me that I didn't have to go back and that his business did enough to support us both. I suppose I just kept that with me, so when Callen was born, I fell into the role of housewife. I didn't really attempt to pursue it again until recently," I stroke his hair aimlessly, trying to think back to that time, which seems so long ago. "Why do you ask?" He stiffens beneath me, like he doesn't really want to say what he is really thinking. "You can say it, you know; whatever you want to say, I have no nice things to say about the man or any justification for how I let my life end up this way."

"It's just…" he stops, pausing his playful musings on my stomach. "I looked you up; on the internet, that is, once upon a time you were everywhere sweet, a real socialite, and then…you just disappeared," he pauses again, contemplating his next point. "And you know he has a way of speaking to you; have you noticed? He makes it seem like his way is the only way, like he uses words and a turn of phrase to get you to bend to his rules, and when you try and tell him otherwise, he just gets angry; it forces you to back down. I physically watched it happen to you," he adjusts himself, so he is now eye level with me, one hand under his head, his free hand resting on the side of my face. "It just makes me think, and I could be wrong. Just…maybe it wasn't your decision at all. You know?" I tear my eyes away from him and think for a long moment. The fact is, I really *don't* remember making the choice.

"Maybe, or maybe it was for the best; I was a new mother after all," I laugh a little, brushing it away from my thoughts, but he doesn't join me.

"Doesn't mean you have to be chained to them 24 hours a day; you're allowed a life sweet, allowed to do the things you enjoy doing."

"I know. Why do you think I am here now?"

"And he is *still* trying to control you."

"And I am *still* here."

"Hiding from him! You are such a strong woman, Catherine, and yet you still cower to him," I don't like this conversation; it's turning my mind sideways and making me rethink things I am in no mind to rethink, especially while I have this gorgeous naked man in front of me.

So instead, I kiss him, deflecting by pulling our bodies closer together and pushing my breasts up against his chest.

"Umm, strong enough to handle all this, huh?" I smile against his mouth, tracing his lips with my tongue while manhandling his giant biceps.

"Oh, definitely strong enough to handle me, sweet girl," Taking the hint for a change in conversation; taking it all the way through the night.

Chapter 13

<u>Jackson</u>

She is mine again…for now. I can pretend anyway, for a little while longer.

I am more determined than ever to win her over and prove to her that I'm worth the risk. Moreover, the idea of not being with her again fills me with a kind of dread I am not used to dealing with, but in addition, I cannot bear the thought of her having to go back to him and live out her life miserable, succumbing to his warped need for control.

We have moved from the studio and are now on location; long gone are the sets built around us. We have a month left to tour the scenic backdrop of Italy to film the final scenes. Catherine isn't in as many of these shots as she was in the beginning, so I am finding myself making the most of the time I do have with her.

She is with us this week for 3 out of the 5 days, and while today is only supposed to be rehearsals, ready to shoot on Wednesday, clearly nobody is in the right mood for work.

"Adrien! Take heed of my wrath and know it was you who brought this upon mankind."

"I will stop you, Helen!" The wind machines blow wildly, full blast into our faces, sending her hair flicking this way and that. Her portrayal of Helen then begins laughing maniacally into the wind, holding her hands out wide to her side.

"And how do you intend to do that, Adrien…" she pauses for a moment before dropping her hands and head in defeat, "When I can't even remember my flipping lines!" It takes a moment to register what she said. Someone from the crew starts to chuckle first. I then follow shortly after as I catch on, placing my hands on my hips. What follows is a chorus of chuckles passing through the rest of the crowd like an echo. "I'm sorry guys, I got so distracted by my hair; it's in my bloody mouth!" She plants her face in her hands, lightly so as not to disrupt the makeup.

Still laughing, I make my way over to her, wrapping her up in a hug and rocking her from side to side.

"My god Helen, you're not conquering anything at this rate," I cry out as I let her go. The crew continues to laugh as they reset the location props.

"Alright guys, we have about 30 more minutes before we lose our light. Can we get this nailed?" Cameron calls out from the crowd. "Hairstylist, can we do something about that haystack?" A girl with a waist belt filled with hair supplies comes running onto the set and starts playing with Catherine's hair.

"For what it's worth, I love the 'haystack' look, very 80s," I offer up a wink, and she giggles at my silliness.

"Haha, not sure Cam will appreciate me breaking out in classic rock, head-banging into the wind machine."

"Ha, I don't know, could suit the character, coming out of hell to a classic!" We're sniggering away while the woman finishes up. When she eventually leaves, it is just us briefly, and it gives me a moment, outside the ear of anyone else, to lean in and whisper in her ear.

"On the rooftop."

"Huh?" She looks at me, confusingly.

"Tonight, meet me on the rooftop of the hotel. Seven," she nods slightly, acknowledging that she heard me, before we both resume our positions for the scene. The company has once again found us a hotel where we can all stay together; again, I think more to keep us out of trouble than for any other reason, but it gives us the perfect excuse to rendezvous without being too inconspicuous. It also gave me time to put a little planning into tonight.

Catherine

I have to say I am a little suspicious of this evening. The last few months with Jackson have been some of the most spectacular of my life. Behind closed doors, Jackson is so passionate and tentative, and not because he is doing anything in particular; there have been no fancy restaurants, no grand gestures, or public displays of affection, just him being him. I know my demands were not easy for him to meet, but he did it, and he did it because I really do believe he cares for me. It truly breaks me to know I cannot give him what he really wants.

The meeting on the rooftop is different, though. He has never planned anything out before; his skill has always been to be naturally charming just by being himself; therefore, our rooms have, so far, been enough.

I have taken the time to dress up a little. Knowing he has made the effort has made me want to do the same. Luckily enough, the door to the roof is located near my room, so I was able to get there without anybody seeing. Sneaking up the fire escape from the hotel, I find myself on the roof, feeling like a disobedient teenager sneaking out of her parents' bedroom. I find the fire exit door slightly ajar, propped open by a fire bucket, and I hear faint music chiming off behind it.

Slowly pushing back the door, it reveals the roof terrace, featuring a small table, a couple of chairs, and a wine cooler at its centre, decorated by two small candles, two glasses of champagne, and a few takeaway containers. The music I can see is coming from his phone sitting in between the candles, and there, standing behind it all, is Jackson holding a single rose, wearing a pair of low-slack jeans and a V-neck shirt. A chagrin smile spread across his face; he probably feels pretty pleased with himself.

Almost timidly, he makes his way around the table to meet me at the door. I am careful not to let the door shut completely as I let it go.

"What's all this?" I ask shyly, feeling a blush creep up my cheeks as he hands me the rose.

"This, all be it a little cheesy, is me taking you out," raising his hand to my cheek, he lightly strokes it with his thumb; then he lays a light kiss upon my lips. "As I can't take you out properly, I thought I'd set it up here. No one will disturb us." Brushing my hair behind my ear, he inhales a sharp intake of breath. "You look stunning tonight, Catherine," Looking into his eyes in the light of the candles, with their flicker of gold reflecting back at me from their depths, I see his sincerity. There truly is more to this man than the small glimpses witnessed in the confines of our rooms, and what I see of it now has taken my words away.

"Come on, I tried, but I'm pretty sure the food is already cold," we chuckle slightly as he guides me over to the waiting chairs. Like a true gentleman, he pulls mine out first and waits for me to sit before pushing it back in again.

"Chinese!" I exclaim as I see the containers, "love it."

"Thought you might; you wouldn't believe how hard it was for me to find a Chinese in Italy!" We chuckle again, and I allow him to lead the way, opening the containers to offer up some of their contents.

We sit and chat for ages; time doesn't seem to pass as we get lost in silly anecdotes, idol chitchat, and childish giggles. After a while, when we have truly stuffed ourselves with food and champagne, Jackson rises from his seat, making his way round to my side to offer out his hand.

"Care to dance, my lady?"

"Now that *was* cheesy!" I snigger.

Returning my grin, he hoists me up out of my seat.

"Come on, we *have* to dance!" Bending quickly to turn the volume up on his phone using its side button, he soon returns upright, bracing himself against me while allowing his arms to glide around my waist while mine rest high up on his shoulders.

We sway almost in sync to the slow music, with neither of us being natural dancers, and as we move my fingers once again intertwine into his hair, grazing my nails through the roots, and lightly scratching at his scalp.

I feel lost, but this feeling of being lost is not like it was before. That place was terrifying and lonely, but here, it's like Jackson and I are the only two people adrift in this world, and that's ok because no one can hurt us here.

"What are you thinking?" He asks while he kisses the top of my head, resting his lips on top of it while speaking into my hair. Closing my eyes, I sigh as if caught in a dreamy sleep.

"I am thinking that this can't be real. You are so caring and sweet; you do and say things so that even when I am alone, your existence to me is like a burning light casting your glow off in the distance, constantly reminding me of the good, to give me hope of something better," I look up into his eyes. "Men like you don't really exist," he captures my lips in his, softly, taking one hand to cradle my cheek.

"We do, sweet girl. I don't know about where you come from, but me, I was taught to treat a woman the way she deserves to be treated; if she acts like a bitch, treat her like it, but when they are as sweet as you," he takes my lips again, "you deserve the world, sweet girl." Seizing my lips again, this time taking my mouth desperately deeper, we let our tongues join in the dance to the tune of the music.

"Truth is, I could say the same about you," he ventures as we take a moment's respite to catch our breath. "I've never met anyone like you: selfless, caring, not to mention talented, and of course, beautiful!" He lists, "I have never wanted to give someone so much, but they want nothing more in return from me than just me being me. There was nothing before you," he wraps his huge arms around me protectively as I wrap mine around his waist. "If all I have done tonight is allow you to escape and give you more fuel for your light, even for a little while, then that's my gift to you. You deserve so much more than this sweet girl; I really would give you the world if you would let me."

Holding back the prick of tears at the corner of my eyes, I continue to sway with him a little while longer, reviling in our perfect moment: it's cold, on a dirty hotel roof, eating cold Chinese out of plastic containers and dancing to music out of the tiny speakers of a phone, with only Jackson for company.

Just perfect.

Chapter 14

Catherine

Something is pulling me. Tugging me backwards. I cannot see nor hear anything from the empty void around me.

"Help!" I call out into an echo. No one is around to answer. Looking back into the nothingness that is pulling at me…it's terrifying—stilling my heart and freezing my bones in fear of nothing.

I began to fight against the pull, dragging myself forwards on all fours, clawing at anything that could give me traction.

The pull became ever more violent, forcing me against my will.

"Please, someone!" Desperation takes over, frantically grasping at anything and everything, but there is nothing, just the emptiness behind me.

Disappearing slowly into the abyss, I see a far-off light flickering off in the distance, but it's too late. The darkness has stolen my voice, and my scream remains my own. Succumbing to the inevitable, my sight goes out.

Bolting upright from my bed, I look around in the darkness of the room. Panting heavily in cold sweats, grasping at the soft sheets around me. Touching something soft and spongy, I wince, struggling to adjust my eyes to the light of the room. Eventually it all becomes clear: the room, huge glass windows overlooking the city still emanating its nighttime glow, and Jackson lying next to me, hand on my leg looking up at me sleepily.

"You ok, sweet?" I bring myself back into the moment as I come to the realisation that everything is as it should be. I calm myself down, settling back under the covers. I edge myself closer to Jackson, who wraps me up in his arms, an instant calm overtakes my body.

"Yeah, just a bad dream, that's all." Cosied up next to my protector, I drift back off into a restless sleep; the feeling of helplessness still remains, hanging over me.

Jackson

I feel like I am running on a clock. Weekends are beginning to feel more like a chore than a luxury; I'm just trying to get through them as quickly as I can so I can see her again come Monday morning. Weeks are ticking away before she is snatched from my arms by the biggest dick in the history of dicks. My chance to intervene is dwindling; I'm not really sure if I had a chance to begin with, driven by one simple thought, *'I have to try.'*

I can't explain it…these thoughts, this projective motivation that tells me I must be near her always, because when I am near her, she makes *me* feel so good, better, complete, that there is nothing else that matters in the world, then to make her happy, to make her laugh, and to make her come so hard, she calls out my name in sexual release. It fills my egotistic pride and makes me feel more like a man: her man. That feeling is addictive, and I want to feel it every goddamn day.

Of course, it isn't long until we are in our final weeks of filming; this being *her* last week, while *I* still have a few more to go. I *have* to make it count; have to make her see that she belongs with me; we belong together; whatever the fallout, whatever the consequences, we'll take them on together, but I can't let this end, not without a fight.

Catherine

It's my final week of filming. It's my final week with Jackson, and I can feel it and see it in his actions. I know what he is doing: he is trying to make me choose him over everything else, but he still doesn't seem to understand that I do not have a choice. If I did, it would be him; of course, it would. I hope he realises that before the end.

Nevertheless, he continues to lavish me with attention. Last night was perfect; it was Monday. Like most nights when it was just him and me, we were in his hotel room. He had set up dinner as usual; we sat, talked, and laughed like there was no end to conversation. Sex, like always, comes so naturally between us; we're drawn to each other like two polar ends of a magnet.

Waking up in his arms, however, has become my favourite thing; it's safe; *he* makes me feel safe; makes me feel like I am *the* most important person in the world just wrapped up in his humongous arms; not to mention the fact that it usually results in morning sex, which, never having indulged in it before, has also fast become my new favourite thing! Nothing has set me up for the day better than a morning orgasm!

With wind machines blowing in my face and a harness tied tightly around my waist suspending me in the air, it has proven difficult to hear what Jackson is relaying to me: choosing to rely on my very limited lip-reading skills to determine if he has finished his line or not.

"What forces from this world can you possibly have?" I can just about make out the sound of a muffled reply through the sound of wind blurring through my ears.

"Ha! Come on, Adrien, show me!"

"Fantastic and cut there, thank you, Catherine. Bring her down, please," Thank goodness, Cameron has really been working us like dogs out here. I understand, though, we're working in a location where we are really strapped for time: they can only close the roads for so long; that doesn't stop the agonising, tired ache from antagonising my body.

"Catherine, can I talk to you for a minute?" Cameron calls as I am finally released from my restraints. I hurry over, with Cameron ushering me over to a secluded part of our temporary set. "Catherine, that was excellent. We are going to do a few more takes from Jackson's point of view, and we are done for this scene, so you don't need to be in the harness for that you'll be pleased to hear," I am! "Listen, we are ahead of schedule, which is good, and believe we are ready to film scene 17 tomorrow, which is your final scene. You feel you're up to it?" What no! We weren't due to film that until Friday: I thought I had more time!

"Umm, I thought we needed those extra shots?"

"We do, but not from your angle; we have some pretty good ones. We will probably have to bring you in for some voiceover in some of the scenes, but as far as shooting is concerned, you're finished."

"Oh ok; well sure, if you feel you have enough already."

"Great! So tomorrow, head straight for makeup; they'll get you prepped; it'll take a few hours. Alright?"

"Sure, thank you, Cameron."

"No problem," he turns back round to face the team, "alright positions! Camera 2, I want you facing here; I need that angle looking at Jackson from the down here, directly faci…" He walks off leaving me to reel in the repercussions of our conversation. It means we have less time than I thought; tonight, would now be our last night together. That realisation hits me like waking up from a hellish nightmare—or as in my life—the impact of knowing I will be returning to one, away from the fantasy bubble we have been living in, away from Jackson.

Off in the short distance, I see Jackson looking at me with a concerned look on his face; my own must be betraying the inner turmoil bubbling away inside.

I catch his eye, and I see him mouth a silent 'are you ok?' to which I nod, schooling my features back to my practiced look of indifference.

What am I going to tell Jackson?

Jackson

It was nearly 8 o'clock.

She is usually here by now.

This isn't like her, but then again, she had been acting unusual all afternoon. I caught a glimpse of her earlier (after her talk with Cameron) looking upset, almost like she was about to cry; then on came her fake persona, the one she uses to hide from the world; she hasn't used it on me for a while though, which has me concerned. I thought I'd try and talk to her about it tonight, but now that she isn't here, I am starting to assume the worst. I found her name on my phone, and I have already shot off a few messages without a reply.

Helen: Hay sweet girl, still coming over?
Today, 19:17

Helen: Hay are you ok?
Today, 19:29

Helen: Talk to me sweet, whatever happened I'll help. Come talk to me.
Today, 19:38

Helen: Where are you? I'll come to you.
Today, 19:49

After staring at the unread messages for a few seconds, I hit the call button.

'Sorry, this person can't get to the phone right now if you would like to leave a message after the beep.'

130

'What the fuck?' Where the hell is she?

Snatching up my hotel key card and phone, I storm out of the room in search of hers, not really giving a damn if anybody sees me or not. Whatever has her upset does not give her reason to shut me out; she must know I care for her and would do anything for her. What has her so spooked she won't even talk to me?

Stopping outside her room, I bang hard using the balls of my fist. Wound up doesn't even begin to explain what is going through my mind right now.

No answer; I pound again.

This time the door flies open, and I am taken aback by the sight that greets me…it isn't Catherine; far from it. In front of me is a very tanned, half-naked man with a towel wrapped around his waist.

"Can I help you?" He asks in a very deep Italian accent. *'What the fuck?'* Rage is now ringing through my ears; I am no longer able to concede any logical thought.

"Where's Catherine?"

"Who?"

"Catherine!" I shout, calling into the room, "Who the fuck is this?"

"Mate, there is no Catherine here."

"Catherine!" I call again. No longer paying attention to the man in front of me. "Catherine get the fuck out here, or I am coming in there."

"Mate, there is no Catherine here!"

"Then you won't mind me having a look," Without waiting for an answer, I push past him into the room, examining it as I go. On the bed is an open suitcase with clothes spilling out—both a set of men's and women's clothing is laid out next to it.

"Catherine?!" I call out again, anger bubbling over and fuelling my rage. It's then I notice the sound of the shower in the next room, taking a few short paces to get there, and before the man can stop me, I have the door open, mentally preparing myself to be confronted by the sight of her hiding herself from me.

Instead, the sight of an entirely different naked woman hits me. Before my brain is able to comprehend the sight in front of me, I feel the tug at my collar pulling me from the room, landing with a thump onto the floor outside the door.

"What the fuck do you think you are doing?" I am faced with the angry look of the room's occupant, and shock very quickly replaces my rage.

"That wasn't Catherine."

"No shit, that is my wife."

"I'm…I'm sorry, I was looking for someone; I thought this was her room."

"Well, it's not; we just got here after a long journey, hoping we could relax before you come barging in."

"I'm sorry, I'm sorry!" Scrambling to my feet, holding my hands up in surrender, "I made a mistake. I thought she was here," he just continues to stare. Taking my queue, I hurry to leave. After successfully slamming the door behind me, I lean back against the nearby wall. For a second, I thought…thought she would really do that to me, the sensations of relief are quickly replaced again with rage and anger, even topped off with a little worry and concern. Where the hell is she? Why has she run from me? In our final days, why would she purposely miss a night together? Not even answering her phone to give me an explanation.

What the fuck did Cameron say to her?

The next day was agony. She was there, acting like her usual imitation of her confident self. Taking in the laughs from everyone around her, all eyes focused on this forgery, I thought I knew her better, but last night has thrown my whole world into question.

"Adrien…" She gasps from her place in my arms. "Why?"

Why? This is such an exquisite question; it applies to so many things in our lives and, as such, very rarely has a satisfactory answer. Why do we do the things we do? Why do we feel that, that we shouldn't? Why do we have very little control over things around us? Why can't we have what we want simply because we want it? Why is Catherine behaving like this? Like she hasn't just blatantly ignored me the whole day and that her disappearing act last night wasn't a big deal and needs an explanation.

I'm filming this scene like I am on autopilot because all I can think about is tonight. What I am going to say to her, because *tonight* is our last night, no more run-throughs, no more retakes; this is it! Tonight, I have to tell her how I feel, that *this* is it for me; I want her more now than I did in the beginning; there has been no boredom, no straying eyes; I only want her, and I know she wants me too; I need…no, she needs to be strong enough to take the risk. I'll be there with her, dealing with whatever fallout she is anticipating; she just needs to say she choses *me*.

I am so lost in a world filled with her that I barely recognise Cameron's call for a cut at the end of the day. It's been a long one; first thing this morning, and it's now 6pm; apparently, he wanted to nail the scene today!

"Alright, I want us to show our appreciation for our amazing lead, Catherine," he begins, calling everyone's attention. "I think we can all agree you have exceeded our expectations after taking you on all those months ago," I see her blush under the compliment.

"But alas, our time must come to an end," Umm, what now? "So, as many of you know, today was Catherine's last day; the rest of the scenes do not require her presence, so I think you will all be joining me in saying goodbye for now, obviously not forever, but we will sorely miss having you on set. Good luck with everything," A group vocalisation of 'cheers' and 'hurrah', echoes around me, bringing my world to a screeching halt. I am still unable to comprehend the scenes going on around me. *'What does he mean on the last day? No, I had one more! GOD DAMN YOU, I HAD ONE MORE!'*

Making my excuses, I disappear off in the direction of the trailers, attempting to realign my brain to focus on what I need to do rather than wallow in the panic that is about to set in.

'I'm going to lose her.'

Catherine

Wow, what a flurry of emotions saying goodbye to everyone on set. It has truly been amazing to get back out into the world, get to know so many new people, and just enjoy myself. I saw Jackson sulk off early, just after Cameron made his announcement, I shouldn't really have expected anything less. I had hoped we could have a mutual goodbye, an exchange of glances to say more than our words could, ushering in a new stage of friendship we could continue to have outside of filming, but I understand why he didn't. Last night I hurt him; after everything he did for me, I still did it, and why? Because last night I was a fucking coward, that's why.

I head to my trailer for the last time; I had already packed up my hotel room this morning and had left my suitcase in there. As I go inside, I look around, collecting up anything I may have left behind and stuffing it into the side pockets of the suitcase. I then take a moment just to soak it all in. For 5 months, I had it all. *'Until next time, I suppose.'*

Behind me, I hear the trailer door open and close abruptly. I don't need to turn to know who has come to find me in the silence. I try and gather myself, relying heavily once again on the ability I have grown accustomed to—of hiding behind a smile.

"Hay you," I begin cheerily. "I was hoping I'd get the chance to see you before I left," I turn, coming face-to-face with what I have done. His face is sunken: eyes red, fists balled up, one at his side, and the other resting on the counter located by the door.

"I um…" he starts, his voice low and monotone, "I tried to come to you last night."

"Really?" I act surprised, a complete falsehood of course, "Sorry, the hotel asked to move me; apparently the room was double booked. It was only one night, so I thought what the hay?" he pushes out his lips with his tongue as he adds.

"I tried to call."

"My phone died, and I left my charger in the old room. I couldn't charge it till I got here first thi…"

"Stop lying to me!" He screams, pounding his fist on the counter, causing me to jump a little in alarm. This has the effect of silencing me. I know I have hurt him; I can see it and offer him no reasonable excuse. This version of Jackson I know isn't him; it's what *I* have turned him into. "Why are you avoiding me?" He adds in a calmer tone. In defeat, I sigh before answering him.

"I'm not avoiding you, Jackson."

"Stop lying!" He cries out again.

"I'm not lying!" I cry back, allowing my emotion to seep through the cracks in my voice. Composing myself, I add, "I wasn't avoiding *you,* Jackson…I was avoiding *this,*" I am trying to hold back the tears, but it feels like the whole bloody dam is about to break. The dejected, devastating cracks that are starting to appear create fractures of regret to descend across my façade, weakening the supports that are keeping me standing before him instead of falling into a crumpled heap on the floor.

"And what is this?" He knows; the look in his eyes tells me he knows, but he needs me to say it and clarify it.

"This…this is goodbye," he looks down, shaking his head, not even being able to look me in the eye.

"It doesn't have to be," he almost whispers.

"Yes, it does," I take another moment; this is too much and too heartbreaking to watch him falter before me. "Jackson, quite honestly, how often do you think we are going to be able to see each other from now on? 3,4, maybe 5 times?" He doesn't answer, continuing to look down towards the floor. "And out of those times, how many of them are we actually going to be alone?" He looks up, capturing my eyes with his in a silent plea. I see the pools of water wallowing in their depths but refusing to fall. We are both, in the moment, desperately trying to keep it together, but even I hear the tremble in my voice.

"Jackson, I didn't come to you yesterday because the last time we were together was perfect; it was just us being us, and when I thought about not being with you anymore I just…I just…wanted to keep that memory of you, just like that. It's how I wanted to remember you—us—exactly as we were: perfect, not tainted with tearful goodbyes, and full of regret for a life we cannot have," It's my turn to look away; that expression of contorted pain he has is making me want to do something I can't, and something I would hate him for making me do. "Because that's what you are to me, Jackson, perfection."

We stand there in a silent standoff for a while, neither of us being able to say anything but not really wanting to leave either, because we both know that as soon as I walk out that door, we are done, and him; the way *I* know him, will be gone from me.

Eventually I strike up the courage to move, taking hold of my suitcase to move past him, heading towards the door. As I am about to pass, he takes hold of my arm, firmly holding me in place. I look up to find his deep-pooled eyes glaring down at me, the hurt clearly evident behind them.

"Don't go!" He whispers, coming forth as a desperate plea. It takes all the strength I have not to crumble to my knees, to beg him to take me in his arms, and to never let me go. I know in my mind I can't; I can't be selfish enough to do that to the people I love, and I can't do that to *him*. I can't drag him into a life that will bring him nothing but misery.

With my last ounce of strength, I bring my hand up to rest it softly on his cheek, gracing him with a weak smile. I tiptoe slightly to plant a small kiss on the corner of his mouth, lingering just a moment too long, and with a trembling lip, I whisper, "Goodbye, Jackson."

I let him go as I head directly out the door, down the street, towards a waiting car that was due to take me to the airport, not *once* having the courage to look back.

Chapter 15

<u>Jackson</u>

Like death. That's what this feels like. Watching her walk out of my life without once having the decency to look back makes me question if she was even real at all. All the things I wanted to say to her went from my mind, leaving only two words, *'don't go.'* That's all I had left, but it wasn't enough to counteract the strong forces pulling her away. That sweet girl who entered my life and captured my heart is gone, knowing full well that she was right. I may see her from time to time, but she won't be the woman I know; it won't be us.

So that's how this feels, like the Catherine I know has died: she has been ripped from my arms and taken from me like some cruel twist of fate, and I am left to carry on as though it never really happened.

The following two days went by like a blur. I needed to work; I needed to continue the film to its bitter end; it continued like her departure meant nothing. I'd walk on set in the morning, still expecting to hear her laugh echoing through the crowds of crew members, still waiting to be graced with her smile beaming at me like I was actually worth a damn. In the evenings, I continued to stare at the clock, waiting for 7pm, anticipation rising in me until reality hits once again and I realise she isn't coming, not anymore.

When I arrive home for the weekend, my mind is hazy. I'm unable to even think straight because, unlike other weekends where this was just a stopover, a time lapse before I am with her again, this time there is nothing to look forward to.

She isn't waiting for me anymore.

Catherine

"Hay baby, how are you this fine morning?" This man has to be *the* most enthusiastic man I know! I honestly don't think I have ever heard him sound serious.

"Hay Josh, I am good. Thank you, yourself?"

"Excellently gorgeous; you got a minute to talk?"

"I have just dropped the kids off; you have me the whole day if you so wish."

"Ooo lucky me!" I giggle at him down the phone; it's good to have someone to banter with. I haven't really spoken to many people outside of my children since I finished Adrien's Hel six months ago! My mum and dad have popped in for a brew and a catch-up a few times, but like usual, they did most of the talking, so I just sat and nodded my replies.

To be honest, I haven't really *wanted* to talk to anyone. Putting on a brave face for my children is a given, but outside of them, I have not been in a very tolerating mood. Pretty sure even William has been avoiding me, even more than usual, that is!

"Come on, Joshy, lay it on me."

"You said it, sweetheart! Ok, so I have a couple of small jobs lined up for you. I know you said you wanted to take a breather, but these are 2 weeks max jobs; unfortunately, you're not really going to start reaping the benefits of the big one until its release, and then the world will know what you're *really* capable of, hunny," I know he has told me this a few times. I think he feels he needs to keep reminding me as reassurance but forgets I am well versed in the world of Hollywood. "I also managed to get you tickets to the premiere of 'Cat-astrophe'. Isn't that great?"

"'Cat-astrophe'? What the hell is that?" he starts laughing at me down on the phone!

"Ha, being a mother, I *am* surprised, babe! It's the latest computer-animated kids' film to be released. Jackson Hunter provided the voice for one of the characters. It's good promotional work for Adrien's Hel if you show up supporting his other films in the run up to the trailer releases. And of course, it gets your face out there. People will start recognising you sooner if you make a few more appearances on the red carpet."

"I see."

"Yeah, I got you 4 tickets too. Take the family, your husband, make yourself likeable, and start using your family connections, babe. It's all about the marketing!"

"Ok, thank you, Josh," Not sure I could sound any less enthusiastic if I tried!

"No problem, sweetheart; I'll send those scripts over; have a read and tell me what you think. Remember it's about getting out there; the more people see your face, the more they will recognise you, and the more you'll be in demand from those top directors."

"Thank you, Josh; I will."

"Great, speak soon, babe!"

"Speak soon."

Umm, a premier, one I know for almost certain Jackson will be at, and with my family too. I know what Josh is trying to do, but for *him,* it'll seem more like rubbing salt in the wound.

I know I have to go; I know I will have to face him in the real world sooner or later, but at his own premier?

It is not only his reaction I am worried about, but also my own. Last time I saw him, I barely had the power to leave, forcing my legs against their will to walk in the opposite direction. After I got back, I spent many lonely nights in tears staring at his name on my phone, willing myself not to click that green button. Eventually, just when I thought I would break, I ended up deleting his number completely, erasing all traces of him from my phone, and taking away any temptation I may have had in the future.

Well, I have a month to reign in my weakness: suppress my desire and focus on perfecting my skill and getting through the night with my dignity intact.

Jackson

"That fucking bitch!" I scream out into my house to no one but the empty rooms, holding up a scrunched-up piece of paper in my hand. "Who the fuck does she think she is?" I'm pacing through the hallway into my kitchen and back again, racking my hands through my hair as I tried to fathom what the hell she was even thinking. Holding up the piece of paper again, I'm still not quite believing what I'm reading, hoping maybe I misread it the first time, but nope, there it is in black and white.

Harry just emailed over the final guest list for the premiere this weekend. Printing it off, I thought I would have a glance over it before heading to the gym to see if there was anyone I knew well enough to make this event even worthwhile. That's when I spotted it—her name was around halfway down the page.

Catherine Carell + 3 guests

Who wants to guess who her 3 guests are?

"Urgh!" I cry out in frustration, once again crunching the paper up into a ball with my fist and hurling it ceremoniously at the wall.

What she is hoping to prove by flaunting her family out for all to see, and at *my* expense*; my* premier! She couldn't even give me a heads up; let me know what she was planning. What's her game?

Or maybe it isn't a game; maybe she really just doesn't care; she has truly moved on, and this is just another publicity stunt to promote herself regardless of those around her—of me, piggybacking off of my fame to promote hers.

I never knew you could be so heartless, Catherine, I thought I knew you.

"Good Afternoon, viewers! Welcome back; I am Samantha George."

"And I am Drew Dunn with Entertainment Tonight, and we are here at the premiere of Cat-Astophe, the latest animation picture event due to hit the big screen by Christmas."

"Yes, Drew, and we are joined by a variety of celebrities and their children all out to enjoy this star-packed animation film. Here, we have Catherine Carell with us. Hi Catherine, and who are these cuties?"

"Hi Samantha and Drew, this is Will, my husband, and this is Axel, and this is Callen."

"Hi boys, how are you finding the red carpet today? Are you looking forward to the film?"

"Yeah, this is awesome!"

"Hahaha, and what about you, Catherine? Now let me get this right; you are not in this one, but you are playing alongside Jackson Hunter in his next film release, 'Adrien's Hel'; due to be released mid-next year. Are you looking forward to that?"

"Of course, I am very impatient to see the final cut; I think it will be an amazing film."

"You must be so proud of your wife, William."

"Immensely."

"And how have you found it, Catherine, working alongside Jackson Hunter?"

"Haha, it's been amazing; there is never a dull moment with him around, that's for sure! Just hoping that what we were trying to achieve as a team comes across on camera as well as we expected."

"So, what brings you here today?"

"I was about to ask the same thing."

"Jackson Hunter! What a pleasure it is to have you here. I am Samantha George."

"Good evening Samantha. Catherine."

"Jackson! Jackson! Do you remember us?"

"Of course, I do, buds. Are you enjoying yourselves so far?"

"Yeah, this is so cool!"

"So, what has brought you here, Catherine? Didn't I think I'd see you again until our own premiere?"

"We're here to support you, dummy! This is the first film that doesn't actually show your face; I thought you might need some emotional support."

"Ha, this one, so funny, isn't she?! Anyway, I'll see you inside. Have fun, boys!"

"Bye!"

"Jackson Hunter there, so you guys got on well then?"

"Famously. Anyway, I think we better head on inside too."

"Thank you for talking with us today, Catherine, and bringing your gorgeous family. I look forward to seeing you again, maybe at your own premier next time."

"Maybe, thank you, Samantha; thank you, Drew."

"And there it is, newcomer Catherine Carell making herself known on the red carpet. She seems nice, doesn't she, Samantha?"

"So nice! Oh there, it's Bethany, Bethany! Entertainment Tonight, can we have a quick chat?"

Jackson

Support me, my ass. I was right; she is here to associate herself with me to elevate her own fame. How can I be so stupid? She never cared for me; she used me, and now she thinks she has me wrapped around her little bloody finger. Ha!

While touring the room, I do my best to ignore her. My eyes, however, consistently betray me, being drawn in by her beauty and the echo of her laughter. God, how I miss that. Making her giggle, her smile. *'Get a grip, Jackson!'*

I became so engrossed in an anecdote a fellow co-star was regaling that I failed to notice I was within earshot of her and her *dear* husband. That was until his familiar tone of upper-class snobbery found my ear, cutting through all other sounds. So much so, my focus was lost to my companion and I became completely engrossed by his voice cutting through the murmuring of the crowded room.

"How much longer do we have to parade around these ponces Catherine? I have much better things to do with my time."

"You are supposed to be here to support *me*…you know? As my *loving* husband, in case you have forgotten, and *I* am here to show support to Jackson. I didn't think it was a good idea either, especially bringing you and the kids, but Josh said it's better in the run-up to our film that we show cooperative support. If we leave too early, then it looks like we have snubbed him, and it'll make him, and not to mention us, look bad. Anyway, we haven't been here very long, just give me another hour or so," she *did* come here for me.

"You have no idea how tedious this is for me, Catherine; I didn't sign up for all this, you did."

"I know you didn't, and I am sorry I got you dragged into it all; that wasn't my intention."

"Yes well, now you owe me; you should feel *lucky* I even agreed to this." Lucky. LUCKY! That son of a bitch!

Taking a peek from the corner of my eye, I see her, a glass of wine in her hand and a smile on her face as she looks out into the crowd, but her face isn't hers; it's the classic one I have seen her hide behind so many times—too many times!

Oh god, how could I be angry with her? She is still living the hell of her life, which she has no control over, forced into situations like this for the sake of appearances and reputations.

I find myself with the ever-familiar notion of being drawn back to her. This need to be close; to feel her skin on mine is fast becoming overwhelming. I am no longer able to keep my attention on the people around me; I only have eyes for her. I need to talk to her, make sure she is all right—shit I don't even know what else…just to be close to her.

"Excuse me, get me another while I pop to the loo," I overhear her handing him her glass as she walked off into the crowd. Grasping at the opportunity, I excuse myself, discretely making my way through behind her. Exiting the main room, I can see her vier off towards the restrooms.

While she is inside, I search around for somewhere quiet. Spotting a dark corridor off to the left, which led off into another corridor that looks like it is for staff only. With the lights off, I hide there in the darkness, waiting for her to start her return to the main party.

A few people walk past before I see the quickest glimpse of her.

"Catherine!" I whisper, loudly, hoping it was loud enough for her to hear. Holding my breath, I pause to wait. *'Shit maybe she didn't hear. Did I lose the moment?'*

No. Her face appears in the entranceway of the hall, peering in curiously. Quickly, I snatch her hand in mine, pulling her in and swiftly dragging her back so we can disappear down the second hallway out of sight of prying eyes.

Once I have her there, however, I am suddenly struck dumb by her presence, forgetting all notions that brought us to this point; I find myself unable to speak. Even as I have her pinned up against the wall, I *have* no words to offer her, just this incessant need to be close to her. With our faces a mere inch apart and our lips almost connecting, I tentatively raise my hand, tracing my fingers lightly across the side of her face. I am hoping she isn't just a figment of my imagination, as I half expect her to turn out to be a ghost of my memories. My hand slides back into her hair as I continue to stare, trying to focus my eyes in the dark, on hers; my body is unable to do anymore, almost in disbelief that I even have her here at all.

Upon seeing my hesitance, she must have decided to take the initiative by acting first, closing the gap and capturing my lips, her hands in fists tight around the open folds of my jacket, pulling me closer. I give in immediately, snapping myself out of my stupor and succumbing to the sensations of lust and want coursing from my lips, spreading to every limb and every nerve. I feel my cock come alive, straining against the constraints of my suit trousers. Hitching her leg up over my hip, I realise she needs this as much as I do, thrusting her hips forward into my pelvis. In an instinctual response, I press mine into hers, pinning her against the wall with it, holding her leg up with my spare hand as I do. I used the bulge in my pants to grind up against her groin, releasing from us both a collective groan from deep in our throats as our bodies once again relished in their intimacy, not wanting to relinquish the connection of our mouths.

Once out of breath, our bond breaks, but our bodies remain, pressed up against each other, holding on so as to never let go. Our faces remain so close that I feel her breath against my lips gliding across their surface; our noses nudge lightly in the tender closeness that is running between us. My hand finds her cheek with the intention of gently stroking it with my thumb…but what is this I feel? *'Is her cheek wet?'*

The sudden realisation hits as I stare wide-eyed at her, still trying to gain focus as I look at her in the dark. *'Is she crying?'* Her hands roam up and down my chest as she tries desperately to recompose herself, but all I can do is stare at this beautiful woman in front of me, to have the strength to hold it together for the world, but not for me; with me she can't, and she knows she never has to.

"I've missed you, sweet girl," No longer able to hold back, she cracks, sinking her face into my chest to try and hide them. It's my turn to break, I'm not strong enough for this.

"Come with me, Catherine, please!" I beg, my voice trembling. "We won't have to pretend anymore; just say you'll come with me," Shaking her head, she pushes me back. Without saying a single word, she sniffs her nose and walks off, wiping her eyes carefully as she heads back in the direction of the toilet.

I have to do something; I *can't* leave without her—not again. Taking a moment to recompose myself, I head back outside into the crowd. I am going to find that jackass and end this; no one will get between us again; no one.

Unfortunately, I didn't anticipate the coming of the crowd to unknowingly intercept me. Past colleagues stopping me, engaging me in idiotic, idol conversation, one after the other, all asking me variations of the same damn questions.

"So, how have you been?"

"What have you been up to, other than pretending to be a cat?"

"What is the next big project?"

I don't care, I don't care, I don't care. I just need to get to him.

By the time I am through the sea of pleasantries, I can see she has already made it out of the bathroom, taking her place by *his* side, his arm wrapped possessively around her waist. *'Not for long, it won't.'*

Pushing my way through, I am nearly with them when I hear off in the distance a…

"Dad, Dad, look who I found?"

"I found them first, Axel! *I* found them, Dad."

Looking round, I see the kids first, dragging behind them an older gentleman and a lady, ones I would recognise without even having to give it a second thought.

"Nanny and Grandad!" The boys cry together, proudly showing them off to their parents like some prize they had won at the fair.

"Mum, Dad, what are you doing here?" Catherine exclaims, embracing them both in a hug, clearly as surprised as everyone else.

"Well, when we heard you were coming, we thought we would tag along, been a while since we graced a red carpet ourselves you know," her mum explains, "Besides, I used to coach Elizabeth Fallan, who was in the movie too," Of course, she did, Caroline LeMond, one of the great voice coaches of her time, married to Christian LeMond, how did I not make that connection before?

"You didn't have to."

"Of course, we did," her father interrupts, "Whatever you need, sweetheart we are here. So, Will," siding up next to her husband, patting him on the back, "how did the takeover go? Were they as disruptive as you anticipated? Your father was over this week and told me you were having a tough time with it."

I watched for a little, taking in the interactions between the families, the relationships between father and child; the grandparents. A sinking realisation hits me like a rock was tied to my feet, and I was plunged into the depths of the river.

It wasn't about her. It never was. She told me that, but I didn't listen. I didn't understand. It was about this family unit, so intertwined their parents have tea in the week for no other reason than to spend it in each other's company. Her father knows details about her husband's work, respects it, and believes in it. Her children love and adore her parents, their fathers, and their fathers' parents, as a complete unit. To break that up would be to break up everything. She doesn't have a choice because she *had* to choose to sacrifice for the people she loves or else risk messing up the lives of everybody else around her.

I thought I was competing for her affections from him, the jackass, to which there is no competition. The truth is, however, is that in reality, I was competing against this, and well, I never really had a chance now, did I?

I watch as her family is busying around her, placing her high up on a pedestal, so high no one else has even a chance to reach her: a glass of wine in hand and a vacant look behind her eyes—no longer wanting to engage in the world passing by around her. She captures my gaze for a brief moment, a silent apology for not being able to do more and for not having the reach to choose me over them. The gaze I offer back, I hope—offers her my condolences and that I do, finally, understand.

Dejected and defeated, I feign a headache and go home, no longer in the mood to entertain. I just want to be by myself to wallow in the truth—the truth I had known all along but refused to believe until now.

Catherine and I *were* meant to be together; what we have *is* real, but the fates are cruel and unyielding, and so we are left to accept the hand we are dealt. Goodbye, sweet girl; I wish you well.

Hello viewers, and welcome to Entertainment News, I am your host, Jane Collins. Tonight, on the gossip rags, Catherine Carell is new to the Hollywood scene...or is she?

Reports indicate that the new actress Catherine Carell is none other than Catherine Carter, AKA Catherine LeMond, the daughter of infamous actor and director Christian LeMond and voice coach to the stars Caroline LeMond.

For those of the 'younger persuasion' who may not have heard of Catherine LeMond, she was a child actress of the 1990s and famous socialite of the early to mid-2000s; there was not a party to be seen at unless she had been invited, and she was fast becoming an actress within her own right, away from her family connections. However, shortly following her famous wedding in 2005 to William Carter, son of the notorious Patrick Cater, Catherine fell off the map, choosing to shun the limelight instead and concentrating on her family. Many rumours speculated at the time as to the reason why; some feared problems following the birth of her first son, caused her to become a recluse!

However, that all appears to be under the bridge. Catherine made an extravagant comeback into the light in a low-back golden one piece on Saturday, bringing with her gorgeous family all sporting tuxes, all in aid of supporting her current co-star Jackson Hunter in his latest project, 'Cat-astrophe'.

She is fast becoming a must-have actress again, already landing voiceover roles in the latest Graham film, and there is talk of her starring in the next Starman movie!

Keep your eyes posted on this one, folks; she is the one to watch!

Chapter 16

<u>Jackson</u>

I haven't gone anywhere for the last few weeks. My ability to care has dissipated. Total distance travelled: bed, gym, living room, bed, maybe a couple of trips to the kitchen in the middle. It doesn't feel right anymore—my home. It's weird. I once loved my house with its white, pristine walls and minimal décor, sporadically dotted with occasionally odd-looking art pieces, but now it feels hollow and empty. This place hasn't felt right from the moment Catherine and I first connected. I just want to be where she is, and nowhere feels right without her in it; for me, she *is* home. Nothing has made me feel as complete as I did when she was in my arms, and I am really struggling now to see a future where anywhere will ever feel like it again.

I know I have a job starting up soon that should keep me occupied, keep my brain from spiralling, and keep questions of 'what ifs' and 'maybes' buzzing around like bees annoyingly reminding me of what cannot have.

I barely even reacted to the sound of my front door opening then closing. I already know who it is; very few people have access to my house.

"Hay Hars!" I call out from my place on the couch when I hear his clicking heels rape against my hard wood flooring. "In here."

"Hay Jack, just came to check in with my favourite A-lister! Everything ok?"

"Yeah, I'm good. Got any news for me?"

"No more than when I spoke to you the other day. I just came to check on you, that's all."

"You're not my babysitter, Hars; I am quite capable of looking after myself," I say it with a small smile.

"Oh really, I would never have guessed!" I chuckle slightly in feigned amusement as he flops down on the couch next to me. "But really, how is everything?" He adds, concern written across his face.

"I'm fine, Hars, why do you keep asking?"

"Because for the past 3 weeks you have said yes to every script I have sent you, if I didn't vet them, you would be double booking yourself for two years! Are you even reading through the scripts before you agree to them?"

"Of course, I am—who do you think I am? An amateur?" I lie.

"Really?"

"Really!" His expression tells me he clearly isn't amused or satisfied with my answers.

"Umm that's interesting," he begins, speculating like he is a bloody detective or something, "because the last script I sent through, *I* wrote personally; quite a read if I do say so myself; it was just two words on a document…'Fuck you!' was all it said, in comic sans font! Quite an emotive script, I thought! I am glad you liked it so much that you agreed to it!" Ok, he caught me. I offered him a large smile for his efforts.

"The words spoke to me," Jesting to his efforts.

"Umm, I bet they did. Now, are you prepared to tell as to why you're not taking your role seriously at the moment? Seriously, Jack, I am worried about you. Is this about that girl we spoke about?" I don't answer him for a while, subtly biting the inside of my cheek, unsure if I should be divulging any information at all for fear of revealing the truth. My silence must have been all-telling, as he doesn't move, continuing his inquiry.

"It is, isn't it? What's happened? Did you find out the 'why' in the end?" I nod my head slightly and turned away, looking blankly into the hollow room, hoping he ends it there before I blurt out more than intended. "Mate, I am waiting on bated breath here."

"I can't, Hars. I promised."

"You ever heard of a 'problem shared is a problem halved?' This thing, whatever it is, is eating away at you, and it isn't healthy, mate. Listen, I am your agent, but I am also your friend. Whatever you say here won't leave this room, *I* promise."

I look at him for what seems like a long time, contemplating my next move. I do need to get this out, even if it is to get some prospective on the whole damn thing, because right now, my head just isn't right.

"What happened?" He probes again; he can clearly see my resolution is breaking. I exhale a deep breath through pursed lips, leaning forward in my seat with my arms resting on my knees.

"She's married, Hars," looking down towards the floor as I expel the confession.

"Shit! And she didn't tell you? That's kinda a bitch move, man. Stay away from that one."

"No, it isn't like that," sitting back again, I am no longer comfortable in my position as I rest my hands on top of my head. "Her husband…her husband…shit he is the biggest dick in the history of dicks!" I dropped my hands to my lap as words seemed to spill from my mouth. The wormhole has been opened, and I am no longer able to stop them. "He cheated on her man, cheated! And not just once; it's constant, like even now. I mean, who the fuck does that? And despite this, he still treats her like shit, like she's his property or something. He tries to control everything she does; he's a manipulative, emotionless fuckwit, and it just makes me sick!"

"Why doesn't she leave him?"

"She can't."

"Why not?" Again, I pause. How do I explain to him her situation without actually indulging in who it is? I must have paused for too long, as it has given him time to think and come to his own hypothesis. "Shit, it *is* Catherine, Catherine Carell, isn't it?" My face must have painted a sorry picture because it is his turn to exhale a long breath, leaning back against the sofa in shock realisation. "Man, you need to leave her alone! The girl is wrapped up in so much social bullshit that her family might as well be the Hollywood mafia. She is untouchable!"

"You think I don't know? Shit Hars, I can't stop thinking about her. I just…I couldn't stay away."

"You continued to sleep with her, even after finding out who she is?" I nod sheepishly. "Shit Jack, what were you thinking?"

"I told you I wasn't, not really. I tried, I really tried, I thought…I thought I could get her away, that we could…but it ended, and now all I can think about is her—about where she is, what life she is living with that fucking dickhead!"

"You really did fall for her?"

"We fell for each other, man. I *know* we did; I felt it! And now I have to live with the fact that despite all that, despite everything we were, we still didn't make it, and it is completely out of both of our control."

We sat in silence for a long time after that. Harry was wrong; it really doesn't feel any better saying it out loud; it just exacerbates this feeling—the feeling of not being in control of my own life and not getting what I want. This is so much worse.

"It makes sense now," he finally states, staring off blankly.

"What does?"

"Why she disappeared from the public scene all those years ago? If William Carter is *that* sort of man, it makes sense he wouldn't want her in the limelight."

"Right? That's what I tried to tell her; this is all his doing!"

"And what did she say?" I shoot to stand up, no longer comfortable sitting, pacing the room like some pent-up animal locked in a zoo. Harry stays on the couch, watching my movements as I tour the room.

"She just laughed it off, like it was nothing. He has her so far under his fucking thumb, she can't even see it, or even if she does, she can't do anything a fuck about it because of everyone else around her. He has her exactly where he wants her, right there playing little wifey while he goes and fucks around, and there is literally *nothing* I can do," I stop pacing, dropping my hands to the side of me in dejection. "She is the most amazing person I have ever met, and when I'm with her, it just feels right, you know? And he…he treats her like garbage, it is so fucking frustrating!"

"I'm sorry man, I have nothing to offer you. For everything I know about that family, I know *that* girl is out of reach, not only to you but to *everyone*! I think you just have to try and find a way to move on; you know, get over her and find someone else."

"I know. I'm trying. I thought, maybe if I keep working, it'll stop me from dwelling on it too much. Keep me focused on my career," I look at him to talk to him directly, "I promise, I'll take it more seriously from now on."

"No worries, tell you what. I'll vet the scripts for the time being; I'll only send on the ones I think might be worthwhile. Make sure we are scheduling breaks in between shootings so you're not burning out. It'll take time, but you will get over her, I promise."

"Thanks, Hars."

"No problem, Jack."

With that, he gets up off the sofa, taking my hand in his. "You'll be fine, Jack; you'll find someone else; you always do," Giving his hand a firm shake, I offer him a pathetic smile in gratitude.

"I know. Thanks Hars," and with that, he leaves, leaving me once again in the white hollowness of my home.

Chapter 17

Jackson

I stare down at the piece of paper in my hand, unsure of how I should be feeling about the words I find printed there. The guest list for the premiere of 'Adrien's Hel'. It's been over twelve months since we finished filming and five months since I last saw her. It's better now and easier. I haven't yet found the enthusiasm to date again; somehow it still feels wrong, but I don't think about her as much; even when I do, it's more a thought of how she is and what she is up to than dwelling on the times that could have been.

This piece of paper, however, caught me a little off guard; it doesn't say anything I didn't expect, but it stilled me all the same.

Catherine Carell + 1 Guest

So, she *is* bringing him. I suppose she has to; wouldn't look very good if he didn't support her in her first major role on the big screen. It's ok. I'm ok. I already had to prepare myself for the evening—the agony of having to sit through two and a half hours of Catherine and me enacting our intimacy for all to see on the big screen. I already know it's going to be torture, but I am getting a little sick pleasure knowing he is going to have to sit through it as well, watching as I get closer to her in those five months than he has in nearly three years. Some petty side of me wants to be sitting in viewing distance so I can watch his stupid face distort in distain as I do.

Catherine

Getting ready in my hotel room, the nerves rack up inside me, feeling just like they did at that very first audition—that overwhelming sensation of butterflies and nausea dancing around my abdomen. Just from the knowledge that he is going to be there, I hug my arms around my stomach as though that action alone will still them.

Breathe, Catherine; just breathe.

What if he doesn't want to see me? What if this all goes horribly wrong and all I am doing with my presence there is dredging up old, painful memories for him? But I have to go; this is our movie, after all! I move one hand from my waist to press it to my forehead, attempting to put at bay all these self-conscious notions.

"You'll be fine, Catherine. With or without his approval," I say this to myself in the mirror while I continue to stare back at my reflection. Dressed in a low-slung pale pink dress that glides along behind me and finishes off with delicate patterns of lace throughout, the hair stylist has already been, completing the look with my hair designed in a stylish up-do and a flower, fashioned entirely out of my own hair. *'Very red carpet!'*

"All eyes on you tonight, girl. You can do this," I laugh at myself in the mirror; now I imagine those same words again, but in Jackson's low, comforting voice, *'sweet girl, you can do this.'* Stemming the tears about to ruin my otherwise perfect makeup, I grab my bag and head towards the door where he will be waiting.

You got this.

Jackson

We are all assembled in the foyer. After previously passing the chaotic sea of fans and paparazzi on the red carpet, we now stand lingering with the rest of the cast and crew, waiting patiently to go in to see our final production. I'm not sure if anyone else has noticed, but I keep poking my head up like a bloody meerkat, just trying to get a glimpse of her; so far, however, she has remained aloof.

"Hay has anyone seen Catherine? I can't imagine she would miss this," exclaims Rebecca, also appearing to look out into the crowd.

"I haven't seen her come in," chimes in Cameron, "Well, we can't wait any longer. Let's head in. We'll save a couple of spaces in case she comes in late," such an unsatisfactory answer. I have no choice, however, but to comply, following the crowd into the screening rooms. Just as we were about to disappear, I heard Rodney next to me cry out.

"Who do you think you are, Cinderella or something? Running a bit late, are we?" He steps out from next to me towards the stunning vision of beauty entering our view, holding up the train of her dress.

"Sorry, I'm late. This damn dress keeps getting caught up," Rodney takes the dress from her hand, helping her to readjust it so it once again flows behind her.

"Well, if it helps you look stunning, Catherine, quite the contrast to your usual get-up, you know, wink wink," she laughs along, patting her hair as she recomposes her demeanour. "Doesn't she look gorgeous, Jackson?"

"A vision, as always," I reply, choosing to take the moment to soak in her glory. Those old notions I thought I had long buried are now bubbling, threatening to resurface. Of course, they are; they were never really buried deep enough in the first place, more like patted down into a shallow grave.

My gaze catches her eye as she blushes under the compliment; those unspoken connections are still like a raging current between us.

As we pass the threshold of the theatre, we find our seats, with Rodney conveniently placing himself between us. The not-too-subtle gesture is not lost on me, and I smile inwardly at his feeble attempts to get closer to her, knowing his efforts are all but in vain.

Suddenly, pulling me out of my amusement, I had the realisation. Quickly glancing around the room to clarify, I then lean past Rodney to catch her attention, blurting out my first thought before I consider who else might be overhearing.

"Where's your husband?" A sly smirk appears across her face as she takes a swift glimpse at me, then backs forward towards the screen.

"Not here," is her only answer before the events of the evening begin to unfold.

We exchanged the odd meaningful look in the theatre, but I wasn't able to talk to her with the great chasm named Rodney, in between us. What did she mean, 'not here'? He was on the guest list. I thought they were coming together! And what was the meaning behind that smirk?

I lose her to the mass of people exiting the theatre as we make our way back into the main foyer, where the afterparty is due to take place. So much excitement and chatter from everyone around me, with an assortment of congratulatory pats on the backs and personal regales of favourite scenes, I'm forced through social etiquette to respond to. I remain patient and engaging, even if my insides are screaming at me to find her as quickly as I can.

Finally, I spot her at the bar. A glass of brown liquid resting happily over ice sits in her hand. She must have spotted me first because her gaze is fixed directly on me, with soft eyes and a gleeful smile that holds a hint of mischief on her face. I can't help but return it as relief washes over me—relief from what I am unsure of, but it's that sensation that tells me everything is ok again, for now at least.

Heading over, I order myself a whiskey and I prop myself against the bar next to her. I attempt to remain indifferent and force a restraint on myself so as to be careful not to indulge my cravings and just take her in my arms where she stands.

"So, um no hubby tonight?" I try to play it off as cool; this is a normal conversation, right? She continues to stare out into the crowded room.

"No, not tonight; he is watching the children."

"You couldn't get a babysitter?"

"Oh, no. We definitely could," she stops mid-sentence to look at me, making sure I know the exact meaning behind her words. "But I did remind him how much he hated the last premier we went to and how *that* one wasn't even mine. I also reminded him that this time I would likely be part of the main focus, and I knew how much he would hate that and how he would be so bored. I told him I didn't mind and gave him the option to opt out. He gladly took it."

"That was nice of you."

"It was, wasn't it?" That beautiful, suggestive smile emerged and spread widely across her face.

"So, um, where did you end up staying in the end?"

"I asked my agent to find out where my co-stars were staying and to book in there. Figured if I was coming alone and found myself having a little too much to drink, it was best if I stayed where friends would be. I am at the Crescent Moon Hotel," That same smile finds my own face now, spreading wider than I thought it was possible…It is the same hotel I am at. "And you know," she continues, "They are so helpful there. As I was leaving, I noticed I couldn't find my key card. I looked everywhere! In the end, I phoned down to reception, and they very nicely told me it was fine; they would print me a new one, which I could pick up when I returned later," I can hear the clear, exaggerated tone in her voice, implying an ulterior motive for her story.

"But when I got here, I looked in my purse, and low and behold, here it is." She pulled a small card from her purse, holding it up between her fingers for me to see. "Bit ditsy, huh?" It is becoming blatantly obvious what she is implying and exactly what her real motivation truly is.

"I see," playing along. "Well, as I am clearly the more responsible one out of us, maybe I should hold onto that key card for a while, just in case you lose it again," she passes it over with a slight flick of her wrist, and I gladly take it.

"I think that is a brilliant idea. Room 227, in case you need to get me home again after too many of these," Tapping the side of her glass with her nail.

"I'll remember that," and with that, she scoots off out into the crowd, continuing to charm her way through the mass of people, her smile beaming throughout, and—I notice—with an additional little swing of her hips.

She did it. She found a way. Not one person will be able to erase this smile as I, too, manoeuvre around the crowds. As the evening progresses and the anticipation continues to build, I eagerly wait for her to once again be in my arms, even if it is just for one night.

Catherine

Too bold. Was I too bold? While waiting in my hotel room, no longer wearing the ball gown from earlier but a long kimono, I started to second-guess our interaction this evening. It was only brief, a few half-spoken words at the bar, but had I been too presumptuous? I assumed he wanted to see me and wanted my key card. But what if he didn't? What if he already has a girlfriend and has moved on from me entirely?

Pacing my room with a glass of Amaretto in hand, I go over it all over and over again in my head.

I want to see him, God, how I do; to once again be wrapped up, encased in his masculine aura, to feel his hands on me, his kisses. How I have fantasised about them, him; us, and what we were.

I shiver at the memories. It's been *so* long—an eternity, it seems—as cliché as that sounds, and I miss him. How could I not? How sweet he was, how he made me feel like the most important person in the world. *'My sweet girl.'* If only I could hear him say that just one more time.

156

So lost in my spiral of thoughts, I barely registered the familiar click of the door lock. Turning to face my visitor, I am greeted, by the strikingly handsome vision of my Jackson, pouting slightly with a look in his eyes I can't quite pinpoint: it isn't sad, nor anger; it's almost a relief, maybe uncertainty? As he enters, he doesn't come to me at first; he doesn't even come into the room; instead, he leans back against the closed door, staring intently at me. He is still wearing his tux from earlier, but the bow tie is now dishevelled, just hanging from around his neck.

This silent stare is beginning to unnerve me. Unsure of what to do or what he wants, I start playing with my glass, rubbing my finger along its rim, engrossed in its smooth lines, and tracing them in its infinite circle.

Unable to hold his gaze any longer, I look away, feeling pangs of self-consciousness gnawing away at me under his glare. It was only after I turned away did he then begin to move slowly towards me, removing his jacket along the way to toss it onto the back of the vanity unit's chair. As he reaches my position next to the bed, he moves to take the glass from my hands, placing it beside us on the bedside table before directing his full attention back to me.

Somehow, however, the sudden weight of the moment rests too heavily upon me and the air is too thick. I am unable to look at him, barely able to even breathe; instead, I allow my head to collapse, resting my forehead against his chest, fully aware of this pressured feeling baring down on me. I feel his hands find my hair, gently stroking through it, threading his fingers into the strands, and then I feel his lips make contact with the top of my head, reassuring me that it's ok. We're ok.

I instantly relax in his arms, the weight of the last year leaving me, allowing me to finally feel safe again and find my home in his arms. I know I don't need to say the words, but I do none the less, bunching my fists up in his shirt, holding on tightly, and whisper.

"I miss you!" So quiet, I am not even sure he heard me. That is until I hear him whisper back into my hair.

"I know, sweet girl," It's then that I find the courage to look up, catching his eyes searching for mine, deep pools of want, call to me across the space between us. Taking the first initiative, I am no longer able to restrain myself, capturing his lips in mine and instantly opening up to the feel of his tongue seeking its mate…it's home. His huge hand rests on my cheek, holding my face to his, completely engrossed in the moment we have been denied for so long.

It wasn't long before my hands remembered how much they wanted him, quickly making light work of his buttons, pushing his shirt off his broad shoulders to let it slide towards the floor, revealing a new addition, ink, to the right of his chest. A beautifully delicate design of a flame, etched into darkness and illuminating a darkened space, the illusion of it makes it appear that the flames are far away and out of reach. The tips of my fingers start tracing the design before moving to more familiar territory; the bumps and ridges of his abs, retracing every muscle like they have so many times before, remembering their tracks, their lines, and how good they feel under my feather-like touch. Relishing in the feel of my caress on his torso, his gaze doesn't leave my face, rubbing his nose against mine, placing light kisses across my cheek and my jawline, relearning what it feels like to be in each other's embrace.

Feeling my renewed sense of boldness, I take a step back from him, closer towards the bed, unwrapping the tie from around my waist that held the kimono in place. I see his eyes follow my hands to survey my body in time for my reveal. Opening up the kimono, I showcase the chosen lingerie I picked out just for him tonight.

It is a pink-laced corset top with matching thong panties, leaving not much else covered. I brought it when I knew I was coming tonight alone, and the thought of being with Jackson again peeked at my confidence and made me bold. It took all my nerves to dress myself in it however, and seeing Jackson's eyes now glaze over with desire at the sight of me (and maybe with a little touch of alcohol for Dutch courage), suddenly that same confidence that propelled me to buy it in the first place returned. Dropping the kimono to the floor, I leave my arms open to showcase my body to him in its entirety, offering myself to him.

I hear him exhale a shaky breath as he narrows the distance between us. One hand grips the side of my face while his lips find my neck. Going to work kissing at the nap under my ear, I move my head to the side to give him better and access, knowing full well how it turns me on.

"On your knees, sweet girl," he mummers against my ear. "On the bed, I want you on your knees facing the mirror," I do as I am told, climbing onto the bed, sitting up on my knees, and facing the mirror on the vanity unit opposite. From the reflection in the mirror, I can see Jackson continuing to undress, never taking his eyes off me, ravishing me with his gaze.

Once completely naked, he climbs on the bed behind me, pressing himself up against my back. I close my eyes as I feel his hands snake around to my front, and I feel his erection pressed up against the top of my arse.

One hand quickly finds my breast, needing it through the corset while the other plays with the elastic of my underwear, his head resting in the crook of my neck—a sigh of anticipation escapes me as I lean back into him, closing my eyes while I relish in the soft caress of his touch.

"Look in the mirror, Catherine," his deep command flows through me, giving me no other option than to obey. Opening my eyes, I catch him glaring back at me through the mirror, and I gasp at our reflection—the sight of us, dressed in only a corset and panties, wrapped up by his enormous form. I thought I would feel self-conscious and shy and would want to cover myself back up immediately, but I don't. I feel sexy and empowered because *I* am the cause of that intense look of desire in this gorgeous man's eyes. I created this scenario, and I am in control of it. That notion alone has me turned on beyond any realm I have felt before.

Taking Jackson's hand from around my waist, I guide it lower, tucking it into the inside of my thong. I hear him chuckle with a low rumble behind me.

"What do you want, sweet girl?"

"Touch me, Jackson," I watch as his hand fully disappears, feeling his fingers pass by the folds of my sex, using my own wetness to slick his fingers before they slide back up again, finding my sensitive clit to play with. In the mirror, I can see my mouth open, and my eyes glaze over as my body succumbs to his touch, sensations of arousal only exacerbated more by the effect it has on me watching the whole scene play out in the mirror.

Jackson's free hand skates to the front of the corset, finding the flimsy ribbons holding them in place and untying them one length at a time until the whole thing flies open, freeing my restrained breasts. Finally able to breathe properly, and now with Jackson's expert hands double-timing my breasts and my sex, I start gasping, crying out loudly into the room as I feel that familiar rise build up, feeling his fingers shift between plummeting inside my body and encircling that sensitive bud.

Shaking violently against the strong hold of Jackson's embrace, I climax, crying out his name as I do, continuing to ride his fingers as he coaxes me through my orgasm.

"Are you ready for me, sweet?" I vaguely hear him breathe into my ear, his own arousal thick in the tone of his voice. Opening my eyes again to see him in the mirror, I utter a "yes."

With this cue, he removes his hand from inside my pants, just briefly enough so he can remove them all together. Then, while still on my knees, he pushes me forward, resting my upper body on my forearms. He uses his cock to tease at my entrance, dragging it across the crease of my arse then down, letting it fall between my legs, using his hand instead to caress my arse cheek softly, encircling it in his palm. Looking up into the mirror, I watch as he takes me in, staring at my body adoringly, his teeth pressed down against his bottom lip. Looking up, he catches me watching, a smile now forming on his face.

"You know how sexy you are, Catherine? I have dreamed of seeing you like this again. How lucky I feel to know that I am the only one who gets to see you like this," I return his smile, adding a little sultry twinge to it while wiggling my butt for added emphasis.

"It's you that make me act like this. It's not for anybody else."

"Then I really am the luckiest man in the world," I see him lean over to the side, trying to reach for an item of clothing on the floor. I know what he is after.

"Leave it. I have it covered. I want to feel you tonight," he looks at me; I can see him ponder the connotations of that for a moment before he sits back up, leaning over me to kiss my back.

"You are sure, sweet?"

"I'm sure, I want you, Jackson," No more prompting is needed. He sits back up onto his knees, lining himself up with my sex, before I feel his cock gently nudge at my opening. Flinging my head back in anticipation, I welcome the rest of him edging his way in, filling me up in a way only he can.

He pauses; in the mirror, I can see his eyes closed as he relishes the pleasure that must be coursing through him. Seeing him *so* on the brink just from being inside me is creating a mixture of pleasurable notions coursing their way through me, heading straight to the source of my arousal. I must have been clenching because, as I relaxed, it causes Jackson to react, moving slowly in and out of my body, triggering the sensitive nerves inside.

It doesn't take long before his movements become more erratic, using his hands on either side of my hips, to move me back and forth with the thrust of his hips allowing for deeper, more impactful penetration with every thrust. Gasping again, I am now on the brink of yet another orgasm, each thrust hitting deep within me and creating a satisfying mix of both pleasure and pain.

"Shit…Catherine…I can't…I'm going to…" his thrusting stops as he pulls out, and his deep guttural roar echoes around the room, spilling his seed out onto the bed sheets. Using his hand to mimic the final thrusts as he empties out.

The room falls silent, other than the sound of our heavy breathing. Both of us, unable to compute anything else until we have our bodies back fully under control.

I recovered first, edging my way out of bed.

"Fuck me!" He exclaimed from beside me.

"Ha, I thought we already did that! Or was that just foreplay?" With a quick smirk aimed in his direction, I offer, "Drink?" I took up my glass from the side of the bed, swigging down a large gulp before moving to refill it.

"Please," he replies shooting me a smile back, grabbing at the top sheet to throw it off the bed, then adjusting himself so he is leaning against the headboard, the flimsy under sheet covering up his modesty.

"Got you the good stuff," I say, while pouring him whiskey and me out another Amaretto. In the brief moment, it took me to organise the ice I had been keeping cool in an ice bucket, Jackson said something that completely caught me off guard.

"I love you," holding the ice between the tongs hanging over the glass, I am left stunned in mid-motion.

"You don't mean that," I countered with a slight, nervous chuckle while I continued with the drinks.

"Yes, I do," he pauses as he searches to find his words. "I have had a long time to contemplate this, and I know the way I feel about you," Finishing up my task, I grab both glasses and head back over, handing one off to him before straddling his lap and focusing his gaze back onto me. Instinctively, his free hand comes to rest on my thigh, and he exhales a deep, guttural sigh.

"You don't. You think you do because right now it's exciting—all this hiding, sneaking around, and sex. Once you see my reality, my boring old life of school runs and society parties, you'll soon see that's all this is," he starts shaking his head slightly, taking a sip of his drink, while I absentmindedly begin tracing the edges of the tattoo on his chest.

"Nope, I don't think I will. I think you're it for me, Catherine. I really believe I was supposed to spend my life with you…" I start to interrupt, but he stops me.

"No, let me talk, please! You *are* it for me, Catherine. I *want* the 'boring' with you…but I *know* now that I am too late. I should have come to find you years ago, but I was too self-absorbed and stupid to open my eyes."

"How could you? We were on different paths," he stops looking at me, choosing to play with the glass placed between us.

"Not really; I was there. In the early part of my career, I was invited to one of your dad's parties. Still a little bit of an unknown then, but I was there; it would have been about 10–11 years ago. We were probably in the same damn room, Catherine, but I wasn't ready for you then! I should have been looking, but I wasn't, and I missed you," the confession tears at my heart, leaving a gaping chasm ripping at its strings.

"Hay, I wouldn't change our lives, Jackson; we are who we are. I have my boys who I wouldn't change for the world, and you had your life. It's who we are," he reaches up to cup the side of my face in his hand; instinctively, I lean into it. He takes a quick glance down to where my hand is over his chest before his eyes find my face again.

"You want to know what it means?"

"Umm?"

"The tattoo. You told me once that I should choose something that is uniquely me, something that means something," I nod my head in reply. "When you regaled your analogy of the burning light, a faraway beacon of hope that was off in the distance. I realised that you, for me, could be represented the same way, the light of my hope, the warmth of a home, but you are so far away from me that you're out of reach, but I know you're there, forever a beacon over my heart." A stray tear escapes my eye, staring at the image—the representation of us forever etched into his skin.

"I *do* love you, Catherine. I *need* you to know that. Not because I expect you to say it back or even feel it back, because I *know* you can't. Just…I need you to know that no matter what is going on in your world, no matter how low you may get or fucked up it is, you need to know there is someone out here who cares for you, who believes you're worth it, and that you deserve the world. Catherine, you need to know someone out here loves you, no matter how far away they may seem." Before I allow any more tears to fall from my eyes, I capture his lips in mine, indulging in this moment with him. In another life, I could have had it all, but in this one, I will just have to settle for tonight.

We didn't sleep at all that night. Chatting and giggling away between bouts of our close intimacy and overwhelmingly mind-blowing sex. I think both of us are acutely aware that this may be our last time, if not for a while, then maybe forever. We don't know when the next opportunity will arise, so we are making the most of it, and although by morning I am sore and exhausted, I am also content. The night was perfect, and by 5 am it was time for Jackson to leave before the array of risers start making their way out for their continental hotel breakfast.

Standing at the threshold of the doorway, we embrace a hold that is full of all the hidden words we are unable to say. There is just silence as he lets me go, cupping my cheek and smiling sweetly before walking out the door, letting it close softly behind him.

'Goodbye…my love.'

Chapter 18

The party was in full swing. Once again, the LeMond annual charity fundraiser is a roaring success, and Christian LeMond's list of celebrity friends is endless. Always the life of the party, he circulates the garden, greeting each of his guests like every single one is his closest companion.

On his rounds, he spots his daughter off to the side, nursing what must have been the same glass of wine he gave her when she got there. Taking the time to stop and spy on her for a minute, he can't help the wash of worry flowing over him. He cannot stop it; she is his only child and has always been the light of his life, but recently she has been distant and reserved, not the confident young girl he raised to take on the world.

He figured these last few years must have been draining on her; he knows her, and knows she likes to keep herself busy. With her boys growing up, she must be finding herself a bit lost. He thought that with her getting back into acting, it would boost her spirits and get her back to her old self, and he thought it was working. Those first few months, he began to see that spark back in her life. Now, however, it's all but dissipated, maybe even worse now than it ever was. He's afraid that if she continues down this path, there may be no way back for his colourful, bright daughter, and she will be lost to him for good.

He spots her husband off in the distance talking to his father, no doubt sharing the virtues of his business. He never did get the appeal—stuffy office spaces, pristine suits, electronic gizmos, each to their own, he supposed.

"Hay Will, Pat, how's it going?" He pats his son-in-law on the back as he makes his presence known.

"I'm good, thanks, Christian. Just telling Dad, the merger went through this week; I have my people moving in over the coming fortnight, and my team is projecting to see a turnover within 6 months."

"That's great news!" He exclaimed while inwardly screaming, *'Boring!'* To no one but himself. "Listen, Will, you seem to spend more time with Catherine than I have recently; do you know what's bothering her? Whenever I ask, she just blows me off."

"Fuck if I know, she has been moping around like that for the last week, ever since she got back from that damn premier!"

"I see. Well, that's it then; with the whole thing sort of wrapped up, she must be missing the action."

"Umm, I doubt it; she *is* still working; she has a couple of voiceovers she is working on."

"Yes, but it isn't the same; physically acting out scenes with co-stars and immersing yourself in a role gives you something to put your heart into. I'll call in some favours and see if I can't get the ball rolling on her next role."

"Please don't, Christian," he intercepts his well-meaning gesture. "Listen, Catherine wants to make her own way in the world; if you intervene, she wouldn't feel as accomplished. Besides, we talked it over after the last one. Big productions like that take a lot of time, and the boys still rely on her at home. It just isn't the right time to keep throwing herself into the big ones all the time. I am sure whatever is going on with her will resolve itself. She is a grown woman now Christian," he pauses for a moment to consider the concerned frown on Christian LeMond's face. Despite everything, he is still his father-in-law, and he is still a very influential man. His business probably wouldn't be where it is now without their association fuelling his connections and negotiations. "I'll go talk to her, but I am sure she is fine."

William leaves his father with his good friend and heads over to his wife. She is still so lost in her daydream and playing with the glass in her hand that she doesn't even notice his approach until his tall form casts a looming shadow over her smaller frame. Lowering himself into the seat next to her, he sits in close so no one can hear their conversation.

"What's wrong with you?" He barks abruptly, not even giving her the courtesy of looking at her but schooling his features to mimic those of a concerned spouse.

"Nothing," her response was short, abrupt, and unmoving.

"Then pull your head out of your goddamn ass! We are at *your* father's party, and you are sitting here like someone has died! You're making me look bad!"

"I am sorry my mood is affecting your social standing," she replies dryly.

"It's not just mine you need to worry about. Your father is concerned; do you want him to know about the sorry state of *your* marriage? Or alternatively, shall we do what we usually bloody do and at least act like we are happy? You're an actress, aren't you? Well, bloody well act!"

"You're right," she gets up from her secluded place, moving past him. Her vacant expression is unable to give his face any attention. "Give me 10 minutes," heading into the house away from the flurry of guests.

Once inside, she moves around the house, trying to find somewhere quiet to discreetly compose herself. Her father's study at the far end of the house catches her eye.

Upon entering, she sits down on the large leather sofa, breathing out a huge sigh of relief for the comforting silence blanketing her.

Spotting the drinks cabinet opposite, she sets aside her now-warm glass of wine to seek out her father's stash. Positioning herself cross-legged on the floor opposite, she peers inside to find several bottles of scotch from various years set out before her.

Taking out the one filled with the most liquid, a vintage of 18 years, and reaching above her to the top of the cabinet for a glass, she then proceeds to pour herself one. Flicking her head back sharply, she downs it quickly, only pausing briefly to let out a horse gasp before pouring herself another.

After her third, she finally gives herself the chance to stop. Staring down at the now empty glass, she thought back to the last time she held a small tumbler like this. It's then that she allows her tears to come. They rolled down her cheeks, flowing freely and unchecked, fully allowing herself to feel the loss.

He's gone now, and with him, so was she. That girl who had hoped for an escape was gone; she was dragged back into this world and put on stage to perform the same tragic tale over and over for the amusement of those around her.

Let them see your smile now, Catherine; your stage awaits.

Jackson

Coming down from my shower, my hair still ringing wet, I head straight for the kitchen, snatching up my already-made smoothie from the counter. I always feel good after a workout. Still feeling the ache in my thighs, it lets me know it's working. Staring down at my phone, also left on the counter next to the smoothie, I can already see I have half a dozen messages flashing up on the screen.

There is never a dull moment when you're a Jackson Hunter! Always somewhere to go; someone new to meet. When I first started out, I used to answer every single one and go to every event I was invited to, but it didn't take me long to realise that it really wasn't necessary, and by keeping it up, it was becoming a full-time job, and becoming a socialite was not on my list of accomplishments I had hoped to achieve.

So, I learned to manage, skim, read messages, reply to those that genuinely interested me, and only attend events that would promote my career or that I actually wanted to attend. That list is now becoming shorter as I get older, however, especially recently, the need to attend parties and play this character has become benign.

I have not lost to the reason why, and it is not what you think. Yes, Catherine is the reason, but only because she opened my eyes to potential: what it truly feels to care for someone, what it's like to be in the company of someone whose opinion matters to you, to do anything to be with them again. If I can't have her, then I want someone or something like her in my life—something that actually gives me motivation to be better and to give more. She set a standard in my life, and I am determined to find it again, and, well, attending nonsense events for shallow people I have no intention of seeing again is not the way forward.

Joe: Hay, I rented a yacht for T's b'day this weekend; you in, right?

Ok, yeah, I'll go to that!

I hear the familiar sound of my door opening and closing. Half turning to click on my coffee machine behind me, I once again face my phone, not needing to even glance up at my visitor.

"Hay Hars," when I see his form come into my peripheral vision.

"Hay Jacky-boy, how are we this fine morning?" Without moving my head, I glanced up with my eyes to catch his face sporting a massive smile addressing me, and I return it with a very amused smile of my own.

"I'm well; you're very cheery this morning."

"I am."

"You care to share with me why, or are you just going to hover over there?" I reach back to grab his now-completed coffee, placing it in front of him.

"I am 'cheery', as you call it, because *you* are going to love me!"

"Is that so?"

"Yes, I have the perfect part for you; it's all lined up waiting for you to audition to finalise." Reaching into his bag, he pulls out a printed script, slamming it down on the counter in front of me.

I started flicking through, becoming more horrified the more I looked.

"I period drama Hars? I am shit at all that old English stuff."

"You'll learn."

"Sex scenes? Nudity? Come on, Hars, this isn't for me," turning it around and placing it back in front of him. In return, he turns it back, pointing to the front page.

"Read the overview," I start reading, still not sure what it is about this one in particular that Harry is seeing…that is, until I do.

"You sure about this?"

"You have to audition as a formality, but as long as all parties agree, it's pretty much a done deal."

"Alright, Hars, sign me up."

Catherine

The boys are at school, and Will is at work. My only company today is the gentle sound of the hoover humming away in the distance as Anita, our cleaner, potters around the house, headphones in, tuned out to all except the mess. Cradling a cup of coffee in my hand, I am curled up on our black-coloured loveseat sofa, staring off into the room, seemingly thinking about everything and nothing at the same time.

'How do you move on from this?'

Fuck if I know.

The sound of my phone disrupts my daydreams, the name 'Josh' appearing on the screen.

"Hay Josh."

"Hay my lovey, how is the most beautiful belle today?"

"I'm good, thanks Josh, you, ok?"

"I am. Listen, I have something for you. I know it isn't what you are after, but I am obligated to run it past you anyway because you have been asked specifically for the role."

"Ok, shoot," I sit up straighter in my chair.

"Ok, so it's a period drama, and it contains nudity and the dramatisation of sex, which you will obviously be involved in."

"Come on, Josh, I thought I made it clear."

"You did, I know; as I say, I have to ask because you have been asked specifically."

"Ok, why me?"

"It's because of your potential co-star, Jackson Hunter," I hold my breath at the sound of his name. "The director is keen to recreate the chemistry you two had in Adrien's Hel, but in a more romantic setting. Essentially, you have been asked to be a pair. If you turn it down, it may impact his chances of getting the role."

A million and one thoughts are flooding my mind, half of me screaming yes yes yes only for the sole purpose of seeing him again, the other half scared: scared of sacrificing my morals just to be with him again, is it worth it?

But then again, my mind flips over my thoughts, buzzing around my head. Am I really sacrificing? I am an actress; it's a job, and I actually had no issues baring flesh before for the sake of a role (as long as it was in good taste, of course), so who's morals am I sacrificing?

His.

Of course, it's his. He was the one who did not like me in that costume before; he is the one who convinced me that taking on voice work was more suitable. *'Why the fuck do I care about what he thinks?'*

"I'll do it."

"You will?" He sounds surprised, his voice elevating a few octaves higher than usual.

"I mean, yeah, I'll audition. I can ask any questions I have and then see if I am happy with the arrangement."

"Hunny, you are a star. I'll let them know and send over the details."

"Thanks Josh. See you soon."

"See you soon, sweetie."

With that, he hung up. My hands are trembling around my now blank-screened phone, and the consequences of my actions are flooding through me.

I'll have to face him and tell him I am doing it and that he has no choice. He has a say in everything else I do, but this is mine, my job, my passion, and I'll be damned if he takes this away from me as well.

Why do I always get flutters of anticipation whenever I know I am going to see him? The same nerves and the same sense of nausea flood through me.

'Get over it, Catherine.' Forcing myself through the doors of the audition theatre.

Of course, it isn't just him who triggers my nerves. It's the producers, directors, and, as you might expect, the nightmarish shadow that follows me— the one that reminds me that if I say yes to this role, there *will* be a fallout with Will. I haven't told him about this audition today, and as much as I won't let him hold me back, it's also not a pleasant notion knowing *that* is what I'm going to have to look forward to later.

Navigating through the main foyer of the theatre, where our auditions are to take place, I easily find the room allocated for us. 'Starmen' written on the door. Through the small pane window, I spot him; looking comfortable and completely at ease, sitting chatting and laughing away with the casting director, one leg crossed horizontally over the other and a hand resting on top of his knee.

Involuntarily, I smile to myself at the sight of him. He looks good and comfortable. I am happy our split has not affected him as much as it has me; as I cannot deny, I have missed him, and I longed to hear his laugh again and see his smile. Just watching him these few seconds has settled my mind more than the time being without him has these last few months.

It seems I am not that inconspicuous, however; he spots me within 30 seconds, spying on him from a distance, and while his smile remains, it warps into the one I recognise, the one he reserves only for me. Almost instantly, he rises from his seat, heading towards me, arm outstretched to get to the door. I beat him to it, sliding through the narrow opening, my eyes focused only on him.

"Catherine, you made it!" He embraces me in a hug, mimicking the behaviour reserved for old work colleagues. I return the gesture, wrapping my arms around him while trying desperately to mask my face from exposing my true desire for him that is threatening to be revealed, simply by the smell of him infusing my nostrils.

"I did!" My voices cracks a little, betraying me. I cough to try and cover it. "You didn't think I'd let you do this alone now, did you?"

"Ha, that would be a *very* different movie!" We chuckle amongst ourselves, enjoying our old on-set banter.

"Umm, well, I do have one condition."

"Oh?" A devilish grin appears on his face. I want to play into it but I am very aware we have an audience.

"No more zombies in the corridors, please? The last one nearly done me in," his head flies back as he bursts out into laughter.

"Ahh, no flying around the set in this one either; we will have to make do without our crash mats!" I join in with his laughter. We take another few minutes to reminisce, fooling all those around us into thinking that we are nothing more than old work acquaintances.

"Alright, shall we get to this then?" One of the casting directors comes up to interrupt our interactions. "I'm Phil; this is Lisa," pointing to a lady behind us.

"Hi," I greet them shyly.

"So, as you know, this is really just a formality. I think we have all seen what you two can accomplish together," we all give off a slight chuckle at the reference. "Did you get the scripts with the highlighted bits we would like to see today?" We both nod. "Good, shall we see what this," pointing to the two of us, "looks like in a more sophisticated setting then?"

"Let's get to it," Jackson adds, his hand bracing against the small of my back edging me towards the centre of the room.

"Ok," Lisa announces, "so for the record we will be recording this for playback later; are you both ok with this?"

"Of course," I answer.

"Great. So, to set the scene, it's a party at your character Catherine's father's house. You are a headstrong, intelligent woman who nobody approves of, past the appropriate age of marriage, but you have no inclination to do what society expects of you. Your father is an influential man, so those around you are forced to tolerate your antics, and as a result, you feel like you hold a certain amount of power there. You are at the party to purposely create tension and gossip because you enjoy creating disgust in the more distinguished classes. Jackson, your character is obviously older, widowed, and plays the role of a sarcastic wit. Those around you take pity on you because they think you act like that because you're grieving; in truth, you are just someone who enjoys…basically winding people up."

"So, neither of us fit into society's box," Jackson interjects.

"Exactly. You are both quite intellectually witty, which is what has drawn you together. We cut into where you had just met and spent the afternoon trying to outdo each other at the party, and now you venture off by yourselves in her father's house. Are you ready?"

"Let's do this," I offer, attempting to get into a character I am not overly confident with…period drama, not my fort-aye.

I start by walking around the room.

"And where do you think you are off to, young lady?" Jackson takes my hand, spinning me around to face him, a sly smile displayed on his lips.

"I am neither young nor a lady, I'll have you know," raising an eyebrow to insinuate the jest.

"I am sure if I lifted up that pretty dress, it would prove the contrary," he encircles me, and I am sure to try and seem intimidating to the character.

"Lift my dress? What you *will* find *there,* good sir, is class, something in which you are severely lacking," his deep laugh emanates from his throat, vibrating out into the room.

"I have a feeling it would not matter to you if I possessed it or not. Class is clearly *not* what drives you."

"Then what do you think drives me good, sir? Society maybe? Money?" He approaches, getting impossibly close but not touching. Even though the moment is written in the script, it has still got me caught up in his aura, taking my breath away as he looks down into my eyes.

"Passion," he almost whispers; the muscles in my neck tense up, and I find it difficult to catch a single breath. He chooses this moment to reach his hand up to cup my cheek, still not touching, just hovering next to it.

"Passion is certainly motivational," mimicking the action of taking a gulp for the sake of my character, feeling those muscles contract against the strain of the tautness.

"Jocelyn, you are, no doubt, the most interesting person I have ever met."

"I am not often associated with the word 'Interesting'."

"That's because those you have met so far are all simpletons. Unable to see the port from the sherry," his actions, now so deliberate for the part, flicking his eyes from mine to my mouth and back again. In return, I open them slightly, adjusting my breathing to feign arousal, which, to be fair, isn't hard to do around Jackson, my chest rising and falling in deep succession. "Jocelyn, would it be wrong of me to want to touch you?"

"Very wrong." Changing my appearance to wear a smirk and tilting my head slightly so his hovering hand touches my cheek, in return he takes it, holding my face in his palm, fingers finding my hair.

"And kiss you?"

"Well, now that would be considered scandalous, Mr Harrison; whatever would possess you to think I would partake in such amusements?"

"Because I think you rather enjoy operating outside of class rules for your *own* amusement. Do you not?" He moves his face closer, his lips suspended above mine, barely a whisper between them.

"Do you now? Do you dare risk finding out *exactly* what I enjoy doing, Mr Harrison?" And with that, he finally claimed my lips with his. I fell into the familiar warmth of his embrace, allowing myself to get lost in it. They can believe all they want, but this isn't acting; this is us re-finding ourselves after months apart.

After our brief connection, we part; he seems to compose himself much better than I can, as he remembers his lines immediately, prompting me to recollect mine.

"You, Miss Jocelyn, are a very dangerous woman," he growls, not moving further from my face than a mere inch or so.

"As people keep telling me."

"Jocelyn!" Phil calls from his seat, reading the part of my 'father'. Pushing Jackson aside, I turn my acting ego into one of panic.

"You must go."

"What happened to the girl who was unafraid?"

"This girl *is* afraid—afraid of the one person you too, should fear. There is no crossing my father, nor will he stand for anyone defaming his daughter. You must go!" He takes a few steps back.

"When can I see you again?"

"You are very forward for someone who is about to die. Now go, I shall try to write to you."

"Jocelyn!" Phil cries again.

"You do not know where I live."

"Then you must write to *me*. Be sure that the letter is addressed to Emma."

"Who is Emma?" He laughs a little.

"She is my maid and closest confidant; she will not tell and will make sure I get it," I go to him, taking his lips again briefly before pushing him out an imagined door. "Now, please, you must go."

"Keep watch for my letter, Jocelyn," and with that, he exits, ending the audition scene.

I hear Phil and Lisa clapping their hands from behind me, tearing my eyes away from Jackson to face them both. I can see a pleased look on their faces.

"Excellent well done; obviously some bits to work on. I can tell neither of you are particularly comfortable in these roles, but that will come. What we have seen is exactly what we wanted to see. The two and from between you flow really naturally, and you're able to portray a very clear attraction between the two characters. It's what we wanted," he pauses for a moment to read through some papers. "Now speaking with both of your agents, they tell me you have no training on anything pertaining to this time period, which means before filming we are going to have to send you off for training."

"Training?" Jackson interjects.

"Yes, so you both," pointing to us, "will need to learn to ride a horse independently."

"I can do that," I add.

"Yeah, no, I've never done that," Jackson admits it, as Phil writes it down on his paper.

"And you will also need dance lessons."

"Ahh man, so my usual dance moves are no good?" He begins to dance around, thrusting his hips from side to side jokingly, emanating a giggle from the rest of us.

"Unfortunately, no," he continues while still chuckling. "We will sign you both up for a short etiquette course as well. As much as I am sure you know how to behave in public, there were certain expectations of the era. Are you both ok with that?"

"No problem," we both answer at the same time.

"Great, do you have any questions for me?"

"Yes," I start. "In the overview, it stipulated there would be nudity with the dramatisation of sex. Can you tell me a little more?" I cough to cover my awkwardness. "Is it full nudity, for example?"

"It isn't full nudity, no. So, for you, Catherine, showing for the audience, it will be mainly from the waist up, and for Jackson, it will be from behind. The scene will be shot with minimal crew and closed sets and shot at angles and with well-placed props to insinuate sex without actually getting fully nude. It is really just one scene in the whole movie. Is that a sticking point for you then?"

"It's a little out of my comfort zone, yes."

"If you're not comfortable doing it, Catherine, don't," Jackson lays a sympathetic hand on my shoulder. "Don't feel like you have to accept the role just because you have been offered it," I look to him in reassurance; he thinks I am here for him, but in truth, he is only part of my reasoning. I really do want the role, not for him but for myself. I know I need to push myself out of my bubble if I am going to succeed in breaking free; taking on a role like this will open up my acting repertoire. I placed my hand on his, offering him a smile to confirm my resolution.

"It's ok, I want to; just know it's not going to be easy for me, that's all."

"Not a problem; in these kinds of scenes, we are usually happy to go with the actor's lead; as long as we get the footage, we need at the end of it," I nod briefly.

"Ok then, I'll look forward to hearing from you," I walk over to the wall to grab my bag. "Thank you for today."

"Thank you, Mrs Carell; we look forward to working with you," with smiles all around I turn to leave.

"Hang on, I'll walk you out," Jackson skips up behind me, opening the door and guiding me out towards the foyer.

As we reach the main room, Jackson gently grasps my elbow, bringing me to a halt as I turn to face him.

"So um, how have you been, Catherine? Is everything all right? Been up to much?" I smile at his attempt at small talk designed to cover his genuine concern.

"I'm good, just the usual nonsense, you know, nothing exciting. And yourself?"

"Yeah, I'm good; not really done much either. Oh, I went to a friend's birthday on a yacht last weekend, which was fun."

"Yes, I saw it in the paper. It must have been quite a party," his face now distorts into a more serious look of disgust.

"Nothing happened, you know, Catherine; with those girls, I mean."

"Jackson, even if you did, it is no business of mine, is it?" His eyes widen in horror; a look of concern, with a small hint of anger, bears down on me, and I can see his façade break. Looking around, he spots an empty room to the side, promptly taking my arm and dragging me off towards it.

Upon entering, he takes my bag, flinging it down to the floor while pinning me up against the wall, hands clasped at either side of my face, directing my eyes' attention to his.

"Catherine, I swear to you, nothing happened."

"Hay," I comfort him, placing my hands flat on his chest. "What you do is your business; you shouldn't even be considering me. I don't expect you to put your life on hold for me, Jackson."

"I'm not. It's just," he pauses to deliberate his next words. "I told you; I don't do one-night stands, and until a girl comes along that makes me feel even half of what you do, Catherine, there's no point," he kisses me softly, punctuating his words with his actions. "You've set standard, now, Catherine and others, well…they just don't quite match up," I smile up at him, and an odd sense of relief, which I have no right to feel, washes over me. '*He is still my Jackson, for the time being.*'

"Promise me you're not holding back finding someone else, over me?" he smiles back, capturing a quick kiss as he does.

"I'm not sweet girl. Now stop worrying about me. Ok?" I nod slightly at him, still not completely convinced. "Are you…are you staying here tonight?" he adds sheepishly.

"Not tonight; I have to get the kids. I only came up briefly, but I'll see you soon, ok?" He nods his reply, using this last opportunity to kiss me again, this time taking me completely, slowly savouring the feel of our connection re-igniting.

"I'll see you soon, sweet girl."

We turn to leave the room; my pulse is pounding in my ears. I am so turned on, and with no expectation for release, the stems of frustration begin to build within me. Heading out the front door to go our separate ways, I linger for a beat too long to take this last moment to stare into those impossibly deep brown eyes, enjoying them and remembering their depth and their adoration until we are re-united once more.

Chapter 19

<u>Jackson</u>

In preparation for filming, which starts in just two short weeks, Catherine and I have been going through what I like to call the 'how to act like a posh twat' lessons, which are, let's just say, tedious to say the least: this fork here, this bow there. We have found ways to make our time more interesting, and it isn't even about sex! We haven't even had the time to, not with us being chaperoned off for day courses here and everywhere.

This *is* about us getting to hang out outside of filming, though, to reconnect, and as much as I still have to reign myself in from touching and, god forbid, kissing her in public, it has allowed us to be ourselves a little and relish in the banter we share as a pair without having to engage it with a group.

Today we are at dance class; this is day one of a three-day course, six-hour days, in which we need to learn four dance routines in time for filming. Towards the end of the day, we have managed to grasp one, the Minuet, I think he called it. We will practice more tomorrow when we have other dancers around us to interact with. The one we are currently performing is slower and more intimate, requiring lots of side steps for us to be in tune with each other's presence so we don't end up stepping on each other's toes.

This kind of dance has forced us to be in closer proximity to each other. It *is* supposed to be romantic, but when coupled with the immense amount of tension emanating off our instructor (who clearly takes his work seriously), it has the very opposite effect on us than expected. You see, at the moment, we are attempting to perform this routine while desperately trying not to laugh at each other's antics. This is proven to be an impossible task, however, because every time I look at Catherine's face: seeing her strained features hopelessly trying to hold in yet another giggle, her lips sucked into her mouth while her eyes hold that amused expression, all as she stares straight up at me, it of course sets me off, it *has* already more than once. I continue to struggle in my attempt to school my expression as it fights against my own bodies need to keel over and burst into laughter.

As part of the routine, I dip her back while she stretches out her arm to the side.

"Catherine, don't forget your lines; extend those arms!" Our instructor calls out from off to the side somewhere.

"Yes Catherine!" I add in a mocked serious tone. "For Christ's sake, don't forget your lines!" With that, she loses all composure, breaking out the giggles she was fighting to withhold. This of course, creates a rippling effect that immediately fractures my own demeanour as I bend over in a fit of hysterics. Over the next few minutes, every time we just about calm ourselves down, all it takes is one glance at the other one for us both to break down again. I am sure neither of us are really sure what we are laughing at anymore.

"If you have had quite enough!" I hear the instructor bark from behind me, clear frustration permeating off him.

"I'm sorry," Catherine gasps in between. "It's not this…I promise…it's just us…I think you can tell we are clearly *not* naturals, and we're a little out of our element."

"Maybe not, but you are going to have to behave like it," he pauses for a moment, tapping his thigh with the long stick he has in his hand, which he had previously been using repeatedly to correct our postures *and* lines. "Hold right there, I'll be back." And with that, he whisks off into a different room.

Upon his return, we see, in his hands, what he went to find; a horrified look falls upon Catherine's face.

A huge dress straight out of the 1700s!

"What is that?" Catherine exclaims in horror.

"This, my dear, is a dress similar to the one you will have to wear while filming, and you will *have* to learn how to move in it. It's all well and good prancing about the studio giggling away, but when you have to manoeuvre with this thing trailing around you, it's a very different story. Go put it on."

"Now?"

"Now, Amanda next door will help you into it," with that, Catherine ventures off, head drooping down towards the floor and the dress folded over her arm, out into the adjoining room; she looks back at me wearing a scowl across her face before disappearing all together.

Around 10 minutes later, after the instructor and I have passed the time in an awkward silence, she finally returns to what is now a very odd-looking assembly. The dress was simply thrown over her own clothes, which previously consisted of just a hoodie and joggers. She holds up the edges of the dress as she walks, clearly uncomfortable as she re-enters the room, her scowl now replaced with a sorrowful-looking pout.

I instantly turn on the spot, looking away from her, clutching at my sides while I crack up in hysterics again, just at the mere sight of the atrocity!

"Stop!" She whines. "I feel puffy!"

"You *look* puffy!" I exclaim in return, punctuating it with yet more laughter.

"Of course, you do; it was the fashion," the instructor interjects, a small smirk written on his face. "Now come on, let's try this again. Don't forget, it's not just you that needs to navigate it." Redirecting his pointing stick from Catherine to me. "It's you as well! Gentlemen, do not go treading on ladies clothing!"

"Yes, come on, you," taking her hands in mine, "let's dance." Flashing her my cheekiest grin.

"If I trip over, you're going to catch me, right?" She looks at me pleadingly.

"Always."

We begin to move around the room again, twirling her around in time to the music as her dress spins out around her. It *is* a lot harder now with the added size and weight. Catherine is so small, it's a wonder she can carry it all!

"Good, good," we hear him calling off in the background. However, I barely hear him at all. I am too caught up in her, with the concentrated look on her face as I twirl her around the room. I could almost pretend that this was us and that this was real. Except for the occasional call of "Catherine, lines!" We both gently giggle at his perfectionism, neither of us really taking it seriously enough for his liking; we are just enjoying our time together nonetheless.

As per the routine, I dip her backwards, holding on tightly to ensure I don't indeed drop her. She screams out despite my strong hold, which flows effortlessly into a sort of cackle while I suspend her mid-air.

"Jackson! Don't drop me!" I chuckled along with her.

"Never; I won't let you fall, Catherine, I promise," pulling her up quickly, she almost seems to jump into my arms, holding her close to me in order to support the weight of her against my chest. I forget where we are for a moment, lost in her embrace as she looks up at me, catching my eyes bearing down on her. I raise my hand with the intent to stroke her cheek, completely lost in the moment, but before we give ourselves away, we are interrupted by our instructor again, breaking away like we are a couple of school children who just got caught by the head teacher at prom.

"Good, you're looking better," he glances down at his watch. "Listen, I have to shoot for the day. You are welcome to use the studio for another hour to practice, but then there is another class on."

"Ok!" we say in unison.

"Great, so I'll see you both in the morning," as quick as a whippet, he grabs his bag and is out the door without even waiting for a goodbye.

"Thank god for that!" I declare, breathing out a sigh of relief. "I wasn't sure how much more of that I could take!" She giggles along next to me.

"What we do, hay?" She comments as we once again take up our embrace to dance. This one, however, begins slowly, a far cry from the coordinated faff we were forced to do 5 minutes ago.

"I'd do anything to spend more time with you," breathing out a deep sigh, "even if it does mean more bloody dance lessons!" She giggles again, leaning to rest her head on my chest. Our dancing immediately changes to a more swaying movement; all thought to our previous routine is lost as we rock back and forth on our heels around the room, with my head resting on top of hers.

"Reminds me of Italy," she sighs. Instant flashes of that time together are now filling my mind, causing me to smirk slightly from the memory.

"We weren't very good at dancing then, either," I light-heartedly joke while we chuckle. I bring my hand up to cup her cheek so I can tilt her head up to mine. Once aligned, I kiss her so deeply and so filled with my desire for her, she has no choice but to return it with the same intensity.

Unable to help myself, I push her up against the mirrored wall behind her, attempting to get close, but…

"This damn dress!" I cry out. "How is anyone supposed to get intimate in one of these?" She giggles as her smile radiates against my mouth.

"I don't think you are supposed to. Keeps my virtue intact."

"And we wouldn't want to break that now, would we?"

"Definitely not," we kiss again, trying my best to thrust my hips against the fullness of the dress.

Once I have taken my pleasure and given in to hers, I release her, but not from my grasp; instead, I pull her to me, continuing our gentle movements as we dance around the room.

"So, um…" I start to ask. "You heading home tonight?" She shakes her head fervently while sucking in her lips.

"I told him I was staying up late and getting up early. Got me a night away," I softly kiss her again, seemingly not having my fill just yet.

"Can I…" I start again. "Can I come to you?" Throwing her head back in laughter, she replies.

"Of course, silly. Do you even need to ask?" My smile is now broad and spreads across my face as I stare down at this amazing beauty before me.

"Oh, I don't know; are you not bored of me yet?" I catch a glimpse of her radiant smile before she rests her head on my chest again.

"Not yet," I kiss her head gently, continuing our gentle swaying until it was time to go.

'No, we are most definitely not bored yet, are we sweet girl?'

Catherine

It's funny how easily we can fall back into our usual routine. The filming schedule is a little haphazard this time around though, mainly due to the availability of some of our locations. The importance of getting this film historically accurate means we only have a certain set of places we can use, and we have to work around more modern interruptions, like the odd car driving by, for example, or the occasional aeroplane overhead.

Jackson's and my routine, however, remain consistent. If we are filming the next day and therefore are staying in a hotel, we always stay together, not that the film company knows that mind you, and as always, we gym it in the morning to cover ourselves. I am back feeling myself, and Jackson is back in full swing. Jackson, the sweet, passionate man I see behind closed doors, is mine again, for a while at least. Each of us, enjoying this short break from reality, even if it is tainted by ball gowns and coat tails.

Three weeks into filming, however, things are starting to go very wrong…

It's Saturday, and we have been shooting at a 17th century house the studio managed to find, but it has been a hell of a week trying to fit in the shots we needed in the time we had the house for, which meant long hours and extra days. Thankfully, the director said he has everything he needs now and has promised a long weekend off next week to make up for it.

It's late when I open the door to the house, exhausted, throwing the keys onto the side table by the front door. It's eerily silent. The darkened walls of the entranceway gave me no clue as to anybody's whereabouts. The boys, I assume, must be in bed, but it seems too early for Will to have done the same.

After removing my shoes and placing them neatly in the shoe rack, I take a few tentative steps into the entranceway, and that's when I see it. An ominous shadow occupying the chaise long to the right of the door; a silhouette lurking in the dark. That's when it rises slowly, and I am confronted by him.

He glares down at me as I enter, dressed in a suit and tie and with a whiskey, in hand. Purely based on this behaviour alone, I know something isn't right this evening. He never waits, and he certainly never acknowledges me; any interaction we have is in passing. This is a direct affront to me.

"You're late."

"I told you I would be. It's nothing you can't handle, surely?" Our interactions with each other, like usual, are short, with that spit of hatred bedded into every word.

"This isn't working, Catherine."

"What isn't?"

"This. This acting. You have proven your point now, enough is enough; you need to start thinking about this family," I can hear the powerful, authoritative tone in his voice, the one that rears its ugly head whenever he aims to get his way, which in truth, I usually back down to, moreover, to avoid an inevitable argument than anything else. Well, not today.

"You know," I gulp. "I have been thinking, and do you know what?" I slam my bag down on the side table for added emphasis. "I think the boys are just fine; they are proud of their mummy. It is *you* that it is not good for; *you* need me here to watch the children whenever one of your hoes comes calling."

"Now you watch your mouth!" He aims his index finger in my direction threateningly, shooting it across towards my face, and I can see from the expression on his own face that I am right; this spurs me on further.

"Too suspicious, right? Keep calling in a babysitter; boys are old enough to realise where their daddy is going when Mummy is away. Do they ask too many questions?"

"Catherine!" His anger continues to seep through.

"What a selfish prick you are! You cannot even hold your dick for one extra night for the sake of your kids!" With that, he charges at me, the force of him pinning me up against the wall, his full strength holding me there, one hand across my wrist pressing tightly on the hardened surface, while his other hovers just below my neck, pressing down hard against my collar bone.

"You had better watch what you say," he growls out between clenched teeth, only a few inches from my face. His whiskey-stench breath lingers within my nostrils, dominating my senses. I have to be strong; I have to stand my ground; I cannot bow down to his wrath anymore.

"Or what, Will? What will you do?" My lips curl up into a snarl while I stand there, staring into his eyes in challenge. I feel his hand shift further up my neck, pressing against my throat, and his hold of my wrist becomes painful and restrictive, but the adrenaline pulsing through me forces me to hold my resolve.

"This is your last warning, Catherine! If you continue with this, you will effectively end this family. I will leave!" The threat is real, but I cannot help but laugh. *'Is this all you got?'*

"You would really do that to this family, my family, your damn reputation just so you can get laid whenever you damn well, please?"

"No, *you're* doing this by choosing to play at your pretend career over this family," my eyes flash red. I attempt to push him back away from me with all my strength, but his hold is hard fast, I cannot move him more than an inch; my fury, however, burns as it explodes out of my mouth.

"No, it's you!" I cry. "It has always been *you*! *You* did this to us! You are the one who chooses to play away with anything who…who showed your cock an interest for the sake of your wallet," my breathing becomes heavy as that adrenaline continues to influence my actions. "You are the one who insists on putting your physical needs before those of his *wife*! Your *children*! You…you took our love, took my *heart*, something that was pure and real, and I gave just for you…and you broke it…you broke *me!* Everything, all this…It is all *YOU!*" The force of my words projects out in a cry of fury, spitting out my disgust at his apparent dominance.

"I mean it, Catherine!" His voice rises to match mine, intimidating me a little, but I know I cannot stop now. My long-lost courage, supported by my rage, is now overriding all other senses. He continues, believing his words and his hold over my body are enough to break through my demeanour. "It's either acting or me. You continue this stupid endeavour, and this marriage is over. Is that understood?" He pauses momentarily; I just continue to stare, still trying to process this whole conversion while calming my nerves and holding my resolve.

"Understood?" He cries again, his voice echoing through the hallway, the pressure bearing down on my wrist and neck becoming ever more restrictive.

"I understand," I reply quietly, dropping my free arm down to my side and slumping against the wall, dejected. My pulse rings through my ears, and my hands tremble.

"Good, now that that's settled, don't expect me home," he lets go and backs away, adjusting his tie and straightening his jacket as he heads towards the door. I watch from the wall where he left me as he gathers up his belongings.

"I'm not going to stop Will; I am an actress; it is who I am, whether you like it or not," he pauses in the entranceway, turning his full front to me, taking on his aggressive stance once more.

"You just said you understood!"

"I do understand. I didn't say I agree," I say it back as calmly as my nerves will allow. "I'm not giving up my life for *you,* Will…not again!" He glares at me for a beat before the realisation of my resolve finally dawns on him, and his body posture drops, accepting my stance.

"Then expect to hear from my lawyers Monday morning."

"*My* lawyers will be expecting them," with one final glance, he turns and walks out the door.

Once the door has closed behind him, my body finally gives up its façade. Hands still trembling, I fall to the floor, my legs no longer able to carry my weight, and I feel the tears form and then fall from my eyes. It feels as though every emotion is flooding my veins all at once, creating an overwhelming overload of senses to course through me.

Relief, pain, anger, hurt, happiness, bereavement, peace, fright, resolve, and confusion are but some of what I am experiencing in the moment.

I can't tell you how long I sat on that floor attempting to reign in my heart; I don't even remember making it up into bed, not that I slept at all that night. Just when I thought the tears were done and I was moving on, they came flooding back in a whole new wave of emotion, falling for both the life I was losing and pre-empting the life I was beginning.

Eventually, the sound of Callen waking up forced me to regain my composure. Whatever has happened and whatever is going to happen, I *will not* let *them* see me fall.

Hello viewers and welcome to Entertainment News, I am your host, Jane Collins. Tonight, on the gossip rags, Catherine Carell and husband of 10 years, William Carter, are filing for divorce!

Carter released a statement this morning claiming that he is filing for divorce due to, and this is a quote, 'due to recent changes in our lives, we have found ourselves at an unreconcilable impasse, and we now have no choice but to go our separate ways.'

This very much implies that it is due to Carell's recent assertion to re-entering the acting world has put too much strain on the relationship. In which I have to say, I agree.

Doesn't it seem odd that after 10 years of laying low, living off her husband's successful business, she suddenly throws herself into, let's just say, a less than upstanding role, leaving him for weeks on end running a business and a home with little to no regard for her family? I even have it on good authority that her latest project is even seedier than Adrien's Hel. I mean, that cannot be easy for a husband to watch! And she didn't even have the decency to use her married name!

We did reach out to Catherine Carell for her side of the dispute, but she has refused to comment.

Well, ladies, it looks like a very eligible bachelor will soon be on the market for a new Mrs Carter. Watch this space.

Chapter 20

Jackson

Something is different this morning.

We are back in the studio this week; we are not due on location now for another 2 weeks, which suits me. We keep a better routine when we can control our environment.

Coming in this morning, however, I was not greeted by my usual smiling enchantress; instead, she was withdrawn; she couldn't even look at *anyone* directly, least of all me. The crew seems to be acting weird as well, all gossiping under hushed whispers; it has me rather on edge.

"Jocelyn, I would brave your father a thousand times over if it got me one more minute with you."

"But sir, my father would not even acknowledge your bravery, let alone stand for it." This isn't right; her tone is flat, and it lacks her usual enthusiasm. What has happened to my Catherine?

"Then I will force him to acknowledge me, even if it is through distain. I will challenge his challenge and call him out on his absurdity," she is supposed to giggle here, but she doesn't. This shell in front of me forces me to break character; I cannot hold it any longer. To hell with who could be watching. Taking her cheek in my hand, I force her face up to look at me.

"Catherine, what's wrong?" She starts to try to force a smile, but it immediately breaks. Pushing herself away from my hold, she walks away, clutching her arms around her abdomen. I am forced to just stand and watch as she makes her way over to the director.

She has a quick, hushed conversation with him; while she does, she happens to raise her hand to tuck a piece of hair behind her ear, which briefly drags the cuff of her jumper back from her hand and lower arm, where I see a glimpse of bruising around her wrist. Noticing the exposure, she quickly tugs the sleeve back down again before he nods sullenly in agreement, leaving her to vacate the studio in silence.

"Ok," he calls out to the rest of us. "Change of plan. We are going to run through scene 14. Stagehands, can you get that set up? All cast members, you have a 30-minute break while we rearrange the set."

I use this chance to take myself off in pursuit of Catherine, seeing her off in the distance as she disappears in the direction of the trailers. Picking up speed in a light jog, I reach her trailer shortly after she does. I pause just outside before knocking to listen in a vain attempt to understand what scene I'll be walking into before entering. What I hear is what I expected—the sniffs and sobs of someone who is crying.

After knocking, I wait impatiently for her to give the ok. After the moment I assume she took to compose herself, I hear a "come in," to which I immediately push open the door, confronted by the sorrowful image of Catherine in front of me.

From seeing me appear at the door, it seems all the need she had to put on a brave face fell as she promptly collapsed, falling into my arms. I do my best to envelope her, wrapping her up with my body, stroking her hair with my hand as her own hands snake around my back.

"Hay, you're ok, sweet girl. It's ok," shaking while she sobs into my shirt, I feel it getting wet with her tears.

Once I hear she has calmed down a little, I attempt to approach the cause of her current state. "What happened, Catherine? Why are you upset? Did he hurt you?" She continues to sniffle into my chest. Silence. "Please tell me what's wrong, Catherine; I hate seeing you like this."

Leaning back a little, still not wanting to let go, I can see her face is flushed red.

"It's over," she quietly announces.

"What is?" Wide-eyed, a slight panic passing through me.

"My marriage—it's over." The panic is replaced by…well by relief and elation.

"That's…that's good, right?" The atmosphere in the room suddenly darkens, a heavy sense of doom lingers as my words leave my mouth. I can see a storm brew across her beautiful tear-stained face. Her hands loosen from behind my back as she goes to take a giant step away from me.

"Excuse me?" I hurriedly attempted to take her hands in mine, desperately trying to bring her back to me.

"It's good, isn't it? Catherine, we can be together now," her features warp into that of distain, ripping her hands from mine and tearing herself away while pushing me back, but for all her strength, she cannot push me more than a step, creating a cavern between us.

"I'm here telling you my life is falling apart, and all you can think about is your goddamn cock!" she cries; her rage replaces all the despair she had a few moments ago.

"No, no, no, Catherine, that's not what I meant," I'm pleading with her. How can I be so stupid?

"Get out! You selfish fucking arsehole!" Pushing me again towards the door.

"Catherine!" Desperately, trying to appeal to her, but it was to no avail.

"Get the fuck out! Leave me alone. I don't want to see you." Knowing how royally I have just fucked up, I feel my own tears threatening to come forth.

"Catherine, please."

"Out!" Dejected by the determination of her resolve and the deaf ears my pleas are falling on: I start to back myself out of the trailer, shoulders slumped. I don't want to turn away from her, and I don't want to miss any opportunity I might have to make this right. She gives me no such opening.

I have no choice but to leave.

What have I done?

Hello viewers and welcome to Entertainment News, I am your host, Jane Collins. Tonight, on gossip rags, more insight into the Carell/Carter divorce comes as businessman William Carter took to social media last night with a simple statement. 'When life offers you a choice…family, always pick your family.' Sparking more speculation into the breakdown of their marriage puts the blame at Catherine Carell's door, with her still refusing to comment on the matter and her social media apparently at a complete standstill.

We will keep you updated on this story as it develops.

In other news…

Catherine

I can't even bring myself to turn my phone on anymore. It has been a constant beacon of alert since the moment the story went live.

I knew it would happen; I knew he would try to get ahead of the media by releasing his story first, knowing I wouldn't even try to retaliate. He knows I love my family too much for that. It is better to let him do what he is going to do to salvage his reputation than drag everyone else through the mud along with me.

By the time I pull into my parents' driveway, I am already feeling physically weary from the mental exhaustion. I know I must look like a mess. After being sent home from the set yesterday, I fell into my hotel room and didn't move from my bed all evening. I spent most of it scrolling through the toxicity of my online status to read the comments others had left behind. It wasn't until the early hours of the morning that I realised I hadn't eaten the whole day. Once I deduced what was an acceptable hour, I got in my car; knowing I had burnt the bridge to the person I truly felt safe with, I decided instead to drive over to the only other place I felt at ease: my parents' house.

Opening the door, my father takes one look at my sorry state and embraces me into one of his almighty hugs, engulfing me in his love. It is then that I allow myself to break down again.

"Sweetheart, come on," I hear him mutter into my hair as I nod, "let's get you in," I am not able to talk through the sniffling mess I have become. He leads me straight through the house into the living room, where I can see his paper and coffee have been left on the little table next to his huge, comfortable armchair.

Guiding me over to my mum's chair, which sits next to his, he glances over at the coffee, then back at me.

"I would offer you coffee, but I have a funny feeling you need something stronger," rising from his chair, "Be back in a tick," he exits the room, returning not 5 minutes later with a glass of wine and a whiskey. "I won't tell your mother if you don't," he jokes, rising from me the smallest of smirks.

"Where is Mum?" I ask.

"Oh, somewhere gossiping with your aunt Clara, no doubt. Who knows where that woman goes!" I offer him another smirk while I reach out for a drink.

Unconsciously, I wince a little as I take a sip.

"That's the best we have; it's your mother's favourite. Do you not like it?"

"It's ok; truth is, I don't really like wine," he looks away, raising his hands in the air, and then allowing them to drop back down in despair.

"Then why the hell do you keep drinking it? You have it every time you come over!"

"I don't know, habit, I suppose."

"Here then," he passes me his glass before leaving briefly to retrieve another one. Upon his return, he sits back down in his chair opposite me. I'm not looking at him, but in my peripheral, I know he is staring at me a little uncomfortably.

"So do you want to tell me what happened?" He probes.

"We just fell out of love I think," I lie. He doesn't believe me as he responds with a...

"Ah huh!" Followed by, "ok sweetheart, just know I am here ready to listen when you want to talk about it, honestly," I look up to catch his worried gaze. He answers my unasked question. "You think I didn't notice? Umm? Notice how sad you have been these past few years. I tried to get *numpty* to take notice and do something about it, but he never did. Starting to realise now the reason for that is maybe because *he* was the reason. Correct me if I'm wrong," I feel a tear escape my eye and roll down my cheek as I continue to look on, taking a large gulp of whiskey to try and control myself. "Sweetheart, know there is nothing you can say that will make me love you any less; you know that, right?" And with that, all the dams broke, and I burst into an ugly cry, cradling my abdomen with my arm as all the floods came pouring out of me. My father leaps up out of his chair and stands by my side, cradling my head in his arms.

Between the sobs of tears, I manage to get out my truth.

"He cheated on my dad." The hands that were stroking my head and forearm stop, all while he absorbs the enormity of my confession.

"What do you mean he cheated on you? When?" His voice has taken on a more aggressively firm tone.

"Nearly 3 years ago."

"Ok," I can hear his voice his increasing agitation while his responses remain calm. "What once, and you forgave him, or what?" I shake my head forcefully against his chest. "Twice?" Again, I fervently shake my head. "So, he has continued to step out on you this entire time?" I nod my response subtly. "With the same woman?" His questions are stern and blunt; I shake my head again, seemingly losing the use of my voice. My dad, however, has not. Letting go of my head, he turns abruptly, breathing out a loud growl while placing his hands behind his own head.

"That dirty lying little son of a bitch. I'll kill him...I'll fucking kill him!" He spits behind gritted teeth. He turned back to me, flames of anger now prominent behind his eyes, now forcefully directed at me. "Why didn't you leave him? Why did you put up with his shit Catherine?" His heated, elevated voice provokes my silence, causing me to hesitate before finding my own voice to answer him.

"Because of this: the fallout; your friendship with his family; our own families' reputation. You would lose a lot, Dad. I couldn't do that to you."

"You think that I think so highly of that sack of shit of a family that I would put their happiness over yours? That they mean more to me than you do?" A hit of realisation hits him as his voice softens and cracks a little. "Did I ever make you feel like that?"

"No, Dad, *you* didn't."

"But *he* did. He made you believe that." I bow my head down in shame. "Why that worthless piece of fucking shit!" He starts pacing about the room. "I won't let him get away with this, Catherine!"

"Dad, please," I manage. "Don't; it's done now."

"Catherine, he is dragging your name through the fucking dirt for the sake of his own goddamn reputation; I won't have it! Why don't you retaliate? Why won't you tell the truth?"

"Because what will it do? Create an army of people who take his side over mine, calling me a liar. It's better to just…let it go, take the hit, and move on. The media will have their fill and forget all about me in time. They have done it before; they'll do it again."

"Uh-uh, nope I'm not having it, Catherine; I won't let him get away with it," he gets out his phone and starts dialling.

"No, Dad, please; you'll make it worse."

"Nope, you don't get to where I am, baby, without making a few friends along the way; by the time I am done, you'll be the nation's fucking sweetheart."

"Dad…"

"Hay! Bobby. How are you?" He calls out in a lighter tone. Pausing while he listens to whoever he is talking to on the other end. All I can hear is the familiar, high-pitched chatter that tells me someone is talking. "Fantastic! Listen, I called 'cause I have a story for you, but you may have to do a little leg work." Another pause. "These rumours surrounding my daughter and her soon-to-be ex-husband aren't true. He cheated on her multiple times over a 3-year period," another pause. "Trust me on this, Bob; this is the truth; he doesn't want anyone to know about it and no doubt has covered his tracks well; but with the sheer number of people we suspect he has been with, there has got to be one that will blow the whistle for the right price, and once one comes forward, you *know* others will follow," another pause. "Fantastic, let me know how you get on, and remember, Bob, whatever you find, this didn't come from us; these girls came forth of their own accord. Thanks, mate; see you soon." And with that, he hangs up the phone, turning back to me rather than sitting back down in his chair, taking my free hand in his. "He will pay for what he has done, Catherine; you mark my words. No one does this to you!"

I smile gratefully at him; it feels good to finally have someone else on my side fighting for me. I am reminded, in this moment, of Jackson, the anguish of which immediately breaks my heart all over again. I *did* have someone fighting for me, someone who cared for me, and what's worse, I took his love and threw it at him like the ungrateful wrench I am. Dad must have seen my tortured expression.

"So come on, some more honesty. Now that we're on a roll, what's been happening the last year or so?" He raises his bushy eyebrows in question, to which I reply with a blank expression. "Well, we had a brief time where I thought I was getting my baby back, but then *this* 'you' came back with a vengeance. I thought it was because of filming, but that dick never let me in on anything that was going on with you. Was it because of him again?"

"Sort of but no, it was someone else."

"Another fucking prick. I swear to God Catherine, line them up because I am getting pissed off here."

"No no, not like that; the complete opposite, in fact. Oh my God, Dad, I think I fucked it all up!" I snatch up my hand from his, putting down my glass so I can cover my entire face with both my palms.

"Talk to me, baby."

"Dad, he was so sweet and loving. He cared for my dad and really, genuinely cared for me. He told me he loved me."

"Who?"

"Jackson Hunter."

"The guy from your film?"

"Yeah, we got close—you know, really close. He tried to get me out, but I wouldn't listen. He came back for me time and time again, but all I did was push him away. I stayed with the wrong man because I thought it was the right thing to do, and yet he never gave up on me."

"When was the last time you spoke to him?"

"Yesterday, I was so rude, I called him an arsehole and told him not to come near me again."

"You were upset."

"I was a bitch!" I cry out.

"Hey hey, come now."

"I *was* a bitch, and now I may have lost someone who actually cared for me."

"If he is half the man you say he is, he will know you were angry and upset; he won't take it to heart."

"But what if I lost him because I was too stubborn?"

"Sweetheart, if he feels for you all that you just said, he won't let one tantrum keep him away, and if it does, he isn't worth your effort. Do you know how many times your mum has screamed and shouted at me over the years? Doesn't mean I love her any less; in fact, I love her more because I know I am the only person she feels she can knowingly do that with, and she won't ever lose me over it."

He offers me a reassuring smile that, for all his words, I still cannot reciprocate, the guilt and loss still too overpowering.

"But listen, baby," he continues in a more authoritative tone, "don't go rushing into another relationship so soon after William. You are in a really vulnerable place right now. You're hurt, angry, and as much as it pains me to say it, you're a broken sweetheart; not to mention, you are in for one hell of a shitstorm the next few months with the media and divorce proceedings; this is not the environment that can form a solid foundation to build a new and good relationship on," he takes my hand again. "Let the waters settle; let yourself fully heal first before you rush into anything. When you're ready, if it's still Jackson you want? Then there will be no residual negativity to follow you into that relationship, and you can give yourself to him fully, with nothing to hold you back. Let your new beginning come from a place that is pure and calm. Make sure you are ready to accept his love, and in turn, for you to return it when the time is right for you," his speech, although rift with negative terms and probably not what I *want* to hear right now, is actually exactly what I *need* to hear, and it centres and calms me in a way I haven't felt all weekend since all this shitshow started.

I look up to him, his concern is still evident in his features.

"When did you get so wise?" I mock with a sly smirk, rewarding me with a smile in return.

"Ha, you don't do as many movies as I have and not pick up some inspirational speeches along the way," we both chuckle. "Listen, where are you living at the moment?"

"The director said I could have the week off, but I have the hotel booked in for the week anyway, so I am just staying there and hopefully find myself somewhere by the weekend; if not, I'll probably end up back at home."

"Nonsense. I won't have it. You are staying here; it isn't far, so you don't have to commute for the kids, and they already have their own bedrooms here anyway. You stay with us while this is all going on, or at least until we find you somewhere you're actually going to be happy. This is *your* new beginning, Catherine; we're doing it right," I smile at him; this is exactly the support I needed when I headed here this morning. "Where are the kids now?" he adds.

"He has them this week; he was due to have them all week, anyway, it seemed a bit pointless to change their routine that is already in place."

"Ok, from next week we will organise proper custody; I won't have him holding that over your head. Your mother and I will be here when you need to work." The weight of the world is literally coming off my shoulders as he speaks, helping me organise my new reality so it begins to make a little more sense.

I get up out of my seat, walk over to his chair, and sit across his lap with my legs dangling over the arm of it. My arms are draped around his shoulders with his head in his neck, while his head rests on top of mine and his hands around my body, just like we used to do when I was a child and upset, and just like then, my father's comforting embrace soothes me.

"Thank you, Dad."

"Anything for my baby. I don't ever want you to feel like you are on your own again. You hear me. Never hide things from me; I will always have your back, ok sweetheart?"

"Ok Dad."

We sit like this for a long while, enjoying being back in my father's loving arms. We only break when my mum comes into the room, a handful of shopping bags in her hands, and we spend the rest of the afternoon catching her up on everything that has transpired.

Well, now I have two in my corner.

Chapter 21

<u>Jackson</u>

She didn't come in for the entire week. It wasn't until the following Tuesday that she graced us with her presence once more. She enters the studio like a vision, sweeping in with her beauty. I know to keep my distance; however, the echoes of our last conversation are still ringing through my ears. It doesn't stop me from observing and watching her while she gives everyone else her fake smiles and they greet her back from what must have been a turbulent week—one where I couldn't be by her side, even though I *knew* that was where I belonged.

Yes, I read the news and watched the entertainment channels last week. As she suspected, they had made her divorce into a media circus of 'he said she said', pinning one family against the other, I can see why she chose to remain silent rather than put her family through it all.

She looks better today, though, calmer; she laughs and jokes with our colleagues the way she always has; it seems that only *I* can see through her façade.

While she is chatting with Portia, she takes a glance past her head, catching my eye and whilst staring back at her, I flinch a little, unsure of where we stand, but she offers me a small, shy smile that tells me we're ok. I offer one of my own back, not quite as reserved as hers, but with a full-on toothy grin, portraying my utter relief.

God, how I have been panicking this week. I honestly thought I had messed us up, that my one comment portrayed me as someone I wasn't, and that I thought nothing more of her than what we found in bed. I need to find a way to talk to her and make sure the air is well and truly clear.

I watch as she finally makes her excuses and wanders off towards her trailer. Like a specialised stalker, I follow, not too close as to alert those around me but quick enough for my anxious nerves, looking around as though spies were among us, waiting to catch me in the act.

Gently, I knock on her trailer door. She opens it herself, a vision of grace before me.

"Jackson, hi," she offers her shy smile again; I realise it is the one she uses when she doesn't know quite where to place herself.

"Hi," I stand there, shifting from one foot to the other. "I just wanted to see how you're doing."

"I'm good, thanks, taking each day, you know?" I stand there nodding stupidly, not saying anything more for a solid minute, while an awkward presence raises between us. It seems odd, this self-conscious canyon that has been erected; it is unnerving. I must conquer it before it has a chance to grow any bigger.

Finally, I can't stand it anymore; looking from left to right quickly, checking that we were in fact alone, I add.

"Catherine, can I come in for a minute?"

"Umm, sure. Just know makeup will be here soon," she, too, looks around nervously.

"It's ok, I won't be a minute," moving aside, she allows me to pass her into the trailer, and I hear the door click behind me. Turning around to face her, fidgety and unable to stay on one foot, changing from leaning on one to the other, whereas she just stands there, arms folded in front of her defensively. I do not blame her for putting her guard up.

"Catherine, I just want to say I'm sorry."

"So am I," she interrupts. "I overreacted last week and blew up when I shouldn't have."

"No, no, you were right. You were there pouring your heart out to me, and my first instinctual thought was a selfish one. Just know I didn't mean it; it was stupid, and I am so sorry," she nods, relaxing her arms a little.

"Thank you," she utters under her breath.

"Would you…umm…would you like to grab a drink later," and straight away her defences rise again. '*Shit!*'

"Jackson, I don't think…"

"No, no, no, not like that, I promise," I hold my hands up to her like I am trying to tame a damn bull. "Listen, I have already changed hotels; we are not even near each other; that's not what I want, I promise. Just…I thought…well, underneath everything we were and what we became, I like to think we also had a friendship, and I figured that's what you need right now. Right? A friend to talk to, someone not connected with him, when you're here away from your family at least?" I pause in relief when I see her stance begin to relax again. "I want to be there for you, Catherine. Please…please let me."

She nods her head again, looking towards the floor as I see the pools start to form in her eyes. Instinctively, I take the two steps towards her, wrapping her up in my arms, cradling her head into my chest, and rubbing her back.

After a short while of just feeling comfortable in each other's embrace, I feel her push back against me as she takes a step away. I let her; she is in control of us now.

"So, how about that drink later…as friends?"

"I would like that," she gives me another one of her smiles through the redness of her cheeks.

"Great, we'll just go straight from here; there is a little bar on the corner, which has…wait for it! Sofas!" Emphasising the last words with an exaggerated 'jazz hands'. Amazingly, she giggles along with my silliness.

"Sounds like a plan," with that, I edged my way out the door of the trailer.

Taking this step back away from Catherine is going to be the hardest thing I have ever had to do: to have her this close but not the way I know we could be and to resist kisses and touching her the way I want, will be torture. It's also a gamble. What if I take this step back and she decides after all this that she doesn't want me like that anymore? But I have no choice; it's what she needs from me right now, and I'll be damned if I let my needs come before hers; she deserves more than that.

After a great day of rehearsals—nothing too sexual—which I think our director had planned on purpose to help Catherine ease back into it all, Catherine and I fulfilled our plans to head to the bar. Dressed in nothing but the pair of joggers and oversized hoodie she wore this morning, she still looks like a vision to me.

Thoughts and impulses are misfiring throughout my brain, wicked contemplations of wanting to take her hand in mine and walk side by side as a couple because now my brain is on overdrive, knowing that technically we can; there is no longer an invisible husband barrier standing in our way. I have to keep reminding myself, though, that this isn't about me; this isn't about what I want; it is about her. Emotionally, she is so scattered and drained that what she needs is a rock…and well, you might as well call me a boulder because I am determined to overcome my own selfishness and be that for her.

"Take a seat; I'll get us a drink," I say, motioning to the empty sofas placed near the front window, figuring the use of the outside world passing by will help with any need for a distraction.

An order of an Amaretto and a scotch later, I am heading over. As anticipated, she is mesmerised watching the street outside, a vacant expression evident on her face.

"Here, it looks like you need this," handing her the drink, I fight all urges to be close to her by taking a seat on the opposite sofa.

"Thanks," she offers politely, cradling the glass like hot chocolate on a cold night.

"So how has it been this week? I can't imagine it's been easy; just seeing the news channels at the moment, I can at least tell that."

"It's nothing I didn't expect. He needs to try and save his reputation."

"While tarnishing yours."

"As I say, I expected it."

"He couldn't have always been like that, though, right? He must have been decent at one point. I can't imagine you accepting anything less."

"He was!" A small smile creeps onto her face while she releases a small sigh as she starts to recall the memories. "We grew up together; he was always the shy boy—very sensitive—and hated growing up in his father's shadow."

"It couldn't have been easy. For either of you."

"When you're the child of a celebrity, you find that you will either enjoy the limelight or despise it. Will and I were on the opposite ends of that spectrum."

"Opposites attract."

"They did. As he grew up, that hatred turned to resentment. He became ruthless, especially in his studies; he was determined to make a name for himself away from his father. But despite everything, it truly felt like he was always enamoured by me; he was different around me; you know? Made me feel special," she stares blankly at the glass in her hand, "I really felt like we were supposed to be together, my theatrics balanced out his conservatism. I thought he loved me."

"He probably did, at some point. Maybe in this case, being in love wasn't enough; your differences in nature were just too different."

"Maybe, or maybe he was just a selfish prick who took it for granted and believed that I would always be there," we chuckle together; it's good to hear her laugh.

"You see the good in people, Catherine. I don't think I have ever heard you say a bad thing about anyone…well, except him."

"Yeah, maybe. I think I just liked the idea that I made him different; I brought out a side of him that he kept hidden, but it wasn't who he was, not really," she laughs a little, "but like you say, it wasn't enough."

"So how did it end…in the end, I mean? What made him walk away?"

"He didn't; it was me," she gives me a sly side eye and a smile as I raise my eyebrows in shock. "He gave me an ultimatum—my career or him. You can guess what I chose."

"You stood up for yourself."

"I did. I didn't think I had the strength to do it on my own, and he scared me a little, I admit, but I did it."

"He didn't take your defiance too well then?" She shoots me a confused look, and I gesture my eyes towards her wrist; the bruise is almost gone now but visible, poking out from underneath her sleeve.

"It got a little heated," she admits, once again pulling the sleeve back down over her hand.

"I'm proud of you, Catherine," she smiles as I continue. "Men like that; they rely on those around them never standing their ground; it's how they are able to manipulate so easily; how they stay in control. I have seen you be the most confident person in the room and then be turned into a shell of yourself by just a few words from him. You have no idea how hard it was to watch." I reach over to take her hand in mine. "Your life is now yours to reclaim; don't ever let someone else make you question yourself like that again."

"I won't. Thank you," she squeezes my hand back. "I think it was you actually, well partly you. You've always tried to empower me; your words always gave me strength."

"No, my love, this was all you. You have always been strong, Catherine; you just needed to be reminded, that's all."

We continued talking into the evening. As promised, I didn't try and force anything on her; I didn't try and talk about us or our future; we just talked about her past. She cried, and I tried my feeble attempt to make her laugh again. As the evening wore on and we had to get back, we shared a taxi, dropping her off at her hotel first before heading over to mine.

I am not going to pretend that tonight was easy: listening to her talk about her 'first love', the life they had; watching her get upset over the things he'd done; eventually I had to leave her at the end of the night; it was important for both of us, I think, that we redefine our boundaries—for now.

She needs time to get over this, and I had to witness that to really understand her properly. The experience has stripped us bare to the foundation of our relationship. From here, maybe we can start to grow.

Hello viewers, and welcome to Entertainment News. I am your host, Jane Collins. Tonight, on gossip rags and wow wow wow, more revelations are coming to light as we look into the home lives of Catherine Carell and William Carter.

After the bombshell interview with Jessica Williams on Monday, detailing her three-month-long affair with Carter—2 years ago, which threw into question many of Carter's initial accusations against Carell, two more women, Fiona Phillips and Victoria Miller, have also come forward with their stories. It seems this whole sordid story is further deeply rooted, as Miss Millar claims her one-month affair was…wait for it, 6 years ago!

Messages are flooding social media outlets in support of Carell, calling her the 'victim' of Carter's countless womanising ways. All while she came to terms with these difficult revelations, she was spotted Tuesday evening with co-star and friend Jackson Hunter at the Outlet bar in central London, where she appeared distraught and in tears, to which Hunter was seen offering his support, holding her hand, and coaxing her through these traumatic truths.

William Carter has, however, uncharacteristically remained silent on the matter. Paparazzi attempted to get a quote from him outside his office yesterday, but they were met with animosity from Carter, with one reporter actually being pushed to the ground by the businessman.

I do believe we are seeing Carter's true colours now, viewers, and on reflection, I am starting to wonder what else Catherine Carell had to deal with behind closed doors. Was Carter's original claim of an 'unreconcilable impasse', simply her defiance and breaking free into her reclaimed acting career?

We will keep you updated on Entertainment News.

Chapter 22

Jackson

The months that followed continued to be the most agonising of my life.

On one hand, the separation proved to be successful; Catherine's confidence in herself grew day by day, and I could visibly see it radiate off of her. By removing from our interactions the expectation of sexual contact and an increased undertone of want, we were able to build on our budding friendship. To genuinely, openly laugh and play alongside each other, on and off the set, has allowed our interactions to reach a new level of normalcy, more natural. Our intuitive banter and endless conversations proved entertaining to all those around us.

On the other hand, having her so close and yet having to keep her emotionally at arm's length proved to be a near impossible task, eating away at my sanity like a disease, consuming me from the inside out. What made it worse was the filming, in particular the one promised sex scene that plagued our tension and brought knots to my stomach. We had to recreate our most intimate interactions together, separated by flimsy pieces of fabric covering my junk and hers. We know all too well how our bodies respond to each other, and having to relive them over and over again without the solace of knowing she will be in my arms at the end of it was excruciating.

I have to keep reminding myself of my promise. The silent one I made for her, her needs override mine, and what she needs right now is a friend, a confidant, and support, and I *will* put her needs first, even if it does slowly kill me inside.

Catherine

I look out into the crowded garden to see so many smiles surrounding me. I hear the exciting chatter of all those around us, and for now, I can finally say I am genuinely one of them. My smile radiates off me as I look out into the sea of familiar faces, most of whom I have known my whole life. There are a few people missing, those who we lost due to their loyalty to our opposing side; those I am sad are gone from my life, but somehow, I wasn't surprised they opted to be with the one holding the most money, notwithstanding those who, of course, are related.

"Happy birthday, darling," my dad comes up behind me, kissing me on the cheek while he grips my shoulders. "Are you having a good time?" I turn to smile at him, grasping the glass of Amaretto in my hand.

"I am. Thank you Dad; you really do know how to throw a party."

"I really do, don't I?" He surveys out into the crowd, and I laugh.

"Big headed, much?"

"Why do you think I always have my parties in the garden?" he chuckles back as he gestures towards his head, increasing its size with his hands, and we giggle again. "It's good to see you laugh again, sweetheart," he adds, in all seriousness, and I smile lovingly at him.

"It's good to laugh."

"How are you settling into your new home?" My home. A place I purchased for my boys and me; a refuge. I moved in two weeks ago, and already it has fast become my safe place—a place I no longer have to hide in; nor a place I have to keep my actions or words in check. It is mine.

I lived with Mum, and Dad for around 5 months. Dad was right; I needed to take my time to heal. I needed to borrow their strength and pick myself up again to find my rhythm as a single mum.

"I love it; it's perfect. Thank you for helping me find it."

"I thought you would; I have good taste," I smile again at his boldness.

The divorce is nearly finalised. We had pretty good grounds to separate; neither of us argued about it. Well, he couldn't; it was plastered all over the news for weeks after the story spread of his countless infidelities. He didn't want to just hand over any of his money, and as it turns out, I didn't want it. I will find my own way into this world, and as I have no intention of taking his boys away from him and he has no intention of sacrificing more of his free time than necessary, split joint custody was quickly agreed.

His family, as suspected, has stopped talking to us, as have his 'groupies'. My father just says good riddance; 'that bad apple has come from a tree with bad roots,' he claims. I cannot help but feel a little sad; however, his mother was always very good to me. It was the fallout I feared, but now that I have lived through it, it really wasn't that terrifying to face after all.

"Happy birthday to…" I hear a chorusing out from behind me, prompting me to turn around to see my mother carrying a cake littered with sparkling candles and surrounded by a barrage of singing partygoers. I look around embarrassed with a smile on my face, and watch as the rest of the guests join in on the ruckus. After watching a few of the guests get shoved abruptly to the side, I see an Axel and a Callen appear through the parting sea of legs, huge smiling grins spread across their faces. I bend down onto my knees, so I am level in height with them, opening my arms out wide to bring them closer into my embrace.

My mother brings the cake in closer as the song comes to an end, putting it in front of me. After a quick glance at Axel and then at Callen, we each hold in a huge breath and blow in unison, so all the candles blow out at once. A roar of cheering and applause broke out across the garden, brightening my smile and reddening my cheeks. I feel my dad's lips touch the top of my head as he brings me closer to him.

"Happy birthday, sweetheart," he whispers as he lets go.

My heart fills with contentment and joy for all that surrounds me. These are the people that matter; these are the people I should have surrounded myself with for all those years.

There is still just one more person missing from my heart, and yet I am unable to find it in myself to fully embrace him. I am starting to question if my fear will prevent me from ever truly doing so.

Later that evening, I'm home. The children, after being thoroughly spoilt by their nanny and grandad and completely worn out, are now tucked up in bed. I have treated myself to a movie, one of my favourites, starring *him,* of course. I like watching him act on screen, secretly pretending he was with me.

As if just by thinking about him, he has been magically conjured up, my phone begins to ring, his name flashing up on the screen.

Reluctantly, I answered the video call.

"Happy birthday, sweet girl," his voice purrs into the phone as his face appears on the screen, immediately putting my nerves at ease and bringing a toothy smile to my face.

"You remembered," snuggling down further in the blanket as I tuck myself up into my cuddle chair.

"I couldn't forget; it's burned into my brain since the day you accidentally let it slip."

Jackson has really lived up to his word through these last 5–6 months. He promised to be a friend to me, and he has, arguably, my best friend. I have been able to pour my heart out to him time and time again, and on every occasion, he has treated me with warmth and understanding, giving me the support I needed in my worst moments. He kept me going, encouraged me to get up and out doing my regular activities, especially dragging my ass to the gym each morning because he *knew* it would keep me motivated, and even relaxed his own regiment in order to keep pace with mine. He has also brought a smile to my face at times I thought I couldn't, made me laugh when there was nothing to laugh at, and involved me in the most scandalous pranks on set to get me through the filming of the toughest scripts I have had to do thus far, but with a smile. He has not pushed me for anything more than this; has not even asked; he has remained the perfect gentleman.

Which is why this phone call has caught me off guard. Although he has been known to call or text occasionally, it isn't usually this late, but then it does make sense now. In one of my weaker moments, I let it slip that my dad was organising this party. I complained that he was making a bigger deal out of it than necessary because, quite honestly, I cannot remember the last time I properly celebrated it.

"Did you have a good time in the end?"

"I did," I am sure he could have heard the smile in my voice, even if he couldn't see it on my face in the subtle darkness of the room. "Dad really does know how to throw a garden party."

"Good, I'm glad. You still there?"

"Nope, I'm home, the boys are in bed, and I'm watching a movie."

"Oh, what movie did you watch?" I am silent for a beat, unsure whether it is wise to indulge in the truth. The silent pondering is obviously making him curious. "Catherine?" He questions with a hint of jest in his voice. "What *are* you watching?" I bite my lip like a little schoolgirl caught out in a lie.

"I *may* be watching '64 Ways'." I see him throw his head back and howl with laughter while I continue to smile into the phone.

"Having a *perv,* are we, Catherine?"

"No!" I feign shock, to which he continues his chuckle.

"Have you gotten to the bit where I am in the shower yet? That's the best bit!"

"Not yet," I giggled slightly.

"Fun fact, when I was filming that scene, it took the director over 16 shots to get it right; my cock just kept appearing in the shot, and he had to keep retaking!" With that, I start crying out in laughter, cackling like a witch. "It's true! Damn, near got hypothermia; I was under the water for so long."

"Ahh, the struggles of having a large dong!"

"Damn right! It's a bloody health hazard!" We both continue our laughter until it slowly dies off into a light chuckle.

He takes on a more nervous demeanour all of a sudden, fidgeting in his seat and unable to look at the screen. "Listen, Catherine, are you…umm…are you going to the premier next week, you know for 'Presents Past?'" I nod my head.

"Yeah, I thought you might, our agents probably told us the same thing, right? Go support our co-star, start promoting 'Jocelyn' while we're at it."

"Something like that," I smile at him; he doesn't return it. I can tell he is trying to say something he is uncomfortable about.

"I…um…was wondering if you wanted to go together?" My expression must have told a thousand truths as he started babbling on. "Just, you know, I hate going to these things by myself; it's very boring, and…you know, we'll make each other laugh; it'll keep us entertained, especially in the limo going in; I hate sitting in those things on my own."

"You know what the paps will think if we arrive together," I mutter, sinking further into the blanket to hide my face, almost ashamed of myself for even saying it. His face drops as he nods his head slightly in agreement.

"Yeah. Yeah, I know," he pauses, once again not looking at the camera. "Catherine, listen. You know how I feel about you; that hasn't changed." I see him rub his face with his free hand as he tries to articulate his words, breathing in a deep breath as he continues. "I know you have had a rough few months, and I completely understand if you're not ready yet, and I'm so sorry. It's just…I miss you. I miss being with you. I want us to start being us again, you know? And…and I want a future with you; I want to see where we end up with no one else standing in our way. I know I am being impatient; you know patience has never been my strong suit," he pauses again, hesitantly. "You know what?" he counters, "Forget I asked, I shouldn't have done, I'm being insensitive. I'll just, catch up with you when we're there…" a sudden rush of adrenaline takes over, and I speak before I have had a chance to contemplate the consequences of my words.

"I'll go with you," he stops to look at the screen directly at me, hope bringing to life those deep browns and raise his voice an octave higher.

"Really?"

"Yeah, I mean, what's the worst that can happen, right? We'll just create more gossip for the rags," he laughs again, hinting subtly at relief.

"Yep, it will that," We fall into a contemplative silence for a while, just staring at each other into the phone before I break it with…

"Oh, quick look," I point my phone towards the television. "It's the scene where your cock is trying to steal the limelight!" And with that, the tension is broken. We start laughing and joking into the night. Finally hanging up the phone at two in the morning, anxiety and excitement building in anticipation for the following week.

Everything is about to change.

Chapter 23

Catherine

It's the night of the premier, and this is it. Not only is it my first real appearance on the red carpet without that stupid ring on my finger proclaiming my attachment to a certain arsehole, but it is also my first appearance alongside Jackson. I am not sure how I feel—nerves most certainly, but whether they are for anticipation or anxiety, I am still uncertain.

I have opted for a long peach-coloured gown, decorated with sequins, a low-slung back, and strapped shoulders. The personal shopper I had helped me pick it out and declared it was the perfect assemble for the 'backward glance' pose on the red carpet, exactly what I need to show off my newfound confidence.

Staring at myself in the mirror, I see myself: the me I was long ago; the me I should have been and the me I will never lose again. Even if tonight isn't what we hope and things do not go any further with Jackson, I know I will be ok because this person staring back at me from the mirror's void is strong, with or without him.

My phone buzzes from its place on my bedside table, and Jackson's name appears on the screen.

Jackson: I'm downstairs; I'll wait for you in the lobby.

It's time. My audience awaits.

Jackson

Sitting on the sofa in the hotel lobby, leaning against the back of it, arms outstretched, I attempt to fake confidence; my leg bouncing up and down like a damn pony ride betrays my nerves however.

This is it. This is the night where we see if Catherine and I can make it, if we can push back against all the shit and the turbulent way our connection began. I have wanted her for so long that the thought of losing her now terrifies me. Every single thought I have is clouded by my selfish need to feel complete again, and if she decides she doesn't want me, I'm really not sure where I go from here.

The ping of the elevator grabs my attention. Glancing over, I see a group of people exiting it—a small family and an elderly couple—no Catherine. Blowing out my cheeks, I change positions, leaning forward with my arms resting on my knees and my spread-out legs looking down to the floor. So much rests on tonight, and the sheer gravity of that notion weighs heavily upon my shoulders. This is my future, the one I see with her and I, the boys. As much as that vision scares me, it is also comforting and brings a small smile to my face. It's the future I want, and it's so close I can almost grasp it. I just need tonight to go well. I need her to see the future I see.

"Hi handsome," I jump at the sudden intrusion into my thought bubble, staring up at the goddess in front of me, looking at me with a glint in her eye and the most beautiful smile on her lips. "Waiting for someone?" She asks coyly. I return her smile, unable to prevent its arrival; her presence fills my body with a warm comfort: I have no choice but to obey its reaction to her. The dress she has on shimmers and dances with the lights above, her hair falling around her face in curls, very similar to how we first met, but this time she isn't hiding behind them; instead her head is held high, displaying her beautiful face, which almost appears to be glowing, radiance beaming out of her like she was the sun itself, all directed for my eyes to gaze upon.

"Just the most gorgeous woman I have ever met," and just to relieve any tension between us from our time apart I add in—in banter of course, "You haven't seen her around anywhere, have you?" Her smile widens to accommodate a slight giggle.

There she is.

I stand up from my place to take a few paces to meet her; now taller, but even with those heels, she has to look up to meet my gaze, those blues now filled with the light of the chandeliers above, captivating my senses. I start to reach up to cup her face on instinct before catching myself, settling instead for a stroke down her arm, lightly tracing her skin with the back of my fingers, feeling the goosebumps start to form on her forearm under my touch. Her reaction to me is still so powerful that her body responds without the will of its host.

"You'll be the belle of the ball, Miss Carell," she doesn't respond; her hesitation has me doubting myself once again, so I try and push on. "Come, our carriage awaits," Gesturing out the double doors towards the street where the limo is waiting for us, I offer her my hooked arm for her to slide hers through.

As we reach the car, I open the door for her (like the gentleman, I am, of course) once inside, I race round to the other side, where our chauffeur has the other door open waiting for me. Sliding next to her, I make myself comfortable in the back seat, a feat that proved near impossible when I look over at Catherine. With her now sitting, I can see her dress has a slit working all the way up the length of her leg, stopping just short of her hips. Forcing down the stone in my throat, I chase away all thoughts currently heading directly south to my groin, *'get a hold of yourself!'*

I am pulled from my spiral of unruly thoughts by Catherine's sweet voice, breaking the building sexual tension between us.

"Now, Jackson, you have to fill a very important role for me tonight!"

"Oh yeah?" My voice cracks a little; I cough to cover it. She held up the offending thigh, showing me her beautifully toned legs and high stiletto shoes.

"*You* have to make sure I don't stake it in these heels! *It's not* a good look going down the red carpet, you know," We both start chuckling, and once again, the air is levitated, for now. It seems our friendship is the only real solid foundation we have right now; any suggestion of anything more brings a heavy awkwardness to our interactions; this immeasurable unknown still hung tenuously unbalanced above us, with neither of us willing to define who we are. What does tonight really mean? What happens tomorrow? Choosing the easiest path, we continue our banter, laughing away at the back of the limo.

It doesn't seem long before I notice we are approaching the venue, as indicated not by the change in scenery, but by the change in Catherine's behaviour. She makes fewer witty comebacks to my relentless barrage of jokes; with the long pauses in between filled with silence, her gaze becomes more distant and glazed over, almost in fear. I also notice her fingers begin the fidget, playing with an imaginary ring that used to take precedence on her left hand, a nervous twitch I notice, one she is not quite out of indulging in despite the vacant spot now taking its place.

I stopped with the jesting; it no longer seems appropriate. I don't blame her for becoming restless; it is her first official public appearance since their separation, and she has chosen to spend it with me.

"You, ok?" I ask, knowing full well she isn't.

"Umm hum," she hums her reply, choosing to keep her focus past my head, looking out the tinted window, already seeing the immense crowd that has gathered outside in the lead-up to the venue.

I am tempted to give her an out, tell her I'll get out first, and let the limo drive around the block so it'll look like we came separately, but this selfish need in me tells me not to. I am so close to having her the way I want, here with me and on my arm, that I don't want to give her an excuse to back away.

"You ready?" Her doe-like eyes shot straight to mine, fear dominating her actions. I take her hand in mine, pulling it away from that damn incessant playing of her left hand. "I won't let you fall, Catherine. I promise," I utter. With glee in my heart, I see the fear dissipate from her features, overtaken with a defiant look of determination, strength and trust.

With a small nod to her head, I let go of her hand briefly to exit the car, only to be greeted by an onslaught of flashing lights. *'Here we go.'*

"Good evening viewers, and welcome back to Entertainment Tonight, live at the premiere of 'Presents Past', I am Samantha Darsky."

"And I am Drew Murphy. We have already seen a large array of stars gracing the red carpet tonight. 'Presents Past's' lead, Grace Loran, has already giving us a few words before the break. If you missed it, don't worry; there will be updates on the website, and we will be summing up the events of the evening tomorrow night on Entertainment News with Jane Collins."

"Oh Drew, look, we have another limo approaching the carpet. I wonder who will be taking the long walk next. Oh, oh, it's Jackson Hunter! Glancing out towards the crowds and giving them his trademark smile, that man can work a crowd with one look, right Drew?"

"That's right, Sam. There is a reason he is the most sought-after actor in Hollywood right now. But Sam, what's this? He's bending back down towards the limo door. Has he brought a date with him this evening?"

"It looks like it, Drew; we were just saying it the other week, were we not? We have not seen Hunter with a woman in nearly 3 years; that's almost unheard of!"

"That is true. I wonder who the lucky lady is tonight."

"Oh, oh, Drew, it's Catherine Carell! I can't believe it! She has been in hiding since the revelations over her now ex-husband earlier this year; could it be these two could actually be a pair?"

"I don't know Sam; I mean, you cannot deny the chemistry these two have shown on and off the screen, and with the critically acclaimed 'Jocelyn' due to be released this coming spring featuring the pair, you never know what went on behind the scenes."

"Ohh, look at them, Drew; look at the way Hunter has backed away from her to give her the sole limelight for the cameras; if that's not adoration, I don't know what is."

"Let's see if we can get an insider scoop. Jackson, Jackson! Quick interview for Entertainment Tonight."

"Oh hi, I remember you. How are you guys doing?"

"We are well thanking you, Jackson, so Drew and I were wondering, what is going on with you and Catherine?"

"Haha, oh you are a gossip! Naughty! No, we're here as friends; we were talking the other day and figured it was pointless going by ourselves, so here we are."

"So no behind-the-scenes romance on the set of Jocelyn; the fans will be disappointed."

"Haha, sorry guys, nothing to report here. Don't get me wrong, we are close, she keeps me out of trouble, mostly."

"Who keeps who out of trouble?"

"Oh, hi Catherine, we were just trying to get the inside scoop with you and Jackson here."

"Ha, what scoop? I am officially his chaperone; this one here is no longer allowed to attend public events—or anywhere actually, unescorted; he gets into far too much trouble!"

"Oh, says you little Miss, 'don't let me fall in these heels!' You're clearly the disaster on legs here, not me."

"Excuse me, what did you say?"

"Ahh, haha, Catherine, stop tickling! Haha, ok, ok, you're not a disaster…Just a train wreck! Ahh Catherine!"

"Haha, seems like you two are close."

"Haha, yes, in all honesty, this guy has been my rock this last half a year. I'm not sure what I would have done without him. He really did pick me up when I was down. I am lucky to have had him in my life."

"You were only down because you fell over from those damn shoes you wear!"

"Jackson! I was trying to be nice! Well now, you should get back to your job tonight then! Making sure I stay upright!"

"Yes mam."

"Jackson Hunter and Catherine Carell are walking off in linked arms, proving to be inseparable there; they must be quite a fun pair to work with. What do you think, Sam?"

"Well, I know I'd want to work with them; not sure how much work would actually get done though!"

"Haha, you're right there, Sam."

"More updates on tonight's premiere, after these messages."

Catherine

Walking into the theatre's main lobby with my arm linked through Jacksons, I am suddenly hit by another wave of awareness; all eyes suddenly become focused on us. Some (the more polite amongst the sea of notable faces) turn back around almost as soon as they see us. Other eyes lingered, their disdained stares openly scouring our bodies from head to toe, then back up again, trying to figure out tomorrow's tabloid heading.

Jackson's tilts his head down, so his lips are pursed close to my ear to whisper.

"We'll circle the room separately, hay? Meet back up before we go in?" I simply nod my head in response, slipping my hand out of the grip on his arm tentatively and heading off in the opposite direction.

This was right, right? We are two separate people, friends, who happen to arrive together; that's what we are and what we look like, right?

So why do I keep seeking him out? Stretching my neck out over the crowds just to gain his whereabouts, only for sheer necessity to know where he is at any given time. Every so often, I catch him doing the same, and every time our eyes lock, he winks, broadening his smile, which pulls from me a blush every time, accompanied by my own flirtatious smile in response.

212

I cannot deny it anymore, can I? I am drawn to him just as much as he is drawn to me. Now that I am here with him, I don't want to be apart. It's time to admit the truth. I have had my distance, away from us, to find out what I really want, given him the same reprieve to recount his own feelings, and look at us in the same room, not 10 seconds walk from each other, yet we cannot stop looking for each other to ensure the other is still within reach. As cliché as it sounds, like two ends of a bloody magnet, no matter how many times you pull us apart, we will always be drawn back in.

The final calls were made to enter the theatre. A subtle panic sets in as I begin scanning the room when I am unable to locate Jackson within the first 5 seconds of doing so. That is, until I hear the soft but deep reverberating tone of his voice and feel the brush of his cheek as his face appears next to me from behind.

"Looking for me, sweet girl?" My smile must be beaming from side to side from the calming waves of pleasure his presence brings to me.

"Well," I tease. "I need my walking aid, don't I? It wouldn't look great if I stumbled into the theatre now, would it?" he softly chuckles, moving himself to my side and offering his arm.

"Your escort awaits," I take it, giving him my smile while he returns his. Butterflies and fairies and whatever other fuck know what mythical creatures perform their dance in the pits of my stomach. Placing my free hand on my abdomen to still them, I realise that this is what it is supposed to feel like when you're with someone you like. *This.*

Entering the theatre, he guides us to our seats, helping me to manoeuvre my dress to sit down before taking his own chair. The movie starts with the lights going out, the sound of the film drowns out all the other voices. I find I cannot focus on the film; however, I just keep glancing over at him, relishing in the random thoughts of him, of how perfect he is, and how he could be mine now if only I had the resolve to take it. *'Take it, Catherine; take him.'*

My selfishness takes control. Looking down at his hand resting on the arm of the seat, I know what I need to do. Sliding my hand down his arm, I placed mine on top of his, interlinking our fingers and squeezing his hand tightly.

In what appears to be an automatic reaction, he squeezes back while tearing his face away from the screen to first look at our intertwined hands in apparent shock, then up to my face, his mouth now morphing into that smile that I love, broadening his chiselled features once more. Taking my hand with his, he raises it to his mouth, planting the sweetest of kisses on the back of it before resting them both back on the armrest.

Throughout the duration of the movie, I feel his thumb encircle and dance across the back of my hand, not once letting go, not really wanting him to let me go either. For me, this gentle affection—to want to touch with simple gestures—is all new territory. Although, with William, I did once think of myself in love, he was never one to show public affection; his exterior was always a reflection of the person he was, stubborn and hard, in complete control over his composure. I didn't realise till now how much I would enjoy this—to need and want someone to show me outwardly just how much they care for me, even in these small, simple acts.

I suppose it's true what they say, you don't really know what you are missing out on until you have it, and the goosebumps now rising up along the length of my arm tell me my body knows exactly what it's been missing; it's precisely the way Jackson makes me feel, and I never want to miss it again.

The movie is over way too soon. In the brief moment, I am forced to break our bond in order to stand, I am suddenly whisked away by the current of people, out of my seat, and towards the doors, leaving Jackson far behind me, seemingly lost amongst the waves of chatter and excitement.

Within minutes, we are in the lobby, ambushed by the array of guests and surrounded by people I am familiar with, mainly from my father's inner circle, all talking to me at once, asking me questions, and introducing me to people I 'really must meet'. I have lost count of how many times I have been stopped to pose for photos with various celebrity faces, getting carried away with the bustle of the lobby.

It is a while before I am able to take a breath, excusing myself from the current group that has had me occupied, made up entirely of men I might add, who have managed to commandeer my time for the last half an hour regaling tales of their latest endeavours in the form of—what I am sure they thought—were witty anecdotes. I quickly found an empty table in order to re-convene with my thoughts. I am not by myself for long, however, before a soft-spoken voice pulses through to my core and a short glass filled with an amber liquid is placed in front of me.

"Popular tonight?" He purrs. Looking up, I am greeted by the perfect smile of the only person in the room I actually want to see.

"Yes, it seems I am."

"It's what happens when you're set to be the next must-have name in a film, not to mention being newly single. Every paparazzi wants a piece, every young socialite wants to be seen, and every man wants a chance; all with you."

"Is that all they want?"

"Usually."

"What about you?"

"Yeah, me to," I laugh lightly, taking a sip of the drink in front of me nervously, allowing the sweet taste to swirl about in my mouth before drinking it down, enjoying the feel of it as it sinks down my throat, and releasing a moan in appreciation as it does.

"Umm, just what I wanted; how did you know?" I tease with a knowing curve to my lips.

"Let's call it intuition. It looked like you needed something strong after dealing with those bunch of wankers." I chuckled again into my glass as I take another sip.

"Oh, they weren't so bad."

"Wankers, every last one of them; I don't think they could have made it more obvious."

"What's obvious?"

"They were all trying it on with you."

"A little green, were you?"

"Maybe," I laugh, downing down the rest of my drink while I stare out into the crowd, gearing myself up to embrace the madness of it once again all before I hear him ask.

"So?" Pausing as though he is hesitant as to what he wants to say next. "It's not so bad, right?" I turn to look at him, but he too is looking out towards the crowd.

"What's not?"

"Stepping out with me, being seen with me—it's not so bad, right?" I laugh, a little louder this time, which prompts him to look back at me, returning my smile.

"No, no it's not so bad." I look away briefly in a mocking act of indifference. "Could be better," I add a slight sense of humour to my tone. It could be courage, impatience, alcohol, or maybe all of the above that prompted my sudden boldness, but as soon as it came out of my mouth, I had no choice but to follow through with my thought.

"Oh?" He replies with the same hint of playfulness. "Do tell me, what can I do to make it better for you, my lady?"

"You could kiss me?" It is daring, but I am convinced now that I know what I want, and I am not prepared to risk losing him for the sake of my indecisions. I can see he was momentarily taken aback; clearly, he was not expecting me to be so blunt with my request, but this was quickly replaced by one of his trademark smirks as he leans down, his face mere centimetres from mine.

"Are you sure this is what you want, my sweet girl?"

"I want you, Jackson," I breathe heavily as my body starts to tremble in response to his closeness, anticipation from his lips that I have missed the company of all this time.

"Then you don't need to tell me twice." Our mouths make contact—an almost tentative touch. His hand finds my cheek, coming to rest between my jawline and my neck, while his other comes to sit on my hip pulling them closer to his own. My hands find their home on his chest, drawing him in closer, turning our kiss into a passionate return home into each other's arms.

From beside us, I hear clicks and flashes of light that briefly illuminate around us, bringing us back into the proximity of the room. Our faces, however, remain only slightly apart.

"It looks like there is no hiding it now, sweet girl," he mutters into my mouth, so only I can hear.

"I don't want to hide anymore," I mutter back, earning me his smile reminiscent of that cat that got the cream, planting another quick kiss on my lips before bringing his face back level with mine.

"God, Catherine, do you have any idea how relieved I feel right now?" He takes a moment to take a shaky breath to pull himself back, choosing to keep his one hand on the side of my face while he rests his forehead against mine. "Can we go now, please?" he adds resulting in the relief of tension through my laughter.

"It will be a bit rude if we leave so early."

"I don't care; I am selfish, and I don't want to share; I just want you all to myself," I chuckle again at his absurdity.

"We can leave later; you know better than I do the social expectations of a celebrity, especially an A-lister like you; you have your reputation to think about," With a huge grin on his face and his other hand now on my forearm, he continues his pleading.

"I don't give two fucks about my reputation right now; all I want is you."

"And we will, I promise." Reaching up to return his affections with a kiss, quickly turning from a peck into a brief dance of our tongues. Smiling against my mouth, he relents.

"Well, when you put it that way, I can wait…not too long though," he warns. "I am not sure my heart can survive being without you for that much longer, nor my cock for that matter." Taking his hand in one hand and my bag in the other, we head out into the eye of the storm, determined not to get separated again.

Jackson

Nothing can take this smile away from me now; it is glued to my face as permanently as if it had been drawn on with a marker. She is here with me, holding my hand, accepting my affections, and welcoming my kiss that I cannot help but offer every few minutes, my lips still in disbelief that they are permitted to capture hers so freely that they must continue to regularly check that this is still the case.

However, as I have mentioned before, I am not a very patient man, and never more so than now, ticking down the time before I can have her to myself. Each over-exaggerated false greeting from yet another irritating guest, who I barely know, making it glaringly obvious all they want is a piece of us, each wanting to take their moment with the next 'big story', get the inside gossip before it hits paper tomorrow. If I see one more person gesture to our hands followed by a 'so how long has this been going on, then?' It may become the last thing they say to me. I am eager to move on from these shambles before that notion even has a chance to take hold.

Catherine is to my right, still holding my hand, currently talking to a woman (she did introduce me, but I took no notice) in quite an overly extravagant manor, her pitch rising a few octaves higher than usual and at a speed faster than I have ever known it. The high-speed gossip is intermittently interrupted every few moments with a giggle or a gasp. I am not listening to the conversation, however; I am happy she is excited, but my patience is well and truly out, and my focus is now on how and when we are to get out of here and how quickly.

Confident in her mannerisms that she must know this person, I am encouraged to take our interactions a little further. I let go of her hand briefly to place it in my other one, then wrapped them both around her waist, hugging her close to me from behind. I rest the palms of my hands flat out on top of hers just above her pelvis, then gently rest my head on her shoulder, kissing it for a tad longer than I should so I can take the moment to breathe in deep her intoxicating smell, before looking up at her companion and smiling, mouthing 'sorry', to her. Definitely not sorry, however, as she responds to this new position by pushing her arse backwards into my hips, emanating from me a low growl as my cock starts to twitch.

"Can we go now? I think I have been a good boy and shared you long enough," I moan into her ear, pouting against her shoulder as she turns in an attempt to look at me. She giggles, using the moment to once again gently push into my groin. Raising one hand up to place it on the side of my face as it rests on her shoulder, she replies with that irresistible smile on her beautiful face.

"Come on, then," With no hesitation, I say a quick goodbye to her friend, then start dragging her away from the party towards the exit, all with her giggling hysterically behind me.

Once we are away from the crowds but not quite to the door where the bouncers are waiting, I stop, then turn to face her, taking her by the hands to pin her against the wall. Absorbed still in laughter, my own smile is a mirror of hers.

"I don't see how this is funny. My balls have been slowly turning an odd shade of blue for the last few hours," I mock, silencing her laughter momentarily with a kiss, although it is only brief as the childish giggles continue as soon as my lips leave hers.

"Umm, I can't even fathom what could be causing that. Maybe we should stop by…"

"Nope, no stopping anywhere else but the hotel. I need you, like…an hour ago." And as if to extenuate my point, I take her hand again, moving closer towards the doors, hearing her snigger again next to me.

It's then that I notice, from the corner of my eye in the distance, the flashing of cameras and the soft hum of voices outside. I stop hesitantly, as I am suddenly hit with the realisation of where we are and *who* we are. She seems to be stumped by the same realisation as the giggling has now come to a stop: she looks out beside me. Gulping, I prepare for the worst as I turn to her.

"Listen, Catherine, the paps out there; you can guarantee they already know what has happened in here. They are all going to want a piece," she nods. "We shouldn't say anything; we just need to quickly make our way back across the walkway to the waiting limo. We can wait until an organised interview to say what we need to do, where it won't be so chaotic. Agreed?" She nods again, gripping my hand tighter as we brace ourselves to take on the onslaught of cameras and microphones.

Our first test starts now.

"And we are back. Welcome back viewers, I am Samantha Darsky."

"And I am Drew Murphy, and we are still outside, lining the red carpet, interviewing celebs on what they thought of the premiere of 'Presents Past.' So far, some good reviews, Samantha."

"Some very good reviews; the feedback so far tells us this will be the film to watch this winter, with lots of nods to the upcoming 'Jocelyn' due to be released next year."

"Speaking of 'Jocelyn', Samantha, I can see the two stars about to exit the theatre, and they are indeed hand in hand!"

"For those of you who are just tuning in, photos have been leaked in the last hour of Jackson Hunter and Catherine Carell kissing at the after party tonight! Romance seems to be blossoming between the pair, as some have reported they have been inseparable all evening, holding hands and embracing for most of the night. So do you think they were lying to us earlier, Drew?"

"Is Catherine Carell even capable of lying? Haha. She seems like too much of a sweetheart to lie, but I can imagine they were not telling us the whole story about how close they have actually become these last few months…wait here they come…Catherine! Catherine! Jackson Hunter! Give us a scoop! What's happening between you?"

"Nope, there they go. One last wave before entering their ride. I don't think they were ready to talk to anyone today, Drew."

"No, I don't think so either, but don't worry, viewers, we will reach out to the pair this week and hopefully bring you an update on the blossoming romance soon."

Chapter 24

<u>Jackson</u>

I slide into the back of the limo shortly after Catherine, leaving behind the deafening sound of clicking and the incessant calling of our names.

"The Crescent Moon Hotel, please; one stop," I call to the driver just as he activated the mechanism to close the privacy window dividing us.

"What about you? Are you not heading back to your hotel?" She asks in mock modesty.

"Let me make this perfectly clear to you, *Miss* Carell, I have *no* intention of leaving you tonight, but it will be far more, shall we say flattering? For me to be leaving yours in the morning in tonight's clothes as it would be for you to be leaving mine in that perfect little number," her smile extends to the far corners of her mouth as she leans in closer.

"Oh! So, you think you're getting lucky tonight then, huh?" She can't help the small, tipsy giggle that escapes her lips as she tries to remain composed.

"Oh, sweet girl, I am already the luckiest man at the premiere tonight; it is *you* who will be getting lucky!" And with that, I push her back slowly so she is lying flat, stretched out across the limo seats, capturing her lips as she goes, and following her down so my body all but covers hers. As her leg bends up to rest on the side of my torso, my hand begins its accent from her heel, gliding its way up a path to her shin and then to her thigh. My heart rate quickens at the feel of her smooth, bare skin under the palm of my hand, getting more excited the higher it reaches.

That is, until I reach the top, where her legs merge perfectly into the broad shape of her hips, my heart all but stops while it struggles to comprehend exactly *what* I am touching—or to be more accurate, what I am *not* touching!

Breaking the lock of our mouths, I hear myself audibly gasp. With my eyes remaining closed in a vein struggled to compose myself. I rested my head on her forehead, too heavy to lift it any further.

"Catherine?" I ask through gritted teeth, and the heaviness of my breath.

"Umm hum," she hums, visibly amused at my reaction, sucking in her lips between her teeth clearly a tactic to stifle a giggle.

"Where is your underwear?" Her attempts to hold back her laughter are fruitless as she releases her pent-up, high-pitched cackle at my expense.

"Well, they were there earlier; wherever could they have gone?" The hint of playfulness evident in her tone was added to, only by her continued giggling. I breathe out a shaky breath and open my eyes to look into her blues; green flashes across mine as notions of both jealousy and arousal flood my body, while I try and rearrange the thoughts surging haphazardly through my mind that I cannot seem to align correctly.

"Are you telling me we were in a room with all those people, with all those *men* hitting on you and you having no panties on?" She giggles again beneath me; clearly, she is thoroughly enjoying my reaction. "You, sweet girl, are very naughty," I lean down once more, aiming this time for her neck, which she obliges me by straining her head to the side, giving me better access. I gently place a kiss there, adding a little suction as I do to the sensitive spot below her ear. "How shall I punish you, sweet girl?" She lets out a loud moan as I continue my onslaught, while inching my hand from its place on her hip to somewhere slightly more central.

Changing tactics, I started gently tracing my fingers along the skin surrounding her sex, around her pelvis, and her upper thigh, dragging my fingers lightly over her pubic hair. She lets out another loud moan as she starts to squirm beneath me, attempting to force my fingers into the space where she desires them.

"Jackson," she pleads, her hands finding their place behind my head, intertwining them between the strands of hair.

"What do you want, sweet girl?" I tease.

"I want you…" she pulls my head up by my hair from its space in her neck, just enough so she can lock her lips with mine. Her breath is thick with lust against mine as I continue to dance the tips of my fingers across her skin. "Please!" The demand escapes her mouth as a heavy plea.

"What do you want me to do, sweet girl?" I tease again, enjoying the responses her body is giving, reacting to my touch, and seeing her face awash with arousal beneath me.

"Touch me, Jackson. I want you…" she doesn't need to say anymore. She gasps as I penetrate the walls of her sex, plunging into her first before pulling back, skimming over the folds, finding her delicate bud at its core, and expertly playing and encircling it. Intermittently, I move between her clit and her entrance, and each time I penetrate, I search for that hidden spot that I know will make her groan into my shoulder.

I watch, entranced, as her hips start moving in rhythm to my fingers. Her moans quickly grow louder as her body's pleasure intensifies. She is close; I can see and feel it. Every time I enter her, I feel the walls tighten and clench around my fingers. I lean in close to her ear again, placing a subtle kiss on her neck before whispering.

"Come for me, Catherine," it appears that was all she needed. Her back arches slightly, and her body tenses as she turns into me, her hand finding the back of my head, grasping at my hair as she holds on, riding through the ecstasy coursing through her.

I hold her steady in my arms while her breathing returns to normal. Her legs continue to fidget next to mine as they do. I don't mind, however, my thoughts are still firmly focused on the fact that she is here, with me…and she is now mine for me to pleasure as she wishes; that this will now be our life, no longer fretting over when the next time will be, when we can meet again, no more hiding. We are us. Finally.

Eventually she opens her eyes, finding mine quickly in the dim lighting of the limo.

"I think I need to be naughty more often if that is my punishment!" she offers it with a smirk.

"Oh, I wholeheartedly agree; the naughtier the better, I think, is the safest bet," I lean down, pouring my whole heart into a kiss she accepts without hesitation, opening up to me so our tongues can meet.

With my guard lowered, she easily has us flipped in a flash, with me on my back while she straddles my waist. Rocking her hips with her bare crotch rubbing incessantly against my cock through my trousers, it does not take long before he is standing to attention, and I am forced to hold her hips in place to stop her from turning me on further.

"Why have you stopped me?" She pouts, stroking the palms of her hands up and down my chest.

"My love, as much as I love this, I believe we are almost at the hotel. So, before we take this any further here, I think it best we wait until we are alone…maybe?" She looks out the window, and the fact that she immediately begins to move off me, indicates that I am right.

By the time I have adjusted my clothes and her gown, hair, and makeup, the limo has pulled to a stop. Within seconds of that, the door closest to her and on the side of the hotel opens, with the chauffeur on the other side peering in with that all-knowing look.

"Madam!" Offering his hand to help her out, while I closely follow from behind. "Have a good evening," I was digging out a couple of notes from my pocket and handing them to him. Jogging slightly to catch up alongside Catherine, I then place my hand protectively on her hip as I guide her across the lobby of the hotel at a quickened pace, letting every goddamn asshole in here know that she is mine.

"In a hurry, are we, Jackson?" she sniggers as we approach the elevators.

"You have no idea," I utter under my breath. She giggles again. I cannot help but join in on her laughter. She looks up at me with this adoration in her eyes mixed with a subtle hint of mischief. She is comfortable showing me her true playful self, unafraid. She is finally ready. "Oh Catherine," I add on. "The things I am going to do to you tonight!"

Giggling again, together, we enter the lift.

Catherine

Entering the lift with Jackson by my side, a ball of almost painful excitement and anticipation builds in the depths of my stomach; his words are like arrows aimed directly at my arousal, emanating heat within its depths with every bullseye.

"Floor?" he asks, finger poised, hoovering over the buttons.

"Four," It is agony waiting for the doors to close, knowing we are the only two currently occupying the lift. I look over at Jackson; he is fidgeting slightly, seemingly unnoticeable to anybody but me. Anticipating his reaction, I fully expect to be pounced on as soon as those damn doors decide to close.

The recognisable 'ding' rings through as the doors finally make their descent to close. Without a second's hesitation, Jackson turns and is on me, lips finding my neck almost immediately pinning me against the brass bar surrounding the walls, hands fixed firmly on my hips.

My hands are frantic in their search to find a home: running up and down his back; his arms; up into his hair; and back down to rest upon his chest. Jackson's hands reached down under my arse, giving my cheeks a squeeze, indicating his intention. I know their calling. I jump slightly, my legs land around his waist, my thighs rest on his hips, my arms are slung around his neck, and his hands find their spot holding me in place under my arse, using the railing as leverage. He brings his head up to make eye contact with mine; this however; does not last a second as our lust takes control, our lips locked in their frenzied attack on our tongues.

"God Catherine," he makes out in between the rapid movements between us.

Another 'ding' and the elevator doors fly open. We stopped momentarily to take in the scene before us, unsure if there would be someone there or not. As it turns out, the doors have opened on the right floor with no one around, so we make our exit, still locked in Jackson's hold.

"Number?"

"119, Jackson, put me down; you can't carry me like this the whole way!" I cry out, giggling, while I attempt to wiggle my way out of his arms. He stops mid-step and looks up at me with a cheeky glint in his eye.

"Is that a challenge?"

"No! Jackson seriously put me down; I must weigh a tone."

"Don't be ridiculous. What do you think these..." gesturing with his eyes towards his chest, "...are just for show?" he continues his stride again, beginning to kiss my shoulder as he does. "I'll be damned if I cannot carry a lightweight such as yourself down one corridor. Plus, it's my duty now; I am officially your boyfriend; I have to look after you; and I cannot risk you injuring yourself in those damn heels now, can I?" I hug his head into my breasts as I laugh at his remarks. A slight panic, however, crosses my heart and stiffens my composure at the mere mention of the word 'boyfriend'. *'Am I really doing this?'* The spark of doubt begins to embed itself in my psyche.

Jackson must have either sensed my change in composure, had incredible intuition, or maybe a little of both as he stopped again in his tracks, turning, and pinning me up against the wall. With the wall now as leverage, he has free rein of one of his hands, which he uses to come up and cup my face in reassurance, looking directly into my eyes.

"I *am* your boyfriend now, Catherine. I am *yours,* and you…you are mine," he takes my lips again to punctuate his words. "But, sweet girl, that doesn't mean what you think it does." Brushing his nose with mine. "I'm not going to control you, and I am certainly not going to hurt you. *I love you!* That hasn't changed. I just want to support you and cherish you, because, sweet girl, you so deserve to be cherished," I start playing with the hair at the back of his head nervously. I hate that I am ruining this perfect moment, but that one insecurity plays out in my mind over and over, gaining in size and momentum like a runaway snowball, and I just can't control myself.

"Until you get bored," I whisper. As if his frustration gets the better of him, he thrusts his hips forward into mine while using his thumb to rub against my cheek.

"Never."

"You say that now, but you haven't seen my other life, filled with school runs and homework's and…"

"I want it all. Catherine, I want all of it. Your children, your family; they are the biggest part of who you are, and when I say I want you, I mean all of you, not just these little snippets," he kisses me again; I can see I have upset him, and I can see he is trying.

"I want the boring. The whole time we were apart, that was all I could think about. What it would be like to come home to a warm house, to you, the boys, to just sit in and watch a film or go over the park on a cold day," he pauses again, tilting his head so that our eyes meet again.

"I am not saying I won't fuck up Catherine, 'cause fuck knows if I know what I am doing or how to be that person," I chuckle slightly, and with a sly smirk, he is encouraged further.

"And those mistakes are going to frustrate you, and you'll call me an idiot, and I'll call you stubborn," I laugh a little louder. "And you'll kick me out for being just as bad as the children," A full smile has come back to his face as we both laugh this time, a half-hearted chuckle at his expense. In a moment of seriousness, he adds, "I am not *him,* Catherine; I will never hurt you," he suddenly puts on a more exaggerated, mock-offended tone, "And quite frankly, I feel a little insulted that you have lumped me in the same jerk pile as that piece of shit just because we share the same type of anatomy; I mean, sounds a little sexist to me…" I slapped him slightly across the chest while attempting to pull off annoyed, all the while still chuckling at his babbling nonsense.

He seems pleased with himself, pleased that he has once again brought me back out of my spiral of self-pity.

"But I do want this, Catherine, and you may not believe me now, but I will prove it to you one of these days, I promise you."

With that, we are back in the realm of happiness. I kiss him, quickly intensifying the spark running between us and taking us back to where we were a few minutes before; only now it is calmer, less frantic. He uses his hips to grind into my pelvis, rubbing up against my bare crotch.

"Shit, Catherine, where's your room?" I peer down the corridor, spotting room 119 around 5 doors down.

"There," I start faffing with the zip on my bag dangling from my shoulder, attempting to dig out the keycard in there while Jackson manoeuvres us to the correct door.

Finding the card and passing it to Jackson, he easily slots it in, pushing his way into the room and slamming the door behind him. Once inside, he once again has me pinned up against the wall, mouths slamming into each other, kissing passionately.

We are alone now. I waste no time relieving him of his jacket that he effortlessly let's fall to the floor; his open-topped shirt makes it easy for me to find his buttons; undoing each one, however, turns out to be ridiculously frustrating.

Once undone and I have pushed it off his shoulders to join the jacket on the floor, I cannot help but pull back to marvel at the scene in front of me. Mouth agape, I stare down at his captivating body, his tattoo, and the grooves and ridges of his chest that my fingers lightly trace over, absorbing the intense attraction I have for him.

"How are you mine?" I whisper, still enthralled by the sight before me. He chuckles lightly at my expense; it is thick with the lust streaming from every inch of his toned body.

"All yours, sweet girl," his hand glides its way through my hair, resting at the back of my head. "I've been yours since the moment we met." My eyes shoot up to meet his, and by their sincerity, I know he is telling the truth.

Two years. Over two years, he has waited for me, never really his, and yet he has waited.

Seeing the panic once again sprinting across my eyes, he wastes no time distracting me, spinning me around in the direction of the bed and chucking me down on top of it. The springs cause me to bounce a little, and I use the momentum to shift myself further up onto the bed, spreading my legs as I wait for Jackson to follow.

He wastes no time removing his trousers before joining me, flinging himself onto the bed. The velocity of the impact once again causes me to bounce a little, and coupled with his cheeky grin he produces as he adjusts himself on the bed to meet me, I can't help but giggle again.

Maybe it's the alcohol, or maybe it's the pouring adoration I have for him that has turned me into a giddy school girl, fooling around with her Jock-like boyfriend, but any and all negative thoughts that are playing about in my mind that seem to sprint to the surface at the first chance they get, are replaced quickly with just this feeling I have with him being here. I never want to let this feeling go again: to let him go.

He finds his place between my legs; lifting one into the air, he seductively removes my shoes, one and then the other. Starting on my toes, he places feather-like kisses trailing a path up my leg. My laughter is soon replaced by a deep groan as he edges closer to my sex, bare and waiting for him, still buzzing from the onslaught of his hands just a little earlier on.

Dancing the tips of his fingers up and down my leg, he brings his head up to nestle in the crook of my neck.

"We need to remove some more of these clothes, sweet girl," I twist my body, moving my leg away from his tender teasing, bringing it up so it rests alongside his torso, then lifting my arm up around his head so my fingers can tease at that irresistible length of hair I find there, dragging his face down to meet mine and for our lips to find their mate.

The movement has been left bare my side, where the zip to the dress is located. Jackson understands this, and while I use my other hand underneath me to hold the dress in place, he uses his to pull down the zipper, gasping as my breasts are released from the hold the dress had on them, only for it to be replaced by his hand, grasping and massaging them. Instinctively, I lean into his touch, pushing my breasts further into his hands.

The hand that was behind his head I edged lower, running it down the length of his chest and stomach, not missing a single on one of those grooves, until they found the elastic of his pants. Impatiently pushing at them, tearing them away from his flesh and uncovering that well-sculpted arse I can't help but seize with

227

my hand, all the while he uses his hand and then legs to remove his pants completely.

With the rapid removal of our clothes, our breathing has now become laboured and heavy, both of us wanting this—correction, *needing* this! I need to feel him inside me. I have missed the way he feels, how he penetrates my core, and the way he fills me; completing me.

Eager to fulfil my body's desire, I push him back with the full weight of my strength, which he does not resist. Straddling his pelvis, I bring down my own to complete the V-shaped puzzle. Resting my hands on his chest, I grind down on him. Our interlocking pieces together create a deep guttural sound to emanate from his chest that I can feel vibrating against the palms of my hands.

"Catherine," he growls, hands on my hips to help guide my incessant movements. I don't need any instructions from here; I know what he wants. I lift myself onto my knees, raising my pelvis up to give me space so I can reach around to take hold of his fully erect cock, lining it up with my entrance, ready for me to slowly push back down. He emits a hiss as the head of his cock enters me; his hands tighten around my hips, and his fingertips dig slightly more into my skin as he continues to slowly guide me down. I fling my head back as that full feeling begins to engulf me, slowly until my hips, once again, lock into his. We don't move for a moment, taking the time to adjust to the tight warmth flooding through us. Flopping forwards, my arms fall to either side of his head, his perfect face framed eloquently by my fallen hair.

As if by impulse, and through no actual thought process on my part, I find myself uttering.

"I love you." It was so unexpected that I scared myself, but I was so quiet that I questioned whether I even said it at all and if it was, in fact, just a whisper in my mind. The sudden change in expression on Jackson's face, however, tells me it wasn't; the look of disbelief is evident. That surge of panic starts to rise again, and I almost give into the impulse to jump off him instantly and run out of the room, if it weren't for his hand coming up to cup my face and bringing it down quickly to seal it with a kiss. Tearing his lips away to barely a centimetre, he whispers intimately.

"Say it again," I shake my head in embarrassment, my hair flying around our faces, but he begs. "Please."

"I…I…love…you," I whisper hesitantly. He brings his hips up; I can feel his cock strengthen inside me.

228

"Again," he whispers against my lips.

Gently, I rise up again, slowly at first, bringing myself back down, feeling the tip of his cock hit a certain spot deep in my core with its penetration.

"I love you," we continue at this slow pace, taking our time to enjoy each other's mouths with the movement of our bodies. "I love you," I say this again as we begin to pick up speed.

"Again."

"I love you, Jackson."

"God Catherine…I love you," he manages between gritted teeth as the arousal and our passion kick back in. I sit back up, resting my hands back on his chest; in response, our movements suddenly change to a more frantic, fast-paced momentum, with pain shooting up the backs of my legs from the continual riding, but we are unable to stop ourselves, needing to feel that release. Moans and cries fill the room around us as each thrust quickens and becomes more powerful.

"Shit…Catherine, I'm gunna…" But I'm first, crying out his name as the familiar wave of warmth and pleasure rises up and courses through my body. Flinging my head back, I start trembling involuntarily and tensely as Jackson continues to thrust upwards, pulling my hips down on him with every one, until he continues to roar out as loud as I have ever heard him.

The sheer exhaustion hits. Jackson quickly catches me, guiding my body down to rest beside him as I lose all strength to hold myself up. Lying side by side, our chests heaving, and hearing the beating of the pulse in my ears, the only sound in the room is that of our heavy breathing as we calm ourselves down.

"I love you, Catherine," Jackson pants, still unable to find the strength to open my eyes. "If I never hear you say those words again for the rest of our lives, I will still die a happy man, because that sweet girl," feeling his lips kiss mine in a soft but poignant touch, "was perfect," I kiss him back, and we fall into a light and contented sleep.

Chapter 25

Jackson

The next morning, she awoke in my arms. Squeezing her gently, I am almost intuitively trying to bring her closer to me. Kissing the top of her head, that wave of awareness courses through me. The motion, however, stirs her from her sleep, and the light, contented sigh that she expels reaches me deep down at my core, filling me with a real sense of male pride.

She is mine.

No more sneaking around, and no more painful goodbyes. I am making a vow right now to never let her go and to never give her a reason to leave.

"Good morning, sweet girl!" she smiles into my chest, pressing herself more tightly into the side of my body, her breasts lying lazily against me, her leg hooked over mine, and her hair sprayed out, cascading over my arm like blonde waves flowing from a stunning, angelic river.

"You know I love it when you call me that," she purrs softly.

"I know; that's why I call you it so damn often. You're *my* sweet girl," I plant my lips on her head again before reaching over to tilt her head up gently, meeting hers with mine in a kiss that feels like it depicts the moment perfectly with its depth and sincerity.

"Umm, morning breath," she smiles against my mouth, and I chuckle back in response.

"Get used to it," I murmur back, sealing her lips once more, cupping the side of her face with my free hand while bringing her closer with the other one wrapped tightly around her body, her arse cheek finding its way home in the palm of my hand.

"What's the time?" She intervenes. Grunting out my disapproval of being interrupted from my morning grope, I reach over to the nightstand, grabbing my phone to light up the front screen.

"'Bout eleven."

"Shit, no time; I've got to get back," she begins to manoeuvre herself off the bed.

"No! Five more minutes!" I grab her by the waist, wrestling her back down to the bed and pinning her down with the weight of my body, then proceed to kiss her all around her face and neck, my prominent morning wood snuggling between her thighs.

"Jackson!" she starts giggling hysterically, mockingly trying to escape my hold while very clearly succumbing to it. The sheet, which barley covers her naked body, rests lightly against her, waiting for a slight tug to expose her fully. Having no free hands to remove it further, I am forced to leave it where it is.

"Do you have to go now? We just got up."

"Check out at 12, and I have to get ready to leave; at least make myself a little presentable before I go," she pauses briefly, flashing me her Cheshire cat grin. "Besides, so do you; you dirty stop out!"

"Excuse me?" I retake her neck again, earning me another round of hysterics.

I know she is right. There is a very high probability of there being paps outside waiting to catch the proof we did actually spend the night together; we *cannot* leave here looking 'dishevelled'.

"Ok, beautiful, go make yourself look respectable. I'll head in after," leaving her one last kiss, I let her up, flopping myself back down on the bed with no attempt to hide my arousal.

"You not coming with?" she asks, flashing me her doe-like eyes and seemingly innocent glance.

"Darling, I shower with you with a hard on like this; you will not be leaving that bathroom anytime soon! Now get that sexy ass in the shower while I work on calming this boy down," she giggles again, then heads on in alone.

God, how did I get so lucky?

She doesn't spend too long there; therefore, it isn't long before I follow suit. The soothing water washes over my body, and while it washes away the reminiscence of the night before, it cannot wash away the memory, and the smile that remains is now a permanent feature of my face.

That is until I re-entered the room, towel slung low around my waist and beads of water still trickling from my hair down my back, chest, and face. I begin trying to make some witty remarks, but I stop in my tracks at the sight of her. She is sitting, perched on the edge of the bed, still wearing the towel around her body, staring intently at the television screen, remote in hand. Clearly the first thing she did as she left the bathroom and hasn't moved since.

On television, there is Entertainment News.

Test number 3.

"Jackson and Catherine were seen entering the hotel late last night and have yet to emerge."

Photos of us start appearing on the screen from the party. Skipping between one of us talking quietly to each other and another of us holding hands, and of course they captured the kiss!

"And as you can see, they were getting quite intimate at the afterparty beforehand. We did attempt to approach her ex-husband, William Carter, for his input this morning. We were, however, predictably shunned by the once-popular entrepreneur. Could it be love in the air for these two passionate onscreen A-listers? Tune in later on to find out what our body language experts think of the blossoming romance…"

"Shit!" she utters, shooting up from her spot in bed, scrambling around the floor in search of something.

"What are you trying to find?"

"My phone, where is my damn phone?" I start scurrying around the floor in an attempt to help. She eventually finds it, catching a glimpse of it as the screen flashes up. Eighteen missed calls, seven of which have come from a 'Josh', the others from Will. "Shit!" she exclaims again, holding her hands up and brushing her fingers through her wet hair.

"Hay, it's ok," I try to fold my arms around her, but she pushes back.

"No, it's not; I didn't think they would go to him. It's so wrong. Why would they do that? Why is it his business? I can't…" I grab hold of her shoulders to bring her back into focus, back into the room with me, and away from the world where this is not ok.

"Catherine, they are looking for gossip, that is all. They wanted him to say something negative about this because *that's* what sells. He is smart; he knew this, and that's why he didn't give them a damn thing. He will probably have some choice words for you. I'm not going to lie, but you're right, it's not his business—not anymore. This is only wrong if *we* make it wrong, Catherine," I can visibly see her take a deep breath to calm herself down, looking at me while she nods her head enthusiastically.

"You're right. I should have expected something unexpected," Taking a moment to think, she adds. "It doesn't change anything. We're together, right?" As if she needs to ask!

"Damn right. And nothing can come between us, not if we don't let it." Nodding again, she breaks my hold, but not to move away; she moves closer, wrapping her arms around my waist and resting her head. Her soaked hair sticks to my equally wet chest, and I return the embrace, holding her comfortingly. "You're strong, Catherine; you can take on those paps, with or without me."

"I am glad you *are* here, though," she adds and I chuckle lightly.

"Always."

Pulling back, she wipes her hand across her cheeks. Holding up the phone, she clicks 'phone'. It does not take that many rings for there to be an answer. I can't hear the other side of the conversation; I do, however, listen intently to hers.

"I know I have just seen it. I'm sorry that they came to you." Pause.

"Yes, it's true." Pause.

"Because I don't have to run every single one of my life decisions by you." Pause.

"We'll quite frankly, I don't give two shits," her voice is rising a few octaves higher than usual. "I am well entitled to move on and have my life, as *you* are well entitled to *yours*. I didn't exactly plan this just to get up your backside, did I? Be reasonable!" Pause. Long pause.

"I think so, yes," she takes this pause to turn and look at me.

"I don't know; I haven't asked him." Pause.

"Well funny enough; *if* you really want to know, we were quite busy last night, and it hasn't exactly come up in conversation." Pause.

"I really don't think you have the moral high ground in this situation here, Will. Or did you conveniently forget about Linda the other week?" Pause.

"The boys are capable of talking, you know? They do tell me about what happened during their time with you. The difference is, I don't give two flying fucks what goes on in your private life; that's your business, and I will expect you to respect mine." Pause.

"I understand that, and I have already apologised. I will talk to Josh and release a press statement along the lines of, 'It came as a shock, but you are happy for me'." Pause.

"Because anything else, they will hound you; they want the gossip Will, if we don't give it to them, they will eventually leave us alone." Pause.

"Fine." Pause.

"See you later!" Tapping the phone to hang up, she then chucks it down onto the bed, using her hands instead to shield her face, visibly trying to compose herself. I stay back, trying to give her the space to do so, but the turmoil inside must have been evident by an unintentional frown on my face, because when she looks up at me, her face warps into one of despair.

"Urgh, this is a nightmare," moving past me, heading towards the window. Quickly attempting to readjust my look, I follow, wrapping my arms around her waist from behind and nudging my chin into the crock of her neck.

"I'm sorry…you know, for my face. It was hard to try and follow a conversation one-sided," I turned my head so my lips could graze her neck. "I just got confused; what was it that you hadn't asked me yet?" She breathes out a sigh, allowing her body to go completely slack in my arms.

"Don't worry about it."

"I do worry. What do you need to ask?"

"He just asked if you were coming back to mine this weekend." I was taken aback slightly.

"Umm…well, of course, I was hoping to spend every minute with you, sweet girl. What is that business to him, though?"

"It's ok, you don't have to; I have the children this week, that's all, he asked if I was introducing you to them. But it's ok. It's too soon for you. They are at his next week; we can sort something out then," I turn her around so she is facing me, and I can see the reservation in her composure.

"Do you want me to meet your children, I mean, like this?" Her eyes immediately find mine, in shock and worry.

"Of course, I do. Jackson, it's just…it's different; it's not…not like this…you know. I don't want you to feel like…" I stopped her mid-sentence, kissing her deeply to stop whatever flow of self-conscious thought she was tumbling down.

"Catherine, I told you, when I say I want you, I mean, I want all of you. If you don't want me to meet them yet, that's fine; I respect your choice, but sweet girl, I *want* to meet them. I *want* to be a part of all your lives. I realise to the outside world this is new, but *we* know this has been growing far longer. This, you, the boys, is it for me now; meet them this weekend; next, a month from now, it makes no difference; I am not going anywhere. I love *you,* and although I don't know them properly yet, I *will* love those boys as well. Whether it's this weekend or some point in the future. You just have to tell me when; I follow your lead, sweet," she nods quickly, acknowledging the truth in my words.

"You're right. We know this is more than what the world knows. For us this is the next step. We follow our own rules, not theirs," she pauses briefly, seemingly taking the moment to find the confidence to say the words. "Would you like to come spend the weekend with us?"

I think my broad smile is the only answer I really need to give. I know she doesn't want to hold back anymore; I just need to lend her the strength to push through these barriers she has had up for so long.

"I'd love to. Give me time to head back to mine. Grab some clothes. I'll meet you at yours, and we'll confront ass-wipe together. Ok?" She smiles back briefly and then heads back to the room, gathering up bits as she goes.

We proceed to get ourselves ready in near silence, knowing how important it is to look respectable in the face of the paparazzi we know are waiting for us downstairs and to be ready to face them together.

Chapter 26

Jackson

Leaving the hotel turned out to be as hectic as we expected. There were at least a dozen cameras flashing outside the doors as we made our exit. It was Catherine's decision to leave as a pair and face the reality of our coupling head-on rather than try to hide it. Hand in hand, we walked our way around the car park, cameras and reporters following us the whole way. The sound of the frenzied shouting from the paps attempting to get their scoop filled the bubble surrounding us. As instructed by Harry and Josh, we didn't answer their mad cries; best to leave those sorts of questions to well-organised televised interviews, where we can prepare our answers and control our environment; that would be for another day. For now, our concentration has to stay firmly on dealing with the consequences involving her family.

She drove me around to my hotel, where I could grab my things and retrieve my car. The plan was to return home, grab a few bits, and meet back at hers before collecting the children from Mr Arsehole.

It turned out that while my home was thirty minutes from where we were staying in London, it was around two hours from hers. It took me a long time sitting in a car by myself, when I really just wanted to be with her. Leaving me alone with my thoughts, playing out different scenarios of how it will go, meeting them, meeting him. A showcase of the various ways I could deck him became the forefront of the majority of my visions; the satisfaction of laying him out brought a sinister smile to my face.

Pulling up outside her house is not what I expected, but then that is entirely due to my own misconceptions, as actually it is *exactly* what a home containing a couple of children would look like. It isn't modern or stylistic, nor is it immaculate from the exterior; it is your standard red brick home, with three windows at the top and two at the bottom, all lined with decorative nets. A goal with a corresponding football takes precedence in the front garden, covered in grass, with the markings of a small penalty box present before it.

I ring the bell, your classic ding-dong, and it isn't long before her form fills the doorframe, now changed into a stunning pale blue summer dress.

"Earlier than expected," she chimes as that breathtaking smile once again finds its home across her captivating features. The one reflected back displays my own contentment as well as a little pride, *'I caused that.'* "Come in; I'll just grab my bag, and we'll get the boys. I have already let them know to expect you."

I cross the threshold of her home, and once again, the design and layout throw me a little. So far removed from the sleek finish my home affords, I have to remind myself that this is not a bachelor pad, nor is it a reflection of the rich I have so frequently come across before.

Looking around, I take in its comfortable soft fabric sofa, the potted plants, the photos of family that litter the walls and shelving space, children's drawings held in place by magnets that fill every free space on the fridge freezer's doors, the toys piled high in the corner, and the games console attached to the T.V. Instead of feeling notions of disapproval, however, I am filled with joy as the realisation hits.

This is a home. Her home.

And this is exactly where I want to be.

The vision of my own home becomes a distant memory.

"Not too disappointed, are you?" I turn to see her staring at me, a couple of steps up on the open staircase. "I told you; my real life isn't that exciting," I see her start to withdraw, but not on my watch. Taking the few strides it takes to cross the room to reach her, I stand in front of her. The added height from the stairs puts her head slightly above mine.

Nevertheless, I reach up to cup her cheek, planting a soft kiss upon her lips while wrapping an arm around her waist as I hold her to me. I bring her down to my position at the base of the stairs, swaddling her up in my embrace. Spreading my fingers wide, I glided them through her silken hair.

"It's not what I was expecting; I'm not going to lie. I can't pretend I don't come from a very different world, but it is exactly you, and that makes it perfect," she smiles again, allowing herself to fall into my body while I hold her up with ease.

"No, it isn't perfect, not yet," she adds, sighing into my chest, "but once we have included bits that are uniquely you into it, it will be." It hits me deep within and strikes right at the core of my heart. We are becoming one, and she is beginning to see it too, our future. Elation doesn't even begin to describe how much that sentiment means to me.

She takes my hand, moving towards the door. "Come on, we don't want to leave his lordship waiting," I drag her back, engulfing her in arms again.

"His *lordship* can wait two more damn minutes; we're having a moment here." Reaching up, she kisses me, which quickly turns more passionate as we make out in the entranceway of her living room, which I am pretty sure, lasted just a little bit longer than two minutes!

Pulling up outside, his house is a stark contrast to Catherine's. His mini wannabe mansion looks dark and uninviting. The lawn is immaculate; there are no toys littering the garden, and a tall fence, sealed in by an equally high double gate had cornered it off.

"Who is this guy, freaking Dracula?" I murmur close to Catherine's ear. She scoffs lightly, elbowing me in the ribs for my effort with a grin on her face, which she attempts to hide beneath the vale of her hair.

He addresses us at the door; a false grin spread across his face as he welcomes us inside.

"Mum!" I hear chorus out from one of the side rooms, followed by the unmistakable sound of feet thumping across wooden floorboards as the two boys come bouncing into the hallway. They collide into her with such force that she was taken aback a few steps. An arm around each child as they talk at her at such speed, and both at once, it was hard to keep track of the conversation. I was left with nothing else to do but stand back and laugh at the chaos unfolding in front of me.

From the corner of my eye, I can see him standing off to the side, his stance and eye-line fixed firmly in my direction. I try not to acknowledge it, keeping my own train of sight fixed firmly on Catherine and her boys.

"Come on, then, you can tell me everything at home. Have you got everything?" She finally breaks through the sea of excited chatter.

"Not yet!" The younger of the boys calls out.

"What do you mean not yet? Come on, you two," she turns to me with a sorry look in her eyes. "I need to go help; will you be ok…" nodding her head in an arsehole's direction while trailing off.

"Of course! Do what you need to do; I'll wait here," Once again, flashing images of my closed fist connecting with his face make their appearance in my immediate thoughts.

As she heads off upstairs, I am left to deal with the SOB still lingering in my peripheral vision.

All of a sudden, his glare turns into an eerily broad smile spanning from ear to ear.

"So…Jackson Hunter," he begins, sounding out my name slowly while popping his mouth to punctuate his thoughts. "I did wonder how long it would take you." Immediately, my defence is up.

"Really? How long did 'what' take me exactly?"

"Before you moved in on *my* wife," I feel the heat start to pulse around my body at his words, *'his wife?'*

"Ex-wife."

"Excuse me?"

"She is your ex-wife, and was I really that obvious?" Fists balled up but remain by my side.

"Obvious that you had a thing for her from the beginning. Of course it was. Even as early as the first time we met, I could see you pined after her. She *is* very beautiful, of course. It has been since *we* were children," Red heat emanates from behind my eyes. "Such a jewel to glance at from afar."

"She is more than that."

"Maybe," he pauses, staring down at his fingernails. "She portrays herself very well. Sweet little Catherine will let you believe that she will give you the world if she could," he pauses again. "I will warn you though Jackson because you really do seem smitten. She isn't everything you can see on the surface. Know her long enough, and her true colours reveal themselves."

Just when I think my fists will no longer contain themselves, with the tips of my fingernails digging into the palm of my hand, logic finally takes over, the fog promptly clears, and I start to see him clearly for what he really is.

Test number 4.

Unable to control myself, I start to chuckle. "Glad of my input, I hope," he adds, "just trying to save you from the same misery I had with her."

"Oh, don't you worry; I am *very* glad of your input." Unclenching my fists, I begin to relax. "So, you have found yourself at a loss, have you?"

"Excuse me?" he remarks, I think genuinely taken a back.

"No longer falling for your manipulations now, is she?" I turn, shoulders squared off to face him full frontal. "Let me guess, did you try her parents first? Finding you could no longer control her directly, you tried to work through her family. But they're not stupid; they can see right through your bullshit, and then you see me and think I'm an easy target, right? New man on the scene, easily scared off, an actor, so he must be thick at shit, right?"

I take a step forward, bringing myself face-to-face with him. He is around my height, but with my build, I easily outgun him, and the intimidation works. His eyes widen as the alarm starts to rise behind them, staring back into mine. "You don't control her anymore, mate. She has broken free from your *shit*! You *lost* her! I suggest you concentrate your efforts on being a father to those boys before you lose them too, because believe me, I will not hesitate to pick up the pieces should you fail," I pause, glancing up the stairs to ensure she isn't coming, and catch a glimpse of the scene unravelling.

"Stop trying to get one up on her; she makes her own choices now," Hearing the sound of giggles from the top of the stairs, I start to back off from him, relaxing my stance and composing my demeanour. Facing the stairs, she doesn't need to know what transpired here. He, however, cannot help getting in one last dig.

"She'll leave you, you know? Once she has got what she wants from you, she will start distancing herself from you, and then she will go," I only award him a side glance and a head tilt, for that is all I believe he is worth.

"And that will be her choice too."

I see her emerge into view at the top of the stairs and his words melt away. I *know* what we are and *what* we are worth. I *know* she is much more than what he makes her out to be, and I *know* we are stronger than what he thinks we are.

I recognise what he is trying to achieve, to plant a doubt in my mind, one that would slowly fester and eat away at us. He is a man trying to hold on to his power with the only thing he has left. His words. And they don't mean shit to me. She is what matters; she and her boys are all I need.

This road for us will be tricky; adjusting to this new life will present its own set of obstacles for me and for them. I am not going to pretend it won't, but we will make this work because, for me, she is worth it, and she is all I will ever want. She is mine and I am hers with equal fidelity, and as long as we believe in that, we will never be apart again.

Epilogue

<u>Catherine</u>

Have you ever felt so full like you could just burst at the seams?

So content that life just couldn't get any better?

Don't get me wrong; these last few years, we have had our fair share of turbulence. Adjusting to our new life as a couple proved difficult, integrating our two very different lives into one.

Jackson had a lot more to adapt to than I did; he admitted one night that accepting two children into his life was harder than he thought it would be, especially after the honeymoon period wore off and the boys deliberately began to misbehave and defy him, something we fully expected, but it was tough nonetheless. We made it through, and once it was *well* established that Jackson was not going anywhere, they settled, and in return, so did we.

Jackson proposed a year later; getting married this last June on a stunning Italian beach was a dream, a true coming together of our two lives, and we have been living our true 'boring' lives since.

Right now, I am held up on the sofa, exhausted after an impromptu trip out to find Axel some new school shoes after his broke yesterday, which turned into a two-hour trek around four different shops to find the 'right' ones. Jackson has taken Callen out to his football game; they themselves have been gone for hours. I am sure they are due home soon, to which I have a surprise waiting for his return—another little something I had to get while we were out.

Speak of the devil.

"Leave me alone!" The yells of Callen come screeching through the house, followed by banging against the hardwood kitchen floor.

"Don't you dare walk away from me while I am talking to you!" Jackson's bellow comes ringing through shortly after. I cannot help but notice the small smirk that threatens the corner of my mouth.

Callen has been going through, let's just say, some changes recently that have left him a little short-tempered, and unfortunately, Jackson tends to be the outlet for his preteen emotional rollercoaster ride.

"I said leave me alone!" Callen comes traipsing through the house, still clad in his mud-stained football kit, a scowled fixture plastered across his face.

"You ok, baby?" I call as he walks by me.

"Don't talk to me!" Not even bothering to look up to address me as he passes by, heading straight up the stairs. Jackson is not far behind him.

"Don't talk to your mother like that!" He stops briefly at the cupboard under the stairs to hang up his coat and kick off his shoes.

"What's happened?" I asked, concerned.

"He started mouthing off to the ref! I mean, don't get me wrong, the guy was an arsehole, but he still needs to learn some respect. I tried Catherine; I really did try and talk to him calmly in the car, but his stubborn ass still thinks he's right!" I rest the palm of my hand on the top of my head, breathing out a sigh before I start to get up.

"I'll go talk to him," I sigh, but he gestures for me to sit back down.

"No, it's fine, I got it," he walks off towards the stairs, ascending them to face his nemesis. Another small smirk graces my face, he *has* got this. I know it seems volatile at the moment, but the two are like two peas in the same pod; they explode at each other, and then the understanding happens; they'll be kicking a ball around in the yard in no time at all, I have no doubt.

Sure enough, not half an hour after Jackson comes slumping down the stairs, I can see he, too, is exhausted as he collapses on the sofa next to me, breathing out an exasperated sigh.

"That boy."

"Everything alright?"

"Of course, he is just *so* sensitive at the moment. It really doesn't take much to set him off."

"You're good with him."

"It doesn't seem like it sometimes," taking his hand in mine, intertwining our fingers, and resting my head on his shoulder, I feel his tense body start to relax.

"You are; you don't give up on him; that's what's important. I know you don't believe it but it's a good sign that he fights with you, it shows you he is comfortable expressing himself with you."

"It don't feel like it," I chuckle, tightening my grip on his hand.

"No, I don't suppose it does," he kisses the top of my head as we sit in silence for a while, almost forgetting about my surprise. "I have something for you," I sit up, reaching over to the small box I left on the table. I can see the creases of his frown forming along his brow.

"It's not our anniversary...nor is it my birthday," he eyes me suspiciously, and I laugh again.

"No, and to be honest, I am not sure you are going to like it, but I have it nonetheless," I pass the box to him, waiting in anticipation for him to open it, nerves dancing on the tips of my fingers.

With his eyes fixed on me via a side glance, he opens a box, revealing the blue and white stick inside. This is my cue to explain; all my pre-planned explanations I had rehearsed to myself earlier, however, went flying out the window as I resorted to a mess of words spilling from my mouth like vomit.

"Well, I've been feeling run down recently and tired after menial tasks I usually have no issues with, so I thought it best I check. I am not sure what happened. I know during our honeymoon I forgot to take the pill a couple of times and thought I made it up the next day. I don't know how far along I am; I only just did the test, so I'm not sure. I know we have never really spoken about kids, and I don't even know if you wanted any of your own; I know you accepted my own well enough, but they are grown up; this is a baby, and I am so sorry if you had other plans..." I trail off as his silence starts to eat away at me. Never have I known Jackson to not have anything to say; he always knows exactly the right words, but now...

We sit there for a minute or so, with him just staring intently at the stick in his hands while I shift uncomfortably in my seat.

Eventually, he utters, flatly.

"You're pregnant?" I suck in my lips between my teeth and nod my head, looking down so my eyes focus on the fluff of my slippers. I hear him chuckle beside me, which pricks my hearing. The chuckle quickly turns into a full-on belly laugh. Shooting my eyes up to look at him, I can see the joy on his face, still staring at the little stick.

"You're pregnant!" he states this again, calling out louder this time into the room. A tear rolls down my cheek in pure relief at his reaction as I start sniggering next to him.

All of a sudden, he launches himself at me, pinning me down against the soft sofa beneath him. Immediately, he begins an onslaught of kisses around my neck, face, and head.

"Jackson!" I screech out in a fit of giggles. He stops, hovering his face over mine before repeating.

"You're pregnant?" I smile up at him while nodding my head; the pure joy emitting from him is infectious. He reaches up to stroke my cheek, and he kisses me, opening our mouths, I feel his love flow through me, elevating both of our happiness.

"Urgh, get a room!" Callen passes by, letting out an exasperating grunt as he does, his disgust evident in our open display of affection. It wouldn't be the first time.

Without moving from his position on top of me, Jackson turns to face his opponent.

"We *have* a room. Thank you very much! Am I not allowed to display how much I love your mother in every room of this house?" A sudden jolt from behind Jackson pulls his attention away from Callen and towards a smiling child now resting on his back.

"Get off my mother!" Axel cries while starting to pound at his back. A cheeky smirk spreads across his face: it appears he saw the scene play out in front of him and thought it was a good time for a play-fight.

"Never! She is my mother now! Urgh!" he growls, quickly grabbing him from behind to toss him to the floor (gently, of course, so as not to hurt him), proceeding to tickle him until he is rolling around on the floor in fits of giggles. From the corner, I can see another body come flying in, launching himself at Jackson.

"Argh!" his battle cry, but predictably, he too ends up on the floor. After some quick footwork from Callen, Jackson also tumbles to the floor, where they all end up in one massive pile of legs and arms struggling to out wrestle and out tickle each other. High-pitched laughter and screeches cry out throughout the house. I just sit up on the sofa watching the scenario play out; any other day I would be amongst them, giving as good as I get!

After some time, the game has to come to a conclusion.

"Enough, enough!" Jackson calls out, prompting the boys to come to a stop, all three of them breathing heavily and lying outstretched on the living room floor.

Eventually, Jackson speaks out.

"Right, we are going out! We're celebrating!"

"What are we celebrating?" Axel asks innocently. Jackson turns to me with a silent question. I nodded my answer, smiling stupidly at him.

"Boys!" Placing an arm around each of them sitting next to him on the floor.

"Your mother and I are having a baby," wide eyes gloss over both of them as they comprehend the information.

"Mum is having a baby?" Axel repeats.

"Yes, which means you two are going to be big brothers."

"Urgh!" Callen interjects, evidently disgusted by the revelation, rising up from the floor, heading into the kitchen. "Another kid in the house! Fantastic!" He calls out as he leaves. Jackson is about to scold Callen for his pessimism but is quickly stopped by Axel, who throws himself into Jackson's arms.

"I'm going to have a little brother?" I bend down to join them on the floor, to which he quickly turns to throw his arms around my neck.

"Or a little sister," I add. His face fills with elation. I turn to Jackson, grinning stupidly. "Two out of three isn't bad," I wink.

"Callen will come around."

Later that evening, after spending a beautiful night at the local restaurant discussing all things 'baby', Callen has taken himself off to his room, game console in hand, and Jackson is putting Axel to bed.

Wearily, I cross the hall to my own bedroom, looking forward to the welcoming sight of my bed. My ears prick when I pass Axel's room and hear him and Jackson having a quiet conversation. I stop just short of the door to have a nose.

"So, when Mum has the baby, what will happen to us?"

"What do you mean, Bud?"

"I mean, where do *we* go?"

"You'll be here, of course; why?"

"Well," he pauses in thought. "When you and Mum have your baby, you won't need us anymore."

"Oh, buddy, no, that's not what happens," I can hear a sniff, which I think comes from Jackson.

"This baby, it's not a replacement, not at all; it's more like an addition. The dynamic might change a little, but our love for you guys won't change, buddy, we simply makes more room, and we will continue to love you all equally. I promise," I smile. These smiles seem to come more often to me now; in fact, I don't really remember the last time I cried.

Who knew life could be this good?

The End